THE LAST FAIRY QUEEN

The Last Fairy Queen

BETH LARRIVÉE-WOODS

Beth Larrivée-Woods

If you believe only in happy endings, then this story is not for you. If you are afraid to put your heart on the line, then please, just shut the book. And if you draw a line between what is real and what is dream, and what is dream and what is nightmare, then tread no further down this path, for the way is dark.

But if you are not afraid of tears and dreams and you understand that every time you give your heart, that it might break, then open the door, turn the page, and dream ... You just might find magic.

From: Seventy-Three Love Poems
for a Fairy Princess
By Evan Taylor

Nyad Dryad love child of a willow tree
On slim white feet you tread the forest paths of my dreams
winding inevitably, inexorably onward through the bare trees
to a place that even I cannot find
that place I fear to go
that place that aches and cries out for you

You walk onward leaving a burning trail of small footprints
that flame and spark in the dry leaves of my fruitless soul
You wind and circle ever nearer
and I cry tears that cannot put out your flame

Ever onward you walk
looking into me with the impossible eyes of a child
not a child
seeing what I cannot face
being what I want

You arrive at my heart
that place I cannot find
and when I finally look, I find you there ...

    and you are gone

All that remains is your flame
and I am alone

Prologue

Sheila watched the small pale girl approach the counter with a piece of paper in her hands.

"Um," the girl looked uncertain for a moment and then seemed to muster her resolve. She held out the piece of paper and said clearly, "I saw the 'Help Wanted' sign out front and I wanted to apply for the position."

Sheila took the resume, looked it over and saw that the girl had no formal experience. But there was something about the kid, some vibe that she liked, a feeling of kinship. "Kristabell is it?" Sheila asked.

The girl nodded.

"Can you come in for an interview tomorrow at two?"

The girl nodded again and smiled, "Yes. I'll be here."

"See you tomorrow then," Sheila told the girl.

"See you tomorrow." The girl kept the smile up as she left the garden centre almost skipping.

Sheila watched, shaking her head as the little back disappeared out the door. The last time she'd had an instinctive gut feeling about someone, like she did for that girl, she had ended up a single mother. She wondered what kind of trouble that little girl with the impish smile could possibly bring?

Part One

Kristabell

Chapter 1

She was hiding behind a rack of terracotta plant pots at the garden centre were she worked, sitting there with her back against the wall where no one could see her, which was ridiculous. *What am I doing here?* She asked herself as she stared at the scalloped edges of the pots. They were the good ones imported from a potter in England. Exorbitantly expensive, but rich customers snapped them up. She remembered placing the order and filing the invoice. She looked down at the inventory sheet that she'd just finished checking over when Tanya and Allan, her co-workers, had appeared on the other side of the rack and started talking about her. It was obviously an ongoing debate.

"Kristabell is a freak," Allan declared loudly and with conviction, obviously not the first time he'd said it. It was a quiet day. There were no customers around to hear him.

"I think calling her a freak is pushing it a little. It's not like she's retarded or like she has a third arm ... but I know what you mean," Tanya responded.

Kristabell felt like crying. It was an ache deep inside that she thought she'd left behind when she'd dropped out of high school, but the last few months it was creeping back. She'd never exactly felt like she belonged, but it seemed lately as if everyone was confirming it to her. Even the people who shouldn't be. Just the other night she'd overheard her parents talking about her in a similar if less insulting vein.

"Do you think she knows that she's not like everyone else?" her father had asked her mother.

"I don't know," her mother had responded, "but the older she gets the more obvious it is." It was late at night and they thought she was asleep.

For eighteen years her parents had taken everything about her in stride, or so she'd thought. An odd child, she'd been what is typically referred to as a hopeless dreamer. She'd spent her life reading books about fairies and unicorns, dragons and knights. She could spend hours lost in the backyard, just watching the trees grow. It was when she was thirteen that her obsessive passion for gardening emerged. It had begun with a simple package of wild flower seeds, but over the past five years her garden had turned into a veritable riot of flowers, fruits, vegetables and herbs. She grew strawberries, violets, kale, roses, kiwi, wisteria, cabbage, lavender, and everything in between. She had planted virtually every available square inch of soil on her parents city lot and had grape, kiwi, and clematis vines scaling every vertical surface.

At sixteen she'd come home from school after having been pushed, intentionally, on the stairs only to limp to her locker and find that someone had figured out her combination and left a dead frog there for her. Of course she'd screamed. Of course they'd laughed. "Hey Thumbelina! Someone get your prince?" a taunting voice had called out behind her. "Thumbelina didn't marry a frog," Kristabell had said quietly, to no one in particular, then she'd blinked away her tears, retrieved anything of value from her locker, and left the school, never to return. There was a limit to how many times she could leave school bruised and humiliated, and she had reached that limit. She just couldn't take it anymore.

She had walked in the door at home and announced that she would not go back and that there was nothing they could say or do that would make her. But even this her parents had simply accepted as though they had been expecting it. Her mother, Fionnuala, was a bartender, and her father, Gavin, was a fire fighter. He'd looked at her calmly and said in his soft Irish accent, "More than one way to get an education."

Her mother's response had been, "Don't need grade twelve to do what I do."

Neither of her parents, it turned out, had finished high school, although her father had done his general equivalency, so they had simply left her up to her own devices.

Kristabell applied for a job at the little garden centre not far from home. When her boss, Sheila, had asked her, "Why should I hire you?" Kristabell had been ready.

"Because I'm good with plants." She brought out a stack of photographs. Her parents had taken the pictures and she, Kristabell, featured in many of them with grubby knees and dirt up to her elbows working in her garden. "This is *my* garden. My parents don't help me with it," she'd told Sheila.

Sheila was blown away. The job had been Kristabell's for the taking.

Sheila liked her and had taken to calling her Sprite. The first time Sheila had called Kristabell that she'd asked, "Why did you call me Sprite?"

"Well, you're a funny little slip of a thing and, what with those big solemn eyes of yours, all that hair, and your pretty, pointy little face, you look for all the world like one of Arthur Rackham's fairies."

That night when she was alone in her room Kristabell had looked at herself in the mirror. She *was* pretty—though not fashionably pretty—with thick wavy, pale ash coloured hair that reached her hips and fair skin that gave her a strange colourless quality. It made her lips, which always looked like she'd been eating cherries, and her eyes, which were a strange intense blue—the colour of storm clouds, or mountains in the distance—stand out even more. Sheila was right. She did look like an Arthur Rackham fairy.

Kristabell often wondered what people, other than Sheila and her parents, thought of her. At school the other kids had generally been cruel to her, making the odd tentative friendship she would form every so often awkward and short lived. Most of the time she had felt too shy to talk to people. She was constantly, unintentionally, frying computers in the computer labs which had always lead to more bullying. She wished that she could move through the world with more ease. She wished that she knew what she was doing wrong, but she was what she was—whatever that was. But then, there had been Evan.

Evan had been her best, and only, friend. A university student, he was Sheila's son and would come home and work for his mother at the garden centre during the summer. Kristabell and Evan had a lot in common from a certain perspective. They liked the same books, movies, music and tended to have the same views, although he had, on many occasions, tried to convince her to go back to school.

The first summer they worked together things had been casual enough. They would go for the odd coffee and trade books, but they were at work together nine hours a day six days a week. It wasn't as if they didn't see quite a lot of each other there, and summers at the garden centre were busy and exhausting. At the end of the summer Evan had asked for her address though, and all that winter they had exchanged letters. Nice old-fashioned paper letters.

When Evan came home again the next spring, he came with a gift. An original edition of *Undine*, illustrated by Arthur Rakham. "My mum always says you look like one of his creatures. I found this at a flee market and I couldn't resist. I know how much you like books."

She had taken it, held it tightly against her chest, and smiled, a soft inward smile that he probably hadn't understood.

Except for her parents and Sheila, no one had ever given her a gift before. No one had ever valued her friendship before.

She and Evan spent more time together that summer, going to movies, bookstores, the beach, and often meeting for lunch on their day off, but if Evan had felt *anything* more than friendship for her, he'd hidden it well. More than once Kristabell had come out of a theatre restroom after a movie to find him standing there with that easy grace of his, Evan had a sort of physical confidence, a comfort in his skin, that Kristabell figured came from being a competitive swimmer—being in prime physical condition—but, that also, maybe, she suspected, came in part from the amount of time he spent in a speedo, being at ease with himself as he was, dancers seemed to have a similar quality—, and there would be an attractive girl there in the theatre lobby, ogling him and chatting him up. The girl would take one look at Kristabell and then say something to the effect of, "Aw, how cute. You take your little sister to the movies. I wish I'd had a big brother like you." And then the girl would make cow eyes at Evan, and Kristabell would make him laugh by rolling her eyes while the girl wasn't looking. But they never claimed to be anything other than siblings because, somehow, after being mistaken for siblings, admitting that they weren't just seemed awkward, although Kristabell couldn't have, at the time, said why. And then he'd kissed her.

After *two* summers of *not* holding hands, *not* hugging ...? They were friends weren't they? And friends touched each other sometimes. But not Kristabell and Evan. Even sitting next to each other in theatres sharing popcorn they'd made sure their arms never brushed, and the kiss had shocked her. She'd been standing on a step ladder in the back of the storage shed putting away plant pots. It was the last week of August. Kristabell had turned to Evan to ask him to pass her a plant pot but instead she'd looked at him and said, "I can't believe I have to stand on the second rung of a step ladder to look into your face without hurting my neck." And he'd stepped up to her, taking her arms lightly in his hands, and kissed her. Not a timid chaste little kiss either. A real kiss. Kristabell hadn't seen it coming. She was so taken aback and overwhelmed by the actual feeling of him kissing her that her response had been confused and minimal. He'd stepped back from her and said, "Krista I ..." And then looking as if he almost might cry, he'd said, "Bloody hell," and walked away.

Bloody hell. Those were the last words he spoke to her.

He wasn't at work for the rest of the day and when Kristabell was leaving he still hadn't returned. She headed across the parking lot to the intersection, waiting for the light to change, goosebumps forming on the backs of her arms. It was a little cool outside and she'd forgotten her sweater. She turned back and headed for the staff room to get it. She walked in and picked up her cardigan, then she heard Evan's voice, "I moved my plane ticket. I'm going back to Montreal tomorrow."

"What do you mean? You're going back a week early?" She heard Sheila's voice through the office door.

Then there was a long awkward silence after which Evan admitted, "I kissed Kristabell."

"I'm confused. I thought kissing was a good thing," Sheila responded dryly.

"Mum you're not serious?"

"I *am*. I *don't* understand. You're good friends. Some of the best romantic relationships come out of friendship. What's wrong with Kristabell?"

"Well *other* than the fact that I live in Montreal and she lives in Vancouver," Evan started his list, "She's a seventeen year old high school drop out, and as if that's not enough she looks like she's about thirteen. It seriously bothers me that I'm attracted to her. I mean, she's what, just *slightly* over four foot eleven? I am a six foot three inch tall, twenty-two year old, grad student!"

"Kristabell is more mature than the average twenty year old Evan. Even you've said that."

There was a tense silence that followed and then Sheila asked Evan, "So what is this then, some kind of snobbery?"

"Call it what you want. I just want to go back to Montreal and get over her before the semester starts."

And then the office door had opened and he'd walked out and seen Kristabell standing there holding her sweater. Evan hadn't said anything, he'd just stood there looking at her then blinked hard a few times and walked away. That was the last time she had seen him. The next summer he got a job tree planting in Ontario. Sheila tried not to talk about him. It was a huge blow to Kristabell's ego, not that she had felt for him then what he'd felt for her. Evan wasn't her type, she'd told herself, but the fact that he found his feelings for her so repulsive that he wouldn't come home just so that he wouldn't have to see her ...? She missed his friendship. She missed his letters. She missed the way his friendship had made her feel ... normal. A part of her was curious as to what it would have felt like if he *had* pursued her romantically, but every time she let her mind go there, she remembered how he had looked at her that last time. No. It was better if she just tried to forget Evan. Forget his letters. Forget their long conversations. Forget how she hadn't noticed until it was too late, just *how* handsome he was. No. *Forget* Evan. The problem was that she *couldn't* forget how let down she'd felt. She tried to distract herself. She took courses over the quiet winter. Anything that caught her fancy. Aromatherapy, herbalism, horticulture, world religion. She wished that she could say she was content but after a long empty summer, she felt like she was floundering. And now here she was, at an all time low, hiding behind the plant pots, afraid to come out because if Allan and Tanya knew that she had heard them talking about her, well ... it would just make life that much more uncomfortable.

"So, earlier today, I found her staring at the begonias," Allan was telling Tanya, "Like she could *see* them growing. Sometimes I catch her singing to the plants. She's so loopy. I wonder if she smokes pot or does mushrooms before she comes to work."

Tanya cracked up at this but she quickly stifled her laughter. Kristabell heard Sheila walk up and tell them, "Enough gabbing you two." And then she sent each one on a separate task and poked her head around the rack of pots. "Come on out Sprite. They're gone," she said in an understanding tone. Kristabell always found it difficult to maintain her composure when someone did something nice for her and this time was no exception.

"Thank you Sheila," she said, blinking and wiping at her face.

"Don't let them get to you," Sheila said looking a bit concerned then, "You seem pretty down lately. Why don't you take the rest of the day off. I'll still pay you for it. Just go. Treat yourself good for a few hours."

"Thank you Sheila," Kristabell said again, wiping more furiously at her face.

"Go on, get out of here," Sheila chuckled good naturedly.

Kristabell walked home. It was one of those perfect late August days when the leaves are just starting to turn, the sun is out and the sky is as blue as it can get. She felt the sun doing its magic and by the time she was stepping in the door she felt comfortable in her skin again. Her parents were at work and she would have the house to herself until around three AM. Kristabell decided that she would have a hot bath, go for a walk, come home, make herself some dinner and eat it in front of a movie. That was, if she could get the DVD player to cooperate. Electronic equipment didn't seem to like her much. Most of the time she could listen to her Ipod without too much trouble but she had to get her dad to download songs onto it because every time she went near the computer when it was on it shut itself down, as if it too knew she was bad news Oh well, at least there were always books.

Kristabell slipped out of her work clothes, pinned up her hair, and then slipped into a tub full of hot water and let her mind drift. *Maybe I'm just tired. Maybe I just need a few weeks off,* she thought as she soaked away the grime and the weariness. Maybe that would explain why she felt so sensitive all of the time. Kristabell stood and let the water run off her body. She towelled dry then let down her hair, relishing the feel of its softness against her bare skin. She sat on her bed and brushed her hair out with her good boar bristle brush for ten minutes before getting dressed. She pulled on a pair of jeans and took out her favourite dress. It was a bit worn, but it always made her feel right. It was pink with flowers embroidered on the hem, sleeves, and collar. The skirt reached to just above the knees. She slipped the dress over her head then pulled on the green wool cable knit cardigan that her mother had knit her, and went down stairs. Kristabell slipped on a pair of brown mary-janes, did up the straps and took her canvas shoulder bag down off the hook by the door. The bag contained her wallet, Ipod, a blank notebook and some pencil crayons, so that if she met a plant that she didn't know she could draw it then take the notebook home and identify it.

It was still brilliant outside and it was only two in the afternoon. There were hours still before sundown. Kristabell headed east toward Queen Elizabeth Park. The neighbourhood she lived in was a neat, tidy, upper class neighbourhood smack in the middle of Vancouver and it had often occurred to her to wonder how her parents had been able to afford the little house that they lived in. Her parents had been very young, 22 and 23, when they had adopted her. Her birth mother had apparently been a bit younger than her parents and a good friend of theirs. They had agreed to raise Kristabell as a favour to their friend. They seldom spoke of her mother except, occasionally, to tell her that she looked like her, and this they always said with sadness in their eyes. Then they would sigh great heavy sighs and say, "But your mother is gone."

Kristabell had always assumed that "gone" meant dead, and since Fionnuala was in every way a mother to Kristabell—she had even breastfed her when she was a baby—Kristabell had simply loved Fionnuala as her mother and let the past lie. Since her parents were so cagey about the past it was probably just as well. All Kristabell knew about her parents was that they had come to Canada from rural Ireland as uneducated young people with no family connections, and had shortly afterwards adopted her. But it still didn't explain to Kristabell how they had come by the house. She glanced back at it as she walked away, her riotous garden setting it apart from the other houses on the street.

Queen Elizabeth Park is one of the highest points in Vancouver and Kristabell liked to climb to the top and look at the view of Vancouver's downtown and the north shore mountains. She had sometimes done that with Evan, but today she just puttered around, wandering the trails in the sort of wooded area that wrapped itself part way around the base of the hill, simply enjoying the feeling of being surrounded by trees. It was in places like this, or in her garden, that she felt most at home. Kristabell had a sudden overwhelming urge to be able to walk away from the world with all of its noise and fumes, celebrity gossip and violence. She had tried to isolate herself from all of the awfulness. To just stay home and leave the TV off, go to work, take a course, and keep her life quiet. But lately it just didn't seem to be enough and it was as if she could feel something deep inside of her that was dying to get out, but she couldn't let it out because fitting in was hard enough as it was. She thumped down on a log and put her head in her hands trying to push the feelings away. She was supposed to be enjoying herself right now, not falling apart.

The feeling became so intense that Kristabell jumped up from the log and began walking quickly, wiping furiously at her face, gasping back sobs, and not really paying much attention to where she was going, just walking randomly and purposelessly through the trees.

Any person who has grown up in a city has a certain awareness of that city around them, and even though this little patch of woods that Kristabell knew so well could make her feel like she was in a real forest for a little while, she had to pretend, just a little, that she couldn't see the flicker of the city at the edge of the woods, and it didn't take Kristabell long to realize, even in her disturbed state, that she couldn't see the city at the woods' edge anymore and, in fact, from where she stood, the woods appeared to have no edge at all, and this would have been alarming enough, if it hadn't been for the man on the large black horse charging towards her.

Chapter 2

The man on the horse, who was wearing armour—not clean shiny armour—and wielding a sword—a really big sword—, leapt down yelling, and ran, at remarkable speed, past Kristabell only to impale another man on his sword. The dead man, the one with the sword through his middle, had been about to knock an arrow to a bowstring. Kristabell had been his planned target.

Kristabell fainted.

* * *

The man pulled his sword free and cleaned it before sheathing it. He removed the breast plate of his armour just as another man rode up.

"Rowan. Did you get the last one?" the big man asked, still seated on his horse.

Rowan passed the breast plate to the other man and said, "Yeah, he's just over there. I think he was going to try to take this girl hostage instead of fighting."

The big man sat on his horse holding the breast plate and looking puzzled as his friend knelt and picked the girl up. "What are you doing?" he asked.

Rowan looked at his friend and shook his head. "Don't be thick Leif. I'm taking her with us. She's unconscious. We can't just leave her here."

"Oh. You mean she's not dead? That's kind of nice."

20

Rowan shook his head again and smiled as he somewhat awkwardly mounted his horse with the girl in his arms. He settled her head against his chest, took the reigns, and they turned, heading back to where their pack horses were waiting on the main road and continued on their way.

"Where do you suppose she's from?" Leif asked.

"I don't know," Rowan admitted. "She's not from the fort,' he motioned to the large stone castle on the hill top behind them. "Other than that, there aren't any settlements for miles and I don't recognize her as being from any of the big families, but she's soft and clean and she smells really nice. She isn't a poor man's daughter. Her clothes are just a little odd somehow though. Fine and well made, but worn too. And her hair ..." which was loose and spilling over his arm. "A farm girl wouldn't have time to stop and brush her hair out like this in the middle of the day."

The two men rode along and speculated like this for about a half an hour, coming to the consensus as they did, that she must have somehow crossed over from the other world, and as they rode and talked this over, Kristabell slowly came to. At first she was dreaming that she was dreaming. In the dream she had fallen asleep on her bed in an uncomfortable position after her bath and she was dreaming that she was being carried by a friendly, though smelly, knight through the forest on horseback. But as she became more lucid she realized that the part about her bed was the dream and the parts about the knight, and the uncomfortable position, were real. There was armour digging into her back and chain mail against her cheek. Kristabell tried to adjust to this highly improbable set of circumstances but she couldn't think straight until she got into a more comfortable position, so she opened her eyes and tried to shift. Shifting, of course, alerted the two men to her conscious state, and it also caused her to over balance, which in turn forced the knight with whom she was riding to hold onto her more tightly.

"Whoa!" he said, shifting her so that she was looking into his face. Kristabell gulped as she found herself staring into a pair of dark, amused eyes. She leaned back just a little so that she could get a better look at his over all appearance. He had dark shoulder length hair and handsome features. A refined nose and good cheekbones. Even with a week's worth of stubble and grime he was ... Kristabell gazed at him for a long moment trying to put her finger on it. He was just a bit ... pretty ... in a way that made her want to keep looking at him. *Cripes Kristabell,* she though to herself. *Stop staring at him and wake up. You're still dreaming!* But she was awake and she knew it. She couldn't tell from where she sat, basically in his lap, but she didn't think that he was a very big person. He was however, really quite strong.

"Are you alright?" he asked.

"Um, sort of. I mean, I'm not hurt. I'm just confused," she paused, "Where am I?"

"You're in the coastal Kingdom of Nova Britannia. My name is Rowan. I'm the captain of the King's Army. This is my second and my foster brother Leif."

Kristabell looked over at the other man. He was the polar opposite of Rowan. Where Rowan was compact and dark, Leif was huge and blond with waist length dread locks, a beard, bright blue eyes and a sunburn. He grinned and waved at her. She sat there stunned for a moment then said, "My name is Kristabell and ... I don't think that I'm from around here."

They rode on in silence for a few minutes before it occurred to Kristabell to ask, "Why were you in the forest and who was the man with the bow?"

"He wasn't a man. Leif and I were ambushed on the road by a group of elves but they were inexperienced and under-armed.

That one ran as soon as he realized they were in trouble and I followed him."

"Are elves ... bad?"

"Always. They are evil. That one would not have been kind to you," Rowan answered, and his voice was hard and stern.

Leif turned to her and said something but she couldn't understand him. It was strange because it was as if he was speaking English but none of the words were quite right and even stranger was the feeling she had that she'd heard people speak like this before and even though she could understand Rowan, his accent and the cadence of his voice were just like her parents faded Irish accents.

"Why can I understand you but not him?" she asked Rowan.

"I don't ... really ... know," he answered slowly, hesitating with each word. "But magic works strangely. Maybe it's because I'm the first person who you met after you crossed the threshold between the worlds. Or maybe it's because I saved your life. Sometimes magic creates special bonds like that, but I'm not a good one to ask. You'd need to talk to a druid to get a proper answer."

"Thank you for saving my life," she told him.

"Oh, no problem," he said as if she'd thanked him for passing the salt. "I would have killed the elf anyway but, I'm glad he didn't kill you first."

"So ... I'm from a different world, magic exists here, and elves are bad, right?"

Rowan turned to Leif and translated what she had just said. She could still understand Rowan even when he spoke to someone else and she felt self-conscious hearing her words repeated. Both men started nodding in agreement. "Sounds about right to us," Rowan told her, but it didn't sound as if either he or his big friend were especially disturbed by the facts. At least, not as disturbed as Kristabell was.

Kristabell tried to absorb these new bits of information. An hour ago none of this could be real, now somehow she had managed to open a door to a ... Kristabell looked around her and back at the hill that was disappearing into the distance. *Had* she somehow walked into a parallel world? Or, was she really lying with a concussion somewhere in the woods having a hallucination brought on by too many fantasy novels? She looked around some more. The lay of the land and the flora were just right for Vancouver, but there was *no* Vancouver. They were riding along a dirt road through a forest on a route that would have been approximately equivalent to King Edward Avenue. Finally it occurred to Kristabell to ask where she was being taken, "Where are we going?"

"Home," Rowan answered in a tired but satisfied tone, then it seemed to occur to him that this was not an adequate response. "We're heading to my family's home. We were fighting north of here but everybody needs to start preparing for the winter, including our enemies. We had a major skirmish a week ago but we've forced them back into the eastern hills. It will take them time to regroup and their supplies and weapons are running low so we have a bit of time to breathe. Hopefully they will stay quiet until the spring, but for now we have a chance to go to our homes, rest, and help with the harvest."

Kristabell thought about her own garden back home and how the vegetables were all ready to be picked and the thought of home reminded her of her parents. She felt a pang at the thought of them worrying about her. Was time passing at the same rate here? She hoped her parents weren't worrying. Rowan seemed to sense her sudden discomfiture and said to her, "Don't worry. You'll be welcome at my family's home. They're good people. They'll make sure you're alright." The way he said it made her trust him although she couldn't think why.

They rode in silence for what seemed about an hour before she asked, "Where is your home?"

"It's not too much further. We'll be there in time for the evening meal."

"Do we keep riding east of here?"

"Yes, and north a little. It's by a lake. In a while, we will be able to see it when the road swings past the west end of the lake. The house is at the east end, high on the hill."

"Deer Lake," Kristabell said mostly to herself.

"Yes. That's what we call it too, but we use the old words. Fiannasmere," Rowan replied, a note of surprise in his voice.

Kristabell sat and watched the forest go by. It was beautiful lush forest. Intoxicatingly lush, with pure clean air flowing out from the shade, and the sounds of birds echoing from within. The trees were massive majestic columns. This was, she realized, old growth forest. Two hours ago, in her existence, this would have been streets, traffic, stores and houses. It almost made her cry to see the beauty of the forest and then to think of it decimated in favour of houses and concrete. As she let her eyes wander deep into the forest she saw a flicker of white.

Now, there is a big difference between what we *expect* to see in our lives, and what we *want* to see, and it took Kristabell a few strange jarring moments to let herself believe that what she was seeing deep in the forest was real, because if she let herself believe only to find herself mistaken, the disappointment might crush her. But as the flicker of white moved closer Kristabell realized that it truly was a unicorn, glistening white and silver in the dappled light. She sat bolt upright and almost overbalanced again, forcing Rowan to put a hand around her waist to keep her from losing her awkward side saddle perch in front of him. "Look!" She had to make an effort to keep her voice down. "I knew it! I knew they had to be real somewhere! I knew that it was impossible to have feelings so strong for something that was imaginary!"

The big man, Leif, looked at her and said something. "He wants to know if you have unicorns in your world," Rowan told her.

"No," Kristabell shook her head. "There is an old story about a flood and a man called Noah who built a ship big enough to save a male and female of all the animals in the world and in the official version there is no mention of unicorns, but in the unofficial version they tried to get the unicorns to come but the unicorns were to foolish or crazy and they drowned in the flood."

"We have the same story," Rowan told her, "Except in our version, it's the king of Babylon, and he sends his son out to find two unicorns and the son fails, so the daughter runs off the ship at the last possible moment just as the storm is really beginning to rage. She's gone for just a short time and comes back with two unicorns. A male and a female. And so they say we have women to thank that there are still Unicorns in the world."

The unicorn disappeared back into the depths of the forest and Kristabell sat quietly as they continued to ride. Her heart was filled with the deep rapture of one whose had a life's longing fulfilled and she was beyond speech, or so she thought, but just at that moment they came to a bend in the road and rounded the western end of the lake. There, like a glowing beacon of beauty and wonder was a castle, high on the hilltop, partially surrounded by trees at the eastern end of the lake.

It was like no castle Kristabell had ever seen before. It was earthier than the pictures of medieval castles she'd seen in books, and nothing at all like Neuschwanstein. It's smooth walls reminded her of old adobe and it had pillars formed of giant cedar logs. There were several graceful turrets, two of them topped with domes like elongated onions, like the ones on Russian orthodox churches, and a high wall from which she could see armed sentinels scanning the landscape. It looked delicate somehow, and golden and ethereal. As they made there way around the lake towards the road that lead up to the gates she could make out great carved wocden doors in a graceful archway. "I can't believe how beautiful it is. I've never seen anything like it in my life!"

Rowan and Leif just smiled.

The awe Kristabell had felt since waking up to find herself in this ... Situation ...? Predicament ...?—she wasn't sure what to call the curious turn her life had taken—was almost encugh to push aside the awkward self-consciousness she felt at riding so close to Rowan, but she couldn't help notice that her presence didn't seem to be bothering him in the least. She guessed that he was just a gentleman and, as it would slow them down if she walked and there was a shield, a bow, a quiver of arrows and a bed roll tied to the saddle behind him, there wasn't anywhere else she could ride. The other concern that was stirring anxiously in her chest was that, despite Rowan's reassurance, she really didn't have any real idea as to what was going to happen to her once they reached the castle, but it seemed as if she was about to find out.

Chapter 3

Rowan and Leif had been, at least it seemed to Kristabell, expected by their family, and many happy loud people awaited them in the courtyard which was lined with apple trees and hip laden rose bushes. The late afternoon sun and the slightly turned leaves gave the scene a gilded surreal fairy tale quality, like a picture from one of her story books. Leif lifted her down from Rowan's horse and held her hand for a moment to make sure she had her balance while Rowan dismounted. The two men were swamped by three women, two teenaged boys and two older men and there was, for several minutes, a loud rush of chattering and hugging. Kristabell tried to hide behind a tree. She listened to the talking, paying attention to the words, and realized that, if she concentrated hard she could understand about three in every ten words that they spoke. Rowan however, hadn't forgotten about her and he pulled her out from behind the tree by her elbow and brought her over to what Kristabell guessed, based on the resemblance, must be his sister. They were joined by the other two women who eyed her with not unfriendly curiosity.

Rowan nodded towards a brown haired woman in her late thirties, "Kristabell, this is my mother Bronwen, and these are my sisters Fenna and Nessa."

Kristabell smiled at them and nodded shyly. She wanted to be polite, she really did, she didn't want to be rude to these people, but right at that moment she wished that the ground would open up and swallow her whole. Somehow Rowan made everything okay.

He looked at the smaller of his two sisters, the one who resembled him, and said, "I think Kristabell is very nervous right now. I found her in the forest today and she doesn't understand much of what we say, although she does understand me. I need you to take care of her for me. Set her up in one of the good spare rooms and find her some clothes that fit so that she has something more to wear while she's here. Make sure she gets to dinner."

Fenna made a comment that Kristabell felt she should have been able to understand but couldn't quite grasp. Rowan laughed and told Kristabell, "My sister says that I'm treating her like an incompetent child and that she knows how to take care of a guest. I'm leaving you in good hands. I need to get this armour off and take a bath. I'll see you at dinner." And off he strode.

Kristabell felt a moment of panic as he walked away but it faded the moment Fenna turned to her and smiled. Fenna was like a female version of Rowan. She said something to her mother and Kristabell picked out the words "trunk" and "east room". Bronwen nodded and smiled, then Fenna took Kristabell's hand and said, "Come."

First Fenna brought her up to a room that Kristabell understood to be Fenna's own bedroom. There was some general clutter, a pile of clothes, a hair brush lying on the bed, a tangled wad of jewellery on a dresser. For a moment or two Fenna fussed at the messy regions of her room as if embarrassed and then abandoned the fussing with a shrug and a grin and rummaged around through drawers and chests until she had found an extra brush, a comb, a small mirror, and a few other oddments that she thought might be useful like hair ties. Then Fenna took Kristabell to the room next door which was, apparently, the east room. She indicated, grinning and fluttering, that this would be Kristabell's room. It was a simple room with the same adobe type walls as the outside of the castle, stone floors, wood beams and wood window frames in the thick walls. The furniture was simple, well made, beautiful, and there was a fireplace with a wonderful carved mantle full of Kells-esque tangled beasts. Fenna placed the toiletry items on the dresser top and Kristabell hung her shoulder bag from a hook next to the door.

It was good when the realization came, of how much worse things could be, that what Rowan had said about his family was true. She was not being forced into slavery or eaten or any of the other more painful or violent scenarios that Kristabell had imagined, and though it had been sheer fluke that she had appeared in this world when and where she had, so far, she seemed to have fallen into good hands. Even communication was not as big a problem as it could be, and as Fenna prattled on, keeping up an almost constant flow of words, Kristabell found that she usually had at least a vague sense of what she was saying. Fenna reached out a hand and again said, "Come."

She lead Kristabell up to a nearby attic and began opening trunks and then closing them again. When she found the one that she was looking for she motioned to Kristabell to come help her move it and together they carried it back to the east room. Fenna was still talking. Kristabell was listening intently. She was pretty sure that Fenna was trying to tell her that the trunk was filled with Fenna's own old, out grown clothes, and that while Fenna didn't think that the colours would suit Kristabell as well as Nessa's would, she didn't think Nessa's clothes would fit. Once back in the room Fenna began taking the clothes out of the trunk and hanging them in the ward-robe. They had been packed with lavender in a cedar trunk and the comforting smell of herbs and wood billowed around the room as Fenna shook out the fabric. There were a couple of dresses but mostly it was filled with tunics of varying lengths and styles and loose linen pants, some ankle length but most about mid calf and everything was in earth tones. Deep reds, russets, creams and browns which, while not perfect, would suit Kristabell well enough, assuming she was even there long enough to need any of it. After the clothes had been hung and the trunk set aside Fenna, once again, with a smile, extended her hand, "Come."

Fenna began showing Kristabell around the castle, naming things as they went. Kristabell tried to pay attention to what Fenna was saying but the castle itself was too beautiful and all she could do was stare, amazed, at her surroundings. The entire castle was elegant, simple and homey, but it also had a grandeur to it, and a golden glow that made it feel humble *and* exalted both at the same time. It didn't feel primitive. It felt idyllic, like a fantasy concocted by Victorian Arts and Crafts enthusiasts or like storybook pictures from the Golden Age of Illustration. Kristabell couldn't even begin to imagine what it would feel like to call a place like this home. Fenna brought her to a window high in a turret. The view of the lake was dazzling. With the sun low in the sky it looked like a divine accident involving a very large vial of gold glitter. A bell sounded and Fenna's hand was extended, yet again, like the hand of a friend. Kristabell took it and Fenna smiled and said, "Dinner. Come," and pulled Kristabell off through the castle.

The dining hall, Kristabell couldn't bring herself to think of it as a dining *room*, was just as comfortably magnificent as the rest of the castle, with carved chairs and a long table that was being filled with simple wholesome food. Cheese, rye bread, apples, some kind of meat, stew with lima beans, and a salad with spinach, more cheese, and nuts, all served in beautifully crafted pottery bowls. Bronwen and Nessa were there already, as were the two younger boys—Dunstan and Gareth, Fenna said their names motioning to them—and then introduced her to the two older men, Mark and Nels. Kristabell was pretty sure

that she had understood correctly that Mark was Fenna and
Rowan's father and Nels their uncle. Within moments Rowan
and Leif appeared. Free of their weapons and armour, clean and
in comfortable looking linen and wool clothing, Kristabell was
able to get a better impression of them. Though Leif looked
a bit lankier than he'd seemed in armour he was still massive
and imposing, and Rowan was lean and lithe. She also realized
that they were a bit younger than she had first assumed. She'd
figured that they were twenty-six or twenty-seven but they
were probably closer to twenty three. Rowan sat down next to
her so that she was between him and Fenna with Leif across
the table from them next to Nessa. Rowan reached for the
bread basket and selected a thick slice for himself then passed
the basket to Kristabell.

"I trust Fenna's got you properly settled?" he asked, smiling.

"Yes, very properly. Thank you."

"Do you eat meat?" he asked her as the platter was passed by.
She shook her head.

"Yeah. Didn't think so. You'll want some of the stew then?"

"Um, yes please," she replied, briefly wondering how it was
that he knew that she didn't like meat. He motioned for her
bowl and she passed it to him as he stood and ladled stew into
both their bowls.

Kristabell was much hungrier than she'd realized and bread
and cheese had never tasted so good. The apples were delicious too. They were a variety that she wasn't used to. She
turned to Rowan, "Thank you ... For bringing me here. I don't
know what I would have done if you hadn't."

"It's nothing. It's what any good person would do, and you
really are welcome here."

"In my world people aren't so quick to invite strangers into
their homes. I really do appreciate this," she told him very
seriously.

"You're safe here in any case. You wouldn't have been, alone in the forest," he said, still serious.

They seemed like happy well rounded people, Rowan's family. There was a lot of talking and laughing as they ate. It was a relaxed atmosphere. No one stood on ceremony. It didn't seem like a repressed feudal society. Kristabell sat and listened to the conversation, picking out familiar words in this strange evolution of English, because that's what they were speaking. She could hear that it had grown out of more or less the same group of languages as the English she had grown up speaking. She picked out several words she knew: goblin, fork, turnip, arrow ... Rowan would turn to her and explain what they were talking about. A battle, Gareth's archery practice, Nessa's goats. As they ate Rowan and Fenna would lean behind her and exchange whispers and gestures. They almost sounded like they were bickering and it ended with what sounded like a refusal from Fenna, and a resigned sigh from Rowan, after which he somewhat tentatively asked Kristabell, "Do you have a husband or ... an understanding with anyone?"

"Oh, no," Kristabell answered shaking her head vigorously, taken aback by the question. No one had ever enquired after her relationship status before. "I um ... I'm only eighteen and that's well ... It's seen as a bit too young, where I'm from Or, rather ... well what I mean is, not too young to ... have some-one, just too young to be married to them. And I, I don't ... have anyone, that is." She blushed.

Fenna reached over Kristabell and wacked the top of Rowan's head then snapped something at him. He grinned ruefully then and told Kristabell, "My sister tells me that I'm being rude I'm sorry if I made you uncomfortable." But he didn't stop smiling. Kristabell blushed some more then turned her attention back to the rest of the table.

They were a big bustling family in a way that Kristabell's family never had been. She and her parents had had good times together. They were a loving family but Kristabell had been raised by solemn parents and she had grown up to be a quiet person. After a time the conversation turned to Kristabell and the story of how she had been found unconscious in the forest. They took turns asking her questions and everyone seemed to be of the same opinion, that she had come through from another world. "There are many stories of this from the old country. They also say that the fairies could walk from one world to another with ease, but that the other world, the one that is closest to ours, probably your world, is hostile now, and difficult to navigate."

After Mark, Rowan's father, had said this, and Rowan had translated for her, Kristabell had looked at him with big eyes. "Please tell me that the fairies aren't evil?" she asked, realizing that they seemed to speak of the fairies in a way that was quite distinct from the elves.

He laughed. "They are nothing like the elves. Some of the Fay are good. Some are ambivalent. They are all non-interventionist or neutral when it comes to our war with the exiled prince. There is a long mistrust between human and fay."

Kristabell nodded, satisfied with the answer she had received. She had read too many books about fairies to have expected them to be good in a black and white sense, but at least they weren't evil. "Unicorns, fairies, elves, and goblins are all things that people tell stories about in the world that I came from, but no one sees them. Some of us hope that they're real, the unicorns anyway, but most people are convinced that they're just stories."

Rowan translated and his family sat nodding and discussing until Bronwen turned to Leif and asked, "Play us some music?" Kristabell understood the whole sentence. Leif nodded, rose from the table and sat behind a large beautiful harp. It was an incongruous image. It was easier to imagine Leif wielding an axe than playing a harp, however, play the harp he did, and beautifully. Fenna sang along sometimes in a beautiful rich alto, as did Dunstan harmonizing with her in his boy soprano. Their music was beautiful and its delicate style reinforced the impression Kristabell had that these people must be at least in part descended from the Celts, or whatever they called the equivalent to the Celts in this world.

The evening was passing. It was getting late. Leif played one last song. A slow one. "This is a lullaby," Rowan whispered to her. The melody made her feel very small, very young, and she wondered if the melody was one that existed in her world as well. It made her miss her parents. Everyone sat quietly for a moment after the music stopped and Rowan's mother said something that Rowan translated as, "Time for bed." Fenna held out her hand and said, "Come."

"I'll find you in the morning," Rowan said to her, "and take you to see Gwydion, our Druid. He will be able to explain things to us a little better, help clear up your situation a little. Okay?"

Kristabell nodded and smiled hesitantly.

"Goodnight," Rowan smiled, and then Fenna lead her away in the opposite direction.

Once up in the east room Fenna opened the wardrobe and pulled out a night gown. She filled a basin with hot water from a pitcher that she had filled in the kitchen on the way up, then closed the window shutters and pulled the heavy curtains over the windows. She went to the door and smiled a goodnight.

"Goodnight," Kristabell said to Fenna.

Fenna's smile deepened. "Goodnight," she said and softly closed the door behind her.

Kristabell looked around the room unsure, for a moment, of what to do then she realized that she really would like to lie down and went about the business of getting ready for bed. She took off her clothes and hung them up, took out the little moonstone earrings she'd been wearing and removed the chain with the ring on it from around her neck. It had belonged to her mother and she always kept it with her. She brushed her hair out then braided it, tying it with one of the grosgrain ribbons Fenna had given her, and went over to the basin and washed her face and hands in the herb infused water with the creamy soap that Fenna had also left for her. She towelled off her face and neck, brushed her teeth with tooth brush and tooth powder, then pulled the nightgown over her head and replaced the chain with its ring on it around her neck. She climbed into bed and blew out the beeswax candle that Fenna had left on her bedside. It was then that the enormity of all that had happened hit. She was not at home. She wouldn't be in her bed when her parents got home from work in the wee hours. They might never see her again. She might never see them again. She could leave her world behind easily enough, Kristabell had always found it an overwhelming assault to her senses, but to disappear from the people who had loved her and raised her without a trace? The idea of them not knowing where she was or if she was alive made her eyes water up. They were stoic people who would cope with her death, they would miss her if she was far away. She wasn't a small child, she was independent and mature and was used to the freedom that afforded her, but she knew her mother and father, and not knowing if she was okay would be the hardest thing of all. Kristabell rolled onto her side and snuggled into the big soft bed. She wiped her eyes on her sleeve and let them close. Maybe this was all just a dream. Maybe she would wake up in her own bed in the real world, but she felt guilty for not wanting to. Maybe she was lying in the woods dying in the real world. Maybe she was already dead. *At least someone will find my body and my parents will know that I'm dead.*

Chapter 4

She dropped off into a deep dreamless sleep and it felt like only moments before Fenna was in her room again opening the shutters on another perfect sunny day. Kristabell blinked, disoriented by the unicorn tapestry on the wall that was almost like the one in her room at home, only this one was the real thing, and the one at home was a cheap reproduction. Fenna had brought fresh water for the basin. She chucked the old water out the window without looking and there was a shout from below. She cringed and shouted an apology, then grinned at Kristabell and tossed her some clothes from the wardrobe. Kristabell climbed out of bed and scrambled into the clothes, a simple deep red tunic with drawstrings to give it some shape, three quarter sleeves with slightly gathered cuffs that buttoned, and a pair of loose brown pants that tied at the waist to make them adjustable. They were comfortable and functional and went well with her shoes. Kristabell splashed her face, unbraided her hair and brushed it quickly, grabbed her green cardigan and then followed Fenna, who was waiting, down to the dinning hall.

Not everyone was there that morning. Fenna's father and uncle as well as Rowan, Leif, Nessa, and one of the younger boys were absent, but there were two older women at the table who were introduced to Kristabell as Deirdre and Gretta. They looked at Kristabell with interest but finished their breakfast and left. Fenna tried to explain who they were and Kristabell was left with the impression that one was the steward's wife and that the other was a great aunt, but she really wasn't sure. Breakfast was oatmeal with honey, goat's milk, nuts and chopped fruit. There was also a dish of hard boiled eggs on the table. It was the kind of food that Kristabell liked and she was hungry. Rowan walked in just as she was finishing. "Good morning," he smiled at her as he helped himself to the food.

"Good morning," she returned.

"Did you sleep well?" he asked.

"Yes, thank you. The room was very comfortable."

"Good," he said, then, "If you don't mind waiting for me to eat, I'd like to take you down to meet Gwydion. He's very old but he's still sharp and he knows more than anyone I've ever met. He used to be the head of the council of druids back during Sven and Freya's reign. He would be fascinated to meet you, and I think it would be a good idea to talk to him."

"Alright," Kristabell agreed to it wondering, really, what choice she had, but she wanted to learn more about this place that she had inadvertently wandered into. She had a barrage of questions surfacing in her mind and it would be nice to spend some time figuring things out. She and Rowan chatted comfortably about nothing in particular for a few minutes then Kristabell asked him, "Do you grow all of your own food here?"

"Mm, We do," Rowan answered her, nodding and swallowing. He described to her the barley and rye fields, the extensive gardens and orchards, the goat herd—largely managed by Nessa—and the apiary. There were also extensive hunting grounds, chickens, and, further out, fields of flax and a large sheep herd. There was a large fine house in the village that belonged to a family of expert weavers. Anything that they didn't produce themselves they could trade for.

Rowan finished eating and motioned for her to follow him. As they walked through the castle she still couldn't help looking around her at the beautiful architecture. There were scroll work patterns of ivy leaves and feathers carved into the pillars and archways. Nothing was overdone, only natural and beautiful. She asked Rowan, "So who, ultimately, is in charge here?"

"Ultimately, my mother and father and someday, either me or Nessa, but it isn't so clear cut as that." He explained the way things were run and from what she understood it was a sort of co-operative communal democratic feudalism which sounded like it should just cancel itself out and implode but they made it work neatly and elegantly. They passed through the courtyard, then Rowan stopped her near the gate and lead her to a small armoury. He belted a sword to his waist, slung a quiver of arrows over his shoulder and picked up and strung a bow. "Why do you need those?" Kristabell asked, nervous of the weapons.

"We have to walk through a small woods but, mostly, I just feel more comfortable having them these days. Do you know how to shoot?" he asked reaching for a second bow, but Kristabell shook her head vigorously and backed away.

Rowan shrugged, nodded and then left the bow.

They headed down the main road but after a short distance Rowan told her, "This road leads down to the village and maybe there will be a time to visit it, but today we're going this way." And he lead her down a side path.

"What about the kingdom as a whole, how is it run?" Kristabell asked, curious now after Rowan's description of the running of his family's estate.

"Well there's the King, but that role is somewhat ceremonial. It doesn't hold as much power as it once did. The majority of the actual management of the kingdom is done by a council of thirty members who are voted in by the people and it is run largely by consensus," Rowan explained.

Kristabell was impressed at the level of forward thinking traditionalism. They had blended socialism, anarchy, and monarchy and come out with an organized system that worked. "Can women vote?" she asked.

Rowan gave her a funny look and asked her, "Why wouldn't they be allowed to vote?"

"Women have only gradually been allowed to vote in my world. We've been allowed to vote for roughly the last 100 years where I'm from, but in some parts of the world women are prevented from voting by their husbands or fathers even though it's technically legal. They don't have any freedom in those places."

"Women here can do whatever they want and as far as I know it's always been that way," Rowan replied, clearly baffled. "The current head of the council is a woman and while women do often maintain traditional roles like household management and child rearing, men do that too, and while there are definitely more men in the army, roughly a third of the archers are women. Men aren't excluded from crafts that are typically female dominated like weaving. My brother Dunstan is doing a textiles apprenticeship. I take it things are different in your world?"

"Yes," Kristabell replied. "In some parts of the world women have no rights. They are seen as the property of their fathers and husbands. In the part of the world where I live we have what is called 'equality' and things are not that extreme at all, but it's still harder for women in some ways. Women are encouraged to go out into the world and do whatever men do but it's a very different world ... I don't quite know how to articulate this but ... it's like the traditional roles that women used to hold because they had no other choice have lost their value, and men are still seen as weak if they stay home to watch the kids and make supper, but women who join the police force or the army often face discrimination. It's all twisted out of shape and people don't raise their own children anymore they just pack them off to day care each morning and everyone works, but women are paid less. Then men and women come home together and fight with each other over who is going to clean the house because ..." She shrugged.

Rowan looked at her, completely appalled. "I never imagined that things could be so imbalanced. Here, work is just work and it doesn't matter who does it as long as you're tired and satisfied at the end of the day. Obviously there are some things that women will always be better suited to, and that it's simply more practical for them to do by virtue of the fact that they have breasts and wombs, men just can't compete there, but we're bigger and stronger, so you're not going to meet as many female stonemasons or blacksmiths either. Obviously there are differences that go beyond size and anatomy but it just isn't that big a deal here. Many choose to eschew gender altogether. I know your world is what you're used to but it sounds ..." He trailed off, not wanting to offend her.

"It's alright. I was never very happy there." She looked around at the woods. They were walking on a path that lead down and around the hillside. The leaves were touched with gold and the air was fresh. They came to a place where they could look out over golden fields and orchards. Kristabell gasped. "It's so beautiful here. It seems so peaceful."

"It would be if it weren't for ..."

"The exiled prince?" Kristabell finished, turning it into a question.

Rowan nodded, and his expression turned tired and bitter all of a sudden.

"I know you probably don't even want to think about that right now but, who is the exiled prince?"

Rowan sighed heavily, "The old queen's younger brother Seamus."

"Why was he exiled?" Kristabell asked as they started to walk again.

"He's power hungry, angry, and underhanded ..." Rowan started then paused as if reluctant to spoil a beautiful morning with the story, but it had been brought up and now it was on his mind so he shrugged and continued. "According to rumour, about twenty years ago he accused his sister Sulamith of something, we don't know what. It was before her reign and whatever it was, if there was any truth to it at all, it was covered up by her parents and the druids and Seamus never repeated it, ever. Instead he brooded and plotted and sought revenge. After many years he succeeded in killing the Queen. He nearly took the throne but the army and the council supported the Queen's son and heir, not Seamus. His plot was exposed and he was exiled. Liam took the throne and has maintained the kingdom fairly and peacefully even though he was, and I suppose still is, very young. I was in the military by the time the exiled prince had formed his own army and tried to overthrow Liam. I had been a page in the castle as a youth, and then a squire, I knew the king when he was a boy and I still like and respect him. There was a large decisive battle about three years ago. I suppose I fought well. That's when the king and council appointed me captain of the army."

Kristabell was quiet for a moment, sorting and compartmentalizing information, including the expressions that had flitted across Rowan's face as he'd related the information. "Are the elves with the exiled prince?"

"The elves are for the elves, but they will jump on any wagon that they think will get them where they want to go, and right now they *are* riding with Seamus."

They rounded a bend in the path and came out in a clearing by a little brook. There was a stone bridge and across the bridge was a little stone cottage. They crossed the bridge and walked up to the door. Rowan knocked and a grouchy voice called out from within.

"It's me, Rowan. I brought you a visitor," Rowan called to the grouchy occupant. The door opened and a funny little old man stuck his head out. "Gwydion, this is Kristabell."

The old man opened his eyes wide for a moment and then pulled the door open wider and hustled them in saying something about Kristabell's name that Rowan responded to with, "Her name sounds strange to you because she came here yesterday from another world." Gwydion ushered them excitedly toward the table and chairs flapping his arms and exclaiming.

The old druid turned out to be more of a scholar and a librarian than anything particularly mystical, he was however very knowledgeable. He had a passion for learning and wanted to hear all about the world that Kristabell had come from and how it differed from theirs. Kristabell and Rowan spent the entire morning drinking chamomile tea and eating biscuits while looking at books and poring over maps. Over the course of the morning they had figured which events had changed the course of history and caused what Gwydion was convinced had originally been one world, to split and become two. The first difference was the unicorns. The second difference was that Christianity had never come into being in Rowan's world. Jesus had instead wandered east, become a Buddhist and founded the "Thousand Years Peace". Apparently there were very few wars in that part of the world but also, curiously, from what they knew about it, very few humans either, just Fay. The Hebrews had largely disbanded, some of them joining the Zoroastrians and the rest of them meeting up with the Romany and travelling the world. Kristabell found a certain amount of irony in that idea. The majority of the Jewish faith had been lost to antiquity. Except for the angels.

"Angels?" Kristabell had said disbelieving.

"You took fairies, unicorns and elves in stride. Why not angels?" Rowan looked at her, eyebrow raised.

"I guess that I've always seen them as being a part of the Christian world which I've never believed in so why would I believe in angels?" she shrugged. "What are they like?"

"I don't know. I've never met one." Rowan turned to Gwydion.

Gwydion was able to understand much of what Kristabell said, not because of any magical connections but because he understood the old languages from which both versions of English had evolved. Kristabell's version contained more Latin and French, and the version native to Rowan's world contained more from the Celtic tongues, but the structure was similar. Gwydion answered Kristabell's question about the angels. "They are reclusive and stay in the mountains. They haven't associated with humans since the plague wars that forced us out of the old country. They are big creatures, stern, with deep blue or crimson feathery wings. They wield swords and wear armour. I met one once when I was in my early thirties. He was fierce and arrogant."

"Old testament angels," Kristabell murmured mostly to herself. A word had caught her ear as Gwydion had described the angel to her though. "What were the 'Plague Wars'?" she asked.

"Hundreds of years ago we lived in the old country," Rowan pointed to a world map that was spread out on the table and being held down by a stoneware teapot and a plate of cookies. It looked like an early map from Kristabell's world and it wasn't especially accurate. He pointed to what would have been the northwest coast of France, Belgium, The Netherlands, Denmark, coastal Germany, Norway, Sweden and the UK and Ireland. "These are the regions that many of the people who live here now came from. One thousand years ago there were sorcerers and they weren't good people. They began fighting in this region," he pointed to the Mediterranean, "using a magic that spread illness amongst the people. They were trying to wipe out each other's armies, but they lost control of their spells and wiped out everyone else too. Our people lived on the edges and we heard stories of what was happening. We fled first to the north, then to the west. About 3000 of us headed west in ships. 2000 or so made it to the new country. Around eight hundred of us settled in this region. My family has been living on this hill for five hundred years," Rowan pointed to a map of Nova Britannia which was a tiny area only slightly larger than Vancouver itself and almost cut off from the mainland by marshlands to the east. The map appeared to have borders even within the borders, like the holes in swiss cheese. "The angels are the ones who stopped the war. They intervened to stop the sorcerers but they annihilated everything and everyone left behind by the plague in the process. Their magic is very powerful and they turned all of this into a wasteland," Rowan motioned towards all of mainland Europe. "They said that the war was so evil that it would seep over into other worlds. We've lived in this part of the world ever since, and remained somewhat isolated."

"It did seep over into my world," Kristabell said. "There was a plague in that part of my world around the same time. They say that it killed thirty to sixty percent of the population. It was called 'The Black Death'."

Gwydion reacted to this as if he had been given a precious gem or a rare piece of art, his eyebrows raised and fingertips together in blissful contemplation.

Kristabell was in all honesty just a little bit confused however. "Didn't you know that? About the plague? I mean others have crossed over. Right? It's not just me. There are stories in my world about fairies crossing over and bringing humans back here with them, because that's what this place is to us. It's the fairy realm, isn't it? We just didn't realize that there was a human population here too. Haven't any other people told you these things?"

Gwydion answered her, speaking with care to make himself understood. "Only the Fay pass between the worlds." He was very serious, solemn even. "We, the druids, forswore magic after the plague wars. It is not stuff for us to possess. We misplaced much knowledge on our escape to here. You are the first person with this knowledge that I have spoken to. We have not, in many generations, met someone from your world."

"Then ... How did I get here? What about my parents? There must be some way to let them know that ... I'm okay? Isn't there?" Kristabell brushed the tears that came aside and looked imploringly at the old druid, but she was sure that he was refusing to answer her. A look crossed his face. A look of conflict. It was a wounded look. As if he had been pierced by an invisible arrow, and he said, "Let it be. You are safe here. Stay near Rowan. Don't walk the forests alone. There is little that can be done about your situation at present. Just ... try to rest easy. I know that it is not as simple to do as it is to say." He looked at her kindly then announced, "Alas, I am an old man and I need my nap. You young people do exhaust me."

Chapter 5

Kristabell left the little cottage following Rowan out into the sunshine and onto the hard packed dirt path. She felt quiet, pensive. Both more and less lost than when she'd arrived. "What did he mean Rowan?" she asked him, stopping on the little bridge and watching the water as it flickered and rushed over the rocks in the stream bed below. She turned and looked into Rowan's dark eyes. She saw a complicated confusion there, and then his face fell and he sighed. "Honestly ... I don't quite understand what he meant or *why* he said exactly *what* he said. Not enough to reassure you. I'm sorry."

She could see that he was telling the truth. Not just that he couldn't clear up Gwydion's statement, but that he was *sorry* he couldn't. Kristabell didn't look away but whispered, not entirely expecting an answer, "How *did* I get here? What happened to me? Why can I understand you? Am I dreaming? Am I a fai. . ." She didn't get the word fairy out. Rowan's fingers flew to her lips and he placed them there gently, but it was enough to keep her from speaking. There was a look close to panic in his eyes and he shook his head but it was a barely perceptible head shake and a new expression formed in his eyes. Understanding. Then he put his arms around her, drew her close and she stood there leaning against him, letting the steadiness of his heartbeat stop her world from reeling. She didn't make any move to leave his arms. She found that she rather liked it there. It was a strange feeling, new, and strange, but not unpleasant. After a few minutes Rowan said, "Let's not talk about this. Let's talk about something else. Tell me about you? What are you good at? What do you like to do?" He pulled away but took her hand and started walking, drawing her along beside him back up the path.

"Gardening mostly. Herbs, vegetables, fruit trees. I know my way around most growing things, although I have no experience with grains. I can cook too, but our kitchens are different and I've never cooked for more than three people. Other than that, I read."

"Read?" Rowan wrinkled his nose. "Old scrolls and documents like Gwydion?"

"No!" Kristabell smiled. "Well yes, sometimes if I'm curious about something but mostly, I like to read stories, you know, for fun. Adventure stories full of romance and magic. Stories that make me forget my own life, or make me feel like there is more out there than concrete and noise. This place is like something out of a story," she said wistfully. "I keep figuring that this must be a dream." She looked at Rowan, into his dark wild eyes.

"It's not a dream. I'm not dreaming. My eyes are open," he said a little cryptically and they walked back to the castle in silence, but still hand in hand.

* * *

They were back too late for lunch so Rowan lead her around the outside of the castle—it wasn't really that far—to the kitchen door. He ducked in and was out within minutes with half a loaf of fresh bread, some goat cheese that tasted like gouda, a little dish of butter, and some figs. As they sat in the shade at the edge of the kitchen garden and ate Rowan told her, "There's a lot that needs to be done right now so everyone pitches in. I figure you're all right if I leave you with Fenna and Thomas in the vegetable garden. They need help hauling cabbages. Just do what Gwydion said, and stay out of the woods."

"That's fine. I like cabbages. I mean from a physical tactile perspective as well as to eat. I have a bad habit of planting too many in my garden at home. I always end up giving half of them to a food bank." Rowan smiled at her and she asked him, "So, other than cabbages what else do you grow?"

"Kale," he answered. "Rutabagas, potatoes, carrots, kohlrabi, radishes ..." The list went on and on, "And in terms of fruit we grow apples, pears, plums, grapes, figs and cherries. There are hazelnut and walnut orchards as well."

"How did you get the variety of crops that you grow? Did you bring seeds and roots with you from the old country? How did you get potatoes up here?"

"Some were brought from the old country others were traded for from the south, or brought over from the Orient by ship."

Kristabell started asking about whether they tilled their soil or if they used no till methods, how they rotated their crops and then started in on fertilizers.

"Woah!" Rowan laughed. "I have no idea what kind of manure we put on the fields or when. I'm not usually here in the early spring, that's beyond me," he paused, "Your hands are so soft and your skin is so fair. I didn't figure you for the kind of girl who would know so much about dirt. I figured you were some rich mans pampered daughter."

"Definitely not," Kristabell shook her head. "Back home I decided that I didn't want to go to school anymore so I worked. I had my own garden, and I also worked at a garden centre which is a place where people go to buy seeds, pots, soil, and plants. My hands are always this soft and my skin always stays this colour. I don't tan or burn."

Rowan nodded thoughtfully.

* * *

Kristabell spent the rest of the day with Fenna and Thom, the head gardener, in one of the very large vegetable gardens that had been cut terrace style into the hillside and surrounded by a low stone wall. There were many cabbages. They loaded and carted cabbages all afternoon and Kristabell was glad that she was used to physical labour because she had never worked so hard in her entire life. That night at dinner she ate ravenously then sat and listened as if in a trance as Leif played his harp. She tumbled into bed and slept the sleep of the exhausted.

Life went on like this for the next few weeks and if Kristabell was dreaming she certainly wasn't waking up. She followed Rowan and Fenna around like a puppy dog, spending mornings with Rowan and Gwydion studying the new world where it seemed she now lived and learning its language. She would have lunch with Rowan and then they would go join Fenna for the rest of the day in the the gardens and orchards, packing fruit, vegetables and nuts into baskets and carting them up to the kitchens to be prepared for winter storage. At the end of the first week she had gotten comfortable enough with the new language that she felt more independent and Rowan would sometimes leave her if soldiers had come to Fiannasmere to report to him. The combination of good food, clean air, and hard work had Kristabell feeling strong and healthy in a way that she never had before in the city of her world, but it was more than that. Kristabell was happy. She felt at ease with these people, with Rowan and his family. They seemed to accept her. Rowan's parents treated her in much the same manner that they treated their other grown children. She and Fenna had become friends too. In fact Fenna was the first person that Kristabell had ever formed such a close friendship with, other than Evan, but when thoughts of Evan surfaced Kristabell pushed them aside with a brusqueness that bordered on cruel. Her friendship with Fenna was different too in that Fenna was a girl and they were the same age. They were both born gardeners and they could be falling down dead tired and still spend half the night talking, lying in one or the other's bed in their night gowns, stumbling around language differences, only to wake the next morning and start chattering away again. Kristabell had stopped going to Gwydion's cottage in the mornings, there was too much work to do, but Gwydion would come find her wherever she was, and quiz her language skills or ask her questions about her world. One day while she and Fenna were digging potatoes—uprooting the plants with a spade and their hands and then reaching down, scrabbling in the rich earth to grab the potatoes and chuck them into baskets for Rowan and Thom to retrieve and put on the cart—Thom had become irritated with Gwydion. "She's a good worker when you're not here bugging her with questions. Off with you you pesky old druid!"

Gwydion had bristled with indignation and bowed to Kristabell, "Perhaps I will see you tomorrow at the midday meal Miss Kristabell." Then he thumped off with all of the dignity he could muster. It was all Kristabell and Fenna could do not to burst into giggles. Even Rowan had pressed his lips together and looked away with his eyes full of mirth.

Nessa, who was two years older than Kristabell and Fenna, stayed, for the most part, with her goats. She could usually be found in the pastures or in the dairy but early on she had told Kristabell, "You stay out of the dairy. You're too much like Rowan and Fenna. You'll make the milk go sour."

Despite the fact that Kristabell wanted to see the dairy and Nessa's goats, she was quite taken with the idea that her very presence could curdle milk. Was it the agrarian version of frying a computer, and did Rowan and Fenna really curdle milk too? It intrigued her to know that Nessa was likewise excluded from the preparation of herbal salves and medicines. Apparently she had walked through the kitchen once when a batch of comfrey salve for wound healing was being prepared and the whole batch had needed to be thrown away as anyone who had used it had developed a mysterious rash and a craving for cheese. They said that it was because Nessa had a prickly personality.

And so, for the first time in her life, Kristabell felt like she fit in. The only dark cloud in her sky was the guilt she felt over her parents. She wished, with an ache deep in her heart, that she could let them know that she was okay, but she also knew that she didn't want to leave this world. She would have nightmares that she was trapped in that other world, miserable, and unable to find her way back to her new world, only to wake up in tears with Fenna shushing her and petting her brow. It was near the end of her second week with them that she became aware of the fact that Rowan was courting her.

She used the word 'courting', because he wasn't flirting with her, and he wasn't trying to get into her pants, but he was paying attention to her. Very pointed attention that had a sweetness to it, and an innocence, despite his obvious designs. One night when she had gone up to her room she had found a little bunch of lavender and vervain on her pillow. She had turned to Fenna and asked if she had placed the herbs there.

"No-o," Fenna admitted thoughtfully. "I told Rowan that you were having nightmares though. It must have been him."

At first the idea had been alarming to Kristabell. She knew how she *felt* about Rowan, but after Evan, she had never expected reciprocation from anyone. She didn't know what to *think* about Rowan. The heart and the mind are two very different things. She knew how she felt when he looked into her eyes, when he smiled, or took her hand. She loved the wildness in his look and the way she felt when she was beside him, but in the world she'd come from, she had been an outcast. Unpopular, friendless, and misunderstood. Sheila at the garden centre had been the closest thing to a friend that she'd ever had, up until Evan, and Evan ... ? She gave the thought a vicious kick and it retreated to the shadows. It seemed unbelievable to Kristabell that someone like Rowan would be attracted to her. She was an eighteen year old high school dropout, what did he see in her? But Bronwen was only in her early forties at the most. She must have been close to eighteen when Rowan was born, so obviously Kristabell's age wasn't much of a drawback in this world. That, and the fact that there was no formal education here. Everything was learned through experience and apprenticeships. Kristabell's skill with plants was seen as a valuable skill by Rowan's people. From their perspective she was mature and educated. It was a difficult shift for her mind to make, and when she let herself *think* too hard about Rowan and everything that he was, she could wind up feeling very confused. Rowan was beautiful and intelligent and kind but he was also the Captain of the King's army. Twenty-three had seemed too young to Kristabell, for a position with so much responsibility and pressure, but after she'd seen Rowan and Leif sparring outside the stables a few times, she had changed her mind about that. One thing was obvious, they knew how to fight, and watching Rowan with a sword was like nothing she had ever seen before. The speed with which he moved and the power he seemed to have access to boggled her mind. It must be said that Rowan was not a big man. Five foot eight at the most, and by Kristabell's guess, no more than one hundred and sixty-five pounds. Leif, on the other hand, was over six feet tall and at least two hundred pounds. They would crash together, sword blades clashing with a plangency that set her teeth on edge, but no matter how fast Leif came at Rowan, he would always be deflected by the smaller man and no matter how well planned Leif's attack, he would always be forced back by Rowan. Each time Kristabell watched, it ended in Leif's surrender. One hot afternoon when she was walking back from the gardens she caught the end of a match. Rowan smiled at her and waved as he headed back to the castle for a bath before dinner. Leif was sitting on a hay bale, too exhausted to get up. Kristabell approached him and asked, "Do you ever beat Rowan?"

He looked at her, his eyebrows knit in irritation. He usually answered her in monosyllables. "No."

"Does *anyone* ever beat Rowan?" she asked.

"No." He answered as if she was asking stupid questions.

"Other than Rowan, does anyone ever beat *you*?"

This time she got a small smile, "No."

Kristabell nodded and walked away. By rights, Rowan should be a cocky bastard, but somehow he wasn't and Kristabell knew that she had fallen in love with him.

The next day she was picking pears and packing them into baskets when Rowan came by driving a cart pulled by a horse and loaded with lunches to take out to the fields. He hadn't been at breakfast that morning. According to Fenna he'd been in a meeting with two lieutenants from a patrol. "Kristabell," he called to her. "I'm taking this out to the fields then making a trip to the mill. If Fenna can spare you, would you like to come?"

Kristabell turned to Fenna. She didn't need to ask. Fenna nodded, smiled and said, "Go." But stuck her tongue out at Rowan.

Kristabell walked over to the cart and Rowan reached down a hand and pulled her up beside him. Once she was seated he flicked the reins and off they went. It was the furthest out from the castle that Kristabell had been since she had arrived and it was nice to sit back and see something new. The fields were being ploughed and readied for fall planting and dry grain was being gathered for milling. There was a bustle of activity all around.

As they made their way along the cart track they hit some ruts. Rowan reached out and slipped his hand around her waist holding her steady. He did it so naturally and so nonchalantly —without pausing as he related to her how he'd been attacked by an irate, seasonally confused, humming bird that morning, making her laugh—that she hadn't thought anything of it. But even after the track smoothed out his hand was still around her waist. Kristabell's first reaction was to think to herself, '*It doesn't have anything to do with me.*' It was like when they'd first met and he'd brought her to the castle on his horse. She'd had to ride somewhere. But his hand was still on her waist and he'd left lavender and vervain on her pillow. He'd asked her to come for a ride with him. He *wanted*, she realized, to be close to her. She let herself relax then shifted a little closer, and Rowan slid his hand a little further around her waist.

They stopped and ate lunch with Leif out in the fields then headed onward to the mill to get flour to take back up to the house. The entire time Rowan asked her questions about herself. He seemed to want to know everything. How she felt about her world and his, what her thoughts were on big philosophical questions, what she wanted out of life. He already knew her fairly well owing to their mornings with Gwydion, but he never seemed to get bored of her or, and this was the remarkable thing to Kristabell, to think that there was anything strange about her. As they rode back up to the castle she asked him, "Do you like being a knight? Do you like fighting?" He sat quietly thinking, and then said slowly, "Most of the time, I try not to think about it. I'm good at it, and right now it's needed, but ... the short answer is no. I'm more like you. You said that you wanted a happy home and a big garden, and ... I guess I have those things. I love them, so if I want to keep them, for the time being I have to fight. Maybe someday it will end.'

They rode the rest of the way up to the castle in silence, but he had slipped his hand back around her waist.

Chapter 6

The time flew by. There was always something that needed doing and extra hands were always welcome. By the time Kristabell had been with Rowan's family for three weeks she was comfortable with the language and although she wasn't particularly articulate, it hadn't been like learning a whole new language from scratch. After a time there was less picking and more preparing of food to ready for winter. She spent two days in the kitchens with Rowan's mother, Fenna, and some of the other women in the household, in addition to the two younger boys, chopping cabbage for sauerkraut.

Kristabell, being an only child, had no experience with younger siblings but she found herself enjoying Dunstan and Gareth's company in a way that surprised her. She'd had no idea how entertaining adolescent boys could be and she found their antics hysterically funny which meant that they always went out of their way to make her laugh. As they'd chopped away at the giant heap of cabbages both boys goofed off trying to get a laugh out of Kristabell until Bronwen finally exclaimed, "You boys are driving me crazy. If you don't pipe down I'll send you to Thomas and let him find something for you to do and Kristabell, if you don't stop encouraging them I'll send you too!"

By the end of the day she'd found herself in a potting shed with the two boys repairing the nets that they used for the peas and the beans. At least out there they weren't driving Bronwen crazy.

Another two days were spent making salves, simples, creams and tinctures with the herbs that had been picked and prepared over the summer. It had been fascinating to be included in this. It was work that was satisfying to Kristabell and she liked the smells of the herbs, infused oils and beeswax. They were wonderful things to work with and when they were done it was nice to see all the little pots of salves and bottles of tinctures lined up on the shelf. Bronwen said that they had turned out better than they had the year before. There was enough beeswax left over that Bronwen told Fenna that if she and Kristabell liked they could make themselves a batch of nice skin cream, so they used a chamomile infusion along with some rose and calendula infused oils that Fenna had prepared earlier in the summer. When they were done they had four little pots of beautiful, smooth, sweetly scented skin cream. One for each of them, and Bronwen and Nessa as well.

There were other times too, over those weeks, when they would take a break, a short breather to unwind and recharge. Picnics with Leif, Nessa, Fenna, and the two younger boys. They would lie on a big blanket in an orchard and eat and talk, sing, tell jokes and riddles. Nessa could be very funny in a dry way. She could make even the dour Leif laugh. Kristabell asked Rowan once when they were alone at one end of the hazelnut orchard loading baskets onto a cart, "Is Leif always so taciturn?"

"No. He's peeved at me. Don't take him personally," Rowan had answered. Kristabell didn't ask further.

* * *

As the equinox neared and they were in the thick of the last truly hot days of summer the temptation to slip down to the lake was impossible to ignore. Nessa, Fenna and Kristabell would wander down before dinner, slip out of their clothes, and gratefully immerse themselves in the cool clean lake, letting the water rinse away the sweat and grime of the day. It was one of those last days. Nessa was lying on the beach snoozing on a blanket, and Kristabell and Fenna were still drifting in the water, all too aware that it might be the last swim until next summer, when Fenna asked, "So, has my brother kissed you yet?"

Kristabell blushed dark pink right to the roots of her hair. She wasn't sure where to start or what to say, because Rowan *had* kissed her. He had continued to leave little gifts on her pillow. A hand woven wreath of barley, a hollow painted quail egg, a little carved wooden bird, flowers. One morning she had woken to find a small dish of perfectly ripe late figs on her night stand which, of course, meant that he had snuck into her room while she was sleeping. Each time he gave her one of these little gifts Kristabell would know that it had been him. He would be waiting to gauge her reaction, waiting to see her smile. She would walk into the dining hall in the morning and he would be watching for her, and when their eyes met she would always smile. She couldn't help it. She would sit down at the table next to him and he would smile back and say to her, "I like it when you smile." And when they'd finished eating his hand would invariably seek hers under the table, feeling for the soft skin on the back of her hand as he laced his fingers into hers. As sweet and simple as they were, those little gifts, and the feel of his hand on hers, left her thinking about him every night as she fell asleep, and each morning when she woke, and well ... if she was honest with herself, most of the day too. And then one night, as dinner ended and everyone had trailed up the stairs on tired feet destined for welcoming beds and much desired sleep, she had found herself left behind, and as she'd walked out into the wide hallway Rowan had been standing at the other end holding a candle, on his way to the west wing where his rooms were. He'd looked at her, and she at him. It was so quiet. So still. He'd walked to where she stood and looked into her eyes. Kristabell had looked straight back at him feeling frozen in the moment as his hand rose slowly to her cheek and he'd slowly leaned forward watching her eyes as he did, silently asking permission. Kristabell couldn't believe how her heart had pounded as his lips touched hers in a warm yielding kiss that lingered, and how she hadn't even realized that she was kissing him back until they'd disengaged and stood there looking at each other in the flickering candle light. Kristabell knew that she wanted to go wherever it was that his kiss could lead her.

"Goodnight ... Kristabell," he'd whispered.

"Good ... Goodnight," she whispered back.

And then he'd turned and walked away leaving her in the dark and then turned back suddenly, smiling and bringing the light back with him. They'd kissed again, a little furiously this time, then he'd pulled back and put the candle in her hands.

"Goodnight." He smiled

She smiled back at him, "Goodnight."

And he melted away into the darkness. For a moment or two Kristabell didn't move and then she'd hurried up the stairs and into bed with her heart pounding for what had felt like hours.

Kristabell shook herself out of her reverie and looked at Fenna who was wringing water out of her hip length molasses coloured hair and talking, "Come. I know Rowan fancies you. I've never seen him so worked up over a girl before."

Still blushing, Kristabell admitted to having been kissed. Fenna splashed around excitedly in the water squeaking, "I knew it! I knew it!"

Later that night as Kristabell lay sprawled over the foot of Fenna's bed, Fenna asked her, more seriously this time, "If Rowan asks you to be his wife, will you say yes?"

Kristabell couldn't give the question a direct answer. First of all, four weeks ago, marriage had been the furthest thing from her mind. Allan was the only male she'd had much contact with over the last year, and he thought she was a freak. And then of course there was Evan, but Kristabell sent that thought packing. She was still adjusting to the knowledge that Rowan found her acceptable and that eighteen, which was generally considered too young to get married in her old life, was also acceptable in this world. Kristabell also readily admitted to herself that she really disliked the thought of a wedding. The idea of all that attention focused on her made her nauseous, and there was obviously no birth control in this world. Most families had at least four or five children. When she walked down to the village with Rowan there were children everywhere. If she agreed to be his wife she would be pregnant before the year was up and as much as she wanted Rowan physically, she had to remind herself of what the end result of sex would be, and she wasn't quite sure that she was ready for motherhood. She would also prefer to know someone intimately before marriage. She looked at Fenna, turning the question over in her mind a few more times before answering. "If I tell you how I feel about this, you have to promise me that you won't tell Rowan. I don't want what I say to you to change what he feels for me, or what he might do."

"I won't say anything, I swear I won't," Fenna promised solemnly.

"The truth is that I don't think I'll be able to answer that question until he asks me himself. If, that is, he's planning on asking me. The idea of a wedding and babies makes me ... well, apprehensive to say the least but ..." she smiled a little, "I don't think I would say no."

Fenna nodded still serious. "If it puts your mind at ease, we no longer have weddings. It is an antiquated tradition that was abandoned during hard times. It is customary to have a feast to celebrate the union after the fact, but it is usually not a terribly formal affair. Just family, close friends, and lots of food."

"If there's no wedding, then what makes me his wife?' Kristabell asked, puzzled.

"His asking you and your consent essentially," Fenna answered. "In theory at that point the relationship would be consummated," Fenna blushed. "But it is your word that counts, and his. It is your willingness to commit to each other and recognize each other as husband and wife that is important. Our law is very specific about this. If he is planning to ask you he will have told our parents and probably Nessa and Leaf. If a girl claims that a man asked her to be his wife just to get his way with her he can get into trouble. The punishment is severe so a man who is serious will cover his ass by telling someone or asking the girl's mother before he asks so that she cannot accuse him of falsehood after the fact if his true intention really was a committed relationship. The same applies to a woman who does the asking. But if the answer is yes, there is no wedding. It's a question of love, not formality and if no love or commitment exists then it is just two people screwing, which is fine. We are not a prudish people, but it always comes with the risk of pregnancy and if a woman doesn't have the resources to care for a child on her own, or a family to support her it can be difficult if her lover cannot support her either. There are farms and other places where single women with children can go and work to support their children, but most people prefer to raise a child with someone they love."

"What about diseases?" Kristabell asked

"What do you mean?"

Kristabell had to explain STDs to Fenna who looked slightly nauseated.

"There is not much disease amongst our people. Unless someone is very old or in the advanced stages of an illness the Fay can usually heal them, and if not they die, which limits the spread of the disease." Then Fenna grinned, "And as for babies, I know that your family is small, but, it's not like that here. You would have lots of help and a good fairy midwife. My mother and Nessa and I would all be here to make things easier."

Kristabell was silent. It was all so strange here. No boyfriends. No months or years to decide if someone was right for you. A kiss could lead to a husband. She wasn't sure if one way was any better than the other. One thing was certain though, regardless of what anyone else thought about a union between herself and Rowan, as far as Fenna was concerned, it was all good.

Chapter 7

It was the end of the harvest and just a few days after the Equinox. The lion's share of the work was done and everyone was looking forward to a break and a chance to kick up their heels. Kristabell, Fenna, and Nessa had gone down to the large bathroom, with the huge boiler and big bathtubs, that was behind the kitchens. The people of this world were not like medieval peasants. They understood the importance of proper hygiene. Soap and hot water were always on hand for proper washing but in terms of bathing there wasn't the same full on preoccupation with it as what existed in Kristabell's world, and it was okay if a proper bath only happened a couple times a week, but tonight was a special occasion and a proper bath was a must. The three of them scrubbed each other's backs and rinsed each other's hair with diluted cider vinegar to make it clean. They cut their fingernails and made sure they were spotless then snuck up to Fenna's room to get dressed.

They towelled their hair then brushed it until it was dry and shining except for Nessa who had a head full of copper curls which she carefully combed out and arranged while damp. Then it was time to actually get dressed. Generally speaking Kristabell liked the clothing from the trunk that had been brought down for her. It was comfortable, earthy and simple, yet beautifully worked. There was one dress that was nicer than the others, long cream linen with green embroidery. The colour wouldn't be great on Kristabell but it was nicely cut and it would still be pretty. In the end she never even got a chance to try it on. Fenna and Nessa giggled as they pulled a different dress out of the closet. It was a fine linen dress in a soft golden pink with a full skirt that would reach her ankles. "This used to be my mother's." Nessa told her. "She gave it to me to cut down for you last week. She said it was the dress that she wore the night our father asked her to be his wife."

This brought on an uncontrollable fit of giggling from all three of them. Even Nessa, who was usually so poised, was having a hard time regaining her composure. Kristabell had had a hard time warming up to Nessa the first week she'd been there, but she'd realized that there was no reason to be intimidated by the tall beautiful redhead with her sardonic manner. Sarcasm and dry wit were Nessa's forte, but she never directed them at Kristabell with the exception of once telling her, "If I didn't like you so much I would tell you that you were dull for giving me so little opportunity to make fun of you, but as it is I can't even think of a good insult to direct at my brother for fancying you. Oh, look. I've made you blush. Well, at least that's something."

Fenna helped Kristabell into the dress, doing up the laces at the back and firmly drawing in the waist that was heavily embroidered with gold, green, and costly indigo silk thread. It had gathered cap sleeves and the band of embroidery on the waist followed the line of the slightly plunging embroidered princess neckline. On the hem and sleeves was a narrow band of blue silk ribbon. Not enough to make the dress look fussy but enough to add to the overall quality of fineness. It was beautiful. Kristabell had never in her life had a reason to put on a dress so fine let alone own a dress so fine. Nessa did her hair leaving most of it loose but french braiding the front then looping the braid into a coronet and tucking pink wax-dipped rose buds into the braid. Fenna passed Kristabell a little pair of soft green, dyed leather slippers. "Here. I outgrew these before

I wore them out." Kristabell sat on Fenna's bed and slipped on the little shoes, then watched as Nessa did Fenna's hair in beautiful upswept braids that were elegantly coiled on the crown of her head, then the sisters put on their own dresses. Fenna looked like a goddess in her heavily embroidered and pin tucked, cream on cream gown which made her eyes glow dark. She looked at least four years older with her hair up like that, and Nessa was like a regal forest dream in a fine moss green wool dress tied with a wide coppery red silk sash. Giddy and giggling they set out down the hall to have a look at themselves in Bronwen's full length glass mirror. It was one of only two in the whole castle. Fenna knocked.

"Come in," Bronwen's voice drifted calmly from inside. Kristabell had never been in Fenna's parent's rooms before. They were comfortable and elegant with an outer sitting room, a dressing room and a bed chamber. Bronwen was in her dressing room. Tall and fair with long golden brown curls and grey eyes Bronwen didn't look like either of her daughters. Kristabell wouldn't have called Bronwen *beautiful*, but she was so elegant that it didn't really matter. She sat and smiled as Fenna asked, "Mum, can we take a wee peak in your mirror?"

Bronwen laughed, "You can take more than a 'wee peak'. Stay and visit with me for a while. I feel like I've hardly seen you three all week."

Kristabell felt her eyes tearing up as she walked into the room with the two young women that she was beginning to think of as her sisters. To be included by their mother only increased her feeling of love for these people. She wondered if Bronwen knew how much that 'you three' had meant to her.

"Stand still, let me look at you," Bronwen was saying to them and Kristabell found it difficult to stand still and be observed but when she looked into Bronwen's face it was as if time had stopped. The expression there made no sense to Kristabell. There was a wistfulness that Kristabell understood but behind that, veiled, was grief and sadness. An old loss and ... compassion? Heartache? And then it was hidden once more, and, back to her usual elegant self, Bronwen rose and embraced each of them starting with Nessa and ending with Kristabell. "Thank you for the dress," Kristabell mumbled as she was enclosed in a motherly embrace.

Bronwen leaned back and looked into Kristabell's face once again, "Well, it seemed fitting. But that dress does need a necklace." And she released Kristabell and strode over to a dresser. Kristabell had put in the little moonstone earrings that she'd been wearing the day she'd come over to their world but the ring on its chain hadn't looked right with the dress, so she had tucked it into her bodice. Fenna and Nessa were both wearing beautiful pieces of jewelry, chalcedonies set in finely wrought silver with gold accents, but the necklace that Bronwen turned around with was something else entirely. On a solid gold chain hung a cut oval sapphire that caught the light and glowed a strange and distant blue. It was encased in a fine filigreed bezel and suspended from the chain, not from a single bail, but from either side on small filigree clasps. Then, suspended from the sapphire on a loop that was gracefully disguised as a leaf was a glowing baroque pearl. "It's from the old country. I want it to be yours," Bronwen murmured as she clasped it around Kristabell's neck. "None of my children have blue eyes. This belongs on you. There. Go look," Bronwen said closing the clasp and stepping back. Kristabell looked in the mirror. She hadn't known what to expect and she wasn't quite prepared for what she saw. She hadn't seen more than just her face in over a month and she'd been so busy that even then, she had only looked to make sure it wasn't dirty, but now ...? The dress and the necklace brought out her eyes in a way that was truly beguiling. She stared at herself. She'd grown in the last month. Lost that little bit of baby fat around her face that had made her look *so* young. She would always be tiny but she didn't look like a child anymore. With the pearl glowing at her throat and the laces on the dress cinched tight so that the tops of her small breasts showed just a little, she looked … desirable. She'd never expected to see herself that way and two things struck her as she looked in that mirror. One, that she *wasn't* a child anymore. And two, if Rowan liked her for more than just her personality, then there was a good reason for it. Kristabell fingered the sapphire with its deep glow and whispered, "Thank you. Thank you so much."

After Fenna and Nessa had had a chance to have a good look in the big mirror, Bronwen sighed and said, "As much as I'd like to stay up here with you three all afternoon, I know that I'll be cross all evening if the tables aren't set up properly. Let us go down now and help set up the courtyard."

They spread good tablecloths over the tables that had been arranged according to Bronwen's specifications. The younger boys helped bring every chair, bench and stool that they could find out of the castle. When Gareth first spotted Kristabell he hooted and yelled, "When Rowan sees you he's gonna …' But that was as far as he got because Fenna had caught and muzzled him and was swiping at his bottom and saying, "Your brother will behave like a gentleman and so should you."

As Fenna and Kristabell decorated the tables with arrangements of dried flowers, baskets of apples and candles, Fenna looked at Kristabell seriously and told her, "A lieutenant from the king's army showed up late last night. Apparently there's trouble. I wouldn't be surprised if Rowan has to leave in a day or two."

It was the first time that Kristabell had felt the full impact of loving someone and then realizing that they might not always be there. Her heart, which had been so light, like a butterfly in the sunshine, sank like a pebble through dark water. She didn't want him to leave. She didn't want to stop seeing his face every day or stop feeling his hand under the table. She was too inexperienced to let her mind wander much passed this, but she didn't want whatever was happening between them to stop. Fenna saw her face fall and said, "I'm sorry. I didn't mean to bring you down. I should have kept my mouth shut till tomorrow."

"It's alright," Kristabell forced a smile, "I knew he would have to leave at some point, I just ..." She trailed off not sure what else there was to say. She hadn't seen Rowan at dinner the night before and she hadn't seen him all day either. She was beginning to worry that he wouldn't make it to the gathering.

People were arriving from the village and the surrounding farms. People who Kristabell was beginning to know a little, although beyond the immediate household she had been introduced as a cousin from Bronwyn's side of the family. All of the families who had a hand and a stake in the wellbeing of the land were coming together to celebrate. It was more like a giant potluck at a hippie commune than a medieval feast and dinner was going full swing with beer and mead and all manner of delicious food being passed around by the time Rowan showed up. Kristabell had been having a nice time but she'd felt a little like she was all dressed up with no place to go without Rowan there. Like yesterday's party balloon, just a little deflated, and then he was there. She turned her head to see him standing there, watching her from a distance as she sat with Fenna at the end of a table. She put down her cup, rose from her seat, and went to him. He was dressed more finely than Kristabell was used to seeing him, and the cream coloured tunic he wore did the same incredible things to his eyes as the colour did to Fenna's. Rowan looked very serious.

"I was worried that you weren't coming tonight," Kristabell said softly.

"Not seeing you tonight would have been the greatest tragedy of my life. I could have stood here and *looked* at you all night and it would still be the best night of my life." He leaned forward and kissed her. Kristabell didn't even think about the people watching as he put his arm around her and lead her back to the table. "I've never seen you like this before. You look like a dream," he whispered in her ear.

"Tonight feels like a dream," she answered. "A good one.'

They ate and danced and talked and really didn't have a care for anyone else that night. Kristabell laughed and screamed in Rowan's arms as he swung her around in the wild folk dances that Fenna had spent the week teaching her, and after the dancing there were torches lit and candles glowing on all of the tables. The beautiful blown glass lanterns that were hung at intervals throughout the courtyard contained lights that flickered and danced like magic. "How are the lanterns lit? They're so lovely," Kristabell sighed. They were sitting close together in a quiet corner. The music was softer now and the tables had been moved back into the centre of the courtyard. The sky was dark and there were little nests of blankets all around the edges that contained sleeping small ones. Adults were seated around the tables, sampling the deserts, drinking and talking quietly but contentedly. Every so often a burst of raucous laughter would erupt from the group of youths huddled around a table at the other end of the courtyard. The evening was cooling off and she shivered as Rowan answered her in a low distracted voice. "Magic," he said pulling her closer to him and looking into her eyes. Kristabell wanted to tell him that she had never been so happy, never felt so whole and wonderful as she did at that moment. She opened her mouth, and words completely failed her. "Rowan ... I ... Tonight ..." She stammered and suddenly Rowan was very serious. He stood and, taking her hand, pulled her with him to the staircase at the corner of the courtyard and up to the gallery above from which the blown glass lanterns could still be seen. He turned to her, pulled her to him and then without beating around the bush told her, "Kristabell, I love you and I can't imagine leaving here without you." He took a deep breath and then asked, looking intense and uncertain, "Would you be my wife?" The words rushed out of his mouth as if he couldn't keep them in another moment and Kristabell, who wanted to cry out, "Yes! Yes! A million times YES!" was having the exact opposite problem. She couldn't get a word out. She knew her answer. She had known for the last week that he was going to ask her and the truth was that it hadn't taken much thought in the end. The only true happiness that she had ever known was here in this world, with these people and, in particular, with Rowan. She wanted a life with him, whatever that would bring. She had pushed aside the part of herself from that other world that told her she was *too* young and that they were moving *too* fast. It was perfect, like a fairy tale. She wasn't a child, and this was what she wanted. She was sure of it.

Rowan's arms were around her waist. She knew he was waiting for her to answer him. She tried to say "yes," but her tongue was still frozen. She looked into his eyes, those dark beautiful eyes, and finally managed to nod and smile, and then she stood up on tip toe and kissed him and he kissed her back and they kissed ... and kissed ... and kissed. Rowan had pulled her against him. She had never felt anything like that before. It was like they were melting together and he smelled so good. Eventually they paused to draw breath and Kristabell blurted, "YES!" and they laughed breathlessly, maybe a little hysterically.

Rowan drew her over to a bench in an alcove covered in ivy. "I have something for you. It used to be my grandmother's and it was the only ring in my mother's collection that I thought might be small enough for your fingers."

He reached into his pocket and pulled out a ring. It was a simple band of what looked like platinum—too bright to be white gold and too clean to be silver—with a channel of bright gold down the centre. He put the ring in Kristabell's hand. "I'm not sure which of your fingers it will fit."

She looked more closely at the little ring. There was a delicate engraving of scroll work and raven feathers in the gold. It was, she realized, the same pattern that decorated the archways and pillars inside the castle. She slipped the ring onto the third finger of her left hand. It was exactly perfect. Everything. The ring, the moment, sitting there with Rowan. And then, like it really *was* a perfect dream, Kristabell reached into the bodice of her dress and drew out the chain with the ring on it. She removed the ring from the chain, it was warm from being against her body, and she placed it in Rowan's hand. Kristabell had never worn the ring on her own hand for one simple reason. It was far too big. It was a man's ring. "I want you to have this." she told Rowan. "It was my mother's." It was the only thing she had to give him, other than her love.

Rowan looked at the ring. It was, in fact, somewhat similar to the ring that he had just given her only heavier, and opposite, gold with a channel of platinum. It too had an engraving on it and this was, of all things, rowan branches, leaves, and berries. Rowan looked at her, so many feelings mixed up there in his eyes, love, longing, a strange sadness that twisted her heart and made it ache for him. He slipped the ring onto the same finger on which she now wore hers. It fit. They sat for a moment, stunned, looking into one another's eyes, dark brown into deep blue, then Rowan took her hand and said gently, like a question, "Come with me?"

Chapter 8

They left the gathering then, hand in hand, laughing, almost running through the castle halls until they reached the door to Rowan's rooms. Rowan opened the door for her then closed it behind them, turning the key in its lock. It was strange to be in his rooms. They were in a receiving room of sorts. There was a table covered in maps, a desk, some chairs. It was all very functional, very masculine. He took her hand again and lead her into his bed chamber and closed that door behind them as well. Rowan lit candles then knelt before the hearth and lit a small fire to take the chill out of the room. Kristabell looked around wondering if it was always as spotlessly tidy as it was now, or if he had cleaned up for her, and then he came to her, gently put his hands in her hair and slowly kissed her. This was alien territory to Kristabell. She wanted to touch his face, so she did and he kissed her again then began carefully taking down her hair, making sure he'd gotten all the rose buds and pins out before uncoiling the braid and loosening it with his fingers. Then he started unlacing her dress. It felt like there were more laces to take it off than there had been to put it on. He helped her step out of it then draped it over a chair. Kristabell reached for the buttons on his collar and undid them then slid her hands under his shirt, feeling the smooth warm skin underneath. He pulled the shirt off, pulled down the bedding, then suddenly, so that she shrieked and laughed breathlessly in surprise, scooped her up and lay her on the bed. He kicked off his boots and breaches and lay beside her kissing her and their arms went automatically around each other. They kissed and caressed one another and it was the most wonderful feeling but the further they went the more the little seed of panic in Kristabell's breast threatened to overwhelm her. There were things she was ignoring, and as much as she wanted everything to be simple and uncomplicated between herself and Rowan she had to face the fact that they were *not* simple and uncomplicated and she cried out, "Rowan we have to stop!"

The look of anguish on his face was almost more than she could bear. "Kristabell? I thought that you ..." He sounded so hurt.

She understood his confusion and said right away, "Rowan I love you so much and I want to be with you every night and have your babies and spend the rest of my life beside you and I want it so bad it hurts. *Please* don't think I don't want this "

"What is it then?" he asked, still confused but looking less hurt. He was stroking her hair and looking down into her eyes.

"It's just that I'm ..." She took a deep shaky breath, "It's just that I'm scared." Kristabell could feel hot tears pouring down her temples and into her hair.

Rowan put his arms around her and said, "You don't need to be afraid. I wouldn't hurt you."

She shook her head, "No, no. I'm not afraid of that, not of you. I trust you."

"Then what's wrong?" he asked, not at all annoyed with her, just concerned and confused.

She tried to think of where to start and it seemed simplest to start at the beginning. "Four weeks ago, my life was *very* different from what it is now, and I lived in a world that made me miserable. Now I'm here with people I love, and I've never been happier than I am *right now*. But I'm terrified of losing this. I don't care what Gwydion says, I can't rest easy. Somehow I brought myself here and I don't know how. I just randomly wandered out of my own world one day. What if it happens again? I know that I did it, but I can't control it. What if I wandered away from *you*? What if we keep on like this and I get pregnant? I could end up alone with a baby in a strange world far away from either you *or* my parents. They don't even know where I am right now and I feel *so* guilty about that. The thing that scares me the most is the idea that, I could be with you, time could pass, we could have a child together, and I could be separated from both of you. Rowan, if that happened, if I couldn't get back to you, my heart would break into a million pieces. How would you feel if you just ... couldn't find me one day."

He had his arms around her and she was crying into his chest. "I'm sorry," Rowan spoke softly. "I should have thought this through more completely and realized that you might feel this way. I forget that you weren't raised in this world. To me you belong here. And," he sighed, "You're probably right. I haven't been doing my most logical thinking lately. I've been living in a dream. Leif says that I'm not thinking with my head. All I've been able to think about lately is how much I love you, and how much I want you."

She looked at him, her deep blue eyes glistening. "Say it again," she smiled faintly.

"I'm sorry." He looked it and she felt bad because it wasn't what she had wanted him to say.

"No, no. Not that," she told him, softly, apologetically.

"You're right?"

"No. The other thing."

"I want you." He couldn't keep the impish look off his face.

"Now you're teasing."

"Well, I'm not thinking with my head."

"What are you thinking with?"

"My heart ... Mostly."

"And what is it telling you?"

"It's telling me that I love you," he said smiling.

"I love you too," she smiled back. She couldn't help it.

They lay there quietly for a short space of time feeling a strange combination of elation, confusion, and disappointment. Eventually Rowan took a deep breath and let out a long sigh. "I have to leave here. Not tomorrow, but the next day, to go to the King's council. There is an army massing on the northern border. Seamus wants to force our hand. There is ... concern. Warranted concern."

Kristabell found it strange to see Rowan change before her eyes, losing the calm quality she always thought of as distinctly his and taking on a tense efficient aura. "I want you to come with me. I have reservations about taking you out on the roads right now, but, I have reservations about leaving you here too. I want to take you to the fairies." He looked at her and even though she didn't want to leave Fiannasmere Kristabell couldn't help feel a little thrill at the idea. Rowan continued talking. "I have a good relationship with their King, or," he shrugged, "as good a relationship as an outsider can have with any of their kind. But some of the fay can walk between the worlds. They will be able to tell you how you crossed over and, at the very least, teach you how to prevent it happening again if not actually teach you how to control and use it."

"But Gwydion said ...?"

Rowan put his fingers over her lips like he had four weeks ago. "I know what Gwydion said. Just *trust* me for now. When we get to Lugh's stronghold things will make a lot more sense. They might even be able to get a message to your parents."

"Do you really think they could do that?" Kristabell wrapped her arms around Rowan tightly and looked into his face intensely.

"I don't know," Rowan sighed. "Fairies and humans have historically had a strange relationship. There is a taboo. We don't get too closely involved with them, they don't get too closely involved with us. Apparently it wasn't always this way but now and for the last several hundred years the relationship has been touchy. We go to them for healing and they come to us for barley flour. It's a strange trade, but ..." Rowan shrugged again.

Kristabell remembered what Rowan had said about an army on the northern border. "If there's an army in the north, then that means you'll have to go fight, doesn't it?"

Rowan's face worked for a moment and his mouth formed a bitter line. He nodded. "I didn't want to think about these things tonight, but whatever happens ..." he paused and swallowed. "If anything ever happens to me, you'll always have a home here. My family will take care of you."

Kristabell felt her tears running again and pooling on Rowan's chest. Even if she wanted to spend forever with him, she might not get to. As if he were reading her thoughts, he said, "This doesn't seem to be a very good time for us, does it."

Kristabell looked up and smiled even as she dripped and said, "I don't think that love considers the convenience of the people whose lives it complicates. But I would rather love you than not."

"Then ... You'll stay tonight?"

"Of course I'll stay," she said softly and kissed him. "I said *yes* didn't I?"

"Yes, you did," there was a note of wonder in his voice but a glint of mischief in his eyes as he rolled so that he was pinning her down. "And even if it drives me insane with passionate, frustrated, lust to have such a beautiful girl in my bed and *not* have my way with her," he rolled off. "I would rather have you beside me than spend our nights apart." He smiled.

"That's good because, I hadn't planned on leaving," Kristabell told him sheepishly.

Rowan laughed and Kristabell was amazed by how good it felt to hear him laugh.

Chapter 9

In the morning when Kristabell and Rowan woke it was difficult to motivate themselves to get up and do what needed to be done in preparation for the next day's departure. They had spent most of the night making out like a couple of horny teenagers, which was an odd and frustrating first night for two people who were planning on spending the rest of there lives together, but it was, simultaneously, a strangely sweet night. They had decided, in the end, that it probably was prudent if Kristabell *didn't* get pregnant, at least not right away, and she knew that if they waited, even just a few days, the risk wouldn't be so high. So they would wait.

Kristabell sat up and swung her legs over the edge of the bed. "We ought to get up. Everyone will wonder where we are and, if your men are here at the castle, won't they be waiting to hear from you?"

"They can wait five more minutes," Rowan said pulling her back under the warm blankets with him and burying his face against her chest.

Kristabell wrapped her arms around him. "Now I'll never make it out of this bed."

He propped himself up on one elbow and said, all the while kissing her cheeks, throat and forehead. "We have to get up though. We have to leave tomorrow." He kissed her mouth, held her for a moment in a tight embrace then got, very abruptly, out of bed. "There. It's done," he said pulling on some fresh clothes. "You wait here. I'll go get you some clothes from your room."

"Thank you. Nothing says 'I didn't spend the night in my own bed,' like sneaking through the castle in yesterday evening's party dress."

Rowan headed for the door grinning. Kristabell heard him cross the outer chamber and unlock the door to the hall. He didn't get far. She could hear him cursing obscenities at Fenna who was laughing hysterically at him. Fenna followed Rowan back to the bedroom with a tray of food in her hands. Scones, butter, hard boiled eggs, fruit and hot milk.

"She was right outside the door. I almost tripped on her," Rowan scowled.

"Mum sent me when neither of you showed up for breakfast," Fenna said grinning as she placed the tray on the table by the hearth. She passed Kristabell the red wool dress and linen shift that had been draped over her arm.

"Thank you," she said with a sheepish smile, pulling the shift over her head then slipping her arms into the sleeves and doing up the buttons that ran the length of the dress. She looked at Fenna who suddenly shrieked and wrapped her arms around Kristabell.

"I knew we were supposed to be sisters!" Fenna blurted out.

Rowan was still scowling at Fenna but he motioned for her to pull up a chair and sit with them while they ate. For all that Rowan and Fenna could be very argumentative, Kristabell knew that of all his younger siblings, Fenna was his favourite. "So I take it everyone knows?"

"Pretty much," she nodded. "Nessa saw you leave together last night, and when you weren't in your bed this morning," she glanced at Kristabell. "Well, where else could you be?" She went on, "Leif's cutting you a little slack. He's down at the stables right now making sure the horses will be ready and Mum is packing provisions. Dad is in the armoury with one of your lieutenants. Oh, and a regiment showed up about a half an hour ago. They're down at the gate house. Brian is with them. He's waiting to speak to you but under the circumstances," she grinned and started to giggle, "They're being very patient."

Rowan shook his head still scowling. "Can you send a message down to Leif? Have him make sure there's a horse for Kristabell. Ask Nessa if she'll loan us Strawberry."

"You're taking her with you? Are you sure that's safe?"

"It'll be fine. She'll be with me and Leif in addition to ten or so of my men. We won't take the main road. We need to speak to the fairies about opening doorways to other worlds and how Kristabell came here. I don't think that either one of us will be able to rest easy," he looked at Kristabell, "until we know that she's safe and that it won't happen again. We also want to see if they can send a message to her parents."

Fenna nodded understanding and sighed, "You're right. I don't like it ... but you're right."

"I know that I don't have to say this to you but, don't mention our reason for going to the Fay. I have an official reason that I can feed to the men and I think that I could trust Brian or Thaylum with this, but you know how twitchy some people can get about the Fay. It is better if they think that I'm bringing Kristabell with me for my own selfish pig-headed reasons." He'd directed what he'd said at Fenna, but he turned to Kristabell and asked, "Do you understand?"

She nodded.

"There is a chance that I'll have to leave you with the Fay. If I do, you'll be safe there. Is that alright?"

She nodded again. Suddenly everything seemed uncertain and while she knew that this had to be done she wished, she would always wish, that there was no war, and that there was no other world. That it was just her, and just Rowan, and he could see this in her face and he knelt down in front of her and put his hands on either side of her face in a way that she would come to associate only with him. "My love," he whispered and kissed her.

Fenna rose to leave but she paused by the bedroom door and looked Rowan in the eye. "I'll kill you if you don't bring her back here safe." She was serious. Then she turned and walked out the door.

Kristabell was relieved in a sense that Rowan had taken her seriously and shared her concern that she might have some kind of mishap and leave the world that they were in but god ... she wished things could be simple. She leaned forward and rested her forehead on his shoulder and he put his arms around her then exclaimed, "Your hair is a mess! Here swivel around."

She turned on her chair and Rowan reached out grabbing a brush and comb off of his dresser and, pulling over his chair, began working industriously at removing the tangles from Kristabell's hair.

She was just a little surprised, "Gosh. You don't pull nearly so much as my Mum used to."

"I have five younger siblings. You have no idea how many times my mother would say 'Rowan! Leif! Brush your sisters' hair for me while I change the baby,' and Leif and I would fight over who got to brush Fenna's hair because Nessa's took forever. But Leif did himself in. According to the girls he's far gentler than me. I always got impatient and started to yank on the tangles so there came a point when Nessa would only let Leif brush her hair. Not even Mum could come near her with a comb. I never figured I'd ever *want* to do this for a girl of my own volition but right now ... it seems such a small thing, but at least I can get the tangles out of your hair."

They sat like that for a few quiet minutes, Rowan absorbed in his task, working his way slowly up from the ends with the comb then switching to the brush, making long soothing strokes. "This is probably just my male pride talking, but I'm sure everyone out there thinks that everything that normally would have happened last night, *happened* last night. Can we just let them keep thinking that? I feel like you're my wife in word if not quite deed."

Kristabell laughed, "Sure. It's simpler that way, and we'll figure things out before anyone knows any different." She turned around and kissed his sheepish cheek.

"I have to go," he said, putting the brush and comb back on the dresser then pulling Kristabell to her feet kissing her and holding her tight. "I'll see you at dinner." He let his fingers linger on hers until the last possible moment then walked out of the room.

* * *

The rest of the day passed in a disoriented blur of activity as they prepared to leave. Kristabell went up to her room and looked through her things. There wasn't much, or at least there wasn't much that she could take with her. The room was decorated with all of the pretty things that Rowan had given to her over the weeks. The barley wreath, dried flowers, a bird's nest that she had put the painted egg into, a heart shaped rock. She put her hair brush and comb into her shoulder bag. She left her Ipod and wallet in for some reason but took her sketch pad and pencil crayons out. She picked up the little carved wooden bird with its berry stained wings and placed it carefully in an inside pouch along with the heart shaped rock. She took the pair of jeans she had been wearing the day she'd arrived, folded them small, then tucked them into the bag. There was a hidden pouch in one of the seams and she opened the Velcro and undid the zipper and carefully placed the necklace that Bronwen had given her inside. She looked through the trunk and wardrobe but most of the clothing there was summer clothing and the weather was changing rapidly. She went to find Fenna.

On her way through the castle as she searched for her sister she chanced upon Rowan's father. He was much like Nessa. Tall, sarcastic, red haired, but he had a sweet streak and when he saw Kristabell he rumpled her hair and smiled. "Fenna's looking for you," he told her. "She's in the front hall." Then he patted her head again and wandered off. She found Fenna who took her hand right away and said, "Come." She hauled Kristabell off to one of the attics. It was a strange reliving of her first day there, only this time she was leaving not arriving and she could understand everything that Fenna was saying. "We need to find you some good riding clothes and a few nice outfits that are passable for the King's Castle. Is the dress you were wearing last night clean?"

"Yes, it's on my bed."

"Good. I'll make sure it's packed. I'll be able to send a trunk to the castle in a couple of days with an armed merchant who's stopping here, so you don't need to worry about having every-thing ready tonight. We just need to find something for you to bring as a change of clothes." Fenna began opening trunks. "My mother keeps everything. It's finding it that that can be tricky. I had a very good riding outfit and I only wore it for about six months before I outgrew it. Ah! Here it is."

It consisted of sturdy grey wool leggings, a deep plum coloured tunic, and a dark brown fitted leather vest. Fenna opened it so that she could see the loose silk lining. "In case of arrows." Fenna told her then pulled a pair of riding boots out of the trunk. "Here try these on. If they don't fit you we'll have to keep searching."

Kristabell tried the boots on. They were too big. Fenna looked thoughtful for a moment then went to the other end of the attic and began opening trunks down there. "Here," she called out. "These ones used to be Rowan's when he was about twelve. Gareth has huge feet so he never wore them, and they were too big on Dunstan last winter but he's grown so much over the summer that I doubt he'll fit them either. If these don't fit we can try the boots that Gareth wore last year.' But the boots fit. Just right.

They closed up the trunks and made sure that everything was neat and tidy as they left the attic then went down to Kristabell's room. "I guess this isn't going to be your room any more," Fenna sighed as Kristabell tried everything on.

"I had just gotten used to thinking of it as my room. That's the funny thing about changes. They're never all good or all bad, are they? You're my best friend Fenna. I've never had a friend like you. I'm going to miss you." They hugged each other and cried and once they had pulled themselves together Fenna passed Kristabell one more dress to try on. "Here. Last one. It should fit but I would be appalled with myself if I sent you off with something that wasn't perfectly appropriate."

That was the moment that it truly dawned on Kristabell that after they talked to the Fairies, assuming that she wasn't left there on her own, she was going to the King's castle as the wife of the Captain of the King's army, and suddenly she felt very overwhelmed, very nervous, and very small. This place had come to feel like home and now she was leaving and she didn't know when she would be back.

* * *

Dinner was ... tense. That would be the only word that Kristabell could have applied to it. Nessa had come hustling up to her with a bundle of indigo cotton just as she had found her way to Rowan's rooms to give her hair a brush and make sure her face was clean. "My *darling* brother," Kristabell could tell by the way Nessa had said the word *Darling* that she was not entirely pleased with Rowan. "Bought this fabric last week because he claims, and I suppose he *is* right," she rolled her eyes, "That it matches your eyes." Kristabell remembered being at the market with Rowan when they'd seen it at the cloth vendor. It was imported and had been costly but he'd said, "I would love to see you in a dress made of this," as he'd fingered the soft gauzy cotton.

And now Nessa was standing in front of her, perturbed. "So he brings me the bolt of fabric this morning asking me if I can make you a dress from it and I say, 'Of course' and then he says it, 'In time for dinner?' and I say, 'In time for dinner!?' And he says 'Please tell me you can do it. I'm so tired of seeing her in Fenna's hand-me-downs.' And then ... he gives me puppy dog eyes." She said the words 'Puppy dog eyes,' as if they were a contemptible offence. "The aunts and I have been sewing for seven hours straight." she said blackly. "And I still need to finish the cuffs. Hurry up! Strip so I can finish this."

Kristabell hurriedly unbuttoned the dress she was wearing and pulled the indigo cotton over her head. The bodice was all pin tucks and the gracefully scooping neckline and volumi-nous hem were trimmed with a fine strip of silk ribbon a shade lighter than the cotton. Nessa began snugging up the laces at the back as Kristabell smoothed and arranged the skirt. Lots and lots of fabric had gone into this dress. "Rowan is just lucky that there are a few competent seamstresses in this house. I must say it did turn out rather nicely. The aunts insisted on a lace up back. Buttons would have been so elegant but they wouldn't stop carrying on about how this way at least you can still wear it in three months when your belly starts to swell."

Kristabell blushed rather furiously and passed the dress back to Nessa, carefully avoiding being scratched on the pinned sleeves. By the time Rowan showed up no more than twenty minutes later Nessa had the cuffs stitched, the ribbon trim applied, and was tying the ribbons at the back for her. Rowan was in uniform now. It was obviously a uniform. Red tunic, close fitting brown pants, brown leather vest, boots and,— this was the first time Kristabell had seen him carry a weapon inside— sword belt and sword. There was a sigil on one arm and badge of gold that must have been his rank on the left breast. His hair was tied back. He walked differently in the uniform, but he looked at Kristabell in the dress and then said to Nessa, "You are the most wonderful sister in the world.' He had a giant smile on his face.

Nessa's answer was caustic, "*No* I am *not* the most wonderful sister in the world. *Seven* hours with the Aunts to get this done Rowan. You *owe* me, and I swear that if you don't get her pregnant in the next month I will string you up by the testicles because *I* wanted to put buttons on the back but the aunts insisted on laces with all those fussy little loops and more pin tucks! I'm going to the kitchen to soak my stiff fingers in hot water and chamomile so that at least I can feed myself at dinner!" And she stormed out.

Rowan scratched his forehead smiling sheepishly at a flushed and embarrassed Kristabell. "I'm sorry. I didn't mean to inflict Nessa the Dragon Woman on you. I only wanted you to have a new dress tonight, and whatever she meant about buttons versus laces went right over my head. Did that make sense to you?"

"Laces are um ... adjustable. Apparently she had to listen to the aunts discuss our reproductive future at length."

Rowan winced, "That *would* get her ire up like a swarm of angry hornets right now."

"Why?"

"Oh, she's angry with Leif. Normally a day of sewing wouldn't do much more than leave her slightly peevish but ..."

"She and Leif are, sort of involved aren't they?" Kristabell had caught them kissing in the back of the stables one day when she had been out in search of Rowan.

"'Sort of involved' would be a fairly accurate description of their relationship. They're lovers. They have had a long standing agreement that when the war is over they will make it official, but Leif feels that it would be irresponsible to start a family right now. The thing is that Nessa's been waiting for four years. She wanted to join the army. She's as good an archer as I am and not bad with a sword, but Leif begged her not to. I guess she gave him an ultimatum last night. Call her his Wife and have a family with her or she's joining the army. Leif blames me."

"Is that why he always seems so annoyed with me too?"

"Yes."

"I just hope that no one is going to bring up *you* getting *me* pregnant at the dinner table. People don't discuss these things in the same way where I'm from." Kristabell blushed again.

"I think that I can fairly safely promise you that no one will." He smiled. "Dinner can be, how shall I put it ... less informal, when men from the King's Army are here, especially the older Lieutenants. If it were just Thaylum things would be much as they usually are but with Brian and Eric here too ..." he shook his head. "I've also warned them that you can be very shy and I've threatened various suspect family members with horrors untold if they do anything to embarrass you."

Kristabell walked up to Rowan put her arms around him and kissed his cheek. "You're very sweet you know."

He laughed, "Let's go to dinner. I'm hungry."

He took her hand and they walked through the halls to dinner. Kristabell stopped briefly to look herself over in the large mirror in the front hall as they passed. The dress was lovely. Not too fine for every day but fine enough for guests. And the colour ... The full tiered skirt ... The softness of it ... It *was* nice to have a dress that was only hers. Kristabell loved it.

Rowan let go of her hand and slipped his hand around her waist as they walked into the dinning hall and Kristabell understood then why he'd wanted her to have a new dress. There were candles lit down the full length of the table and every candle in every candelabra on all of the sideboards around the room were lit as well as the oil lamps suspended from the ceiling. There was food running the length of the table. Pies, stews, vegetables, braided bread, deserts, and wine in glasses on a sideboard. The room had been decorated with garlands of holly and ivy. Kristabell remembered, belatedly, what Fenna had told her about it being customary to celebrate a union after the fact with a feast. Most of the household was there. Aunts, uncles, and cousins too. Fenna was wearing a tidy new red tunic with deep burgundy slacks. She looked very elegant. People were milling about enjoying the wine, talking and, obviously, waiting for Rowan to appear with Kristabell. When their presence was noted by the occupants of the room wine glasses went up and a cheer went round. Kristabell felt herself shrink and she literally tried to hide behind Rowan who held her in place with his hand. It reminded her of the day she'd arrived and he'd had to pull her out from behind a tree. "I knew you would try to do that," he whispered in her ear and she couldn't help smiling.

After that there were no speeches or toasts to be endured and the meal proceeded without incident. Kristabell wondered if there would have been toasts and speeches if she had been a normal girl from their world instead of the mysterious stranger she was, with no family of her own, a strange way of speaking, and no history. Rowan introduced her to the soldiers who were under his command. They were, like Rowan, dressed in uniform, as was Leif, who was even more distant than normal that night. She was used to seeing soldiers at the castle as there had been a steady stream of them coming and going to report to Rowan ever since her arrival, but they had never stopped to look at her. Now the men present looked at Kristabell with some curiosity. Fenna had told her at one point that Rowan was considered at court to be a very good catch. She supposed they must be curious about what sort of girl he had chosen in the end. She spent most of the meal with a shy smile on her face, not speaking, holding onto Rowan's hand under the table, but the atmosphere was subdued. Even though an effort was being made to have a merry evening, no one could fully push aside the knowledge that an army was being built somewhere north of them to keep a war that everyone was weary of going. Fenna was down because Kristabell was leaving, Nessa wasn't her usual self and Leif was sitting at the other end of the table. Every time Kristabell caught either Bronwen or Gwydion's eye they either gave her a loaded complicated look, or they turned away.

After the meal was over the men, and Nessa, sat at one end of the table discussing war, and the women, and Dunstan, gathered around the hearth sitting in the comfortable rockers and settees (no couches in this world). It wasn't romantic, but it was inevitable. Fenna had taken out an embroidery project. It was soft ultra fine undyed linen and she sat making neat little stitches that became ivy leaves and vines as Kristabell watched. She tilted her head and leaned it on Fenna's shoulder feeling sleepy in the warmth of the fire. "When I'm done the embroidery, I'll give it to one of the aunts or to Nessa, and they will cut out the pattern and make a baby dress from it," Fenna whispered.

Kristabell fingered the soft fabric as the needle flashed up then down then back up again pulling the smooth embroidery silk with it. "When I come home will you teach me how to do this?" she asked in a low voice.

"Of course," Fenna's reply was soft and sweet as she tipped her own head so that it was resting against Kristabell's.

After a time one of the older knights left the group of men and approached her. He had been introduced to her earlier. His name was Brian. She stood as he approached. He was tall, as so many people in this world seemed to be, with grey hair, slate coloured eyes, and many scars. He held out his hand to her and she gave him hers. He took it and bowed over it before releasing it. He smiled at her and she smiled back. "You have the same gentle smile that Queen Sulamith did. It is no wonder Rowan picked you."

Kristabell blushed and he chuckled. "Rowan warned us that you were shy. I do not mean to embarrass you, although we made rather relentless fun of your poor husband today."

"How did he take it?" She asked smiling.

"With grace and good humour and only a little irritation," he paused. "It's what makes the men of the King's army so devoted to him. They would follow him anywhere. He's also better with a sword than anyone I've ever seen. He's liked *and* respected."

"He seems so young to me," Kristabell sighed, feeling overwhelmed.

"Don't ever assume that your husband isn't up to the task. He might be young but he's the most competent man in the army."

Kristabell nodded.

* * *

It was late, or perhaps it wasn't so much late, as that Kristabell was tired and wanted to be in a quiet room alone, or not alone, but alone with Rowan. *Strange to be alone* with *someone,* she thought to herself groggily. But there was something she wanted on this last night here. Something she wanted to hear, and that meant that she would have to ask Leif to play. She knew that he would, but in the five weeks that she had been there she had made no headway in understanding the big man. She had often gotten the impression that he resented her, and after what Rowan had told her just before dinner she suspected that her impression was correct. She had messed with the status quo of his world. She walked up behind him and rested her hand on his shoulder. When he turned he seemed surprised to see that it was her. He stood and towered over her. "Leif, I was wondering ... I mean ... if it wouldn't be too much trouble for you to play your harp ... and if you would rather not I would ..."

He cut her off and asked more gently than she expected, "What would you like me to play?"

"The lullaby you played the first night that I was here?"

"It would honour me to play that for you."

"Thank you," Kristabell whispered and he nodded.

She slipped into the empty seat that had appeared next to Rowan and listened to the sad, slow, sweet, melody, and as Leif played, Kristabell couldn't keep the tears off her face. The song reminded her of her parents and all that was happening to her now, that they were missing.

* * *

As she lay down next to Rowan that night she whispered, "What will tomorrow bring?"

He pulled her closer to him. "I don't know, but as long as I wake up next to you it will be alright." He kissed her then sighed, "I hate the conflict between desire, responsibility, and duty. I wish that we could have some time together and have everything be simple but ... that's not going to happen." He kissed her again. "We have a long day tomorrow. We need to sleep."

"Goodnight my love," he whispered.

"Goodnight ... My love," she whispered back, and nestled more deeply into his arms as he pulled her in, and they went to sleep.

Part Two

Rhiannon

Chapter 1

T he weather had turned. A heavy drizzle was coming down and everything felt cold and dank. Kristabell shivered as she climbed reluctantly out of the warm bed and began pulling on the sturdy travelling clothes that Fenna had dug out for her. Rowan was already dressed and was buckling on a sword belt. He watched her pull on the boots.

"I haven't seen those in years," he chuckled.

The castle was quiet as they walked to the kitchen for a quick breakfast. There was a fire blazing and fresh bread with butter waited on the table. It was still very early. Rowan wolfed his food down. "Take your time. Eat a good breakfast," Rowan said to her. "I have a few things to do, just come down to the stable when you're done eating and we'll leave from there." He kissed the top of her head, hugged his mother and sisters who had just walked into the kitchen, then strode out the door.

Kristabell sat at the big table and ate bread and figs and drank some of the fresh milk that Nessa had just brought in from the dairy. Nessa, Fenna, and Bronwen sat with her but they didn't talk. When Kristabell stood to go Bronwen rose and looked into Kristabell's face. "I've always felt that I should have had three daughters ..." A strange sad expression passed over Bronwen's face and she opened her mouth as if to speak but then thought better of it, closed her mouth, hugged Kristabell, said goodby, and then left the kitchen.

Fenna and Nessa walked down to the stable with her. She felt heartachy and uncertain and was relieved to see Fenna wiping at her face first. She turned and hugged Fenna hard then hugged Nessa who was getting more sombre looking by the moment. "You'll be fine," Nessa was saying gently. "Nothing bad will happen while your with Rowan and Leif." And Kristabell wondered what, exactly, was showing in her own face to make Nessa say that.

"Thank you for letting me take Strawberry." Fenna had introduced Kristabell to Strawberry the previous afternoon. Strawberry had been Nessa's horse as a child but she was far too tall now for the little skewbald mare with the pink vaguely strawberry shaped mark on her nose. Strawberry was gentle, easy to ride, and according to Nessa, darn near impossible to spook. In short, perfect for someone like Kristabell who had never ridden in her life.

"Don't worry about it. She's the only horse here that I would let you take even if Rowan hadn't asked first."

Kristabell slipped her foot into the stirrup the way Fenna had shown her, pushed herself up and swung her leg over, then Rowan was riding up to her on his own massive black warhorse. Kristabell stared at him for a moment. He was wearing a sort of light armour, was armed to the teeth and looked efficient and dangerous. It was a part of him that Kristabell didn't know. Unbidden the memory of Rowan slaughtering the elf in the forest the first day, the first moment, she'd known him came to her. It just didn't jive with the Rowan she knew.

"Hey ... hey ... Don't look at me like that. I'm still me," he said as he pulled off his gloves and manoeuvred his horse next to hers.

She nodded and he reached across taking her face in his hands and kissing her then wiping away the tears that she couldn't seem to get a handle on. "I love you," he told her and looked into her eyes and smiled so that she would smile back like he knew she would. "We have to go now. Did Fenna show you how to canter and what to do if we break into a gallop?"

She nodded.

"This might be strange for you, just remember that I love you. Okay?" he was still looking into her eyes.

Kristabell nodded again then Rowan pulled his gloves back on, took hold of Strawberry's bridle and kicked his big war horse into a trot. Kristabell pressed her feet into the stirrups as Strawberry followed suit. They rounded the corner of the stable to where several of his men were waiting. Rowan signalled them to follow and they fell in behind. She looked behind her as they turned down the road that lead to the gatehouse, at Fenna, standing alone now in the rain. Kristabell raised her hand in farewell and Fenna's hand went up in response. Kristabell's greatest hope in the world at that moment was that someday Rowan would bring her back and that they wouldn't need to leave, ever again, then Fenna was out of sight and there was a lurch in Kristabell's heart.

When they reached the gatehouse, forty-eight armed mounted men in uniform waited in formation. There was a small barracks in the gate house that had been sufficient to house them for the night and now they stood stock still awaiting orders. Rowan motioned to Leif to come wait with Kristabell and she watched from where she sat, on Strawberry's back with Leif next to her on a giant dun horse, as Rowan handed out orders. He didn't bark or yell. He wasn't a cold bastard but even though he wasn't loud or aggressive Kristabell could hear in his voice and see in his look, an iron expectation of complete obedience. It *was* strange. Ten men peeled away from the main group and started east at a brisk pace, then Rowan selected six from the main group who immediately lined themselves up on Leif's other side, then Eric, whom she had met the night before, rode away in command of the twenty nine remaining men.

Rowan turned to the small group of men who were left behind. "Brian has already explained to you what we are doing today. Are there any questions?" He gave them a moment. "No? I realize that this is somewhat irregular but I do expect you to be courteous and watch your talk while my wife is with us, and thank you for volunteering. Thaylum, Cole. Take the point. Fredric and Ivar, I want you at the rear. Lets move." And that was it.

They followed the main road until they came to a narrower track that angled to the northwest. Kristabell watched the men as they rode. They were all tall Scandinavian or Celtic types. The darkest hair she could see was a light golden brown with the exception of Rowan and a very young man at the front. The one Rowan had called Cole. He was a bit shorter too with a solid build. He had black hair and pale skin with big brown eyes. Not dark, wild, almost black eyes like Rowan's, but soft sweet dreamy eyes, like a cow's eyes or a seal's eyes. He had turned in his saddle two or three times and stolen surreptitious glances at her and when their eyes had made contact he'd grinned and given her a goofy salute. They were all wearing the same light functional armour as Rowan. It wasn't like the armour that you would see in a museum in the world that she had come from, although it had obviously evolved from it. These people might not have the technology of her world but they were not without their own sophistication. These were highly trained men. Each had a sword at his side a quiver of arrows at his back and a crossbow or bow at hand. Some, like Rowan, had a row of small daggers sheathed in their saddles. Kristabell suspected that they were for throwing and she also suspected that only the ones who could throw with deadly accurate efficiency would bother carrying them. Despite the fact that this was a casual ride she could see the men constantly scanning the deep cathedral like forest, always on alert. Rowan was restless and would ride to the front and stay there for a time then pull his horse to the side letting everyone pass, taking the rear.

"Is he always like that?" she asked Leif, who was still beside her.

"Yes. Very much so."

Brian, who rode on her other side, added to this, "He is always this diligent. He never assumes that every man is doing his job. He makes his presence felt and it keeps the men diligent. Nothing would be so humiliating as having your commander do your job for you."

She watched as Rowan rode once more to the front of the line. She had asked him once how it was that he had come to be a knight. "My grandmother, my mother's mother, has been the elected head of the King's council for the last fourteen years," he'd told her. "It is common with some families to send oldest sons to be pages in the King's castle. I think in part because my grandmother was there and because my father had done it as a boy, it was simply something that my parents saw as a part of a boy's education. I didn't want to go and I told my parents that I wouldn't go without Leif. I don't think that they expected us to find places as squires and then make careers of it, but I don't think that they expected a full blown war either."

She looked at Rowan again. He looked so much older, stern even, sitting astride his war horse. Brian's voice broke into her thoughts. "Do you know how it is that your husband came to be Captain of the King's Army?"

"Rowan told me that he fought well in a particular battle. I don't think he's very comfortable talking to me about fighting.'

"Is that all he told you?" Brian asked.

Kristabell told him everything that Rowan had said. "He said that it was three years ago. He said that, he 'guessed' he'd fought well."

"That's really *all* he said?" Leif questioned in an incredulous tone.

"That's all," Kristabell said softly, looking ahead at Rowan's back. "Why, is there more?"

"Not *only* more. For him to say that 'he guessed he fought well', is the understatement of the century," Brian told her. "He won the battle for us. He stopped what would have, most definitely, been a decisive loss and turned it into a decisive win. We had received faulty intel. Rowan suspected it but no one else did. He said that it didn't add up over and over in the war council. He was twenty and had made it to the rank of Lieutenant already. He was in command of a small regiment that included Thaylum, Fredric, Cole—he had just joined—, Leif here, and about twenty others and even though he wouldn't disobey orders he secretly came up with a backup plan just in case he was right and we were being double crossed. And we were. Our army departed, so we thought, to intercept the enemy but we didn't find them where we thought we would. We were ambushed and forced against the base of a mountain. Rowan saw it coming from miles away and broke his regiment off from the main body of the army. We were being picked off by archers from above. When it was apparent that we were losing we realized that the double cross had come from the top, and that the entire army had been handed over on a silver platter. The captain of our army, a man named Tor, had changed his colours and was killing off his own men. Now you have to understand that when the exiled prince turned against the kingdom he took certain people with him. Supporters who, for various reasons—desire for more power, dislike of the Fay, a hankering for more land or more money—would rather have a new system. Although we didn't see it until it was too late, Tor was one of those who had turned. He and Rowan had never seen eye to eye. Tor recognized that Rowan was popular amongst the men and that he had remarkable skill and promoted him in the hopes of controlling him that way. He recognized that Rowan would be a dangerous enemy, but Tor always hated the Fay and while he was never public about it, it was known that he was not unfriendly to the idea of forcing them out of the kingdom." Brian paused before asking, "You're er ... new, to these parts? Am I correct?"

Kristabell nodded.

"Well," Brian continued, "What we have now is essentially two overlapping kingdoms. It has worked for eight hundred years and there is no reason to change, but some feel differently. When the battle was, as we saw it, a complete loss, and all we could do was try to go out with a bang, Rowan's regiment snuck into the fray and attacked from the behind. At the same moment, what looked at the time to be about half of Seamus army, turned and started attacking their comrades. Rowan had managed to procure some eighty enemy uniforms, still don't know how he did it, and Rowan's regiment plus the eighty men hidden in the enemy ranks managed to break an opening. The archers from above didn't know who to shoot at any more. It was mass chaos but we managed to gain the upper hand. Rowan single-handedly fought his way to Tor after that. He fought Tor in single combat. This was a man in his prime who was bigger, and more experienced. Rowan took him down."

"He killed him?" Kristabell asked, her voice small and thin.

Brian nodded.

"The first time I ever saw Rowan, he was killing an elf who was about to kill me. Sometimes I find it difficult to reconcile his two sides."

Kristabell sat quietly astride Strawberry's back thinking about everything, the tall armed men in front and behind, Rowan, the story Brian had just told her. *Knights. I am surrounded by Knights.* Something that didn't even exist in this capacity in her world. She was, for all intents and purposes, married to *a knight.* She loved him and she would follow him anywhere, but it didn't make the situation any less surreal. In the world she had come from she would never have attached herself to a military type.

At what felt like lunch time they stopped. Rowan rode up to her and dismounted with ease, "Are you very stiff from riding? Here let me help you." And he reached up and took her waist as she swung her leg over Strawberry's rump, so that she wouldn't stumble as she dismounted, not that Kristabell was ever particularly clumsy, but he was right. She was stiff from sitting, especially in this cold damp weather. She was glad of the heavy green wool hooded cloak she had been given. Rowan opened her saddle bag, took out a wooden box and passed it to her. "Fenna packed you a nice lunch. The rest of us got bread, apples, and cheese."

He took the reins of the horses and lead them a little way off the path, stopping near an old moss covered nurse log where they could sit and eat. Rowan pulled a piece of oiled canvas out of his own saddle bag, spread it on the log and sat leaving room for Kristabell. He was right about the food, Fenna *had* packed her a nice lunch. Leftovers from last night's dinner. Lima beans that had been baked into a casserole with potatoes, cheese, butter, onions, and marinated greens, and a piece of apple pie. She had no idea how sitting on a horse could make her so hungry but she was glad to eat and sat silently, concentrating on her food. "We'll be at the stronghold in about two hours. The men will make camp outside and I'll take you in."

They ate then walked for a few minutes, hand in hand. Kristabell pretended that they were alone as Rowan walked her back to Strawberry, kissed her, and then made sure she was comfortably mounted. She couldn't help notice, though, the way they were watched by some of the men. That odd curiosity. Thaylum, even at dinner the night before, had looked at her with a sad fascination. Sometimes she wondered if there was something that everyone else knew that she simply wasn't privy to, but she told herself that she was being paranoid.

* * *

They had left the track that they'd been travelling on and were forced now, by the narrow trail that they were following, to ride single file. They didn't stay on the trail for long and came out onto a path. The path, obviously, rarely saw cart wheels or even horses hooves as it was mossy and grassy green. They followed the path for maybe five minutes, the moss muffling the sound of the horses hooves, when Kristabell saw Rowan stiffen. He gave a signal then cantered back to where she was riding between Leif and Brian, took hold of Strawberry's reins and lead her off the path and deeper into the trees, his eyes scanning the forest all the while. He drew her horse around to the other side of a tree trunk as thick as a small house, then turned to the others who had left the path at his signal. Rowan motioned to the two men at the front to go ahead on foot and make sure the path was clear.

"What is it?" she whispered to him, feeling uneasy and not only because of Rowan's sudden order to move them off the path but because of the achy feeling in her bones.

"I'm not sure but I thought that I heard something that was out of place up ahead. I'm not taking any risks today.' He didn't tell her not to worry, he just reached out and touched her cheek then rode over to Leif. She couldn't hear what they were saying. Brian gave her a reassuring smile but she had an uncomfortable feeling. Like there was a dark current moving closer to them, closing in. The two scouts had returned. Apparently there was a small band of elves and men on the path ahead, about twenty of them. Rowan cursed. Kristabell could see the worry in his eyes. He didn't like being in this situation. He turned to Leif, "We'll skirt around to the north. There's a grove there and the elves don't like the groves, then it's not far to Lugh's stronghold."

Leif nodded.

They began picking their way north through the dense undergrowth of the forest. The going was slow and tedious. There didn't seem to be any sign of people but there was a hum in Kristabell's head and the ache in her bones was getting worse. She looked back and one of the knights who was taking up the rear looked back at the same moment. She saw him loose his crossbow. "Rowan," Kristabell's voice shook as she said his name, the pain getting worse and fear creeping through her. Suddenly Rowan reached over and grabbed her, pulling her onto his horse with him.

"Ride west!" he shouted, "They're on us at the rear!" He ordered his men to turn. They rode as hard as they could through the forest, low branches whipping them. "Stay down," he told Kristabell. She held on to the horse's mane, staying as low as she could and holding on tight with her legs. Rowan's bow was in his hands and he was loosing arrows rapidly. She could hear the arrows hitting their marks and the sound made her want to vomit. They broke out of the underbrush. *This must be what Rowan referred to as the 'grove',* she thought.

But it wasn't a grove anymore. The trees that had been standing in the mossy area that was free of underbrush—beautiful, magnificent, majestic trees—were being pulled down by men as elves stood by watching. Oak, birch, rowan, cedar. The oaks looked as if they must have been hundreds of years old and there were standing stones in the centre of the grove, but they had been toppled. Kristabell realized that this was where the pain, that was running through her body now, was coming from. The trees were screaming in her head. Rowan shouted an order to cut west across the edge of the grove to get them back to the dense forest where there was more shelter. Kristabell caught sight of an elf, crossbow in its hands raised to shoot but too slow, as Rowan loosed an arrow and the crossbow fell followed by the elf. The elves were strange and almost human looking. They had bloodless skin, black eyes and hair that had an unnatural depth of colour, with faces that could almost be beautiful yet somehow weren't. They looked *hard*. Like the closest thing to a smile they were capable of was a sneer of malice.

They hurtled back into the dense forest. Two of Rowan's men fell. Arrows were falling all around them. Another man fell. Leif leapt from his horse, sword in his hand and placed himself between the advancing elves and Kristabell and Rowan, who was still loosing arrows at rapid speed, but it wasn't enough. They were outnumbered and surrounded on all sides. Kristabell could feel terror and panic filling her breast. Rowan had dropped his bow and now had a death grip around her middle and his sword in his other hand. "I'm sorry my love. I'm so sorry," he whispered. Leif was backed up against Rowan's horse as elves and cruel looking men closed in on them. Kristabell had no idea what she was doing, but something was building inside her and it felt familiar. It built until she couldn't hold it in but now she knew what it was and she welcomed it. She let it loose and felt the world shift around them. She grabbed hold of Leif's armour and then grabbed the reins and pulled hard. The forest, the elves, the men with swords and axes all disappeared.

Chapter 2

Leif crashed to the ground. She had inadvertently pulled him off balance when she'd drawn him through the portal. They were silent, stunned, relieved, and completely terrified all at once. As they crossed through Kristabell had felt pain, sharp and overwhelming, lance through her temples and she was fighting to maintain consciousness. She looked up and exclaimed, "Oh! I know where we are. That's the roller coaster at the P.N.E. fair grounds." Then, she promptly fainted.

* * *

She opened her eyes then closed them. She'd had a brief view of someone's garage door. They were in an alley. She could rest for a moment longer. Rowan was talking, "I'm *so angry* with myself." He was throwing bits of gravel at the garage door, hard. Kristabell could hear them ricocheting around the alley

"For crying out loud Rowan, stop throwing bloody rocks," Leif growled. "You almost got me in the eye with that one."

"I'm sorry," Rowan sighed. "I just got six men killed and now we're in a strange world with an unconscious girl and I'm *pissed off*! Especially at myself. I've never fucked up like this in my life!"

"You couldn't have seen this coming. We all agreed with you that we were taking the best route. We all believed that the risks were minimal. You talked this over with Brian last night for an hour. Elves haven't been spotted in those parts for months. Even if you hadn't brought Kristabell, you said that you *still* had to talk to Lugh. We would have run into trouble no matter what."

"I know, but I *did* bring Kristabell! You *know* what they would have done to her. I couldn't ... I ..."

"Rowan this is a war. You know that there is every possibility that Seamus might attack our home some day to try to get to you. I don't need to tell you that. You know that! You've said it yourself. Does it really bother you any less to think of Fenna or Nessa being raped and tortured? If you had left Kristabell behind *that* would have been a risk too. And as for what just happened, every one of us believed that if we could just make it to the grove, that we would be safe. Everybody knows that the elves are weakened in the groves. I can't for the life of me figure out what Seamus could possibly be hoping to accomplish by desecrating one of the groves. It's against the law. Both Fay and human, and the Fay will see it as an act of war."

"He wants the trees for their power and," Rowan paused, "I'm willing to bet that he had some clever plot to try to lay the blame at Liam's feet. Nothing would please him more than a conflict between Lugh and Liam." Rowan threw another rock and Kristabell heard it hit Leif.

"Piss off Rowan! I know you're angry but none of us saw this coming. It's not something we could have predicted. None of us saw this as a high risk journey. We expected a mellow morning ride, and none of us expected you to go back to the King's city without Kristabell. A run in with a band of approximately ninety elves and men in those parts is unprecedented. You kept her safe longer than anyone else could have and she got us out of there. Now lets just accept it and deal with the situation at hand!" Kristabell had never heard Leif talk so much.

"He's right you know." she mumbled. She was lying on her side half on the gravel and half on Rowan's lap with his cloak under her head. She could hear the wooden roller coaster and screaming in the distance and Rowan's horse chomping on weeds next to her head. The world was spinning a bit but otherwise she seemed to be alright. She sat up so that she was sitting between Rowan and Leif, who were leaning against a garage door with their legs stretched out in front of them. Rowan was sitting there looking tortured and guilty, his eyes dark and angry. Kristabell tried standing and he was up in a flash making sure she didn't fall. She held out her hand to him. "Come," she said softly. "We need to get out of here. We look like escapees from an S.C.A. convention and we need to get this horse out of sight."

Rowan hesitated to take her hand so she reached out and took his. She could see it in his face. He was hating himself for what had almost happened and punishing himself inwardly. "Come," she said more gently. "I know where we are. I know someone who can help us."

They started walking. Leif took the horse's reins, leading him along as they went, heading west down alleys, avoiding the major streets, toward Trout Lake. It didn't take long. No more than an hour, but Kristabell could tell that it was a stressful hour for Rowan and Leif. This world was overwhelming at the best of times even for the people who lived here, but despite being battle hardened warriors, Rowan and Leif were scared shitless. Kristabell thought that they were going to pee themselves when a Mac truck boomed by as they were waiting for a light to change. By the time they made it to Sheila's house they were exhausted. Kristabell lead them down the alley and through the back gate into Sheila's garden. It was an impressive garden much like Kristabell's own garden at her parents house, with every inch of the small city lot given over to plants. The horse was munching on Sheila's kale. "Oh dear." Kristabell sighed as she thumped down on the back porch steps. "This is my boss's house," she explained to the two men. "She will, at least, be able to help us get to my parents' place. We can figure out what to do from there, but I guess that you've figured out that we can't walk across the city like this. We draw too much attention and we're not supposed to have a horse here."

The two men just stared at her dazed and then sat down on the ground right where they were standing. It would be an hour or two before Sheila would be home from the garden centre so all they could do was wait.

Chapter 3

When Sheila did come home it didn't take long for her to realize that there was a horse in her back garden. She came to her back door and looked out in dismay at the horse that was nibbling her Japanese Maple, then she saw Kristabell. Sheila looked spooked at first then she almost yelled, "Kristabell! Sprite! You're supposed to be dead!" And Kristabell was enfolded in a sudden tight hug.

"Where have you *been*? Are you alright?" Sheila asked in a tone of incredulity and relief placing her hands on Kristabell's shoulders as if for further confirmation of her reality.

Kristabell was tongue tied, unsure of where to start or what to tell Sheila. "I've been stuck ... Away," she said uselessly. "I've had a little trouble. I was wondering if you could give us a ride to my parents house?"

Sheila stared at her in dismay, "You don't know do you." It wasn't a question.

Rowan came to Kristabell's side. She was teetering and getting paler. He put his arm around her waist and looked at her with concern.

"Who are these people?" Sheila asked in a tone of suspicion.

"This is Rowan," Kristabell told Sheila trying to settle on how to clarify her relationship with him without feeling awkward calling him her husband. "He's my boyfriend. And this is his brother Leif. Their English isn't so good," she said, and she could hear her voice getting thinner and thinner, then she asked, "What don't I know Sheila?"

"Oh God," Sheila said heavily, then, "You'd better come in.' She stepped to the side and let them into her kitchen. "I'm going to make some tea. Make yourselves at home. Take off ... Whatever you need to take off to be comfortable." She glanced at the swords and armour, "And don't worry about the horse." There was a note of forced nonchalance.

Once they were all settled comfortably around the kitchen table with cups of milky tea in their hands and a giant pile of weapons and armour stacked on the back porch Sheila was ready to talk. She looked at Kristabell. Sheila, Kristabell realized, was not entirely unlike an older plumper version of Fenna and it made Kristabell feel suddenly homesick. *Homesick for where?* She wondered.

"There isn't any way I can say this that will make it easy to hear." Sheila looked at Kristabell sympathetically. "The day that I sent you home from work early, there was a fire. Your parents are dead."

Sheila passed Kristabell a newspaper from five weeks earlier. The front page read, "Family Dies in House Fire. Police Suspect Arson." There was a picture of a burned out shell of a house surrounded by a lovely, somewhat charred garden. Kristabell stared at Sheila in disbelief, unable to speak or move.

"Your parents were positively identified. There was a third smaller body in the house and you left no dental records so it was presumed to be you."

Kristabell's breath was coming in great gasps. She didn't know what to do. They were dead. Her parents were dead. Rowan and Leif were in the dark but she couldn't talk. Suddenly she jumped up, ran to the sink and vomited. "No,' she gasped leaning on the counter. "Why would anyone do that? They didn't do anything to anyone." Rowan was beside her trying to hold her hair out of the sink. Sheila ran the water and turned the garburater on which made Rowan and Leif jump, then wet a clean cloth and passed it to Rowan. He nodded a 'thank you' and wiped Kristabell's mouth for her.

"Are you okay?"

"I don't know," she answered, tearing up.

"What's happened?" he asked her holding her face between his hands.

"My parents are dead," she sobbed. "Someone set fire to my house the night you found me. They've been dead all this time. They didn't deserve that." He put his arms around her and she sobbed into his chest with her legs threatening to give way beneath her. *Breathe*, she told herself, *just breathe. You can't fall apart right now.* She tried to get herself to stop crying, tried to get her breath to come steadily instead of in hiccuping little gasps.

"I'll fix dinner," Sheila said quietly. "And you can stay here as long as you need to."

Sensing that they were in the way Rowan moved Kristabell to the old loveseat that was at the other end of the kitchen and sat there with her, shhing her and stroking her hair, waiting for her to stop shaking. After a while she leaned her head back with her eyes closed, took a deep breath and listened to the sound of Sheila moving around in her kitchen. A fridge opening, the glass bottles and jars in the door rattling as it closed again. The crunch of a knife slicing through celery, the creak of an oven door.

"So, what language are you speaking?" Sheila asked after a time.

"It's not so much another language. More an alternate English."

"Is it some strange British or Irish dialect?"

"No," Kristabell sighed. "If I tell you ... If I explain this, you'll think I'm crazy."

Sheila laughed, "There is a horse eating my climbing roses I've got Sir Lancelot and his brother Beowulf in my kitchen and don't think I haven't noticed that you and your *Boyfriend*,' she emphasized the word, "Are wearing what look to me like matching wedding bands." She looked up from the vegetables she was chopping. "At this point the only kind of explanation I'm gonna believe is a crazy one."

"Okay. Here goes." Kristabell explained as best she could starting at the beginning. Rowan could understand her but she had to do a bit of translating to keep Leif in the loop, but it wasn't as if he didn't know the story so the big man mostly sat at the table drinking tea.

Sheila whistled long and low when Kristabell finished. "It makes sense in a way. It fits with all the old Celtic legends and old fairy stories. My old Scottish granddad used to claim, with the utmost seriousness, that he had spent a night dancing drinking with, and being *pleased* by fairy women. His brothers always said he was three sheets to the wind but he always believed it was real."

Kristabell got up off the love seat. "Are your plates still in here?" she asked, opening a cupboard, finding the plates and taking four down. She needed to do something to make herself feel normal. The cutlery was where she remembered it being as well, so she set the table.

"I have to say it, you've managed to find yourself an awfully nice looking husband."

Kristabell blushed and looked over at Rowan who seemed to have picked up on the fact that he was being talked about. "He'll do," Kristabell said smiling.

"So how old are they?"

"Leif's twenty two. Rowan's twenty three."

"Shit. They're younger than I thought they were."

"Yeah," Kristabell nodded. "I think people grow up a little sooner in that world."

"Like you." Sheila looked at her.

Kristabell nodded. Her brain was starting to work again. "Sheila? Did Evan leave any clothing behind that these guys could borrow? I have something that I need to do tomorrow, and I need them to blend in a little better."

"Sure, yeah. He never takes everything. Let me get this lasagna in the oven then we can go up and have a look."

Evan, it must be said, for all that he could be very academic, and a bit of a jock, was very much a punk and, what with Leif's waist length dreads and Rowan's long hair, it was probably just as well. Sheila passed Rowan an old Pixies concert T-shirt, black jeans and a purple hoodie. "I'll have to hem those jeans. Tell him to try them on," Sheila said sticking her head back in the closet then passing Leif cargo pants, a black turtleneck, and a really bad ass leather jacket. "I don't have shoes that will fit you." She said to Rowan as she passed Leif a pair of Vans, "But at least this way your foot wear won't match." And with that done they went back downstairs and ate dinner.

After the entire lasagna, salad, and a whole loaf of kalamata olive bread had been consumed Sheila announced that she needed to do something mundane, so they loaded the dish-washer, which amazed Rowan and Leif, but if they thought that was cool it was nothing compared to the television. "So much for mundane," Sheila commented dryly as the two men sat transfixed by the eight o'clock news. When it was over, and Leif and Rowan had gone out to put the gear and the horse in the garage, Kristabell said to Sheila, "I don't want to stay in your house any longer than I need to. Someone killed my parents and faked my death. I don't even want to think about that too hard and I don't want to put you in any danger by being here, so if you don't mind giving us a ride downtown tomorrow morning, there *is* something I need to do there, then we'll find our way back here during the day, get the horse and the gear from the garage before you get home from work, and then I'm going to try to get us back home."

"So you won't stay in this world?"

Kristabell shook her head. "In Rowan's world I have a family and a home and a chance at happiness."

"I was planning on semi-retiring next year. I was going to ask you to manage the garden centre for me."

"I would have liked that," Kristabell smiled. "I'm sorry about your garden."

"It's alright. It's fall. It wouldn't have been nice much longer anyway. I'll just think of it as free fertilizer."

* * *

Sheila gave Kristabell and Rowan the spare bedroom. Leif was sleeping in the living room armed to the teeth. Rowan's sword, for that matter, was propped up against the night stand as they lay there talking.

"I keep telling myself that if I hadn't been with you I would have died with my parents and that at least they died too soon to really worry about me. But I still feel so cold and hollow inside. I'll never see them again. Hear their voices ... all those little things. They loved each other. I can't imagine them together anymore. They're just gone."

Rowan ran his fingers over her cheek and stroked her hair, "I know. I know how you feel. I think you talked to Brian a few times over the last two days."

"I did," she confirmed.

"When I was young I was his squire. He taught me to fight. Taught me to be a gentleman. He was like a second father to me. He was a good person. That's why he took an interest in you. He told me that he liked you, that he thought I'd made the right decision in asking you to be my wife. After all the flak I took from Leif over it, that felt really good. It meant a lot to me. And he died today. He'll never meet our children. Right now I can't even guarantee that we'll ... I feel ..." he paused, took a breath. "It's like your parents. I want a life where we know that the people we love are going to be there to go through it all with us and I can't even keep *you* safe. If I'd gone straight to the fairies with you instead of taking you to my home, maybe we could have helped your parents."

"You couldn't have known the kind of trouble we were going to run into today. It's a wonder that you stayed as clearheaded as you did, what with the trees screaming in our heads like that. And you couldn't have known that someone would go after my parents."

"We would be prisoners right now if you hadn't opened a door into your world," he said flatly.

"This isn't my world anymore, and we would be prisoners if you hadn't kept me safe long enough to get us out of there, and now, even though everything feels really horrible, at least we're together."

"I know ... I know ..." he whispered. "But today was different. I've lost men before. It comes with the territory. I'm a soldier in a war but today, I had a personal agenda."

"So what are you saying?" Kristabell whispered.

"I don't *know*." She could hear the agony in his voice, could hear him breathing hard in the dark, trying to quell emotions that were threatening to overrun him. "Kristabell, I'm confused and I'm not used to it."

She could tell that he wasn't used to talking to someone like this, to being this open. Admitting that he was angry with himself to Leif was one thing, but to admit that, for the first time, he doubted himself, *was* different and if he couldn't admit it to her then who could he admit it to? She wrapped her arms around him as tightly as she could and buried her face in his neck hard. She held on to him like that for a long time until eventually they slept.

Chapter 4

When Kristabell woke Rowan was already awake watching her. There was resolve in his eyes as he kissed her. "Waking up with you makes everything a little bit easier."

"I love you." She smiled and ruffled his hair. It was as if a healthy scab had formed over everything that had been so raw and immediate the day before and it *was* just a little easier to be objective.

They dressed, went downstairs and ate breakfast with Sheila, then headed out to her car. The horse was still in the garage along with the gear. Sheila gave Kristabell the key. "Here, just slip it under the back door before you go."

Kristabell had slung her shoulder bag across herself under her cloak before leaving the previous morning, and the bag and all its contents had made it safely across. She wore her jeans with Rowan's old boots, the plum coloured tunic and a borrowed wool cardigan from Sheila. Seeing Rowan and Leif dressed in the clothing of the world that she had come from was something else altogether. Rowan looked like a rock star and Leif looked *Big* and *Bad* and somehow more menacing and intimidating than he did in armour with a sword. Kristabell couldn't stop grinning at them. If Allan from the garden centre saw her with Rowan and Leif, he wouldn't dare call her a freak. He'd be too scared.

Rowan and Leif had, obviously, never ridden in a car before and they almost needed to be coaxed into Sheila's little Honda

Civic. It was, to them, like so many things in this world, both frightening and fascinating at the same time.

"So. What's the address you need to get to?" Sheila asked as she turned right onto Knight Street heading downtown.

"550 Burrard." Kristabell answered looking at the card that had been in her wallet for years.

Ever since she was little her parents had drilled her, "If anything ever happens to us who do you call?" She had figured that it was just the paranoia of two overprotective parents with no family and few friends, but the card with Smith, Flanagan and Flanagan printed on it was always on the fridge and from the time she had started kindergarten she'd had one with her, either in her backpack or in her wallet. She didn't know what to expect from the visit but this was the sort of circumstance her parents had planned for, so she figured that before she left this world for good, that she should do this. Sheila pulled up in front of the huge modern office tower then turned to look at Kristabell, "I'm never going to see you again am I Sprite?"

Kristabell shook her head, "I've found my place and it's not in this world."

"If you ever need me, you know where I am," there was a look in Sheila's eyes for a moment, a look of what might have been.

They got out of the car and stood on the sidewalk. "Goodbye. Thank you," Kristabell threw her arms around Sheila.

"Goodbye." Sheila gave Kristabell one last complicated look, and then got back into her car. For the briefest moment, as Sheila pulled out into the busy downtown traffic, Kristabell thought about the photograph she had found on Evan's dresser top the night before. It was of herself. The day she had climbed into the blossoming cherry tree in Evan's yard and he had snapped a picture of her from his bedroom window. It was soft and white at the edges as if it had been, many times, held in sweaty hands, and spotted, as if it had been cried upon Kristabell banished the thought.

"Let's go," she said to the two men who were standing on the sidewalk gawking at their surroundings. "Stay close. This place might be a little weird."

She took Rowan's hand and Leif followed closely behind as she lead them through the automatic glass doors and into the seamless foyer that, like the mouth of a concrete giant, seemed to swallow them whole.

Chapter 5

Kristabell had to admit that even she found the interior of the giant office tower unnatural and disorienting. They took the elevator up to the twenty-fifth floor and stepped out into an expensive looking reception area. As Kristabell approached the mahogany desk a receptionist watched her dubiously over the top of her glasses. "How may I help you?" The receptionist asked in a professionally dismissive tone that was followed by an expression of alarm as the woman took in Rowan and Leif. Kristabell looked behind her at the two men who in their discomfiture were looking quite hostile. "My name is Kristabell O'reilly," Kristabell said turning back to the receptionist but that was as far as she got.

"Oh," The receptionist perked up. "Yes. We've been expecting you. I'll let Mr. Flanagan know you're here. Just one moment." Her tweed suited figure disappeared and reappeared within moments. "Mr. Flanagan will see you right away." She lead them into an eccentrically Victorian looking office where an exceptionally good looking red haired man was waiting. He rose from his desk chair to greet them and as he came around his desk Kristabell was taken aback to find that he was only about four feet ten inches tall. "Hello," he smiled. "It's good to see you alive. I was sorry to hear about your parents. We had no idea where you were so when we first realized that you weren't killed in the fire we had one of our people fake your death. We thought you would be safer if your enemies thought that you were dead. We didn't freeze your bank account in case you needed money but we had to do some finagling to make sure that no one *else* was tracking your account either. I know that you haven't used your account so I'm very curious to know where you've been." He looked at her with inquisitive bright green eyes.

Kristabell's mind was taxed. She was stressed and over-burdened. "What are you and who are my enemies?" she demanded ungracefully.

"Well, I am a lawyer, of sorts, and as for your enemies, they would be the exiled prince Seamus and his followers."

"Why would they be *my* enemies?"

He looked at her, slightly taken aback. "You don't know?"

She turned to Rowan, even though she knew that he would have an only partial grasp of the conversation, and said in the alternate English, "I don't like it when people say that to me."

Mr. Flanagan smiled and began to speak. He too had switched to the language of Rowan's world, "That explains where you've been and why you haven't used your bank account."

Kristabell felt like she was going to explode. "What don't I know!" she almost yelled dropping the pretense of regular English altogether. "I have no idea what's happening or why I'm here. All I know is that my parents told me that if anything ever happened to them that I was supposed to come to you!"

"Come with me," he said gently. "This will explain things." He lead them to a little room with a security lock. "Are you fine with these two?" He glanced at Rowan and Leif.

"Yes. I trust them."

Mr. Flanagan opened the door and motioned to the table within. He left them through an inner door and returned carrying a metal box the size of a shoe box. He placed it on the table, opened it, then pushed it towards Kristabell. She looked in. There were two envelopes and two small boxes. One of the envelopes had her mother's writing on it. She picked it up, opened it, and read.

My Dearest Kristabell,

If you are reading this, it means that your father and I are dead. I wanted you to know that we loved you like you were our own child and that you made us smile and lifted our hearts. That is why we called you Kristabell. It is not the name your mother gave you, but you were like the funny little fairy in the movie about the boy in the green tights. You were our own little fairy. I'm sorry that we didn't share more with you. We were never sure what the right decision was, but you always seemed to know instinctively who and what you were so we thought that perhaps it was safer if we didn't tell you. I'm sorry if it was the wrong decision. There is a letter enclosed from your birth mother. It should explain everything. If you have any other questions Mr. Flanagan can answer them for you.

Love Fionnuala

Kristabell wiped her cheeks with the back of her hand, "Are my parents really dead then?"

"I'm afraid so," the lawyer admitted.

"What does it say?" Leif asked.

She slid the letter to Mr. Flanagan. "Can you read it out loud? I can't."

He read and translated the letter. Kristabell looked over at Rowan seeking comfort in his glance but the look in his eyes was guilty and ashamed. He seemed reluctant to meet her eyes. She looked into the box and took out the other letter. It was in the script of Nova Britannia which she still had trouble deciphering. She looked to Rowan but he wouldn't meet her eyes. She turned to Leif. "Would you read this to me?" He nodded. "Thank you." He broke the seal on the letter and began to read.

Rhiannon,

Right now you are just a tiny baby, and I have had only one hour to hold you, but already they are here to take me away from you, back to the world where you were conceived. I feel like my heart is being ripped out. By the time you read this you will be a grown woman of nineteen. They tell me that that is the age of adulthood in this world. It seems strange to me, as I am only seventeen. I am sorry for exiling you to this strange place. Gavin and Fionnuala will love you. They have lost much as their punishment for helping me conceal my relationship with your father. Your father and I loved each other. Lugh doesn't know that you exist and my parents have made sure that he never will. All I can hope is that your presence in the universe will come to some good. Your father and I, we wanted to break the taboo. We were idealistic and in love. We wanted to prove that there was no harm in fairy and human being together. We would unite our two kingdoms with an heir that was neither fairy nor human, but both. In losing you I have lost both my heart and my hope. My beautiful little girl. I love you.

Your mother,

Sulamith

Kristabell's face was streaming tears. Rowan wouldn't meet her eyes or hold her hand under the table and, strangely Leif was having trouble maintaining his composure and kept brushing at his eyes as well. He'd barely made it through the letter. The metal box was empty save the two small boxes. One was the size of a book, the other smaller. Both were made of elegantly tooled leather. Kristabell took the small one first and opened it. Inside was a platinum ring in the shape of a little heartsease blossom with rose and green gold accents. The petals were formed of amethysts, and tiny aquamarine dew drops were set on the leaves. There was a little piece of paper in the box with her birth mother's writing on it. She passed it to Leif, "It says that it was a love token from your father to your mother. It is fairy metal work. Very fine, but it will last forever."

She took the ring out of the box and slipped it onto the middle finger of her right hand where it sat on her pale slim finger like it belonged. Then she opened the last box. Inside was a circlet set with a crescent moon carved from an opal that was full of flashing colour and caught up in a net of silver Celtic knotwork. She lifted it and placed it on her brow. Rowan was looking at her now, his eyes filled with remorse. She wasn't ready to deal with what she saw there so she looked away. She took the circlet off and placed it carefully back in its box. She took the box and placed it in her bag with the two letters. Mr. Flanagan lifted a briefcase onto the table. "This is your parent's money. I suggest you use it to disappear. We are a small outfit but we try to help those who come to this world seeking refuge. The house you grew up in belonged to me. I liked your parents. I wish I could have done more. If there is anything I can help you with, just ask. There is more magic in this world than it first seems."

Kristabell nodded. "Do you think that it's safe for me to walk around the city?"

He tilted his head considering, "I can't guarantee your safety anywhere. But for a few hours, if you don't linger long and you keep those two nearby," he glanced at Rowan and Leif. "It should be fine. Elves haven't been spotted in the city for weeks. Not since the fire. Just be cautious."

"Thank you Mr. Flanagan. I'll be gone from Vancouver by mid-afternoon."

He gave her a serious considering look, "If you decide to return to Nova Britannia go to your father. You would be safest there."

Kristabell nodded, eager to be away where she could have some space and think. "Goodbye," she said rising from her seat. He shocked her then by kneeling before her and telling her, "It was an honour, my Queen."

* * *

Once they were out of the office tower and back on the sidewalk Kristabell followed the random path on which her feet set her. She couldn't think straight. She didn't know what to think. She didn't know who she was. She was numb and distracted. Everything she thought she knew, including Rowan, seemed unsteady like old neglected beams that could collapse under her feet. She wandered on in a blur until suddenly Rowan pulled her back. A car whizzed by. She had almost walked out into moving traffic.

"Kristabell. We can't just wander like this."

"My name's not Kristabell!" she snapped not meeting his eyes. But he was right. She needed to be somewhere quiet where she could gather her wits. They were just coming back to Georgia Street. She rounded the corner and headed into the lobby of the big posh hotel there. She approached the desk. "I need a room." She paid in advance using the emergency Visa that her parents had given her that was attached to their account, not wanting to draw attention by taking cash out of the briefcase, and unable to use a debit card without frying the machine, then with Rowan and Leif trailing behind her, she headed for the elevators. She wanted to cry. She wanted to yell and scream at someone, at the world. She didn't want this trail of pain that lead up to her. She opened the hotel room door, held it open for Leif and Rowan, and let it fall closed, thinking that it would be quiet now, but the noise in her head wasn't so easily silenced. Rowan reached out a tentative hand, touched her shoulder but she rounded on him, "You knew! YOU KNEW!" she yelled getting louder and angrier. "Didn't you think I had a right to know who I am? Didn't you think that I would rather hear all that from someone I love? I *trusted* you!" She hit his chest with her fists as he stood there looking helplessly lost. She looked into his eyes. She saw sorrow, love, remorse. She turned away from him, ran to the bedroom sobbing and slammed the door behind her.

She threw herself on the bed and cried. She cried for her parents whom she had lost and for the mother that she would never know, and then, like a lost child who will never find home again, she cried for herself. After a time the tears slowed and she took out her Ipod. She turned it on and it immediately lost its charge so she took it over to a wall socket, plugged it in, put in her ear buds and lost herself to the music.

***

Leif stood with his back to the room looking out the window, marvelling at Kristabell's strange world. *Or ...* Not *Kristabell, and ...* not *her world*, he thought. Leif had, for one brief instant, an urge to round on Rowan as, she, Kristabell—not Kristabell—had, but when he turned and saw Rowan sitting, elbows on his knees, hands clasped behind his head, staring at the floor between his feet, Leif stayed his tongue. He had known Rowan for his entire life and this was the first time that he had ever seen him look dejected. With a long heavy sigh Leif sat on one of the fine plush chairs next to the couch Rowan had occupied. "Look, for what it's worth, I'm sorry I've been such an ass over the last few weeks. It was ... unreasonable of me to expect you to deny the way you felt for her just because of bad timing. I've been unfair ... to both of you. And you were right about Nessa."

They'd had a fight in the armoury about it five days earlier when Rowan had told Leif of his plan to ask Kristabell to be his wife and Leif had tried to dissuade him. It had been more than a fight actually. It had turned into an aggressive shouting match that had nearly become physical and only hadn't because their cousin Lewis had come in and gotten between them. Leif still regretted what he'd said when Rowan had refused to back down. "How are you going to feel if you're dying on some battle field knowing that she's at home with *your* baby waiting for *you* to come back to her and you know you're *never going to make it*!"

Rowan had yelled back, "I'm gonna feel like *shit*! I'm gonna feel like *dog meat*! But at least I'll know that I was man enough to put my heart on the line for her!" And that's when Lewis had gotten between them and Rowan had left the armoury with angry tears on his cheeks. Just as he was walking out he'd turned to Leif and said, "It's my heart I'm risking in the end, and if she loves me enough to put her heart on the line too, then I want her *that* much more. Maybe *you* don't love Nessa as much as you think you do." They were brothers. They were best friends. It was the only real fight they'd ever had.

Rowan sat up and looked at Leif. "You know, you and Kris ..." he started to say Kristabell then sighed. "Let's just say that, I'm not the only person who's been holding my tongue I'm positive that Gwydion knows who she is and pretty sure that my mother does too. I have no idea why they left it up to me to figure out except ... that perhaps they, like me, felt that telling her would make her unhappy. That, and put her in even more danger than she's already in. There's something about her that just makes me want to protect her and make her happy."

It was disconcerting to see Rowan this way. He was accustomed to Rowan's usual highly competent decisive actions. Uncertainty was new. Leif had seen him prove himself on the battle field a dozen times over, he was a brilliant strategist, his plans had won them many victories, but even Leif had to admit that he didn't know what to do with this information. A half Fay Queen would change everything, and Seamus would either want her dead, or want her as his pawn, and either situation would be bad news for Kristabell ... Rhiannon ... Whoever she was.

"For the record, I've only known since the night of the harvest gathering. I'd already asked her and she'd already said yes." He passed Leif the ring. "That was the tip off. She's had it since she was a child. And I didn't know about your parents until today. Krista ... She never used their names when she talked about them. She just called them mum and dad. I'm ... sorry."

Leif pushed the thoughts of his parents away. He'd grown up thinking that they were dead. He was used to the idea that they were dead. Except ... that all this time they had been alive, and now ...? They were dead. Everything was the same. *Everything* was different.

"Are you going to go talk to ... Her?" Leif asked Rowan.

There was no answer.

"You *need* to talk to her," he pushed.

Rowan let out an explosive sigh and for a long horrible moment Leif thought Rowan might cry, "And say *what*? Find some brilliant new way to make things *worse*?" His voice was hoarse and he had ground the heels of his hands into his eyes and leaned back on the couch like that.

Leif decided that he would rather go talk to the crying girl in the other room than stay there with Rowan. The truth was that he actually did like her. Not the way Rowan did, but there was a quality about her that reminded him of something that, until now, he had been unable to place. If he had taken the time to get to know her better he probably would have figured out who she was on his own and he would have made the same choice as Rowan. Keep things quiet, and get her to her father. He knocked on the door to the hotel bedroom and waited. There was no answer. *She probably thinks it's Rowan*, he thought to himself, and slowly turned the handle.

* * *

When Leif came out of the room a short time later he took one look at Rowan and said, "Go. Talk. She needs you."

* * *

Modern music was one of the few aspects of this world that she would miss. She flipped through her Ipod and listened to her favourite songs one last time savouring the gritty intensity that existed in rock and pop but that didn't always come through in folk music. She remembered listening to music with her dad in the living room. He'd put on a CD and say, "What do you think of this?" They'd sit, listen, talk. She lost herself in the memory. She wasn't surprised when she saw the door opening, but she was surprised to see who was opening it. He closed the door behind him and sat awkwardly on the edge of the bed. She pulled out the ear buds. He was quiet for a few moments before asking, "Your parents, what were they like?"

She stared down at the Ipod in her hands for a moment before answering, "They were sad and quiet. They took pleasure in small things. My mother liked to care for me physically. Make me food, brush my hair, make sure my fingernails were trim and clean, knit me sweaters. My father would take me for long walks. When I was small he would carry me up high on his shoulders. He was a firefighter, which is about as close as you can get to being a knight in this world without joining the military. That's all I really knew of them. That, and that they loved me."

Leif nodded quietly before telling her, "Gavin and Fionnuala were my parents. They disappeared when I was three. My father was in the Queen's army. My mother was one of her ladies. No one knew what happened to them. My father was Rowan's father's cousin. That's why I was raised by his family."

Kristabell felt like all the sorrow of the worlds, the pain of every lost child, was lodged in her chest. She reached out, unable to speak, and took Leif's big rough hand in her own much smaller one and sat quietly beside him. "I feel like bursting back into tears. If I think too hard about this tangled web it threatens to swallow me whole, but right now, I'm just going to be glad that I have a brother." Then with a start she re-membered, "The lullaby!" And tears did roll down her cheeks then, when she thought of whose arms had rocked her, and whose voice had hummed that melody when those very arms must have been desperately aching for a different child.

Leif smiled. It was a sad smile. "He used to sing that to me. I can't remember the words just the melody. It's his harp that I play. I think that he wrote that song himself because I haven't been able to find out the words from anyone."

"It's stupid of me I know, I've noticed things that are too obvious to ignore but, my life, this world ... They haven't left me a very confident person. I've noticed the way some people look at me and I've wondered if maybe my connection to your world might be more than accidental and it is *stupid*, I *know* it is, to have ignored these things, and to have told myself that it was just my imagination, or that I was just being paranoid, or that it was just wishful thinking, but one thing that I shouldn't have ignored is how much like our father you are. You're just like him. Your manner. Your face. Even through your beard I can see it. I know that you don't like me ..."

"No ..." he cut her off and for a moment his face worked. "I like you just fine. The way I've treated you has nothing to do with you and everything to do with my own issues. I like you just fine. I've been rude." He paused again before asking, "Am I really like him? Mark always said that I was but I was never sure if he told me that just to comfort me or if it was true."

"He had short hair and always needed to be clean shaven for his work. But I'm willing to bet that if I could have seen him bearded or if you were to shave, that I wouldn't be able to tell you apart immediately. For the last month I've thought about it so many times but I kept brushing it off."

They sat in silence until Kristabell passed Leif one of the ear buds. "Put this in your ear," she told him as she scrolled through the menu and stopped at Fleetwood Mac. "My Dad downloaded this for me. He was always really into music. This was his favourite."

At first Leif thought that the Ipod was magic but once he started to pay attention to the music he was completely drawn in. They sat together listening to everything from Hard Rock to Freak Folk and talking like any brother and sister would. Eventually Leif sighed and looked at Kristabell, "It's good to know. It's good to finally know what happened to them." Then he sighed again and, like a lecturing older brother, told her, "You know, you're wrong to be angry with Rowan. He's the best of men and I would follow him anywhere. He doesn't deserve your anger. He's out there torturing himself right now. He loves you. He's afraid of losing you. Everything that he knew, he figured out for himself *after* he'd already asked you to be his. He never told anyone, not even me. He couldn t. If you were caught by Seamus's men you would be tortured for information and you can't tell what you don't know. He was doing the right thing by not telling you and I can't imagine that he planned on keeping it from you for long. You need to give him a chance. You need to hear him out."

"I didn't mean to yell at him. I wish I hadn't. He told me two nights ago to trust him and that everything would make more sense when we reached Lugh's stronghold. I didn't realize ... Everything is just so ..."

"It's alright. He'll understand." Leif rose to go.

"Here." Kristabell pulled out her other ear bud and passed it to Leif. She gave him her Ipod and showed him how to use it. "It'll maintain its charge longer if I give it to you. When we go home it won't work for long. Keep it plugged into the wall until we leave here." Kristabell sighed, "It was a gift from my Dad." Leif took the Ipod reverently, unplugged it from the wall socket, and left the room.

Kristabell laid down and curled up on her side. This was much bigger than she had ever imagined it could be. When she had first met Rowan she *had* fantasized that maybe she really was from his world and now she felt like an extra piece to an already completed puzzle. When Rowan asked her to be his wife she had felt as if she finally belonged somewhere. But she remembered the strange look in his eyes when she had given him her mother's ring. She remembered Rowan's mother and the sadness that would sometimes creep into her eyes when she looked at Kristabell. And Gwydion, all of the things that he had almost said to her and then changed his mind about. Rowan knocked at the door then. She knew it was him. She didn't say anything but the door opened slowly and he came in. He sat down next to her. "I don't know what to call you," he said softly, sadly.

"I don't know who I am. It's funny, I've spent my life not knowing and being okay with that. I knew that I was adopted but my parents never told me about my origins and I never asked."

"I was going to tell you," Rowan said looking into her eyes. "I was about an hour away from telling you. I had it all planned out. As soon as we passed the barrier into the stronghold I was going to take you to the hollow tree near there and sit with you, and tell you everything that I knew. I didn't want you to find out like this, I wanted to wait until you were safe."

Rhiannon thought about the fact that her safety was now such a huge issue and how Rowan must have felt about that. All of the extra pressure and responsibility he'd shouldered on her account. "Rowan, this is all too much for me," she said, overwhelmed.

"I know. And for the record, I didn't fall in love with the Queen's daughter. I fell in love with a girl who loves cabbages. In the beginning all I knew was that you were half Fay. I didn't figure out the rest of the story until the night I proposed to you."

"How did you know that I was half Fay? *I* didn't know."

"I knew the first moment I touched you. I could feel your magic with my hands. And when you came to, we could understand each other. That was another pretty good tip off. It's the dryad blood. But also, the colour of your eyes and the fact that your body hair feels like rabbit fur," he shrugged. "I figured that you were some poor Fairy woman's half human bastard child taken to the other world to conceal her folly, a changeling. I figured that you had wandered back to your world of origin when you found your magic, which tends to happen at around this age. Only the Fay can cross between the worlds. You have to understand though, that in our world it's frowned upon to have Fairy blood. The truth is that other than Fenna who is, as of yet, only a little bit fay, you're the only other human Fay cross I've ever *officially* met."

"What are you saying Rowan?" She looked at him wanting him to just come out and say it. He didn't usually beat around the bush about anything and right now she really wished he would be direct.

"Yesterday when they were tearing down the grove, you and I were the only ones who could hear the trees screaming in our heads."

"You're like me?" She looked at him incredulously.

He nodded. "No one outside our family knows."

She heard it. "Our family," and it made her feel less displaced. Less lost.

He continued, "Fenna, Nessa, and Leif know, but not the boys. Gwydion knows, and of course my mother and my grandmother, but I'm not sure about my father. We don't talk about it at all. My grandmother told me when I was sixteen. It was she who took a fairy lover. It was just for one night and my mother hasn't got a hint of Fayness about her, but I guess it skipped a generation. I was brought up hiding it and I assumed that it wouldn't please you to know. It didn't stop me from loving you, so I figured that it didn't warrant mentioning. I'm sorry."

By the time he was finished telling her this they were sitting side by side, fingers laced, kissing softly. She leaned back and looked into his eyes. "I'm sorry that I shouted at you. It wasn't really you I was angry at and I *do* trust you." She kissed him again then asked him, "What about the rest of the story, how did you figure that out?"

He unlaced his fingers from hers and took off the ring she had given him. "Here, pass me the ring I gave you." She slipped the ring off her finger and passed it to Rowan. "Look at this." He tipped the rings so that she could see that the hallmarks inside the were the same. "This is the stamp of the royal metal workers. The patterns on the ring I gave you are the symbols of my family's home. We took the symbol of the raven. This pattern," he motioned to the ring that she had given him, "Is, of course, rowan branches. The rowan tree is the symbol of the House of Lugh, the King of the Fairies of Nova Britannia. This pattern is carved all around the door of his house. The house that you and I are both descended from. So you see, you and I, we were meant to be." He gave her one of his calculated side-ways smiles and she felt like she was back at his home sitting next to him on a cart or at the table.

"Does this mean we're cousins?"

"Our grandparents are first cousins. We're not too related. Not so related that it matters."

Kristabell sat silently thinking for a moment, feeling her confusion like a physical ache.

"I didn't realize that you were the queen's daughter until you gave me that ring," he said very soberly as he passed her ring back to her then slid his own ring, the one that had been Kristabell's mother's, back onto his finger. "As soon as I saw it I knew, and everything fell into place. Seamus' accusation of the queen and what that accusation must have been. It was 19 years ago and you're 18 years old. Your resemblance to the Queen, it isn't so strong a resemblance that one would necessarily assume that you were related to her, but when you smile you look like her, and you have the same way of gazing softly into the distance like you're seeing something wonderful that no one else can see. You're smaller than she was with darker hair and eyes, but there is a quality about you that is very similar. Even more uncanny is your resemblance to your grandmother and sister. It was when I saw the ring that I realized not just what you are, but *who* you are. Your mother must have had the ring made as a love token, but been unable to give it to your father. Your existence, if it becomes known, will cause major political upheaval. Based on the laws of Nova Britannia, both Human and Fay, you are the rightful Queen *and* heir to the Fay throne." Rowan sighed. "I didn't know what to do with this knowledge. Being who you are puts your life at risk. If anyone who would oppose you finds out about you ... I don't know." He shook his head. "That's why I wanted to take you to your father. He would at the very least keep you safe, but we didn't make it there. I didn't tell you because *I* wanted to keep you safe, and there is a part of me that wishes that I could have kept this from you forever. I love you the way you are. I don't need a Queen, but I need you. When I asked you to be my wife, I figured that we would settle down at my family home, make babies, grow barley, and be happy. It was selfish of me, but for the first hour after you said yes, a part of me believed that if I ignored who you were it would go away and I could have the girl I fell in love with."

"I love you. I'm so sorry that I shouted at you," Kristabell whispered.

"I would have shouted too. I'm sorry that this is happening to you. If I could take it all away I would." He sighed and moved her hair so that it was all falling down her back then brought some of it back over her shoulder again almost as if he wasn't fully aware that he was doing it. "I still don't know what to call you."

It was on her mind as well. Kristabell was the name she had carried in this world and she was leaving it. Her birth mother had given her a different name. A beautiful name. "Kristabell feels like a child's name to me and even though I still occasionally feel like one, I'm not a child. Rhiannon is a beautiful name, and it *is* the name that the woman who gave birth to me wanted me to have, but I don't quite feel like Rhiannon yet either."

Rowan nodded then sighed again, "Someone somewhere knows who you are. The fact that your house was torched is pretty clear evidence of that. The fact that someone from our world has been looking out for you all this time, and that even Gavin and Fionnuala never told you about your origins suggests that even here, you were in some danger. You may not have a choice. You may have to come forward. In the end it may be safer than trying to hide and spending your life looking over your shoulder. Whatever happens, whatever you have to do, you have my allegiance and my support. I would fight for you."

"I know," Kristabell sighed looking into Rowan's eyes not really wanting to think over the weighty implications of his words.

They sat in silence for a few minutes before she spoke. "I think that I need a half an hour to pull myself together before we leave here but, would it be alright, do you think, if I show you a little bit of this world before we leave it for good?"

"I would like that," Rowan smiled.

"Well I'm going to take a bath before we go. I'll bet this place has a gorgeous bathroom and I paid for it so I might as well use it."

Kristabell grabbed her bag and went to the bathroom. She closed the door behind her and took off her clothes while she ran the water. She brushed all of the tangles out of her hair then kept brushing until it shone. She looked at herself in the mirror. *Rhiannon.* She tried it out in her head first then said the name out loud, "Rhiannon." It was easy to apply the name to the image she saw in the mirror. She really had changed in the last month. She noted again, as she had in Bronwen's mirror, the refinement and maturity that hadn't been there before. She examined her features, the deep blue eyes and red lips. The angles of her eyes and cheekbones gave her a beguiling, almost mischievous yet oddly solemn look. Was that the fairy in her? She closed her eyes, watching the angle of her dense, long, ash coloured eyelashes for as long as she could before her eyes closed all the way, then pulled them open again. She ran her hands over her body. She wasn't proportioned the way some small women are. Proportionately speaking her arms and legs were long. She was built more like a tall slim woman only slightly miniature. She let a hand travel over the soft hair between her legs. She'd thought that everyone had soft body hair like that. She turned off the tap, wrapped her hair in a towel to keep it dry then stepped into the big bathtub and soaked.

The hot water did its magic, loosening all of the horrible knots in her stomach and shoulders. She pushed all of the things in her life that she couldn't control to the periphery and let her mind play over the name once more. *Rhiannon.* It felt right in a way. She moved on to other things like how she was going to get them home. There was a feeling that she'd had of something building in her both times she had crossed now. It was a feeling that she had been scared of for years now and, like desire, she had pushed it away. She was pretty sure that she just needed to tap into that feeling again, and that when the time came, she would be able to do it. She turned to more pleasant thoughts though. She was, as it turned out, strongly connected to Rowan's family both by her adoptive parents and her biological parents. That made so much sense when she thought about it. Kristabell didn't feel the stigma against her lineage that Rowan did and to her the idea of being half fairy gave her a sense of pride. It explained the strange otherness that she had battled with her whole life. Now she was able to enjoy the fact that she wasn't a freak. She was magic. She pulled the plug, rose from the water, towelled dry and brushed her hair once more. Brush in bag, she dressed quickly and left the bathroom.

"Let's go get something to eat," she said to Rowan, who was looking out the window in disturbed fascination at the city sprawl below. "After we eat there's only one thing I want to do, then we'll go back to Sheila's, get the horse and go home."

Kristabell went to the elegant walnut desk, took out paper and pen and wrote two notes. She opened the briefcase and took out a wad of cash. It was probably more than she needed but she didn't want to risk running out. She then placed one of the notes inside the briefcase and locked it placing the key in a separate envelope along with the other note that she had written. Once they were in the lobby she took the briefcase to the concierge. "Could you please have this couriered to Sheila Taylor, at Buds and Blossoms Garden Centre at Cambie and Forty-third?"

"No problem Miss."

She took out some bills and asked, "Will this cover the expense for a rush delivery?"

"It certainly will."

She handed him the cash and told him, "I don't need change."

The busy sidewalks made Rowan downright twitchy and by the time they arrived at the little restaurant that was tucked in a basement on the edge of the bad side of downtown Kristabell's hand hurt from how tightly he had held it. Leif on the other hand didn't seem phased. The restaurant was a funky little place with a bright earthy interior and the most delicious raw vegan food in the city. Kristabell ordered them kale stuffed nori wraps, smoothies, and romaine tacos stuffed with walnuts, avocado and fresh salsa. There was mellow reggae playing on the stereo and the combination of the good food and the happy atmosphere were restorative.

"I don't think that I could cope in this world," Rowan commented between bites. "It's too busy. It's overwhelming. Food's good though."

"What you've eaten so far is completely non standard," Kristabell said thinking of the vegetarian lasagna they'd eaten the night before at Sheila's. "Meat between buns is closer to the norm."

"Oh. Yuck. And here I was thinking that the food would be a redeeming quality."

"In a way I'd like to try coping here," Leif admitted. "There are some things about this world that I find compelling, and my father lived here for almost twenty years. It would be interesting to see what his life was like."

"But how do you get used to the noise, the concrete, and the hustle?" Rowan asked.

Kristabell took a long pull on her smoothie then admitted, "I've never become fully accustomed to it and I've had it around me my whole life."

"What was that thing we watched yesterday?" Leif asked.

"Oh. The television?"

"That thing was terrifying. What were those images we were seeing?" This was from Rowan.

"There's a civil war on the other side of the planet," Kristabell told them, hoping that it was an adequate answer.

There was a girl sitting at the table next to them with teal dreads and big hazel eyes. Kristabell had noticed her glancing their way every few minutes. She wasn't sure what had drawn the girl's attention, whether it was Leif, Rowan, or the three of them together, then the girl seemed to come to some kind of decision and said, "I hope you don't mind me asking but, what language are you speaking?"

Kristabell had forgotten that they weren't speaking standard English. "Um, I guess you could say that it's a rare British dialect. You'll probably never hear it again."

"Oh," the girl said then asked. "Does he speak English?" nodding and smiling at Leif.

"Not really," Kristabell answered.

"Would you mind asking him if he's free tonight?"

"Actually, we're leaving town this afternoon. Sorry," Kristabell told the teal headed girl apologetically.

"Too bad," the girl winked at Leif as she rose from her seat to leave.

Kristabell told Leif that he'd just been hit on by the blue haired girl.

He raised his eyebrows. He turned and watched the girl make her way out of the restaurant then turned his attention back to the table, "As I said, there are certain aspects of this world that I find compelling." He smiled.

They laughed.

Chapter 6

If all of the books in the world are going to be burned and you can only save a handful of them, which ones do you save? It's a common enough question, but this was essentially Kristabell's dilemma. The only thing that made this easier was that the books were not actually going to be destroyed so she could pick books that were important to her personally without taking the rest of the world into account. She thought about her book shelf at home, the books that *had* been burned, and tried to think of the ones she loved best as she dragged Rowan and Leif through the massive second hand book store. She figured The Comic and Book Emporium was her best bet.

The Prydain Cronicles by Lloyd Alexander, or the Fionnavar Tapestries? Joan D Vinge's Snow Queen cycle or A Wrinkle In Time? There were so many she loved. But in the end, when push came to shove and it was time to leave the store, the books she couldn't leave behind, the ones she couldn't walk away from, were The Last Unicorn By Peter S. Beagle and Faeries by Brian Froud and Allan Lee. She lucked out when she couldn't find Faeries on the shelf and asked the guy behind the counter if they might have a copy somewhere else. He pulled one out from under the counter, "This is hard to come by these days. I've heard rumours that they might do a reprint."

She ran her hand appreciatively over the pristine cover. It was an original edition still in excellent condition. She flipped through looking at the pictures. "That one looks like you"

Rowan pointed to one of Allan Lee's paintings. Kristabell asked the man behind the counter to triple bag the books then tape the bag closed. As they left the book store a helicopter flew over the city. Leif and Rowan stopped to watch the helicopter, but no one else on the side walk except for a three year old boy seemed to notice it.

She took them to Granville Street Skytrain Station and paid for transfers still using the cash from the briefcase. She really had taken too much. The escalator down to the train platform was long and steep with strange, cool, metallic smelling air creeping up to meet them. "Why do they call this a *Sky*train? I feel like we're travelling into the bowels of the earth," Rowan asked.

"You'll see when we come out of the tunnels," Kristabell replied. "We'll get off at Commercial Drive. It's not far to Sheila's house from there."

They stood on the escalator as it travelled down. Leif behind Rowan, Kristabell in front leaning against Rowan's chest. It *was* strange, but it was also good to be there with him. They looked for all the world like a perfectly normal couple. It felt right, and complete, to have a chance to say goodbye to this world with Rowan, so he could see that part of her.

They rode the train into East Vancouver and as it glided along on its elevated track Leif gawked out the window in amazement at the stadiums, skyscrapers, and congested, car filled streets. Rowan, on the other hand, was miserable aboard the train. He hadn't been happy in Sheila's car either but this was far worse. He was jumpy and paranoid. He stayed close to Kristabell maintaining a death grip on her hand but in the end it was Rowan's paranoia that saved her life. Just as the doors slid closed at Main Street Skytrain Station a stranger slipped onto the train. His hair looked as if it had been artificially touched up with chemically dyed low-lights and his skin was damp and pale. Not a luminous pale, but something closer to a cave dwelling frog's underbelly. It made those passengers near to him squirm and recoil fractionally, the way one does when a big slug is found in the lettuce that is being prepared for dinner. He wore a black leather trench coat—stereotypically reminiscent of a certain turn of the century science fiction movie—but with her back to him Kristabell couldn't see him. Leif's attention was entirely absorbed by the modern city flying by outside the window, but Rowan noticed him right away. He lowered his face to Kristabell's ear and momentarily rested his cheek against hers whispering, nearly inaudibly, "Don't turn. Stay still. There's an elf behind you." Then he kissed her cheek casually as he drew away.

Kristabell froze. There was a nebulous cloud of death behind her pressing against her back like a cold blinding mist. She broke out in a cold sweat and her mind started gibbering uselessly at her. She fixed her eyes on Rowan's face hoping to find some clue as to what was happening behind her. If the elf was looking for *her,* he wouldn't have to see her face to identify her. There weren't any other small women with hip length ash coloured hair on the train. With her heart pounding she watched Rowan reach casually into the denim jacket that he was wearing over the hoodie. Neither he nor Leif had left the house unarmed that morning. Kristabell had watched them carefully concealing a dagger here, a knife there. She'd had reservations about this, but she had also recognized her own fear that something might be out there, and a knife was better than nothing. Although there was also the very real prospect of somehow being caught by the police with concealed weapons.

It happened then, more quickly than it seemed like it ought to have been able to. Rowan had kept his hand in his jacket, not looking directly at the elf, just waiting. Kristabell was terrified, obviously. It could be nothing, but it probably wasn't, and the seconds stretched. They were standing holding on to the poles that were anchored in the floor and ceiling for that very purpose. Kristabell's back was to the greater portion of the train and she was between Rowan and the elf partially blocking the elf's view of Rowan. The train slowed as it pulled into Commercial Drive Skytrain Station then it came to a stop and the people on the train began to scream. Rowan's movements were a blur. Kristabell barely saw him throw the knife. A gunshot sounded, sending Kristabell's already pounding heart into a frenzied overdrive, but the bullet clearly hadn't hit her because the doors on the train had opened and she and Rowan were running with Leif hard on their heels. Kristabell caught the barest glimpse of the elf lying on the floor of the train with a gun in his hand and a knife handle sticking out of his eye.

Luckily it was mass exodus from the Skytrain station and it was relatively easy for them to slip away, but Kristabell knew that now they really had to get out of this world. Rowan and Leif didn't have proper I.D. which was problem enough, but Rowan had just killed someone and it may have been caught on a surveillance camera, although Rowan had thrown the knife so fast that she doubted if anyone on the train had seen it clearly, so this wasn't a likelihood, but still. They moved as quickly as they could without drawing attention to themselves. "We have to get to Sheila's house, get the horse, and get out of here as fast as we can. This neighbourhood is going to be crawling with police in another few minutes," she told them as they reached the alley behind Sheila's house and broke into a run. Kristabell unlocked the garage and they rushed to the pile of clothing, armour, and weapons and began frantically changing clothes. Kristabell removed Sheila's cardigan and pulled on the vest drawing the laces tight, pulled off the jeans and then dragged on the wool leggings. She would have stayed in the jeans but the wool was more waterproof and once they were back in the forest she would need it. The men were still gearing up so she helped them with buckles, fingers working frantically. Rowan was finished first. He saddled the horse who, luckily, hadn't been taken away by the S.P.C.A. or the City. Kristabell locked the garage then ran to put the garage key, along with the key to the briefcase under the door of the house. When she ran back to where Rowan and Leif were waiting they looked at her expectantly. "I can't pull us through here. I have to get away from the houses and the concrete," she told them. "We should go down to the lake."

They were just south of Trout Lake and there was a group of willows on the eastern edge where she thought maybe she could get them through the threshold and back to the other world.

"You ride with Kristabell, I'll run. We'll make it a little faster that way," Leif said to Rowan.

They rode to the end of the alley and cautiously crossed to the other side where the park began. Once on the grass Rowan urged the horse into a gallop and headed for the eastern edge of the lake. It didn't take long and with the trees around her and the lake and the earth, she could indeed feel that now familiar feeling of magic building in her. She could see a police car in the distance. Panic was taking over. The officer got out of the car just as Leif ran up to them. "Here we go!" she shouted as the magic filled her near to bursting like a roaring surf in her ears. She let it rip through her, and with barely a notion of what she was doing, pulled them across away from the world where she had been born, and back to that *other* world.

Chapter 7

As they crossed the threshold from one world to another, the pain that made Kristabell's head feel like it was collapsing in on itself was unbearable and she screamed. The forest around her swam for a second or two before she blacked out. When she came to, she was lying on the forest floor under the branches of a giant cedar. She could see the horse standing nearby. Incongruously, she thought to herself, *I wonder if Rowan has a name for that horse?* Which in turn lead to the thought, *Where is Rowan?* She turned her head and tried to sit up. He was lying right beside her and she knew immediately that something was very wrong. He was grey and his breathing was shallow. "Rowan!" she half shrieked, half gasped.

His eyes opened a little and he smiled at her. "Not ... feeling so well," he managed breathlessly.

"What's wrong? Tell me!" she asked, desperate to know what to do.

"The weapon that the elf tried to kill you with ... its projectile ricocheted." He stopped to breath. "It's lodged in my shoulder."

Kristabell looked at Rowan's shoulder. It was messy and bloody, but he wasn't bleeding hard. She looked around the clearing wondering where the hell Leif could be and hoping that he had gone for help. Rowan started to speak again. "Elves enchant their weapons so that, if a piece is lodged inside you, it kills you if it isn't removed. They do it to arrow heads ... spear points ... I guess that they do it to the weapons of the other world to."

Kristabell could see Rowan trying to focus on her face. "Have to get the thing ..." he took a shuddering breath, "out of my shoulder soon."

Kristabell choked out a sob of panic then launched herself into action. She ran to the horse and began searching the saddle bags for anything of use. She found a small box filled with packages of herbs and some clean cloth. There was a small bottle as well. She unstoppered it and sniffed then took a small swig. Some kind of hard liquor, vodka she thought, strong enough to kill bacteria. She caught up the small cock pot and snatched two of the daggers that were sheathed in the saddle and ran back to Rowan.

He said the bullet itself would kill him, she told herself, *so just get that out and decide what else to do after.* She opened the liquor bottle and poured it into the pot dowsing the daggers as she did and leaving them in to soak. She dipped a corner of the cloth and began wiping Rowan's shoulder. It was a mess and not because of the bleeding but because he had tried to get the bullet out himself. There was a bloody knife lying beside him and there was blood on his hands. She took the daggers out of the liquor then tipped some onto the wound hoping to get it a little cleaner. She wiped it again, then very gently probed the wound with one of the daggers. Rowan wasn't a big guy, not for what he was, and more lean than bulky, but his shoulder muscles were still well developed, dense, and corded, and it wasn't deep but it was difficult to find exactly where the bullet had lodged. Then she remembered that the bullet hadn't hit him directly and changed her angle so the blade reached down into his deltoid. She felt metal scratch metal. Kristabell took a deep shaky breath and, willing her hands still, she reached for the other dagger. She moved the first dagger along the surface of the bullet until she felt the knife slip past it then carefully, aware that she was cutting him more as she went, she slid the other dagger tip in. She found the bullet and using both daggers, she gradually levered and wiggled it out. She lost her grip at one point but managed to find the bullet again and draw it out. She could see it. She plucked it out with her fingers and it burned where it touched her skin. "Rowan ...? Rowan ...?" The whole time she had been digging around in his shoulder he had barely moved. She took the leftover liquor in the pot and poured it over the wound. He twitched slightly. She felt his brow. It was cold. She took off her cloak and draped it over him then checked the wound. It was bleeding more heavily now but still not enough to be alarming. Tanya had fallen once, at work, and landed on a plant pot which had shattered and pierced an artery. Kristabell knew what arterial bleeding looked like. "Rowan!" She tried to get him to respond to her but all she got was a flutter of eyelashes. She felt his pulse and it felt slow to her but she was no doctor, she didn't know. Rowan still felt so cold that she thought maybe she should try to light a fire. The sky was dusky. She must have been unconscious for a long time. She scrambled around the surrounding forest looking for firewood and kindling that was dry. Not an easy task in a temperate rain forest during the wet season. As she went she grabbed bits of lichen from the trees and several willow branches. She sat down and tried to set the smallest and driest of the kindling burning but she wasn't used to a flint and all of her sparks died away. "I can travel to different worlds but I can't start a bloody FIRE!" she shouted, and suddenly the kindling burst into a tiny bundle of flames. She carefully added larger and larger pieces of wood to the flames until she had a fire. There was a little creek running nearby from which she filled the pot with water. She brought it back to the fire above which, with a little experimenting, she managed to suspend the pot. Kristabell examined the box of herbs. She smelled them all trying to find the ones she could use. She recognized yarrow, its smell was unmistakable. She put a small handful in the pot along with some rose hips. She added the usnea (the lichen) she'd collected, to the pot then set about peeling the willow branches and adding the bark to the water. Usnea to fight infection, willow for fever and to fight pain, yarrow to stop bleeding and rose hips for the vitamins and bioflavonoids. It was all she could do. Once the water came to a boil she set it aside and let it steep then turned to check on Rowan. His breathing was so shallow and he was still cold. In the twilight she could see that the wound was oozing an acrid smelling black foam. Kristabell took the little pot and poured some of the liquid into the wound rinsing away the black foam. She'd seen a spoon in the saddle bag so she retrieved it and gently spooned some of the liquid from the pot into his mouth. He swallowed so she gave him more. It took a while but she managed to get about a half a cup into him. She poured a little more over the wound. "Rowan ... Rowan." She would say his name, checking to see if he was responsive but if he could hear her he was too far gone to respond. Leif was still nowhere to be seen.

Kristabell was shaking with fear and worry and despite the fact that she had kept her head all this time she had never really managed to stop crying, and now that she had run out of things to do the panic was setting in. That was when she saw the unicorn. It was watching her from about three metres away, glowing softly in the shelter of another giant cedar. Kristabell sucked in a breath and sat transfixed. The unicorn nodded its head towards her as if beckoning her forward. She rose and tread softly towards the unicorn. Kristabell had no way of knowing as she approached the impossibly beautiful creature, that a nimbus of multicoloured light danced and flickered around her, rising, almost like flames or aurora, from her person. And so focused was she on the lavender silver radiance of the unicorn, that she didn't realize that it was as drawn to her as she was to it. She didn't know how you were supposed to greet a unicorn so when she was only a metre away she dropped into a deep curtsy and bowed her head. When she stood the unicorn had closed the space between them and it began to gently nuzzle her face with its velvety nose. Kristabell placed her hands on the sides of the unicorn's face and revelled in the warm velvet. It was exactly as she had always imagined it would be. Her tears came unbidden as she stroked the unicorn's neck and touched its silky silvery white mane. "I need help," she cried into the unicorn's warm cheek. "I don't know what else to do and I'm lost." She stepped back leaving her hand on the unicorn's cheek. The unicorn nodded to her.

Kristabell thought that she must be crazy for asking but she asked anyway, "Can you go to my father?" She swore that the unicorn lowered its head again in assent. "Will you take something to him? A message of sorts?"

Again a nod.

Kristabell ran back to Rowan and, gently shifting his head, she untied the cord that held back his hair. She checked on him as she did. Still cold. Still breathing, but barely. She returned to the unicorn and took the heartsease ring from her finger. "Can I tie this to your mane?"

The unicorn lowered its horn to her.

"You want me to tie it to your horn?"

A nod.

She slipped the ring onto the cord and looped it three times around the unicorn's horn feeling almost sacrilegious as she did, then she tied the ring with three knots thinking all the while, *Three times lucky*. The unicorn gave her cheek a quick nuzzle then galloped off into the forest and disappeared. Kristabell hurried back to Rowan's side. He was shaking and she had no idea if this was good or bad but she herself was freezing in the growing darkness. She put more wood on the fire then began removing the rest of Rowan's armour so that her body heat would actually make it to him, then she pressed the remainder of the clean cloth to his wound, covered both of them with her cloak and his, pressed herself against his side and held on as tightly as she could.

She tried to think good thoughts. She desperately wanted him to be well. There was a terrified ache around her heart and she didn't want to go on without him. She loved him too much to lose him like this. She let out a frustrated cry of rage at the unfairness of it then tried to hold him even more tightly. She took a deep breath and closed her eyes. Somewhere very deep inside, so deep that she suspected that it might be beyond herself in some nebulous unfathomable way, she could feel the energy, the life of the forest. She concentrated on it until she could feel it flowing into her and she let it back out again, in hope and fear and love, and for a moment the world was incandescent and then, not unexpectedly, she blacked out.

Chapter 8

When the Fairies came Lugh himself was with them. Night had only just fallen and there was a little fire burning in the small clearing that the insistent unicorn had lead them to. In the clearing, under the branches of a cedar tree, was a man, well known to them, almost one of them, and in his arms was a small woman with long ash coloured hair that was draped over his arm. The woman, barely more than a girl, was unconscious, although unconscious would probably be too soft a word for her state. Comatose or nearly dead would be more accurate. The man, it could be told by his face, knew that she was slipping away. Lugh, the King of the Fairies of Nova Britannia, approached the fire and knelt. "Who is she, Rowan?" the King asked the Knight.

"My wife," Rowan answered quietly.

"I mean, what is her name?"

"Her mother, Sulamith, wanted her to be called Rhiannon. I think that is the name that she would have you know her by ... If she could answer for herself."

It could be seen now, in Lugh's face, that he understood who she was. He took her hand in his and placed the little ring back on her finger. Then, still holding her hand, he closed his eyes and reached inward. Deep into the forest.

Chapter 9

It was dim and soft. She could smell fresh air, and the ocean. She tried to remember where they had gone to sleep that night but, no matter, Rowan must be beside her. She told her arm to move. It was a little slow but it reached out. He wasn't there. She tried his name but it came out as a moan. She tried again. "Rowan?" she whispered. Something was nagging at the back of her mind when she remembered that she had eyes and that she could open them. There was a girl with *very* familiar deep blue almost cobalt coloured eyes and long thick coal black braids smiling into her face. "You're awake!" the girl said.

"Rowan?" In her muddled state she seemed capable of only one word. "Rowan!" she called, hearing the hysterical edge in her own voice.

"It's okay," the girl told her. "He's close by. He just went out for some air."

And Rowan came striding into the room and straight to her putting his arms around her so tightly that she couldn't quite breathe. But that was okay, breathing was overrated. At that particular moment, she didn't really need to breathe. He released her a little so that they could see into one another's face. His hair was loose, making him look a little wild. He stroked her brow. "Do you have any idea how worried I've been?" He was looking into her face, smiling in relief as his eyes glistened. "They kept telling me you would wake up, but it's been four days." He kissed her forehead and let her go a little further.

"The last thing I remember is tying the ring to the unicorn's horn then lying down next to you. I had gotten the bullet out of your shoulder and given you herbs. I cleaned the wound and built a fire. I didn't know what else to do. I thought you were dying." She took a deep breath before asking, "Why have I been asleep for *four* days?"

Rowan smiled at her, "This is Nimue. She's your sister. She can probably answer that better than I can."

The girl was looking into her eyes and smiling. "You tapped into the life force of the forest to heal him, but instead of letting *just* the life force of the forest flow through you, you also let your own life force flow out of you. You healed Rowan completely. There isn't even a scar but you almost killed yourself. Luckily you were right behind the stronghold and we found you only minutes after Rowan woke up. You would have died if my father hadn't been there to heal you, and even after that there was still damage to your life force. You have been using your magic in fear and frustration and this is very wearing. But you will recover, and we will teach you, so you won't hurt yourself again."

She reached up a hand to the girl who looked to be about two years younger than herself. The girl, Nimue, her sister, reached out her own hand tentatively and they let the tips of their fingers touch. It was like touching the unicorn. This was something that was, in the life that she had lead as Kristabell, supposed to be impossible. A Fairy. Her *sister*. When their fingers met an aura that almost looked like butterfly wings intensified behind Nimue. It was then that she noticed the soft green iridescent pattern of ferns and vines starting on her hand and travelling up her arm. "What's this?" she motioned to the markings.

"The forest left its mark on you. There are many dryads in our lineage. You must take after them," Nimue answered then asked, "You must be hungry. Shall I bring you some food?"

"Yes please." Then, looking out at the darkness, she asked, "Has it been night long?"

"No, not long," Rowan answered. "It's only a little after the evening meal."

"My father is in a council meeting, but he is very anxious to meet you. Shall I send word to him that you are awake?" Nimue asked.

She laid there and thought about it for a moment. It wasn't that she didn't want to meet her father. She did, very much so, but it seemed too soon. She had just woken up. She was still lying in a bed and he was in a meeting. Perhaps it would be best if for now he simply knew that she was awake and they could look forward to meeting in the morning. "Would it be very horrible of me if I asked you to wait until morning? If I could have the night to get my equilibrium back? I wish very much to meet him, but I'm a little overwhelmed."

Nimue nodded, "Rowan has told us the whole story. I understand and so will our father. I will go get food." Nimue left, closing the door softly behind her.

Pulling herself up to sitting, she looked around the room. It wasn't so very different from the rooms at Rowan's home but this room was perhaps a touch more fanciful. There were reminiscently First Nations carvings around the room, in the door and the window sills, and there were stained glass doors leading to what she guessed was outside—where Rowan had been—all in themes of suns, moons, birds, and animals. The doors would be beautiful when the sun was up. She was sitting in a big four-poster bed with carved posts, a deep, dusky, purple gossamer canopy, and deep blue and purple wool blankets. Rowan was sitting next to her on the edge of the bed. She leaned into him, trying to breathe in his solidity, and sighed as his arms closed around her. "We're here. We made it."

"You can't imagine how relieved I am now you're awake. I was so worried. I thought I was losing you," he said to her.

"Where's Leif?"

"When we came back across you fainted so I kept the horse and headed straight for Lugh's stronghold with you. I didn't realize that I had been shot until I had ridden some distance but I couldn't keep going and you were unconscious. If I had realized that I was injured sooner I wouldn't have sent Leif off, but I was anxious to send word to King Liam of our return, and I needed to make sure that someone I trust is in command of the army. There aren't many people who I trust more than Leif." Rowan smiled then, "I have some good news," he told her, "The band of men and elves who were desecrating the grove were attacked by a contingent of Fay knights only moments after we disappeared. Two of the six who were with us didn't make it but Brian and three of the younger men are here recovering from their injuries."

"They're alive! Here?"

Rowan nodded

"It feels like I've been gone for a long time. So much has changed but it's only been six days since ..."

Just then Nimue came back in with a tray of food. "I brought enough for all of us," she said. "I happen to know that Rowan has barely eaten in the last four days and, well ... I'm always hungry," she grinned. "I hope you don't mind if I stay and eat with you?" Nimue placed the tray on the bed and, sitting cross legged at the foot, proceeded to prepare plates for each of them that consisted of what looked like blueberry muffins and little dishes of baked apple topped with roasted hazelnuts and dried fruit with clotted cream and honey. "The hazelnuts are from your house," Nimue told them as she buttered the muffins and passed them each a plate.

They ate and talked. Nimue was effervescent and charming and each time she became excited about something the winglike aura behind her became brighter. "Did you notice that we have the same eyes!?" Nimue exclaimed excitedly.

"I did. It was the first thing that I noticed about you. Are they from our father or are they a throwback from a grandmother or something like that?"

"Our grandmother," Nimue said, then, "It's so much fun to have a sister. I didn't have any siblings before, and I know that you've had a hard time of it in some ways, I cried my eyes out when Rowan told us about you, but this feels really wonderful to me."

"It feels wonderful to me too. I've never met someone who shares so much of the same blood, and it *is* rather wonderful to me too."

Nimue touched her fingertips then said, "I'll see you in the morning, and if you're well enough maybe I can show you around?" She picked up the tray and said goodnight as she glided out the door.

And they were alone. The silence after Nimue left was uncomfortable. Rowan shifted and turned to her, suddenly boyish and uncertain. What unspoken words were hanging in that silence? He looked down and pleated the blanket with his fingers then smoothed it out. He repeated the action and then said to her, somewhat awkwardly, "I know that you said you needed to get your equilibrium back. I don't know ... Maybe you wanted to be alone ... or you're tired? I can go ... if you want me to."

She knew that it wasn't what he wanted. She knew that he was only asking because he was uncertain. Because in the four days she'd slept, *so much* had changed. Because now she knew she was a Queen. She could hear in his voice that he *would* go if she asked him to, but she could also hear in his voice, that he hoped that she wouldn't. And she didn't want him to go. "My equilibrium is fine. I've never been more sure of you, and everything that I was worried about six days ago is in the past. I don't need to be worried about those particular things now. I have new things to worry about." She shifted so that they were face to face. "Everything is going to change tomorrow, but ... we don't need to think about that now. The past is dead and the future hasn't happened yet. Tonight ... I want ..." She took a deep breath and looked into his eyes, blushing as she worked up the courage to say what she meant. "This is hard to ask for ... I love you, and I want to be in your arms. You asked me to be your wife and I said yes. I want you to be my husband. We have tonight. Let's make it so that no one can take this away from us." And a kiss was the only possibility in the silence that followed.

Tentatively at first, their lips touched, as if gently seeking out possibilities and then finding them, little sparks that leapt and flared until the fire was lit and then they were simply two people desperate to be together. Rowan stopped kissing her for a moment and told her, "When I first found you in the forest, I didn't know that I would love you, but I remember looking at your face and thinking, *When this girl wakes up I want her to be lovable.* And when you woke up, I knew you were my match."

The sensation of his warm skin against her whole body was like the summer sun. If she were a tree she would have stretched her branches up to him but as it was she was a young woman so she put her arms around him and kissed him back as if she could drink his warmth into her and grow with it. She wondered briefly, fleetingly, what *she* felt like to him. Was it just Rowan? Was it the two of them together? How could something as simple as touching be *so* sweet? She looked up into his eyes. The feel of his body on hers was making her dizzy. She felt as if she were evaporating, as if her edges were flying apart, like dandelion seeds on the wind. "I trust you. I love you," she whispered, drawing him in and finding something delicious and pure that moved through her and beckoned her to follow, like a clear stream flowing deep into the heart of the forest. She felt an urge to rock her hips against him and she followed it, matching his rhythm. She stroked his hair, chest, shoulders, and reached up to meet and return his kisses, like rich soil taking in the rain. All she could think of, all that mattered, was Rowan's mouth on hers, their bodies moving together, and the strange beautiful feeling that was urging them on and higher to some as yet unknown but much desired place when suddenly, there it was, singing through her, incandescent, like being filled with golden light, like the sun through spring leaves. She couldn't help crying out wordlessly as the feeling carried her away. Rowan closed his eyes, and for three of four heartbeats, gripped her tightly, his rhythm abruptly changing, and then they were still.

He rested on her for a moment or two then rolled, pulling her with him and cradling her against his chest. "Rhiannon," he whispered. They lay there together bathed in the comfort of each other's bodies, the feeling of their skin touching, and the uncomplicated rightness of what they had just done. Rowan's lovemaking had that same sweet innocence that was *so much* a part of being with him. "There," he whispered. "Now it's binding. We're just two half breed fairies who love each other. I'm your husband, and you're my wife, and that's the way it is."

"Whatever else happens, I love you," she smiled at him with her chin on her hands and her hands on his chest, looking into his face.

He stroked her cheek. "Rhiannon," he said the name again and when he said it it felt like her name. Not, she thought to herself, that she felt defined by *his* use of the name, and not, she hoped, that she was letting him define her. If anything it was the other way around. In agreeing to spend his life with her he was quite possibly giving up the chance to go home, grow barley, make babies and be happy like he wanted. Although the baby thing, she supposed would happen inevitably, regardless. But it still felt good when he said her name. "It feels right to hear you call me that. It feels like my name now. It's as if Kristabell died in the house fire with her parents and Rhiannon is the person that I am now. It feels like a good way to move on."

"It's the name that I gave to your father when he asked who you were."

"What is he like, my father?" she asked.

"Well, most of the time he's pretty self-contained, sometimes even stern, but now that I know more about his past, I'm not so sure that it's his true nature. He has a sense of humour that comes out every so often, and over the last few days there's been a softness to him. I don't want to make you feel uncomfortable but he's spent every spare moment of the last four days watching you sleep."

"Is he like Nimue?"

Rowan shook his head, "No, not at all. You and Nimue are like a cross between Lugh's mother and your own mothers. Nimue's mother was a selkie, but she found her skin and left when Nimue was about six. Lugh takes after his father who was pure water Fay; undine, nymph, Gwragedd Annwn, but his mother is half Dryad half Sylph. The Dryad and Sylph show more in you and Nimue than it does in Lugh and the sylph line is where those deep blue, lose myself for hours, eyes come from." He smiled as he traced the line of her brow.

"And you? Tell me about you?" she asked.

"Oh, my grandfather is a Dryad. Our great grandfathers were brothers. One settled with a Sylph and the other met another Dryad. That's why my grandmother begged my mother to call me Rowan when I was born. She said that it was obvious even then that I had taken after that branch of the family. When I was sixteen and my grandmother told me about my grandfather, it was in part because, what happened to you, unintentional bouts of magic, only much smaller scale, were happening to me. Turning all the milk in the dairy sour, making trees bloom out of season," he rolled his eyes. "Typical fairy stuff. So she took me here, to Lugh's stronghold, and asked if they could teach me how to use my magic and control it. I stayed here for a couple of months and learned what I could do and what I couldn't. It was a good time."

"So what *can* you do?" she asked, tracing a pattern of ferns and vines that spiralled over his shoulder and chest now, and trailed down his arm. The markings were the same as on her hand and arm and they hadn't been there before. They originated in the place where the gunshot wound had been

"It marks me as Fay," he said watching her hand move over the markings. "Your magic spilled over, but it wouldn't have stuck if I hadn't had magic of my own for it to cling to. In a way it's for the best. No more hiding, no more pretending. But as for your question, my magic isn't as strong as yours. In fact not many can do what you've done. I'm not much of a healer, but I can become nearly invisible as long as I'm near trees. I can track almost anything through the forest—except for another Dryad—just by feel. I'm faster and stronger close to the forest. I can hear, taste, touch, smell, see better in the woods. The only thing that was throwing me off the day we ran into Seamus' men were the trees, as you put it, screaming in our heads. I couldn't hear a thing over their cries. It crippled me and it made me realize how much I depend on my Fay senses."

"I know what you mean. In the other world the forests are so diminished. I felt like I was deaf in that world with only the noise of cars and televisions to make things worse. When I'm here I feel awake and receptive. I feel more alive."

"Being with you makes me feel more alive," Rowan whispered lacing his fingers into her hair. They kissed softly and melted, once again, into each other's arms.

* * *

It was some time in the wee hours of the night, cradled in sleep's warm arms, when all is still and wrapped in velvety star pierced silence that Rhiannon opened her eyes to the dream. It was unlike any dream that she had ever had before. Her dreams tended towards stressful, down the rabbit hole, chaos. This was not stressful. There was no chaos. It was a peaceful void that stretched into infinity and the feeling of it reminded her of the scene at the end of the old movie that had been made of 'The Never Ending Story' in which the Childlike Empress is sitting in the darkness with Bastion holding the last grain of sand that was once Fantasia, and it glows like a tiny star, casting a beautiful light on their faces. The dream was like that. A beautiful hopeful light in a darkness full of possibilities. After a time she realized that somehow Rowan was with her and it was she who held the light in her hands. "It's beautiful," she whispered to him, looking into his eyes. "What is it?"

"It ... life," he whispered back serious, incredulous.

"Did we ... Do that?" She felt that the dream deserved more eloquence, but those were the only words that presented themselves for her use.

"I think so," Rowan replied.

"What does it mean?" she asked.

"It means that we have something worth fighting for."

Chapter 10

In the morning when Rhiannon woke she reached out and found Rowan then curled into his side, warm and sleepy under the blankets. She didn't open her eyes, she simply let her mind wander delicately and slowly over the events of the previous night. The sound of Rowan's voice saying her name, his touch, the dream. It was like opening a box of something delicious then sitting and contemplating how good it will be before jumping right in and eating it. Just spending some time *knowing* that you have it.

She felt Rowan stir and his arms went around her. She sighed. After a few minutes of lying like that Rowan asked Rhiannon, "So, are you going to open your eyes?"

She smiled with her eyes still closed, "I'm just savouring this."

"Very well, but you have to open your eyes before the sun moves, or you're going to miss this."

Rhiannon opened her eyes and drew in a breath, then let it out slowly. The sun was shining through the stained glass doors and the room was ablaze with a myriad of vivid colours. Purple moons, red glowing suns, and deep indigo ravens flying across an azure sky over a sea green ocean. The doors formed an arch with two windows on either side completing the curve. These were filled with green leaves and yellow and orange flowers. Wild poppies. The images of water, sky and flowers were enough to stay with them for the rest of their lives but the feeling of lying together bathed in all that colour was beyond compare. A living rainbow. Absolutely breath-taking. "I don't think that I've ever experienced a morning this perfect. This ... Everything ... It's beyond anything I've ever felt before. I don't know what to do with it all. I feel like I'm over-flowing." She laughed and they lay there together smiling into one another's faces. "Last night ... I had a dream ..." She paused trying to find words, but she didn't need to.

"I know. I was there," he said.

"So it's real then. I still have the feeling of the dream inside me. It feels scary and wonderful and right all at once."

Rowan nodded. "That about sums it up, doesn't it."

"A baby," she whispered.

He nodded again, serious, "A baby." And for a few moments they let the silence stretch, but sitting up and smiling once more, Rowan took her hand and pulled her up. "Let's open the doors and go out into the sunshine together for a few moments before anybody comes and makes us go to breakfast or anything like that."

He passed her the blue and pink embroidered night gown that the fairies had put her in. It was finely stitched and gathered with tiny pleats and seemed almost too beautiful for sleeping in. She slipped it on as Rowan pulled his tunic and pants on. These too were obviously made by the fairies and had a simple fineness to them. Rowan passed her a heavy shawl then opened the doors. She reached for his hand and they stepped out into the sun.

It was about two weeks, now, passed the equinox, and the air was crisp bordering on cold, but one could feel that it would be warm by mid afternoon. Many of the leaves had turned gold and there were flashes of brilliant red here and there in the still largely green forests. They were right on what would have been the Burrard Inlet in the other world. "What do they call it here?"

"They call the settlement a stronghold and this particular one is usually just referred to as Lugh's Stronghold."

Rhiannon looked around at the buildings. They looked like the great great grandchildren of Salish plankhouses and Haida longhouses. Still simple and elegant but sleeker and vaguely multicultural looking. Rhiannon and Rowan were standing on a patio together, Rowan behind her with his arms around her. They stood looking out on the water and across at the dense old growth forest growing on the opposite shore.

"I have to warn you about something before I lose my chance," Rowan started in a tone that combined amusement and exasperated embarrassment. "Do you remember how a certain amount of, talk, reproductive speculation, giggling, and silly jokes went around the day after we became a couple?"

Although Rhiannon *had* been sheltered from the worst of it, and Rowan had taken the brunt when she wasn't around, she did indeed remember. "Yes," she answered laughing.

"The fairies are worse," he said bluntly. "And half of them have a sixth sense, so there's no hiding anything from them *and*, they all know that you were a virgin when you got here because of the unicorn."

"Oh," Rhiannon answered as her cheeks grew hot.

Rowan moved so that he could see her face then laughed, not unkindly, "You blush so easily. That world really did leave you in quite a state. There was sex all over the place there, and yet I don't get the feeling that the overall societal relationship to it is very open. I just don't want you to feel too embarrassed." He leaned his forehead against hers, smiling.

"I guess I'll survive. I wouldn't undo last night even if it would save me all the embarrassment in the world, so I'll just have to face it," she smiled sheepishly and as if on cue knocking could be heard from within.

"If that's Nimue we're in for it," Rowan muttered letting go of her waist and taking her hand as they returned indoors, closing the doors behind them. He went to the inner door and opened it. Nimue stuck her head in and, seeing then both up and decent, hustled in with a dress over her arm and a big pitcher of steaming water in her hands.

She smiled a big irrepressible grin which Rhiannon didn't think could possibly get any wider but after two seconds in the room it did and she burst out, "Whoa ho! It's a good thing you waited to do *that* until after you needed a unicorn's help. I don't even need the sight to tell that you're knocked up. It's written all over your face!"

"See what I mean?" Rowan's mouth quirked. "Just be glad she didn't do that in front of your father."

Rhiannon was beet red and laughing so hard that there were tears running down her cheeks. "After that I think I can take just about anything," she told Rowan who hugged her tight and laughed along with her.

"Leave her alone so that I can help her dress. Breakfast is nearly on," Nimue said, still grinning while she swatted at Rowan, the winglike aura glowing madly behind her. Nimue opened the door to the little room off the bed chamber and left the pitcher on the wash stand within. It was just a small, well ventilated room with a composting toilet, some hooks for clothes, and a basin—much like at Rowan's family home—but Rhiannon headed into the little bathroom happy for five minutes of privacy.

When she emerged refreshed, Rowan headed into the bathroom with a fresh pitcher of water. Nimue had laid out the dress and some underthings. "Here, let's brush your hair before we put the dress on. Gran would kill me if I let it get snagged. She chose the fabric to go with my eyes," Nimue prattled on as she worked through the tangles in Rhiannon's hair. "So it should look just as nice on you. I think we're almost exactly the same size although you may be a hair taller so Gran hemmed it a bit longer than she would have for me."

Rhiannon slipped into the delicate embroidered underthings then picked up the dress. It was made of silk and velvet in dusky intense blues. Storm clouds and clear evening skies. It was a simple dress with sheer elbow length sleeves and a velvet bodice. The silk skirt fell to her ankles as she carefully lifted it over her head and let it fall around her. She didn't want to step into it for fear of dragging it on the floor—even clean as it was—and the skirt swished and fluttered as she turned to allow Nimue to fasten the back for her. "Isn't this a little fine for breakfast?" Rhiannon asked.

"No. It befits your station," Nimue answered as she fastened the many tiny shell buttons, suddenly very serious. "You have freed me from a burden that I did not want, and I am sorry for you, but trust me, it is expected of you to present yourself this way." She knew that Nimue was telling the truth. Nimue herself was wearing a pink silk empire waisted gown with a short string of freshwater pearls suspending a wild rose, delicately carved of rose quartz, just below her throat. Engraved silver cuff bracelets were on her wrists, and her shining black hair was neatly braided, coiled and pinned.

Nimue went over to the bureau and opened the top. She took out the box that held the circlet with its crescent shaped opal. Nimue opened the box and presented it to Rhiannon. With shaking hands and pounding heart she lifted it from the box and placed it on her brow. Nimue stood behind her and clasped the sapphire necklace around her throat. Rhiannon understood now why Bronwen would have given her something so precious, and why she had looked at Kristabell/ Rhiannon with so much angst in her eyes. There was a full length mirror in the room which made Rhiannon realize that this really must be a very special room. She walked up to it and looked. It was just her reflection. She knew this, but in a world where seeing your entire reflection is something that only happens once a month or so, a look in a mirror, especially during a time of so much change and turmoil, takes on more significance. Rhiannon looked, and the heir to a Fay throne looked back at her. Eyes glowing, moon shining on her pale brow, hair caught back in a net of silver knotwork and a dress made out of twilight. With a sapphire and a pearl both shining at her throat, she looked like the evening sky, and it was then that she saw for the first time the opalescent flickers that danced, sometimes, along her arms, shoulders, and occasionally her brow. Looking at the fern patterns spiralling up her right arm she realized with a finality that was like a stone in her stomach, that she was not *just* a fairy, which would have, in and of itself, been fine, she was a Fairy *Princess.* She could not escape her fate, and this terrified her.

Rowan emerged neat and clean-shaven, hair combed and tied back in a low loose half ponytail. He looked into her eyes and she saw that mixed look of love and sadness there. She knew now, how he must have felt the night that he'd asked her to be his wife, only to realize all of the painful complicated obligation and danger that would come with her. She flew into his arms, so hard that he grunted but he held her tight. "Please don't let this change how you feel about me. Please remember that whatever happens, at the end of the day, when the door is closed and the world has gone away, that I'm just a halfbreed fairy who loves you. Rowan, I'm so scared."

Chapter 11

Nimue interrupted them, "If you don't stop this, I'm going to cry too, and Rowan, you know how upset my father gets when it rains in the dining room."

"She's right," Rowan said to Rhiannon, "Lugh doesn't like it when it rains at meals so cheer up." He kissed her cheek. "We'll be together all day. I won't leave your side," he told her.

"Do come," Nimue smiled. "My father is very anxious to meet you. We'll go see him before we eat and our grandmother and Rowan's grandfather will be there. It will be nice, you'll see. Please do come," she coaxed.

As they walked through the longhouse Rhiannon looked around at the carvings and decorations. Totem animals and trees surrounded by knotwork. Stern copper suns, serene silver moons, and ravens soaring amongst the stars. Strange, beautiful, and mystical yet earthy and warm. The elemental nature of the Fay was evident in everything they passed, from greenery filled nooks that contained nothing but great earthenware bowls filled with water to the stained glass windows placed at intervals along the halls in golden bursts of flame that sparkled when the sun shone through. She wondered, as they walked, how the fairy population would differ from the human population in this part of the world, and then it occurred to her to make sure that she understood something correctly, "So, in both the Fay and Human kingdoms, the law states that the reign is passed to the oldest acknowledged offspring of the current king or queen regardless of who the other parent is, neither court make any specifications to rule out Fay or Human blood, or a child born of an unacknowledged relationship, and the letter that my mother left me is proof of acknowledgement, correct?"

"Yes and your father acknowledged you as soon as he knew who you were," Rowan answered.

"But isn't my brother already the acknowledged king of the Human realm?" she asked trying to find a loophole to get out of this.

"No. He's not the rightful king," Rowan sighed. "You're the rightful queen because you were your mother's oldest acknowledged child while she was alive. It's just that no one knew that you existed and I'm pretty sure that she had a choice between giving you up and seeing you die. Her parents weren't quite anti-Fay, but they weren't revolutionaries either. Her letter to you however, states that you are her child, and names you, which qualifies as acknowledgement. Your father and I both agree that your mother left you that letter in the hopes that she could somehow bring you back here some day, but she was killed before she had a chance to try."

They came to a stop outside of a set of elegantly carved doors. Rhiannon couldn't move. "When I was in the other world with my parents, they used to tell me that I looked like my birth mother, but it never even occurred to me to wonder if I even had a father who was anything more than an ejaculation, and now he's a real person who loved my mother and he's on the other side of that door. It seems ironic somehow."

Nimue opened the doors and Rowan pulled her through. She didn't stumble. She walked into her father's private sitting room like a lady, with grace and poise. When Rowan presented her to Lugh, her father, she suffered a massive bout of uncertainty and in her consternation, completely unsure of what to do and dizzy with it, she remembered that her father was a king, and rather than look into his eyes, rather than face, immediately, what she may or may not see there, and in part because her legs felt suddenly very weak, she sank into a low curtsy and bowed her head as she had with the unicorn.

"Child," came his rich warm voice from above and he bent, took her hands, and drew her back up to standing. She did look into his face then. He was tall and very handsome with sea green eyes and ash coloured hair, probably the only feature they had in common, and he was, as Gavin had been, very young to have a grown daughter by the standards of the world she had recently left. No more than thirty seven at her guess. She stood as he inspected her, and his stern face softened. "You do look like your mother a little. More so, now that you're awake, your mouth ... you have her pretty feminine mouth, and the angle of her cheeks ..."

She had known that he would say something like this, and say it with sadness and loss in his voice. "I know," she answered softly.

"If I had known ... I would have taken care of you. I would have *never* left you exiled in that world. I would have done anything that I had to. I've always wanted you Rhiannon. Can you ever forgive me?"

He put his hand on her shoulder and Rhiannon stepped into his embrace. She didn't worry about the tears that were staining the front of his blue silk tunic and after a few moments she stepped back and told him with sincerity, "I'm here now. There is nothing to forgive."

"I'm going to go outside for a moment," Nimue hurried from the room just as a few raindrops began to fall.

Lugh chuckled, "When she was a baby we were almost permanently damp. She had colic." He smiled. It was a sad smile, but it was, at least, a smile. "We will have time to talk more later," he said to Rhiannon. "But for now, just tell me if you are well. Are you feeling recovered?"

"Yes, largely ... I think." She smiled and tried not to blush thinking of that other thing that she knew was already sapping her energy and making it difficult for her to gauge whether or not she really was truly recovered.

"You will never know what a shock it was for me to find that unicorn on my doorstep with that ring, and then to find Rowan in the forest with *you* in his arms." Lugh was silent and thoughtful for a moment, "Rowan has told me much about you. I admire you. I've missed everything. Your whole life. I do not wish to imply that I am giving you my approval in saying this to you, because you don't need my approval," he smiled ruefully. "And I think that you may understand my perspective quite well on this, and perhaps it is not necessary for me to be quite so reserved and cautious in my expression of happiness on this subject, and I *will* get to the point and say it ... But, is it not serendipitous and rather wonderful that of all the people in the world who could have been there for you at just the right moment, that it should be Rowan? It makes me very happy that you've settled with him."

Rhiannon smiled, looked at her feet and only blushed a little bit.

Lugh smiled, "Rowan warned me. I am embarrassing you. I will stop before Nimue comes back in and says something truly embarrassing."

Rhiannon laughed, "I am discovering that Nimue has a talent for it."

"That, I think, is a very generous way of putting it," Lugh chuckled, then said, "Come I would like to introduce you to your Grandmother."

Rhiannon looked around, for the first time aware of more than her father's presence in the room and aware, suddenly, that Rowan was not right next to her but had stepped aside slightly to give her and her father space and was standing not far off with a man who she assumed, based on the resemblance, must be his grandfather. Lugh introduced her to her grandmother Morgana, a little woman who did indeed appear to be the source of both her own and Nimue's blue eyes and small stature. Dainty and ageless with silver streaked medium brown hair, she and Rhiannon were eye to eye with each other. "Oh, my love," Morgana said softly putting her arms around Rhiannon.

She had never had a grandmother before and this was new. She felt a lump forming in her throat and a wave of that lost child feeling swept over her as she stood in the older woman's embrace and wondered what she would be like today if she had been brought up in this place, if Morgana had been there her whole life to care for her, and if Lugh had been the father who had raised her, which in turn brought on a wave of guilt, sadness and loss for the parents who *had* raised her, cared for her, and loved her. *But now you're here, and life is changing so quickly, and you're not a child and ...* her mind hovered protectively around the little light deep inside her for the briefest of moments before she brought herself back to the people in the room. She pulled back and looked at Morgana who said, "I've always felt that I should have had more grandchildren."

"What's the matter Gran," Nimue came back in smiling. "Aren't I enough to keep you busy?"

"Nimue, you're enough to keep seven grandmother's busy," Morgana said kissing the girl's rosy cheek. "But I think that I will enjoy having a tiny baby to love and coddle. Three granddaughters will suit me quite well." The older woman smiled and gently patted Rhiannon's cheek.

Rhiannon had to take a deep breath to steady her pounding heart. These people were her family in a way that was more immediate than anything she had ever experienced before and she wasn't used to it. She turned to Rowan and smiled. He was grinning at her as he walked over to where she stood and said to her quietly, "See what I mean? No privacy around these people." He slipped his hand around her waist, "But in a day or two you'll see that the Fairies love great stories, have no shame, and are obsessed with *anything* to do with fertility. So we may as well just give up now and admit to everything."

Morgana's eyes twinkled with merriment, "I think she'll be a summer solstice baby, a very auspicious omen." Rhiannon felt like she was blushing so hard it would be permanent.

"Mother please," Lugh interceded. "The poor girl was raised by humans. She's been through much and she hasn't even eaten breakfast yet."

"Ah well, a young woman in her condition must eat," Morgana twinkled.

"You mustn't mind my cousin," the older man said to her. "She has always been irrepressible. Nimue gets it from her."

"It's alright. I really don't mind. I'll stop blushing some day," Rhiannon said putting her hands to her hot cheeks.

"Rhiannon, this is my grandfather, Merlin's Shadow."

Rhiannon looked at Rowan's grandfather. He was darker than Rowan with waist length braids. Most of his skin seemed to be covered with the fern-like patterns that now marked both herself and Rowan. He looked somehow wilder than the others.

"Merlin's Shadow spends most of his time in the forest, but he always seems to show up for a visit when I'm here," Rowan commented.

"I had always hoped that Rowan would settle with a Fairy woman, but I think that this is more fitting. You will understand each other better as you, like him, are neither Fay nor Human, but both."

"I think so too," she said in agreement, liking the quiet steadiness of the older man. Rowan must have inherited it from his grandfather.

"Nimue tells me that breakfast is ready," Lugh announced. "Let us go and eat."

Meals were a communal affair in the Fairy stronghold and there were three long tables in the large dining hall that, although she was rather turned around and couldn't be sure, Rhiannon got the distinct impression was at the centre of the longhouse. There were stained glass skylights and tall carved pillars all in the same themes as the rest of the building. The hall was filled with Fairies who were as varied in elemental type, cultural heritage, and ethnicity—Rhiannon *was*, she decided, going to apply the word ethnicity to them—as the human population was unvaried. She passed by a beautiful seemingly normal Japanese woman with long blue back hair and flowing silk robes that were tied with a wide blood red silk sash, but as she drew near and the woman smiled, Rhiannon noticed the not unattractively pronounced canines and the glossy black fur that grew, close and short, over the woman's hands and small slightly animal looking bare feet. *A Kitsune*, Rhiannon thought awestruck, looking for and seeing the red fox's tail peeking out from the folds of her lilac robes. The woman winked at her and Rhiannon smiled, too delighted to do otherwise. But her eye was caught, then, by an exotic blue man dressed in bright Indian prints. Indian, as in from India. *Is it the Fay from the orient that the majority of the trade is done with?* She wondered and continued to let her eyes scan the room. Approximately a third of the Fay in the room had a more local look to them. Lots of Dryads but, go figure, they *were* in the middle of a temperate rain forest. There seemed to be somewhat distinct types even within the Dryad population though. Some had chestnut hair, golden skin, freckles and hazel eyes. These were more European looking and dressed in green and wore crowns of leaves, but the others, the ones like Merlin's Shadow, looked like they had been a part of these forests since antiquity. There were others still, not Dryads but birdlike, delicate creatures with sharp eyes, easy smiles, and raucous laughter. They were feathered on their shoulders and had short cropped black hair of the same inky shade. There was a pair of them sitting together and Rhiannon couldn't tell, so androgynously charming were they, if they were two girls, two boys, or one of each, but whatever they were, they were obviously besotted with one another as they repeatedly landed soft little kisses on the other's cheeks and head and gazed longingly at one another. Her eyes continued their tour. There were Phookas with adularescent shining eyes—and who had left random parts of their bodies in animal form, disdaining to look fully humanoid even for meals— and Gnomes and petite red haired Sprites that reminded her of Mr. Flanagan, and many green and blue tinged, shimmering, watery looking Fay. There were Goblins too, although they were neither frightening nor unattractive but lithe, quick and slim, with greenish skin, slightly hooked noses and a look of mischief in their amber eyes. There was a Green Man, and a few little Boggles, three feet tall with round tummies, but for every distinctly identifiable Fairy present, there were as many who were, like Rhiannon, considerably less distinct and more human looking, and many too who had the look of Old country Nymphs, Sylphs, Rhine Maidens and their male counterparts. Suddenly a small pack of river otters ran through the hall, tripping people as they went, then turning into black haired children. They were scolded for being late by a woman decked out in black and red wool and abalone jewellery who looked First Nations. Rhiannon wished the kids would turn back into otters and then run around some more, they were so cute.

Lugh lead them through the room and to the head of the centre table. They sat and the meal commenced. Fairy food was very much to Rhiannon's liking. Little cakes of nuts, seeds and honey, fruits, cheese, eggs, and best of all, no meat, although some at the tables were enjoying smoked salmon. She tried to concentrate on eating and ignore all of the curious glances and thoughts that she could hear coming her way She was quite impressed with herself for maintaining her composure throughout the meal as she found herself in a position that was unexpected and uncomfortable, both from the perspective of someone who had been raised in the world that she had been raised in, and from the perspective of a human of *this* world. In her former life, *if* she had acquired a boyfriend, she wouldn't have hesitated at having sex with him, *if* she had been in love. She wouldn't have wanted to wait for marriage, but she was willing to bet that she would not have been in any rush to get pregnant either. Birth control would have been a definite. But that wasn't the life that she was living anymore and she could, for the most part, let go of those ideas. Except, that she would have had time to get used to being sexually active *privately*. Even if they had been able to stay longer at Rowan's home and she and Rowan had indeed consummated their relationship there, she would have had at least a couple of weeks before everybody *else* knew that she was pregnant. She would have had time to adjust to *that* idea privately. But here everyone knew, what were to Rhiannon, *very* personal events. It shouldn't even have been possible for her to get pregnant last night let alone know about it so soon, and she knew that it had something to do with being Fay, but other than that she was in the dark. She was going to have to ask Nimue about it when she had a chance, but for now every blasted Fairy in the room was whispering about her and broadcasting thoughts so that even the ones who wouldn't have been able to sense that she had been recently deflowered and was now pregnant to boot, knew. It wasn't immaturity or squeamishness, she simply wasn't accustomed to having her private business be ... well ... public. Between her not-so-very private business and the fact that she was their new heir, they were avidly curious about her.

Their thoughts popped randomly into her head. Many were aimless and silly, "How romantic." and a bunch of gossipy thoughts along the lines of, "She's pregnant already! She was a virgin when she got here." Those made her want to sink under the table, but others were more thoughtful.

"She looks more like Lugh than Nimue does."

"She's with child. A good omen."

"Human mother ... Not too sure about that."

"Mated to the Captain of the King's army? Could mean trouble ... even if he does have Fay blood."

"Where does her allegiance lie?"

Rhiannon tried to think of an answer to that question as she ate, because she suspected that sometime soon, she would be expected to answer it.

Chapter 12

After breakfast had been eaten Lugh explained to her, "Under different circumstances I would have liked to have given you time to learn our ways and adjust to life here, but time is not a luxury that we have. There *is* an army massing in the north, and we are still recovering from the desecration of our Grove." Rhiannon had to remember to ask someone what the significance of the groves were before she embarrassed herself with her ignorance. Lugh continued. "The council is meeting in an hour and they have requested your presence. I realize that we are throwing you into this very quickly, but as much as I wish it could wait, I don't think that it can. Your existence and your lineage will present hurdles for the minds of some of our elder council members and it may be an awkward and tedious meeting, but before we go, there are others with whom we should speak." Lugh looked to Nimue. "Please, go fetch our guests and bring them up to meet us."

Lugh lead them out of the dining hall, down a corridor and up a flight of stairs to what appeared to be a small private meeting room. It was a bright and simple room with a polished wooden table at its centre that could seat about ten. They sat and waited. "I will let you explain," Lugh said to Rowan who in turn looked at Rhiannon, his eyes gentle yet serious.

Rowan took her hand. "I know that you will not like this. I know you well enough to know that this is not the life that you would choose, but Lugh and I have talked this over to the point of exhaustion and the one thing that we keep coming back to, is that the best thing for everyone, for all of Nova Britannia, the Fay and the Humans, for you and I, and everyone else who is caught between, is to start where your parents left off. We are going to have to head a revolution. If we want a world that we can live in, it's the only way. I contacted Gwydion and asked him to come. He's been here for the last two days and he knows more than he's ever let on about the events surrounding your birth. He's better connected than I'd ever realized. I'd always known that he had spies but ... Anyway, he can tell you more later, but the bottom line is that Seamus knows you're alive, and he's hunting you. We have a choice between running or fighting, and right now the odds are in our favour if we unite the kingdom and give him a fight. If we run he'll probably win the war, and then he'll have the resources to keep hunting you forever. I know that you don't want to be a Queen, but the good ones never do, and I know that you have more fight in you than you let on." He looked at her, serious, meaning every word.

It made sense to Rhiannon even though it filled her with dread. The idea terrified her, but in a way, ever since she had discovered who she really was, she had known that this was going to have to happen. She nodded to Rowan.

He continued, "We have to figure out who we can trust, who we can count on, and then we have to turn the Fay council in your favour. We will have to tell them who your mother is. They're stuck with you no matter what, but if you have the Fay kingdom behind you in an absolute sense, morally and in spirit, it will make things that much easier," Rowan said. "Gwydion and Nessa will be here in a few minutes along with the four of my men who survived the run in at the grove. Just sit and listen for now. That's all you need to do. All that my men know right now is that you are Lugh's daughter by a human woman," Rhiannon looked a Lugh. He was serious and self contained until he sensed her eyes on his face, then he smiled at her softly and sadly. Rowan continued. "I need to find out where they stand on this subject, and I'm not quite sure how to do this." He looked at her, sombre and thoughtful for a moment or two then grinned impetuously. Rhiannon shook her head and smiled back. It never seemed to matter how low she felt, when he smiled at her like that, she couldn't keep a straight face.

There came sound of feet on the stairs and the door opened. Nimue ushered Gwydion, Nessa, Thaylum, Cole, and Brian into the room and waited for them to find seats before taking one herself. Because she would have felt awkward if she hadn't, and also in part because of the dark circles under Nessa's eyes and the fact that suddenly seeing her sister-in-law made a familiar feeling of love, family, and belonging flare in Rhiannon's heart, she was up on her feet and hugging Nessa before the taller woman had a chance to sit. Nessa laughed her rich sardonic laugh. "I missed you too," she said, returning the embrace. Nessa had obviously made her decision. She wore fitted leather pants and a tight leather vest over a utilitarian linen shirt and tall riding boots. Her copper curls had been tightly reigned in and were tied in a braid down her back. There was also, of course, the requisite sword belt, although Rhiannon couldn't help notice that Nessa's blade appeared to be lighter and slimmer than the swords Rowan and Leif carried.

When all were seated Rowan launched strait to business, "Hans is still causing trouble I take it."

Thaylum answered, "Yes Sir. He keeps fighting with the people that we're staying with. They sedated him." Rhiannon noted that Thaylum seemed neither alarmed nor surprised by this treatment of his comrade and neither did the black haired Cole.

Rowan nodded, not particularly phased by it either, then Lugh spoke up, "This may seem perhaps a trifle ..." a slightly wicked smile played around his eyes, "Manipulative. However if no harm comes to him, and his attitude is improved by the experience, why don't we leave him with Lyla for a few days. Have her wipe his memory of the last week and a half and she can show him a good time while she's at it. I try not to encourage the Nixies but I have, on occasion, found it useful to take advantage of their predilection for, how shall I put it ... using and confusing men. Lyla is *mostly* harmless and generally quite gentle in her methods."

Rhiannon knew what Nixies were and, in the lore of her world, the beautiful water Fay were not particularly harmless. Rowan's mouth quirked almost imperceptibly but Rhiannon caught it. "Have it arranged," he said to Lugh then moved on to more pressing matters. Casually, as if it couldn't possibly have been a calculated movement, Rowan crossed his arms pushing his sleeves up and resting his elbows on the table as he did. Rhiannon watched the eyes of the others, in particular the eyes of thé three male soldiers. Thaylum didn't react, although his eyes did rest momentarily on the exposed fern pattern that extended far enough down Rowan's arm to be visible with his sleeves up. Cole's eyebrows went up as the pattern caught him, and his eyes widened then flicked to Rowan's face and then to Rhiannon's hand which was also resting on the table, but then he schooled his features and pretended not to have seen. And then there was Brian whose face showed perhaps, a more exposed surprise, but also understanding and acceptance. Rowan spoke, "It may already be obvious to you but, for many reasons, my life and my allegiance are currently in a flux. I have something that I must ask of you that goes far beyond the duties of King's Knight but first, I need to know where you stand on the topic of the

Fay and, in particular, the taboo? I know I have no right to ask this."

Again Rhiannon watched their expressions. Her eyes flicked briefly to Nessa's face which showed avid interest but Nessa knew what was going on and was, like Rhiannon, simply observing. The three soldier's expressions were fascinating, however. Cole's look was immediately hooded, and Brian had a considering look on his face, as if he actually had to think the question through. Thaylum on the other hand was open and forthright. It was almost as if his answer had been dying to get out of his mouth and now that the question had been asked there was nothing that he could do to stem the flow of his words. "The taboo is horse shit and you know it! The Good King here obviously knows it too if he's had a half human daughter hidden away all these years. I would know what she was from a million miles away. The Sylph blood is like a beacon. Those eyes and that skin." There was that look again on his face, that same sad fascination that Rhiannon had seen before when she had wondered if everyone else knew something that she didn't. "My children have eyes just like that," Thaylum said softly. "They get them from my wife."

"Your wife?" This came from Brian in an incredulous tone.

"Six years ago I took a Sylph for my wife. We were in love. I've never told a soul. No one. Not in six years. We have a little house in the woods at the base of the mountains. She lives there with our children, and I go there to be with them whenever I can." Thaylum looked directly at Rowan. "I know that Merlin's Shadow is your Grandfather. I've known for some time." Thaylum was a handsome man in a rugged, green eyed, freckled way. Rhiannon guessed that he was about twenty-six. With a nose that had obviously been broken a few times and a collection battle scars he looked the polar opposite of the delicate Sylphs she'd seen at breakfast, but he sat straight, and there was an ease in his shoulders now, as if the thing he'd been keeping in had never quite allowed him to exhale all the way.

Rhiannon looked at Cole whose expression was no longer hooded but it was however, so complex that she couldn't really get a sense of what he was feeling outside of the intensity of it. He gaped at Rowan for a moment then looked at Thaylum and exclaimed, "The trees and the sea Thaylum! Why did ye never tell me!" his warm brown doe's eyes big and bewildered.

"For the same reason the captain's never told us that he's a quarter Dryad. It would be career suicide, and I have a family to support."

"Well then, I guess under the circumstances it wouldn't bother any of ye to know me mum's a Selkie." His tone was so fragile as he spoke the 'never to be spoken' words. He looked almost as if he had expected to drop dead, as if an arrow could have flown in and taken him through the heart, but there was no explosion, no one had died, there was only silence.

It was Brian who spoke into the silence and all eyes were on him. He held up his hands, "Now, as far as I know I'm all human, and I've never been with a fairy woman, but Rowan, if you're trying to find out where my allegiance lies?" He raised his eyebrows and looked at Rowan, but then instead fixed his gaze on Rhiannon. She smiled. "Lady, when you smile like that, I would know you anywhere," he said to her. "The Kingdom hasn't seemed right since Sulamith died, and I would know her heir if I were blind. My allegiance lies with my Queen. Lady, you have my allegiance and my sword. I would follow you anywhere."

It didn't take Thaylum and Cole any more than ten seconds to put all of the information into place and when they did they stared at Rhiannon, both men realizing full force that a half Fay queen was the answer to their fractured worlds. She was the bridge between their hidden lives, and freedom.

"Lady you have my allegiance and my sword," Thaylum was the first one with the words out of his mouth with Cole on his heals.

"Gentlemen," Rowan smiled. "It appears that the Queen has an army. Now we just need to make it bigger." He continued more seriously, "For the next week I am going to try to maintain my position as Captain of the King's Army from a distance. I think that it's obvious where my allegiance lies," he looked at Rhiannon, "however it would be impossible for me to maintain my position for long with this," he motioned to his arm. "I would lose the support of some of the men and it would alert certain members of the council to where my sympathies lie. Like you two," he looked to Thaylum and Cole. "I have been *very* careful to maintain a front of political neutrality over the years. What we need to do now, we need to do fast. I've given Leif command of the army in my stead. You can trust him and he is aware of what is happening. It was his parents who raised Rhiannon in the other world. I sent him back to the King's City with the message that my wife had been injured during the run in with the elves and that I would return as soon as she was well enough to travel, which gives us some leeway. Lugh has also sent a contingent of Glaistig to slow Seamus down. If what we are doing is discovered by the wrong people we will be arrested for treason, but what we need you three to do is go back to the King's City and root out our strongest sympathizers and eliminate those who are sympathetic to Seamus. When the time is right, I need you to be in a position to secure the King's castle. I know that this seems daunting, but Gwydion and I have a plan. All we have to do is convince the Fay council to support us."

"You have my support and I will use what power I have to convince them," Lugh said.

Then Gwydion spoke for the first time, "I have been keeping an eye on the Human court for some time and I have much to share with you that will be of use. You certainly won't be alone in this, and the task is far from impossible."

Rhiannon listened to all of this with mixed feelings. Fear, guilt, pride, and anxiety because despite being surrounded by confident, competent, hopeful people, when it boiled right down to it, it was she who would have to turn the council, and as if on cue Lugh announced, "The council will be meeting momentarily. We should go now."

As they rose to go Rhiannon looked at the three knights and addressed them, "Thank you," she said softly. "Thank you for understanding."

"Lady," Cole said in an equally soft tone. "You don't need to thank us for anything."

She offered him her hand and he took it and bowed over it and then they left for the council hall.

* * *

The council hall was a large round building back from the water and surrounded by trees with an arched entry that was carved with a motif of acanthus leaves and rowan branches. The building was beautiful, serene and natural looking in neutral tones and graceful curved lines, Art Nouveau meets Coast Salish. Inside was a vast hall with a skylight in the centre and carved wooden pillars all around. The pillars, Rhiannon understood, represented the various races of Fairy and they vaguely resembled Totem poles, only these were less symmetrical and had as much Celtic knotwork and botanical themes as actual depictions of creatures. There was one that was obviously a Dryad, a naked female tree with knotwork chains spiralling up into her branches. It was beautiful.

Rhiannon, Rowan, Lugh, Gwydion, Brian, Thaylum, Nessa and Cole walked in and found seats at the large smooth round table. The council was not yet present, however, almost the moment they were seated, the members walked in single file and seated themselves. There were thirteen in total and a variety of Fay, but largely the more human looking types. It was then, looking at them, that the answer to a question that had been forming in Rhiannon's mind came to her. Over the last five weeks, before coming to the stronghold, Rhiannon hadn't seen a single First Nations person. Not one of the indigenous people who had, in the world she had come from, been there long before the Europeans had come. In fact most of the humans she had seen fit the Celtic, Anglo-Saxon, Viking, Germanic profile. Red, blond or golden brown hair and mostly blue, green, and grey eyes. There were a few people around who looked more Mediterranean or black Irish, but not many, and several of those people had turned out to have Fay blood. Cole, Rowan, Fenna. She had assumed, incorrectly, that Rowan's dark hair and eyes had come from some distant Mediterranean ancestor. She remembered the history that Gwydion had taught her though. Mediterranean Europe had been wiped out in the plague wars. Rhiannon looked around the table at the council members. She knew where the First Nations tribes were. They had absorbed the Fairies. It explained the longhouses, the carved canoes on the beach, and the long black braids that so many of the Dryads seemed to sport. West Coast Fairies.

The meeting of the council got underway with very little formality as one of the elders dove right down to business, turning on Lugh in an accusatory tone, "Explain yourself Lugh. How is it you feel you have the right to strap us with a half Human heir?"

It was an old wizened woman holding a well worn grey stone in her hand and wearing black and red robes and abalone—like the otter mother in the dining hall—who had spoken. "That's Stone Keeper," Rowan whispered in her ear.

"She's a Kushtaka from the north and the council Chief. She's a bit outspoken, but she's wiser than she lets on."

Lugh smiled a wicked sardonic smile that made Rhiannon realize just what an elegant creature her father really was. "Don't feel your disdain too sharply just yet Stone Keeper. I didn't just strap you with a half human heir. She is also the rightful Queen of the Human realm."

The room was silent for such a long time that Rhiannon began to feel frightened. She reached for Rowan's hand, her heart pounding, and then to her surprise the Fairies began to bicker. They were caustic and disgruntled, but more in the way that one would expect if their tax dollars had been wasted. It wasn't the rage Rhiannon had feared. Just a bunch of self righteously indignant, opinionated Fairies.

"You've handed the kingdom over to the humans!"

"What will she be like as a leader if she can't understand what it is to be Fay!"

"She's already partnered to a Human and pregnant with his child! You've polluted our people!"

It went on like this for nearly a half an hour and Lugh did nothing to stop it. Rhiannon watched and noted who was loudest in their protests and who sat back looking thoughtful and vaguely amused. It was indeed the older members who were loudest. She watched the Kitsune that she had seen at breakfast. The woman sat back with a deceptively passive smile on her face. "Her name is Yuka," Rowan whispered in her ear as he noticed the direction of her gaze.

There was another across the room. A tall man, perhaps a few years younger than Lugh with slim antlers and moss green hair. His eyes were green too with no apparent whites or irises, but he did not protest Rhiannon's presence either. After a time Rhiannon got fed up. She was a puppet, nothing more. There was nothing to carry on about. She had not picked this horrible *not* accident of her birth. She was nauseous and peeved, so she stood and silently wandered the hall and after a minute or two all eyes were on her and the bickering had stopped. "Thank you. That was rather childish and unnecessary, I'm glad you've stopped," Rhiannon commented not quite sure where her mouth was taking her but, on impulse, going with it. "Now, I really am horribly ignorant. You'll have to forgive me for it, but I'm hoping that no one will mind a little digression. You see, I was wondering, who was here first?" They all looked at her, puzzled. "Who was here first?" she repeated. "Human or Fay. And if it was Fay, were they just a group of Dryads? I'm curious."

Silence. Eventually, seeing that no one else was going to answer Lugh spoke up. "Many Fay came to Nova Britannia from the old country, and many humans. There were some settlements of people, some Dryads, Kushtaka and Selkies, although those aren't the names that they went by then, but it was a vast forest and those from the east were tired and diminished after the journey that brought them here. There is little recorded information from that time. It was eight hundred years ago. We adopted the ways of the people who were here, their houses, their canoes, but were they all Fay or human? I don't know."

"Oh," she said brightly. "That's very interesting." She continued to wander, running her hands over the pillars as she passed. "The world where I grew up is very different in some ways, but in others it is very much the same. The land is very similar, and some of the races of humans. Far fewer Fay however, and no Unicorns that I've seen. Some events have been the same, but much of our histories have played out differently. People from the old countries, or Europe as we call it, did come to the area that is geographically equivalent to this place, and although they came much later, *when they* came, they found a people already living here, and horrifically, they tried to wipe them out with disease. Those people used to live a life that was very much in tune with nature. They have thick dark hair, warm skin tones and dark eyes. Before the Europeans came they lived in longhouses and they still carve canoes and tall beautiful pillars." She ran her hand over a pillar carved with a raven. "They are also, coincidentally, really very human. There are stories of the Fay in the other world, almost every culture has some variant. I used to read them obsessively. I didn't know that I was Fay. In some of the stories they say that the Fay needed Humans to reproduce. They say that the Gwragedd Annwn often took Human men as husbands. It's fascinating to find here, that Selkies pair with Water Nymphs and Dryads with Sylphs," she looked around the room with wide eyes, noting all of the uncomfortable looks. "But pair a Human with a Fairy?" She circled another pillar examining it. "Did you know that I can open a doorway into that other world. That's how I got here. I did it on my own. No one showed me how. I can also heal someone so well that they show no scar. Did you know that I can even start a fire without a flint. I thought that was pretty neat. Now I don't mean to be base or crass, but everybody knows what you get if you mate a horse to a donkey right?" Her audience nodded like bewildered children. "You get a mule, and everybody knows that a mule isn't viable. But if a Fairy has a child with a Human, because they're in love, and they want to be together, do we call that child something different and ostracize them ...? I think that would be cruel." She gave them a hard look. "And just in case there is someone in this room who doesn't know, I think that I have pretty conclusively proven that I, unlike a mule, am viable." Rhiannon said it in the driest tone she could muster and was so insanely proud of herself for not blushing that she could actually feel the little coloured flames dancing on her arms and shoulders, and as if to prove a point she raised her hand and let the lights dance on her fingertips. "Now as for my question, who was here

first? I'm pretty sure that if we could travel back into antiquity, we would find that they were human, and I'm pretty
sure that they are still here. In fact I don't think that it's a
matter of Fay versus Human. Do you want to know what I
think?" She didn't give anyone space to answer, she just
ploughed on through. "I think that some of you have just as
much human blood running through your veins as I do. I don't
think that there *is* a difference between us. If there were, I
wouldn't be here."

Rhiannon had arrived back where she'd started. She looked
around the table. Some were looking into their laps like
chastened children. Yuka, Stone Keeper, and the antlered
green man had satisfied smiles on their faces, and the rest
looked shell-shocked, as if they were in the process of re-
adjusting their world view, except for Rowan, Cole, and
Thaylum, who were grinning proudly. She took her seat, and
before anyone else could speak she asked, "Lugh ... Father.
Would you tell me about my mother? How did you come to
meet her?"

Now all Fairies love a good story, and she had Lugh
cornered. It was time for a tale.

Chapter 13

Lugh looked reluctant to speak but, knowing that he must, he began his tale. He looked around the table for a moment and the past rushed into his eyes so that all could see, and then he spoke, "When Sulamith and I were found out, I thought, I believed, that she was lost to me. I did not know then that anything had come of our love." He looked at Rhiannon apologetically. "When I first saw her on that rocky beach I knew that I was in dire trouble. From that moment, though she did not at first know it, she had my heart. She was sitting on a large rock in the light of the setting sun. She was beautiful, as beautiful as any Fay woman, but solid and earthy. I was hiding from her under the waves. She couldn't see me, but all I wanted was to show myself to her, and touch her golden hair and her alabaster cheek, and look right into her sky blue eyes. She was tall and noble, and I was sixteen and I *wasn't* thinking with my head. I came out of the water and spoke to her. I can't remember what I said to her but she was sweet and innocent and kind and I couldn't help it. I loved her. We met there every night for a month. Her lady in waiting and one of the King's men would act as a lookout for us. I would slip back into the sea if we thought there was a risk. We would talk and talk. We were young and idealistic and we realized as we went how much we had in common. It seemed too good to be true when we revealed our love to one another and both recognized that a union between us would unite our two kingdoms, that if we produced an heir it would be a child that both Human and Fay could follow. We decided to consummate our relationship. Our plan was to go into hiding together and, once we had a child, to make our union known. We assumed that we had years before our parent's reigns would end and that it would give everyone a chance to adjust to the idea of a new kingdom, but we were caught. We were on the beach together. We had just made love. I had given her a ring, and brought for her the circlet of the moon because that is what she was to me. The moon pulling the tide." Lugh blinked hard and took a deep breath. "We heard a cry in the woods, and swords, and she said to me, "Quick hide!" I slipped under the waves. She pushed the ring and the circlet under the blanket, but her younger brother and four armed men took her bodily away. Her lady in waiting, who was crying, came and took the blanket that we had been on together. She found the ring and the circlet. I watched her hide them on her person. It was the last time that I ever saw Sulamith." Lugh was silent for a moment or two but the force of his memory conjured, for a brief moment, an image of Rhiannon's mother as he had seen her, sitting on that rock in the sun that first time. It hovered in the air before him, and he looked at it with such longing and tenderness that Rhiannon realized that he had never really gotten his heart back.

"A week later a druid brought a message. Its meaning was clear. Any attempt to see or communicate with Sulamith would be considered an act of war. Going public about the relationship I'd had with her would also be taken as an act of war. Either action would result in Sulamith being immediately arrested and executed for high treason. My father was furious. I was forbidden any attempt to rescue her and I couldn't think of a way to do it without unduly risking her life. I never saw her again and I wasn't with her long enough that last time to realize that she had conceived." He was silent for a space and all eyes were on him. "If I had known what she would go through ..."

Rhiannon couldn't help herself. She stood and went to him. He wasn't the father who had raised her and she didn't put her arms around him, but just stood beside him with her hand on his shoulder. Her right hand. The one with the heartsease ring on it and the ferns and vines spiralling up her wrist. He took her hand in his and gently squeezed her fingers. He was even younger than she had thought. When he spoke again his voice was steady. "I don't have a very complete picture of what happened to Sulamith after this, but Rowan tells me that Gwydion can shed some light on this time, and what went on in the human court."

No one could be unmoved by Lugh's story and all eyes turned towards the old Druid with avid curiosity. Rhiannon wished that she could hear this story alone without the circle of eyes that would continually check on her, look at her face and see if their were tears. Of course there were tears. What did they think she was? But that was half the point of starting this in front of the Fay council. They needed to see what she was, even if all they saw was a delicate little fairy gardener who couldn't keep her cheeks dry. The story alone would be enough to make them follow her, but hearing it with her, for the first time, would make them an inescapable part of her tale and she would have their support.

Gwydion began his part of *her* story. "In order to go onward with this tale I will have to take a step back and explain Sulamith's family to you. At the time of these events I was the head of the Royal College of Druids and I was well acquainted with the royal family. Sulamith's parents were staunch traditionalists. They were not unkind but they had always believed that the status quo must be maintained and that they knew best. Sulamith was a quiet gentle dreamer, and she was their pride and joy. They trusted her and they thought that they knew her, but she had a passionate heart and had dreamed of change even before she met Lugh. Sulamith and Lugh would have succeeded if she had been an only child, but nobody could deny the effect that Seamus, her younger brother, had on the court. He was in short a sly, narcissistic, psychopath. At the age of eleven I found him drowning a litter of puppies in a bucket. Dismayed I asked him why, and he told me that it was, 'An interesting feeling when their lives left their bodies.' At thirteen I once found him with the daughter of one of the court ladies. He had tied the little girl to a tree and was pulling her toenails off. It was quite some distance from the castle but the little girl's screams..." Gwydion shook his head. "I brought her back to the castle with me and the whole matter was very carefully covered up. Seamus plotted and schemed and by the time he was fifteen he had a solid grasp of concepts such as bribery, blackmail, and extortion. I think the best example of his character though would be what I discovered from a young woman that I found crying in an alcove. She was one of the queen's ladies and she was bleeding profusely. I didn't know what was wrong with her and I didn't ask, I simply did what I could for her and then brought her to you people. It was nineteen years ago. Some of you may remember her." Gwydion stopped almost as if unwilling to continue but then forced himself onward. "Once she was recovered enough she told me her tale. She had become pregnant by one of the King's Knights, but he was a younger son and unable to support her, so hearing of this, though she did not know *how* he'd heard, Seamus approached her with an offer. Let him have his way with her and he would, as he put it, 'Make it so that she didn't have anything to worry about.' I do not like to say this part out loud," the old man said suddenly. "There is such an ugliness to it that it burns the heart, but it is an illustration of the Exiled Prince's character that does not bear forgetting. He brutalized the girl to the point of

miscarriage then left her to bleed. She told me what he said to
her when he was done with her. 'There. You'll bleed out in
about half an hour, then you'll have nothing to worry about.'
Apparently he laughed. Seamus believed that he was entitled
to anything that he could take, as long as he didn't get caught.
A significant amount of time and resources had to be put in
by the king and council to hide his crimes. This happened
only a week before he exposed Sulamith to their parents. He
had an amazing amount of contempt for her. I think that
Sulamith made him feel what a scabby dirty person he was
inside and he wanted to see her crawl." Gwydion looked at
Lugh and shook his head sadly, "Nothing good happened
during that period. It was what could only be called an evil
time. Once it became apparent that Sulamith was pregnant
she was hidden. At this point the king approached me and
asked that I open a door to the other world to hide Sulamith
and later exile her child. I refused. I explained to him that in
order for a human to have access to the kind of power that
was required to open a doorway, a human sacrifice was necessary, and that since the plague wars all druids have sworn an
oath, a fairy binding, literally preventing them from taking
this kind of action. I instead suggested that it may perhaps be
best to accept the course that Sulamith had plotted for us.
This lost me my position at the college, as I now knew what
was happening, and Sulamith's parents thought of it as a
terrible embarrassment and a huge risk. I was threatened with
torture and death, so I left and kept very quiet. Caitlin,
Rowan's Grandmother, was at the time just a lesser council
member, but she understood that I was leaving and offered
me a place at her Husband's family home where I have been
living very quietly for the last nineteen years, and while I *was*
out of the *court*, I was not out of touch." The crafty old
druid's eyes twinkled. "I have, you see, my spies, and the
court is riddled with them. There are more people hiding in

that city who would have been sympathetic to Sulamith's cause than I think anyone realized. What happened in the end was that a Fairy woman was captured and tortured until she agreed to open a door to the other world. Sulamith was taken there to have her child and then the child was left behind. I did what I could to make life easier for Rhiannon and the people who raised her. I had a few contacts in the Broad River Stronghold who were able to put Gavin and Fionnuala in contact with Flanagan, a Wood Sprite who makes his home in the other world, and I was able to have wards put on their home. I always wished that I had been able to tell Sulamith of this and that I had been able to do more. From what I understand her parents controlled her by threatening the life of her child. Behave or we can and will have the child killed. Then after Seamus had gotten the old King out of the way he used Rhiannon as his trump card to control Sulamith as well. Somehow, she managed to be a good queen despite the unhappy life she lead. But Seamus had power at court. He was ruthless, brilliantly evil and very dangerous, and if we believe even for a moment that he hasn't still got some of that power we are kidding ourselves." He looked at Rhiannon. "Six weeks ago I received word from one of my spies that you had been killed. Then the very next morning only hours after receiving that message Rowan showed up at my door looking, might I say, quite pleased with himself. And who do you think he had with him?" Gwydion chuckled. "It was hard to hide my surprise or know what to do about it, but when I saw the ring that you had hanging around your neck, I knew that he would figure out who you were eventually." He looked at Rowan and Rhiannon. "I remembered Sulamith's unhappiness and I hesitated to bring so much sadness to you when you and Rowan were so obviously happy together. I thought that perhaps you were safer if you didn't know. I knew that Rowan was the safest person in all the worlds for you to be with, and when he told me that he was taking you to Lugh, I knew that it was only a matter of time before all of this came out."

Chapter 14

Hearing the story had been for Rhiannon much the same as finding cut that her parents, Gavin and Fionnuala, had been burned to death. She felt physically ill. She returned to her seat and pressed her face against Rowan's shoulder thankful again for the shelter he offered, and that she wasn't going through this alone. But her parents, all four of them, had lost *so so much*, and now Lugh was left behind to deal with the fallout from his decision to leave the water and talk to the beautiful girl on the rock in the sun. Rhiannon wondered if he had regrets and then wished she hadn't. Her heart could hardly bear it. Stone Keeper was the first to break the silence after Gwydion had finished speaking. "I think that under the circumstances it would be appropriate to adjourn for now. We can reconvene later today or perhaps even tomorrow morning. I think that we all need some time to absorb the things that we've learned here today."

Lugh seconded the motion. "Yes. I do not think that we would be delaying overmuch if we waited until morning to make decisions. I for one, am too overwrought to be useful at this time and it is well past noon. We all need a break."

The meeting was adjourned. Rowan put his arm around Rhiannon's waist and lead her out of the great hall and into the warm sun. He lead her down to the beach and they sat on a log together watching the waves and feeling the sharp wet breeze that came up off of the water. "Both of my mothers had their children taken away. What if that happens to us?" she whispered to him.

Rowan looked into her eyes and took her face in his hands, "Rhiannon, I will never let that happen. I swear to you that I will do *anything* to keep that from happening. I made a mistake once and I won't do it again. I can't bear the thought of you worrying about this." He kissed her and wiped away her tears then they watched the water in silence for a time before they heard voices.

"Just this way ..." and, "Thank you," drifted down the beach towards them and soon Nimue, Cole, and Thaylum were approaching. Nimue spoke first, "I didn't suppose that either of you would be up to lunch in the dining hall, but I figured that you would still need to eat, so I packed a basket full of food. Cole and Thaylum told me about the meeting and showed me where you were. We'll leave you if you need to be alone, but if you'd like, we could stay and have lunch with you?" The three stood there, waiting uncertainly.

Rowan smiled at them. It was a tired, sad, wan, smile, "You'd better stay. The company would do us good."

"Yes, stay," Rhiannon agreed. "The food will taste better if you stay." Nimue nodded and began spreading the large blanket that she had tucked in the top of her basket, then passed Rhiannon a soft wool shawl, which she accepted gratefully. It was an odd time to find themselves, suddenly, in a social situation, sitting in the sun with other young like-minded people. At first the others were, Rhiannon could tell, unsure and self-conscious around herself and Rowan. It took her a moment to remember that she was a Queen and that Rowan was a military hero and Thaylum and Cole's commanding officer, but Rowan was used to this and broke the ice with ease. He turned to Thaylum, "We fought in the same regiment for *three years* and you never let on once! Your bunk in the barracks was right next to mine."

"I thought about it," Thaylum chuckled. "But the time never seemed right. Once you get used to keeping a secret, I guess it becomes a hard habit to break even if you know that someone else is keeping the same secret."

Rowan nodded. "So how is White Feather anyway? I haven't seen her in six years. I'm right about that aren't I?" Rowan said it with a smile.

"Yeah." Thaylum answered sheepishly, "She felt a little guilty disappearing like that, but we didn't think that we had any other choice. Sometimes she's lonely, but she really likes having her own home and she loves being a mother." Then Thaylum smiled indulgently, "And I have to admit they're pretty cute kids."

Nimue had finished spreading out the food. Rhiannon took a plate and helped herself. When they were all sitting and eating Thaylum commented, "The only drawback to spending time with the Fay is that, sometimes I would really like some meat."

"I like fish!" Nimue and Cole both piped up at the same time and then both laughed.

"Crazy Selkies," Rowan poked fun at them.

Rhiannon felt herself smiling. She let herself remember waking up that morning with Rowan, bathed in colour, and the feeling of the goodness that was happening in the midst of all of this sadness and upheaval. She closed her eyes and let the sun shine on her face. Cole and Nimue were defending their love of fish when something occurred to Rhiannon, "Do you two have a seal skin that you can slip into?" she asked, thinking about what she had heard about Selkies and their seal skins.

Cole and Nimue shook their heads sadly, "Only full blooded Selkies are born with a seal skin." Nimue answered.

"Where does that leave you?" Rhiannon couldn't help asking.

This time Cole answered, "It leaves us always longing for the sea in a way that we can never truly have it. My brothers all joined the Navy because they have trouble leaving it. I joined the army to try to distract myself from it. It eases the feeling to admit to it out loud though." He smiled a little and, like Nimue, turned and looked over his shoulder at the water. Rhiannon saw their eyes meet and she wondered what had passed between them.

The five of them lounged on the beach and spoke of things that they had never been able to speak of openly before. "I can't help wonder how many of us are out there," Rhiannon sighed. "Half Fay, Fay involved with Humans, Human's with Fay? Does it happen more than anyone admits to?"

"I think it does," Rowan answered. "So many times it's happened to me, that I'll feel a sense of kinship to someone, or have a flash of understanding, only to look away from that person as if it's automatically assumed that we don't talk about this. We just repress it. I've often suspected, but we've been conditioned not to seek confirmation."

Cole nodded, "The same thing happens to me especially when I'm near the sea. I think that there are more chance meetings between Humans and Fairies than it seems. I think that there's an attraction that we can't deny. My mother always finds her skin and swims away, but after a few months, she always comes back. She says she can't help it. When she's with us she wants the sea, when she's in the sea she wants us."

Thaylum had been listening to all of this quietly. "I think Cole's right about there being an attraction. I remember meeting White Feather for the first time. It was completely by chance. I was on my way back to my family's farm which is about five days east of here. I was on foot and I'd stopped to make camp. There's an old hollow tree not far from the main road, about twenty minutes walk into the forest. It makes a good shelter so I often used it as a place to make camp, and that's where I met her. I had never seen anything so beautiful in my life. She was incandescent and gossamer, sitting on a log stroking a unicorn. They glowed in the twilight. I stared and stared and then I stepped on a twig and the unicorn bolted. She looked up and I told her that I was sorry, that I hadn't meant to chase the unicorn away. I felt like a clod but she smiled and walked towards me, so incredibly light on her feet, and she said, "I've made soup. If you have some bread, we could share?" At the time it seemed so strange to me that she wanted me just as much as I wanted her. I felt so ordinary, but she told me that to her I wasn't ordinary." He stopped and grinned, "We barely left that hollow tree for three days. It was summer. It was perfect."

They sat for a time basking in sunlight and good feelings before Rhiannon asked the question that had been burning inside her for quite some time, "So, we pretty much know first hand that nothing bad happens when Humans and Fairies come together, so why the taboo? Where does it come from?"

"I don't know but I wish it didn't exist," Thaylum said bitterly.

Cole nodded agreement.

Rowan looked thoughtful, "I asked Gwydion once when I was about seventeen. He told me that according to the Druids, who have knowledge that goes back to the old country and even to the time of the Plague Wars, that it was the Angels who started the taboo just before they retreated into the mountains. But no one knows why they did it, or why we've adhered to it for so long."

"The Angels?" Cole screwed up his face in incredulity. "I wasn't even sure that they were real."

Rhiannon piped up then, "Gwydion told Rowan and I that he'd seen one. There is something that's bothering me though. In the other world, where I was raised, there is a concept there called science. I don't think that I'm articulate enough to explain exactly what it is, except that it's a way of doing and explaining things without magic, and according to the science of that world, if two creatures can mate and produce viable offspring, then they are the same creature."

This brought on a long thoughtful silence followed by some good natured joking about viability. Then Rhiannon just had to ask, "I wonder what a Human Phooka cross would be like?"

This brought on gales of laughter. "Oh ... Rhiannon ..." Nimue gasped out, "Only a Phooka could love a Phooka, but maybe ... someday we'll see."

The sun was getting low so they packed up reluctantly and left the beach, knowing that it was the last time that they would spend a relaxed afternoon in the sun for a long time.

Chapter 15

Against all odds the mood from the beach survived through dinner. Thaylum, Cole, Nessa, Brian and Gwydion had been invited to stay in Lugh's house which was the largest of the twelve longhouses in the stronghold and with Nimue, Morgana and Merlin's Shadow there, it was a pleasant, if somewhat subdued, meal. Rhiannon was not surprised to find Lugh absent. She suspected that the council meeting had been more traumatic for him than for anyone else. She suspected that he was swimming in a sea of regret. Rhiannon let her thoughts skirt around the subject of her father as she ate and instead focused on ignoring the eyes she could feel inspecting her and not letting the weight of those eyes weigh down her every movement. She had made quite an impression at the Council meeting and the hall was filled with talk. Most of it in her favour. She finished her plate then whispered to Nimue, "Do you think that it would be an invasion of his privacy if we went to say goodnight to Lugh, to our father? I don't like the idea of him sitting alone right now." She looked into her sister's identical eyes and the feeling was unsettling and satisfying at the same time. Like coming home to a home you never knew you had.

"No, it would not be an invasion," Nimue answered softly. "Let us go to him. He was very sad after the meeting. I think that it would please him if we went to see him, just the two of us." Nimue twined her fingers with Rhiannon's and Rhiannon whispered to Rowan that she would see him in their rooms later. The sisters left the hall together, hearing the whispered thoughts of dozens of projecting Fay telling them that together they looked like two sisters from a tale, from a story, so much alike except for their dark and fair hair. Ebony and Ash. They looked like two sisters to which much would happen, and there was a ring of prophesy to those thoughts which both Rhiannon and Nimue tried to ignore.

As they walked down the long hall together Rhiannon asked Nimue, "What are the Groves?"

"Sometimes when a Dryad is very old, instead of waiting for their body to die they wander out into the forest and go back to their element. They let go of the life they've lived, put down roots and change their existence. It isn't very common, and usually only the wisest go this way, but they usually begin to congregate in the same clearing until you have a Dryad grove. They are places of peace and wisdom. We care for them, and go to them when we need guidance or inspiration, or just a quiet place to get away from our parents. Not that the trees communicate anything except perhaps acceptance. Most of the Fay have an exceptional few, who go back to their element at the end, and sometimes Sylphs and Water Fay do this in the Groves as well, so that the trees might breath them in, or drink them up with their roots. No one has ever desecrated a grove the way the exiled prince has our grove. It was eight hundred years old." There was a deep sadness in Nimue's voice as she spoke.

"Do the Fay live a very long time?"

"Long enough. As long as the Humans, maybe a little longer."

"Oh. I just wondered. There are stories in the other world." Rhiannon paused then blurted, "I wish I hadn't asked about the grove. I didn't need another reason to feel sad."

"Do not feel sad. Let us be happy together." Nimue turned and hugged Rhiannon so that the dim hall outside their father's rooms was filled with coloured lights. And then she reached out and turned the handle.

* * *

They sat with Lugh, quietly, by the fire. He smiled wistfully and listened to Rhiannon and Nimue talk softly about their childhoods. Rhiannon could see that he had been crying. He was *so* young to have been through so much, and she wondered what it had cost him to let go of her mother—of Sulamith—after they had been found out. She knew how she would feel if she were expected to let go of Rowan, knowing that any attempt to stay with him would result in his death or the death of her child. It was all too easy to put herself in the shoes that her biological parents had walked in. It was impossible to assign any blame. It was difficult for both herself and Lugh to maintain eye contact for long, but she could sense that while it was painful to him when she looked his way, that he found it comforting to watch her, and listen to her voice, so she sat next to Nimue on a low bench by the warm fire so that he could sit and watch her and, maybe, ease his losses, if only for a while.

* * *

It was a relief, after she had said goodnight to her father, to be behind closed doors with Rowan. She removed her jewellery as he helped her undo the forty five buttons on the back of the dress and then she pulled on the blue night gown and hung the dress in the large carved wardrobe. Throughout the course of the day at least nine new perfect dresses had been hung there and while at one point in her life owning dresses that looked like they had been spun by magical silkworms would have been an enchanting concept, now it only made Rhiannon feel more pressure. She flopped down on the bed with a hair brush in her hand realizing how good it felt to slouch after maintaining a state of extreme poise. The circlet, that she had worn on her brow all day, hadn't let her forget to hold her head high and walk smoothly. Rhiannon wasn't clumsy. She wasn't the sort to stumble and trip, but it was another thing altogether to maintain a flawless grace, which apparently she had if she was to believe all of the whispered thoughts that she had heard as she had entered the dining hall that evening. But now she just wanted to be herself and she slouched gratefully and sat there doing nothing and holding her brush. "Here. Give me that," Rowan said, sitting cross-legged on the bed behind her and taking the brush from her hand.

"I don't think that I've ever felt so drained in my life. Carting cabbages all day is less exhausting than this. I'm not used to this. I don't like being the focus of everything that's being said and thought."

"You did fine," Rowan said, running the brush rhythmically down the length of her hair. "Actually, I think that perhaps you may have done more than just turn the council in your favour, I think that you may have made them love you." He ran the brush through her hair a few more times then rose and put the brush on the dresser top.

Rhiannon pulled herself into bed and Rowan grinned at her as he got in next to her, "I was so proud of you today when you put all of those old Fairies in their places. You were every bit a queen and they could all see it."

She smiled softly, "I don't know where that came from. They were being ridiculous and I wanted them to shut up and accept the situation. It isn't only about me, and I thought that if I could make them see that they're the same as me, that it might work."

"It did work," Rowan answered but then changed the subject abruptly and smiled. "But lets not think about all that.

Lets be selfish, if only for a little while, and think only of us."

"Alright. I can handle that," she smiled back, and they whispered sweet nothings in the other's ear until the rest of the world ceased to exist, and when they lay together dropping off to sleep, she asked Rowan, "Next year, at the end of summer, will you take me home for the harvest?"

They both knew that this wasn't something that he could promise her, and he didn't try to. He could be dead next year, they both could be, but it was the intention that mattered, and it mattered to both of them. They held on to one another in the dark and he whispered, "There's nothing in all the worlds that I want more." And then they slept.

Chapter 16

Rowan was shaking her shoulder gently and saying her name but Rhiannon didn't want to wake up. She was too tired. "Come Love. You have to wake up," he said to her. "I let you sleep through breakfast. You need to dress quickly and eat."

"Okay, Okay," Rhiannon mumbled struggling towards wakefulness. "I'm just so tired. I didn't think that I would start feeling it so soon."

"You've been through a lot, and you drained yourself badly when you healed me. I'm sure that those must be contributing factors. And ... Maybe we should have waited." He had a slightly guilty look on his face but also a tender smile that told her that even if he thought that it may have been prudent to wait, that he wouldn't have wanted to.

"I know that you don't mean that," she smiled.

"No, I don't. I'm glad of everything that I have with you. I'm glad of everything that we get to experience together, good timing or not. I would rather love you and know you fully, even if the future is uncertain, than hold back out of fear or prudence, no matter what anyone else thinks. I've spent a good portion of my life being responsible for others and always keeping my head. I don't want to keep my head around you, although I'm learning to strike a balance." He smiled and she smiled back. "Come on," he said taking her hands and pulling her up. "There is hot water for you to wash up and there's breakfast in the sitting room. The council meeting shouldn't be so exhausting today. We'll have lunch on time and maybe you can rest for a while this afternoon."

She nodded and swung her legs down over the edge of the bed so that the tips of her toes just touched the floor. She slid off and headed for the bathroom. Once she was dressed, this time in a pale silk embroidered dress in the softest shade of whispering dawn, simultaneously rich, glowing and ethereal with a scooping neckline and sleeves that fluttered, she sat at the little table in the sitting room and ate jam and biscuits with hazelnut butter and drank fresh milk while Rowan caught her up on the events of that morning. The council had reconvened late the night before and had unanimously agreed to support a revolution. They had also met for a brief pre-breakfast talk and had the day's agenda outlined. The Fay, it seemed, acted decisively once they had their minds made up. Rowan, who was in uniform this morning, had met with his men and they were ready to do what they had to. All that was left was to meet with the Fay council.

Rhiannon felt like a fallen leaf trapped in a rushing current headed for a cliff. Helpless. Useless. Impotent. She struggled against the feeling like one would struggle against well tied bindings while lying on the tracks of an onrushing train. Uselessly. But Rowan was looking at her and talking so she tried to focus on what he was saying, "I *know* that you know it has to be this way. I know that you know ... that if we're going to make this country over anew that I'll have to maintain my position as Captain. I can't step down just when all of this change is afoot, especially because of *us*. It would be seen as cowardice and the truth is that I don't trust anyone else to be able to do what I've been able to accomplish with my Fay abilities and connections. If the Fay and Human armies are fighting together ... I know that I don't need to say it. I'm like you. I'm from both worlds. It has to be this way. But if we can unite this kingdom, then I can win this war for you."

The train hit. Rhiannon closed her eyes tightly and squeezed her lips together until the storm passed and she could speak without bursting into tears, "I know my love. I know. You don't need to tell me." And he didn't need to, but it was said none the less.

When Rhiannon and Rowan arrived at the council hall everyone was already assembled, including Rowan's men. When Rhiannon walked in they all stood. Each of the thirteen Council members that represented each of the thirteen strongholds rose and waited for her to be seated. It was going to take her a long time to get used to this kind of thing. She lowered herself to her chair and her heart pounded and her hands were sweating. She didn't want to be there. She wished for home. For Fenna. For Rowan to be there with her. But she wasn't at home. Or was she? Everyone was looking at her. She took a deep breath and then addressed the room in general. "Good morning," she said, unable to think of anything better to say and unsure of what the protocol was.

"Good morning it is." It came from Stone Keeper who forged ahead without ceremony, "Before we get down to the business of where our allegiance lies, we would like to ask you where, exactly, does your allegiance lie?" The question was of course directed at Rhiannon.

She looked around the room, at the people seated around the table with their eyes trained expectantly on her. She had been expecting that someone, at some point, would ask her this and she was glad that she had her answer ready. "That is not a clear cut question, so I won't give you a clear cut answer," she realized, as she spoke, that this was a very Fay thing to say. "As the heir to the Fay throne my allegiance is to my father Lugh. As the rightful Queen of the Human realm my *responsibility* is to my people. However, as the future

Queen of a united Nova Britannia, I believe that it will be imperative to create a land where *everyone* can live lives of peace, dignity, and relative freedom. You must understand though, that this is something that I have never had, even in the relative obscurity of the other world. I will never know it unless we succeed, but I believe that it is a worthwhile cause."

She'd said it quietly and very seriously so that they had to lean forward and pay attention to each word. They weren't elegant words but Rhiannon knew that they were the right words and she watched as Stone Keeper looked around at the other council members who were nodding their approval. The old Fairy smiled. "This is an answer that pleases us. We have little choice in the matter but before we swore our allegiance to you we wanted, at the very least, to hear what you would say." Stone Keeper rose and bowed to Rhiannon, "You have our support."

Rhiannon inclined her head to the council, "Thank you." Again, not elegant words. Nothing profuse or flowery. Simple words, but she meant them, and they could tell.

It was Lugh who spoke up at this point, "The truth is that we have little choice." He looked at Rhiannon, "Our hand has been forced and your appearance at this time is fortuitous. The desecration of our grove was an act of war on the part of the exiled prince and we cannot ignore it or the fact that he was attempting to create conflict between ourselves and King Liam. It would be folly to alienate an ally, and at this point it is in our favour to have a strong united Nova Britannia. If we do not unite and make a stand there is a good chance that Seamus will win the war and if he does he will drive us out of our homes and kill us while we flee. He has an army massing on the northern border that outnumbers our own fighting force. But we have maintained a position of political neutrality for long enough."

"The council agrees. What do you propose we do?" Rhiannon found herself put on the spot. Stone Keeper had directed the question to her which annoyed Rhiannon, as they all knew that she had been in this world only a matter of weeks and in the stronghold only a matter of days. Not only that but Lugh was *still* king. She suspected that this was, again, an attempt to sound her out. A test. "As you all know I was not raised in this world and I do not, as of yet, understand its subtleties. But my husband was born here. He has spent half of his life in the human court and seems to have the respect of this one as well. Years of his life have been devoted to fighting the exiled prince. He is already the Captain of the King's army. If anyone is competent to lead a victory against my uncle," she swallowed the thick feeling in her throat, "it is him."

Rhiannon felt like she was handing Rowan a bomb. She knew that this was the only choice. She knew that even if she hadn't been Sulamith's lost child, and he could have left her behind at his family home without her presence there putting the rest of his family in danger—for she realized now that had been what he'd meant when he said that he had reservations about leaving her there—that Rowan would still have ridden away from her at the head of the army. But somehow, now, being all tangled up in it made it all feel that much worse. But Rowan was expecting the job, and even before their short horrible conversation that morning, she had realized that to keep the military in line, to avoid the possibility of a coup, they didn't have a choice. She turned to him. "My love," she whispered as softly as she could, really just mouthing the words.

He nodded. "I know," he whispered back, then looked down for the briefest moment.

The green man with the slim antlers and the strange eyes, Fern was his name, addressed Rowan. "I suppose the question is then, do you have a plan?"

Rowan stood and smiled and Rhiannon understood that even though he was in some ways a reluctant hero, he was, none the less, in his element. "Liam would step down from the throne in favour of Rhiannon without hesitation, of this I am certain. He loved his mother and he would respect Sulamith's wishes in this. The trick will be to show the people that Rhiannon has the support that she needs to keep them safe, to avoid a revolt, and to secure the castle against Seamus' supporters."

"And how do you propose to accomplish this?" Fern asked dubiously.

"With a little espionage, an army of 2000 Fay knights, and the Angels."

"Angels?" The word was spoken around the room with incredulity, doubt, and confusion.

Stone Keeper raised her eyebrows, smiled, and rolled her stone from hand to hand, "I think that we are intrigued. You had better explain."

Rowan nodded. "Willingly," he said, and then began, "As many of you know my grandmother is the head of the human council and that, when combined with my own position, means that I have a certain amount of support at court. What I propose to do is send Thaylum, Cole, and Brian back to the King's City along with Gwydion and Nessa who will remain in hiding. They will ensure that the castle is secure in time for my return. No accurate information will make it to Seamus during this period, Gwydion's spies will see to it, and the people who would support Seamus rather than a half Fay Queen will be removed through," he paused, "various methods. My men understand what needs to be done and they know who they can trust. They will have seven days but the task is far from impossible. In seven days' time Rhiannon and I will ride to the King's City with the aforementioned two thousand fay knights. Lugh has assured me that it can be arranged, and this is where the Angels come in." He paused and looked around the room for a moment, making sure that everyone was with him before continuing, "We don't want this to look like a Fay take-over, so we need something more, something to awe the people of the city with and to show the council that a united kingdom is our best hope at accomplishing peace, and I know that arriving in the city with Sulamith's lost child *and* the Angels will send this message."

"How will you find the Angels and convince them?" Lugh asked. "It has been years since anybody has seen them."

Rowan turned to Gwydion, "I think that you had better explain this part."

Gwydion sat quietly for a moment before beginning. "According to the knowledge of the Druids, the angels retreated into the mountains just after the plague wars. Many of our people had already left the old country by the time this happened, but a small group of Druids stayed behind for a time. The information that they brought with them when they arrived here was incomplete, but the implication was that the angels retreated because they thought that Humanity would be better off without them. They felt that they had misused their power and that what they had done to stop the plague wars had brought shame upon them. But, apparently, long before the plague wars they lived amongst us peacefully. They had been gradually withdrawing for some time but we don't know why. Many years ago, I met an angel and tried to question him about it. He became very angry with me and all he said was that if we ever found out why they had left us, that we would hate them forever, then he flew away. But something tells me that they might be willing to help us now." Gwydion reached down and brought a piece of cloth up to the table. He unfolded the cloth. Inside were three feathers, each longer than Rhiannon's arm, all variegated crimson and gold. "I found this one outside of my cottage," he lifted one of the feathers, "just after Rhiannon had left for the stronghold. I found this one outside of her bedroom here, and I found this third feather outside of the council hall yesterday afternoon." Gwydion's eyes twinkled. "Ladies and Gentlemen. I think our Queen has a guardian angel."

Chapter 17

Silence ensued. Rhiannon hadn't been aware of any angels watching over her at any point in her life and the sight of the huge brilliant feathers had been as much a shock to her as anyone else in the hall. They adjourned the meeting for lunch and after they had eaten Rhiannon went to rest. She didn't sleep per se, but she lay still for an hour and forced her mind to shut down.

At first when she had lay down in the dim quiet room the reality of her life tried to swallow her whole. She didn't want to be a monarch. She wasn't cut out for it. The idea of being at the centre of something so big and having no choice in it, no say, no option but to push through even if she lost who she was, even if it would destroy what made her the person she was ... ? "No!" she cried out loud, curled protectively around her middle, and instead thought of Rowan, and the fact that he would always love who she had been, and she thought of their own private act of rebellion, for that, she realized, is what it had been. It had been their choice. Theirs. No one else's. Theirs ... and only theirs. At the end of the day she still had this. At the end of the day there would still be love. So she focused on that until the only thing she was aware of was her breath and her heartbeat and she lay there, not moving, not thinking, and after a time there was a soft knock at the door. "Come in," she called sitting up slowly and swinging her feet over the edge of the bed. It was her grandmother, Morgana.

Morgana smiled. "Are you feeling better?"

Rhiannon returned the smile halfheartedly, "I can pretend that I am." She didn't feel like lying just at that moment.

"Do you feel up to a walk in the woods?"

Rhiannon nodded. "Yes, that might help." She stood and walked to the wardrobe to see if there was something more functional to wear than a silk dress. She pulled out a purple wool skirt, an undyed linen blouse, and a short, light, magenta, felted wool coat with a peplum that was nipped in at the waist and had a very flattering fit. She hung the yellow dress, feeling relief that at least she didn't have to get used to servants helping her dress, and quickly pulled on the more practical clothing along with a pair of dainty, soft, brown leather shoes. She did up the single button on the front of the coat so that it showed off her tiny waist. She knew what the aunts would say about that, but a quick glance in the mirror had her feeling more like herself, free of the circlet, in clothes that were okay to get dirty. She walked out into the sitting room. Nimue was there as well and together the three of them struck out through a rear door and into the forest.

"I decided that it was high time that someone show you how to use your magic properly. Especially now that you're pregnant," Morgana paused, nimbly navigating the stepping stones across a small stream. "I know that there are very pressing matters afoot, but none of that does anyone any good if you're put in a position of having to use your magic and you hurt yourself again." Morgana brought them to a quiet mossy spot next to the brook and had them sit. "Now I know that we always speak of the magic as if it's ours and we do, each of us, have our own spark of it, even the humans, but we do not really posses the magic we use, in fact you cannot posses it. The only thing we posses is ability. Some of us more, some of us less. You have more," she looked at Rhiannon, "and you have a good instinct for it as well, but you need to learn how to let it flow." Morgana paused, "Now close your eyes and think of reaching deep."

Rhiannon didn't have to reach far. She could already feel the forest all around her, like a green aurora, floating and cascading. "I can feel it," she said out loud.

"Can you feel the stream?" Morgana asked.

Rhiannon searched and felt it, cool and soothing like a caress. "Yes," she answered.

"Now look inside yourself for the life force of your child. It won't be big but it will be bright."

Rhiannon didn't have to look for it. She didn't need to be told what to look for. She could feel it all the time. She nodded.

"Now look for your own life force," Morgana told her.

Surprisingly, it was much harder for her to isolate her own life force. It took a few minutes, but eventually she realized that the opalescent nimbus that was playing and dancing amongst everything else, was her. She drew it all in until it was a crystalline shimmer within herself then said, "Okay."

Morgana took her hand and suddenly there was a grass coloured, effervescent sparkle there. Nimue took her other hand and there was another sparkle, this one blue and gold, autumn leaves on a lake. "Now you have to hold on to your own life force, and that of your child, or they will flow out of you. Nimue and I will help you hold on so that you will know what that feels like. Now relax and let the energy of the forest flow through you. Don't let it build up or try to hold onto it, that will hurt you. You can't contain it you can only allow it."

Rhiannon tried to do as she was told, understanding now, simply by feel, what had gone wrong when she had crossed between the worlds and healed Rowan, and why she had passed out. She held on tightly to her life force and to the little light deep inside her and let the beautiful green light of the forest flow through her.

"You're holding on tightly enough. Nimue and I are going to let go."

And suddenly she was doing it on her own and it had the same feeling to it as when she was five and her dad let go of her bicycle seat. She could feel all of the life and the magic of the forest flowing through her. This was what she had been unknowingly yearning for five years ago when she had started planting flowers in her yard. She let the flow of energy slow then stop and opened her eyes. It was October but all around them wood violets had bloomed and released their scent. Rhiannon smiled, amazed, feeling as if a missing part of her had returned, and the broken part of her had healed.

"That's better, isn't it?" Nimue smiled.

"Much better," Rhiannon agreed.

"Let us walk a little." Morgana said, leading them off deeper into the woods and marvelling at the carpet of violets underfoot. They strolled quietly for a while. Rhiannon watched Morgana and Nimue, their small stature and cobalt eyes making her feel very much related to them. It didn't take long for questions to begin surfacing in her mind. Questions about the things that had been happening to her that she didn't understand because she had been raised by humans. Like her pregnancy. She remembered when she was almost fifteen, she had been listening to the girls at school complain for a few years before it had happened to her, and she had gotten her period. Her mother had talked to her quite a bit about it. It made sense to Rhiannon now, why Fionnuala would have had such an intimate relationship with her cycle. She had come from a world with no birth control. If you wanted to avoid a pregnancy, you had to know your body well. When you were fertile. When you weren't. No rolling on a condom or popping a pill. She remembered her mother telling her, "When you're wet and restless and you think about boys all the time, that is when you can get pregnant. But after when the texture of the wetness changes you are no longer fertile." Fionnuala had used the proper biological names for the phases of a cycle. Looked everything up and explained it all in a detail far greater than what Rhiannon had gotten even from sex-ed in school. But Fionnuala had also said with the utmost serious-ness, "Learn your body and your cycle, but save this way of doing things for when you are with someone you love and trust. A husband, or someone you plan on staying with for the rest of your life. The idea of you getting sick with something terrifies me. I know that you are not the type of girl to have indiscriminate sex but still, in the beginning, until you are both tested always use a condom. Do you understand Krista-bell? Save the way I taught you for someone who you love enough to have a child with."

She had nodded at her mother with big eyes, but had said, "Mum no one is going to love me that much, boys don't like me. I'm strange." Rhiannon would never forget the look her mother had given her at that moment. It was like a photo-graph in her mind. Fionnuala had been exquisitely pretty. Strawberry blond curls that she had piled haphazardly on top of her head, ultra fair skin with just enough freckles to be adorable, and pale green eyes surrounded by her pale straw-berry blond eyelashes. She was built, and carried herself, like a ballet dancer. Her neck and shoulders were delicate, elegant and so refined. Everybody liked her mother. She had made a killing in tips as a bartender. But that afternoon sitting with Kristabell on her bed in the big pile of pillows together, her mother had looked ... so sad. She had almost cried. "Oh sweet-heart. Oh my love. Don't say that. It's not true. It's just that when someone loves you it will be genuine, not a passing fancy. They will never love you for the wrong reasons."

Rhiannon looked back and saw what had been a very normal teenaged moment, but the memory had caught her unaware and the sudden desire to have Fionnuala by her brought on a torrent of tears. Morgana and Nimue took her hands quietly and the three of them walked between the towering trees in the cool autumn air until the tears stopped and Rhiannon finally said. "I have an instinct for what I am without an understanding. Now that I know what I am, some things are obvious, but others ...? I want to make sure that I'm not making assumptions. I don't want to make mistakes, but things keep happening to me and I can't quite make sense of them because I wasn't raised to it." She hesitated a moment, "Like getting pregnant the other night. If I were a normal human that wouldn't have happened. My cycle is like clock-work, like the moon, dependable. I was expecting my period in a few days. I shouldn't have been able to get pregnant that night but I know that I willed it to happen. In hindsight I know exactly how I opened myself to the possibilities and made myself fertile, because deep down inside I *wanted* it to happen, but I had no idea that I could do that, or that I *was* doing it until it had happened and the next thing I know I'm having this incredible dream, and that isn't something I'd expected either, and I'm guessing that it's because I'm Fay, because my mother told me all kinds of interesting things about getting pregnant, and *not* getting pregnant, but she didn't mention anything about beautiful dreams or getting pregnant any old time just because on some not quite un-conscious level I'm longing to have life inside me. I'm not crazy or making assumptions right? It's a Fairy thing isn't it?" she was near tears again.

Morgana smiled, not unkindly. "It is, 'A fairy thing.' As you put it. It is related to our ability to interact with the natural world instead of simply being affected by it. We are not governed as closely by its laws. We are a part of them. We can bend the rules. Some of us, like you, can break them."

"So you're saying that it's not black and white or night and day. There is no rule that says all Fairy women can do this."

"There is no rule. The truth is that rules and laws make most of us itch just a little, but as you apparently pointed out yesterday, we do have a certain amount of human blood flowing through our veins."

"Was that only yesterday?" Rhiannon murmured to herself.

"Time is a strange thing is it not?" Morgana didn't expect an answer.

Rhiannon nodded absently.

"The truth is, I suspect, that even the most Human of women have some connection and interaction with the natural world but they are not, however, raised exploring it in the same way. Unpredictability, chaos, and anarchy have always been qualities inherent in the Fay, along with our predilection for the natural world, and as such I'm afraid that you will have to find your place in it, on your own. There is only so much that I can teach you. I can't tell you what you can and cannot do. I have a suspicion that you have been using your magic in small ways for some time, and that you are realizing this. Now that you know how to hold on and let only the magic flow, practice, *carefully*. I'm sure you've figured out that if you don't hold on tightly, you will risk your life or your child. It was prudent of you to wait until you were here, and safe, to conceive. I will admit that I am curious as to what made you wait?"

"Just an instinctive fear that somehow, because I didn't understand what was happening to me, that getting pregnant could be bad."

Morgana looked at her very seriously, "It's a good thing that you listened to that instinct. If you had been pregnant when you healed Rowan in the forest you would have died. Enough of your energy would have been tied up that there wouldn t have been any left to have sustained you until Lugh arrived."

Rhiannon nodded, feeling pulled down by the gravity of what Morgana had just told her as much as she had been buoyed up by the feeling of coming into her own only minutes earlier.

They continued walking. Nimue would look at her periodically and smile tentatively as they passed by trees like skyscrapers and ferns almost as tall as they were. Green and gold. The smell of leaves dying and decaying. An ending. Rhiannon watched Nimue whose face was so similar to her own. Nimue's face was perhaps slightly more heart shaped with less definition to her cheekbones. Her lips too were more bee stung and her eyes rounder, more soulful, less mischievously solemn than Rhiannon's, but their noses, chins and foreheads were almost identical, and just like Morgana's. Her sister. Different mothers or not, they were still connected. As if sensing Rhiannon's train of thought, or perhaps more than sensing it, Nimue took her hand and for the sake of saying something Rhiannon asked, "Why is this called a stronghold?"

"Here I'll show you," Nimue said leading them a short way further into the trees. Then she held up her hands. "Can you feel this?"

Rhiannon held up her hands and felt a strange, sticky electric feeling in the air. Nimue took her hand and pulled her through. When they turned around Morgana had disappeared along with all traces of the Fairy settlement. They stepped back through and Morgana reappeared. "Humans and Elves can't pass through it. They are simply deflected. They never even notice it happening to them they simply wander off. When we found you the other night you were just over there." Nimue pointed to a spot a few metres away. "Rowan was too sick to get you any further but he knows about the barrier and is able to pass through."

"How do we keep it running?"

"In shifts. Three people at a time. We always have it up."

They stood then, looking around the forest. It was pristine. Rhiannon reminded herself again of what would be on the other side, in the other world—houses, streets, cars—then looked again at the giant pillar-like trees and the mossy ground. There were huckleberry bushes with bright yellow leaves that glowed in the places where the sun actually reached the forest floor. She looked up at the sun's rays slanting in through the trees and shut her eyes, held on to what was important, and let the magic flow for a moment then gently brought it to a stop. She opened her eyes still looking up and simply drank in the beauty of the forest, when something caught her eye. A flashing fluttering bit of colour drifting down to them. Rhiannon held out her hand and a small, downy, soft, crimson and gold feather came to rest there. The three women looked up. Rhiannon couldn't see anything but she could sense that someone was up there high in the trees, and she didn't think that it was all in her head. "Hello?" she called out. "I know you're up there." Then, "Are you molting?"

A stifled snort of laughter came from high above. Morgana raised her eyebrows and Nimue clapped her hand over her mouth.

"Why don't you just come down?" Rhiannon called up to the trees.

There was a rustling high in the branches then with great speed a gold and crimson streak flew towards them. Rhiannon didn't have time to be frightened. He was crashing to earth in front of them then straightening up before she'd even had time to blink. He wasn't entirely what she'd expected. The angel was nearly seven feet tall with enormous crimson and gold wings. He had golden hair and eyes and he was stunningly beautiful with perfect skin and a dazzling smile. He carried a long sword, beautifully worked and deadly. All of this she *had* expected, but she was taken aback by the blue jeans, the tailored black leather vest that left his muscular arms bare, and the black and white Puma trainers.

Chapter 18

"Hello," she said to the angel. "My name is Rhiannon."

"Yeah! I know!" he said, as if he found the fact that he knew amazing.

He reminded Rhiannon of a celestial Keanu Reeves. Only Keanu Reeves from Parenthood or Bill and Ted's Excellent Adventure. Thankfully it didn't last and the angel pulled himself together ... a little.

"My name is Raphael, and no, I'm not molting. I just have a bit of eczema." He scratched at a wing.

This is weird, Rhiannon thought to herself for the first time since all of this had started, then asked the angel, "So, how long have you been watching me?"

He smiled at her again. "I took over about four years ago. My mother was doing it before me. I used to sit in the willow tree outside your bedroom window when you were still living in the other world. I've had a hard time keeping up with you over the last six weeks. I lost your trail a few times. I'd have felt awful if anything had happened to you." The last words few words were spoken more seriously.

Rhiannon was still caught on the fact that he had been sitting in the tree outside her bedroom window for four years. It wasn't as if she had ever closed her blinds. There was a giant tree outside her window, in theory blocking it from view. She thought of all of the things that she had done in that room that hadn't been meant for anyone else to see. Not just changing her clothes or looking at herself in the mirror undressed. There was more than just sitting on her bed naked, brushing out her hair. There were things that any lonely teen-aged girl might do in her room when she thought she was alone. She knew she was red and she felt all sweaty. "You've been sitting outside my *window*?!" she asked in alarm.

His response was even more alarming, "Yeah! But don't feel embarrassed, I didn't mind." He winked at her.

"They say angels don't have genitalia in the other world," Rhiannon mumbled.

Raphael grinned, "Oh, we have genitalia. Believe me. I'd know."

Rhiannon looked at Nimue, "Great. I've had a teenaged angel jerking off outside my bedroom window for the last four years."

The angel was still smiling, "Like I said. Don't feel embarrassed. I didn't mind."

Even Nimue was doubled over, red faced, and laughing hysterically.

The angel continued, "The truth is that I've been trying to work up the courage to talk to you for years. I guess ... I've lost my chance." His face was suddenly soft, wistful, sad, and in a glance, in one alarming look, Rhiannon knew that the angel was in love with her.

The three women stood there and looked up at Raphael. To an onlooker they would have seemed tiny next to the massive angel. Morgana cleared her throat, "If you don't mind sharing with us, how exactly did Rhiannon come to have a ... Guardian Angel?"

"That's a long story," Raphael said, suddenly serious. "I'll tell you if you have the time?"

Morgana looked up at the sky. "It is nearly time for dinner. Would you object to dining with us and telling all of us your story over the evening meal? I assure you, you would be perfectly safe with us, and very welcome."

Raphael glanced questioningly at Rhiannon as if for re-assurance.

"You would be very welcome, and honestly, right now, we need you. Your presence would honour us." She smiled at him, though it was difficult for her, and he seemed to relax and make up his mind.

"Alright, then I'll come."

***

Dinner was an interesting event that night with more Fairies staring at them in the dinning hall than ever, but this time Rhiannon couldn't blame them. Raphael was something to behold. Gwydion's reaction to him was that of pure academic bliss. Lugh stared at first in rapt admiration. Rhiannon had a hard time gauging Rowan's reaction to the angel, but she thought she caught a hint of jealousy. *It would take an angel to make Rowan jealous,* she thought to herself. Over the meal they told Raphael of their plan. He was aware of much of it. He had watched the council meeting through the skylight and had been able to hear most of what was said.

"So what do you think?" It was Rowan who had asked, "Do we stand a chance? Do you think that the Angels will help us?"

"I for one am more than willing to join you. There is a certain amount of discontent amongst the younger Angels and I think that you might well convince some of them, al-though I suspect that the older ones will stay in the moun-tains. On the whole I think that the plan could work and I'll lead you to our city. It may not be easy once we are there, but I think it would be worth trying."

Rhiannon had for the most part left the logistical aspects of planning up to Rowan. It was what he did after all, and he was efficient and competent, but sometimes it made her feel guilty, as though she wasn't pulling her weight.

"We plan on leaving the day after tomorrow. How long do you think it will take us to get there if we take horses?" Rowan asked Raphael.

"I injured a wing a few years ago and had to walk up the mountain. It took me three days to make it home but I'm not used to walking long distances. With horses and strong legs, I'd say two days.'

Rowan nodded. Rhiannon could see his mind working, fitting information into its proper place. They were finished eating and tea was being poured when finally Lugh asked, "Please do tell us now though, how did you come to be protecting my daughter?"

"Certainly," Raphael agreed, carefully looking behind him and stretching his wings. "Actually, it started before either of us was born." He looked at Rhiannon. "You and I are the same age. I'm just a few months older than you. When my mother was pregnant with me she would feel restless at night so she would go flying. She loved to fly over the King's City at night and fly around the towers of the castle. You have to understand that this was forbidden, but my mother has always been a bit of a rebel.

"One night as she flew past she could hear crying so she landed on the roof of the tower. She was just curious but we all know where curiosity can lead. Anyway, if it's forbidden to fly over the city then actually talking to a Human is absolutely out of the question, but talk to Sulamith she did. My mother and Sulamith had a lot in common. They were the same age, they were both expecting their first child and they were both rebels. They became friends and when it came time for Sulamith to be taken to the other world my mother followed her and told her that she would watch over you and bring news of you. For many years my mother lived something of a double life. She flew to the other world a few times a week always careful to make sure she wasn't seen, then went to Sulamith and told her about you. When I was nine I started going with her on these trips. I remember being fascinated by you and the few times I met Sulamith before she died had an impact on me. She was beautiful and so sad. She might not have known you, but she loved you, and seeing how happy it made her to hear about you made me believe that there was no reason for us to isolate ourselves. Humans might not be perfect, but they are capable of so much love. More, it seems to me, than the angels." He continued to tell the story, continuing to address Rhiannon. "When I turned fourteen and I received my sword it became apparent that you needed more than the occasional check. There was one month just after Sulamith died when we killed three elves in your back yard so my mother and I took turns watching over your house almost constantly. Things got a bit better after you grew your garden. Did you know that it was magic?" Raphael asked Rhiannon.

"Not at the time, no."

"Oh, well. Once it was going full bloom, the elves couldn't get near the house and things got easier. I took over so that my mother could rest, not that she could ever let it go al-together. In some ways she loves you like her own." He paused and blinked rapidly a few times. "Things had been quiet over the last couple of years but two months ago I noticed a small group of men and an elf casing the house so I stepped up my watch. The night you disappeared was terrible. I didn't know what to do. You hadn't come back from your walk but I couldn't risk flying in broad daylight so I had to wait until it was dark to go looking for you. I searched for hours, so when I couldn't find you in the woods, where I was sure you had gone, I headed back to your house. When I got back it was already engulfed in flames. I went into the house to try to find you. You weren't in your room. I tried to get to your parents but the fire was too hot. I felt that I had failed you." Rhiannon looked at the angel who now had tears falling down his face. She passed him her napkin which had gone unused through the meal. "Thank you," he said, taking it. "I went back to the woods to look for you. When the sun rose I found a few of your hairs and I could feel a residue of magic so, on a hunch I crossed over and I found more of your hair along with a dead elf, and then I lost your trail. It took me weeks to track you down and I found you the night of the harvest dinner at Fiannasmere. I tailed you when you left two days later and even managed to cross over and follow you through East Vancouver in broad daylight. I got a couple comments on the wings, but its not a bad part of the city for a guy like me. I killed an elf in the back yard of your friend Sheila's place but I lost your trail again the next morning when you went downtown. I waited for you to come back but I had to hide from the police and I missed you, so I waited for your friend to come home and I asked her where you had gone."

"What did she say?" Rhiannon asked.

"She was quite funny actually. She invited me in for dinner and made some cryptic comment about people called Lancelot? And, Beowulf I think? And then she said 'Why not Angels too?' We talked a bit. After nine years of watching you I can speak the language of your city fairly well. She told me that you had gone back to this world. She said to say, 'Thanks' for her, if I found you, and that night I flew down to the lake, crossed over and found you just as the Fairies did. I think the rest is obvious."

"Thank you," Rhiannon said to the Angel. "You've saved my life several times over and I have nothing that I can give you that would come close to repaying you for all that you've done."

Rhiannon didn't want to look into Raphael's face. She didn't want to deal with what she knew she would see there, but she felt that she owed it to him. She looked up into his eyes, unable to keep the sadness out of her own, and felt the hurt in the angel's eyes. Regret. Love. Loss. There because of her.

He held her gaze and said softly, "I've never expected repayment."

Rhiannon nodded then rose to leave. She couldn't stay there, not with everyone watching. Not for another moment. "Please excuse me. I suspect that tomorrow will be another exhausting day, and I am tired. Goodnight." She left the dinning hall and walked quickly back to her rooms.

* * *

She had been dressed for dinner in the yellow silk dress, complete with circlet and sapphire and pearl necklace. Once she was in her bedroom she removed the jewels and unlaced the dress, no buttons, and hung it in the wardrobe. That was as far as she got. She walked to the bed and curled up on her side. It was confusing and uncomfortable and hurtful to know that for years someone had been sitting outside her window loving her. But Raphael had never acted. It made the sting that Evan had left behind burn in a way that it hadn't in months. She cried, wishing that she could get the image of her mother's face out of her head. Wishing that Rowan would come and hold her and remind her that there was beauty without sadness in the world, and let her talk to him about this so that it wouldn't feel so much like it was crushing her. It wasn't purely Raphael's appearance that had brought this on. He was simply the straw that had broken the camel's back. He was one more person looking at her with sad eyes. It was one more sad story that ended with her, and she wished that she could undo it all. Then Rowan was there and his warm arms went around her. He kissed her head and brushed her tears and her hair out of her face. He held her tightly until she stopped crying, even though it took her a long time. If he hadn't been there she would have cried herself to sleep. After she stopped he didn't say anything. Just covered her cold skin with a blanket and held her a while longer. Rhiannon looked into his eyes after a time, and saw only love. She smiled and ran her fingers over his forehead.

He smiled back, a little ruefully, and said to her, "I don't envy your Angel."

"*My* Angel?" She said, eyebrows raised.

"Oh he's your Angel alright and I'm not sure how I feel about that, but I don't envy him."

"And why is that?" Rhiannon asked.

"Because he's loved you for years and he's lost his chance with you. I wouldn't be him for all the worlds."

Rhiannon sighed. "It makes me uncomfortable and heart-sore. He wears his feelings so openly. I'm not sure what to think. I wasn't sure if we could talk about this."

Rowan's mouth quirked, "Honestly ... If I'm telling you the absolute truth, for the first five minutes all kinds of imma-ture, hotheaded things flew through my mind but ..." he paused for emphasis, "I like to think of myself as a reasonable person, and reasonable people think things through. By the end of dinner I just felt sad, maybe a little guilty, and quite sure that we're doing the right thing."

"Why guilty?" she asked in a gentle tone.

It was Rowan's turn to sigh, "Because he was there first. He was devoted to you, he protected you and he lost track of you for a few short weeks, and I stepped in and took his place. For half of his life he's been thinking about you and hoping, and now, just like that, you're out of his grasp."

"But Rowan," she paused for words, "He's had his chance. He's seen *so* much of me over the last four years that it's embarrassing. In fact I think he may have permanently disabled my ability to blush. But he's also seen me cry. He's seen me lonely, and in desperate need of a friend, and he sat outside my bedroom window and *did nothing*. He had his chance, and I love *you*."

They were sitting now, cross-legged on the bed, face to face in the light of the candles Rowan had lit when he came in. He put his hands on her cheeks, leaned forward and kissed her. "I know," he said. "And so does he. And I can see how his lack of action would make you feel hurt, but I can't help seeing it from his perspective. He probably sat outside your window and cried *with* you. It's what makes me certain that we're doing the right thing by going to the Angels. If he hadn't been fighting hundreds of years of conditioning, do you think that he would have hesitated?"

"No," she admitted softly.

Rowan continued, his voice growing passionate, "If we succeed in bringing the Fairies, the Angels, and the Humans together, then in some ways it makes all of the sadness that everybody has had to bear for so many years just a little less unbearable. Suddenly there's a point, beyond mere survival, to all of this."

Rhiannon nodded and they sat quietly, not needing to speak for a few minutes, when one of those questions that surfaced periodically in Rhiannon's mind, always at the wrong time, came up for air. It wasn't a great time for the question but it would have to do. "Rowan? Why didn't *you* show me how to use my magic?"

She trusted him and she knew that he would have a good reason, but his track record for sharing information with her wasn't stellar. That being said, she knew that he would tell, if she asked. She wasn't sure in the candlelight, but she thought that she saw him blush. She squinted and leaned closer to his face and he chuckled embarrassment.

"Uh ..." He scratched his forehead. "I wouldn't know where to start. I mean, I understand the basics of how it's different for women but ... It's not the same for us at all and, oddly, telling you makes me feel like I'm giving you the intimate details of being with another woman."

"Have you been with many other women?"

"Let's talk about magic!" Rowan said returning with enthusiasm to the original topic.

"Okay so tell me how it's different for guys?"

"I wasn't raised in a stronghold so my grasp on the finer details isn't good. It gets me into trouble sometimes, but other than Nimue, and that's more of a brother sister relationship and it always has been, I've never been close enough to any Fairy women to discuss this. My understanding of the way women use magic is that they ..." he hesitated, "let it into themselves."

"Yeah. That's the way it works," Rhiannon said wondering what the big deal was.

Rowan laughed again. "Okay, well, if you think of it more like making love ..."

Rhiannon got it right away and cut him off, "Women let it in. Men immerse themselves in it."

Rowan blushed.

"You're funny," Rhiannon told him and laughed. "I'm right then?"

"Yeah."

"So the other night, I wasn't the only one getting tangled up in magic and willing this baby to happen? It didn't feel like it was only me. It shouldn't have happened you know? In fact I'm sure you did know. You probably asked Fenna when my last period was before you asked me to be your wife. Correct?"

"Yeah, I did ask Fenna," he looked sheepish. "And, no, you weren't the only one getting tangled up in magic the other night, but I didn't know that we could do what we did either.

It wasn't entirely conscious, but somehow, to me, the fact that we were both, not entirely consciously, doing the same thing is awfully wonderful and I just keep falling more madly in love with you."

Rhiannon smiled. How could she not. Rowan smiled back.

"I have one more question. I have to ask while I have a chance because I can't ask some things in the middle of dinner."

"Go ahead," Rowan said, still smiling.

"Why don't you coach me more on what to expect in council meetings? How do you know I'll say the right thing. I feel like I'm floundering sometimes."

"I don't need to coach you," he said without hesitation. "You and I have spent hours talking. I don't think that you realize how concisely you express yourself or how often the things that you say seem to be coming straight from your heart. It endears you to people. If I were to coach you your responses wouldn't be unguarded and natural anymore and you would lose some of your appeal. If we want to sell you, so to speak, to the human kingdom ... well, let's face it, you're not a symbol of strength, with the exception of the Fay power you'll bring with you, but as you are, without anyone telling you how to act or what to say, the people will *love* you. They'll love your story. They'll love the fact that Seamus hasn't beaten you down, that you survive as a symbol of what Sulamith wanted, because the people loved her. All you have to do is be yourself, and be brave."

Chapter 19

They sat and talked and kissed for a while but after a time Rowan looked her in the eyes and smiled pure mischief. "The moon's full," he said significantly.

Rhiannon *knew* the moon was full. She could always feel it when the moon was full. It called to her and filled her with desire most of the time, although she had to admit that now, the feeling was, she stopped, considering it ... *like* calling to *like*. But what of it? Everyone seemed to ignore the full moon. While as a little girl she had gone out into the back yard and twirled under it, she had soon realized that other people didn't do this. In the city, sometimes you could barely see the moon from all the light pollution.

Rowan stood suddenly and went to the door opening it to the outside. She could hear a penny whistle tentatively striking up a tune and the husky notes of a flute. Rowan strode to her and took her face in his hands. "Come out with me," he said intensely, insistently, his dark eyes glowing.

"Rowan I'm ..."

He cut her off, "Please. You won't regret it. Trust me. Come out." His eyes pleaded with her as he stroked her cheeks with his thumbs.

She nodded, "Alright. I'll come," she agreed, not sure what she was agreeing to. Rowan was at the wardrobe in a flash passing her the linen blouse and purple skirt that she'd worn earlier. The skirt was cut from a circle and and came to just passed her knees. It had a broad waist band. Buttoned over the simple blouse it showed off her tiny waist and with three stripes of red, blue, and yellow silk ribbon trim at the hem it looked made for twirling. She hadn't even pulled on shoes or a coat and already he was drawing her towards the door. "But Rowan I need shoes!" she squeaked as she noticed that he wasn't wearing any.

"You'll be fine, just come," he said pulling her out into the night. He was elated, exited, as she had only ever seen him the night he had asked her to be his. She let him pull her into the forest, past the buildings and deeper, but she could see lights ahead and she thought to herself, *Of course. What do Fairies do under the full moon?* That was an easy one. *They dance.*

She could see lights through the trees as they made their way through the forest. Firelight, torches, blown glass lanterns with dancing flickers inside them and Rowan was right, she wasn't cold. A drummer and a rich contralto voice had joined the penny whistle and the flute. Rowan pulled her to the clearing and she stopped, hesitating in the trees, looking around. At the bonfires, the lights, the small but growing crowd of people already dancing in the centre. Not organized folk dances or anything so orderly as that. It was more like a rave crossed with an exotic midnight carnival. There was a wood sprite walking around on his hands and an eight foot tall Phooka with the head of an enormous weasel breathing fire. As the sound of heavier drums joined the music Rhiannon looked to where the musicians stood. It was Nimue who was singing which, for a moment, surprised Rhiannon as her own voice was a light passable soprano. Nimue's voice was all dark rich velvet. There was a Raven girl with a bodhran and a tall dark man playing conga drums. Yuka, the Kitsune, had the flute and Cole was there opening a small accordion case and staring periodically at Nimue. A man who looked Romany was tuning a guitar and a Nixie fiddle player, and a wood sprite with something that looked like Celtic pipes of some sort, were picking up the tune. Nimue shouted something over the music as the song neared its end and the rhythm made a tight change. The music morphed and a faster more intense song started as more bodies gathered in the clearing, whirling flickering undulating in the firelight. Coloured fairy lights glowed overhead. She watched a Sylvan girl twirling and swaying to the music, her loose hair flying and her nearly transparent dress revealing the silhouette of her willowy body against the fire.

"Come on," Rowan tugged at her hand.

"I ... I ..." Rhiannon stammered.

"You're not the heir to the throne here. Just let go tonight. Everyone will sleep till noon tomorrow. Tonight there are no rules."

She looked at him and he stopped tugging at her hand.

"Come my love. Come dance with me. Please," he said softly, pleading again.

She let him pull her into the firelight and as she did she heard Cole's accordion join the melody. With a voice like an angry street kid, proud, forthright, devil may care, he joined Nimue on the second chorus harmonizing with her. Rhiannon borrowed a little courage from that voice and let go just a little. She looked at Rowan. He was one of those people who just knew, intuitively, instinctually, exactly, what to do with his body when the music played. She let go a little further and felt the drums through the forest floor. Her heart pounded in response. Rowan took her hands and pulled her closer and that was it, the music took over. She could hear Nimue and Cole's voices weaving together with more confidence and she threw up her hands and followed until all that was left was the music, the fire, and Rowan and they danced as the moon spun overhead. The throbbing drumbeats kept everyone on their feet. As the night spun by she saw Thaylum sitting in the trees watching, and caught sight, through the forest of bodies, of Nessa dancing with the green antlered man. Rhiannon let the rhythm and her sister's voice tug at her heart as Rowan pulled her back into the dance and the gypsy guitar guided her hands. She swung her hips and pounded the forest floor with her feet. She grew hot and pushed back her hair, undid the top buttons on her blouse and rolled her sleeves then let go once more, relinquishing herself to music more intense than anything she had ever heard before. *This is what it is,* she thought, *to be Fay. This wildness. This freedom. This is a homecoming. This is a part of me. Of what I am.*

As if he'd heard her thoughts, as if even dancing were not enough for the intensity that they felt, they ran hand in hand away from the clearing with the music still guiding them, and in the hollow of a tree they lay down, bare skin against the forest floor and the moon above.

"You're glowing," Rowan breathed looking at the multicoloured flickers rising off her skin and floating around them.

"So are you. Like amber in the sun," and he was, like bits of it were caught in his loose hair and reflecting off his skin. And she pulled him down to her and the dance continued until they cried out together and lay there under the spinning moon, staring into one another's eyes in the light they had made together.

* * *

Rhiannon wasn't sure how long they'd lain there. Years, minutes. It didn't matter. "I love you. You know that right? I know I say it, but I need to know that *you* know I mean it," she whispered.

"I can feel your love leading me into forever. I know that you love me every time you look at me," Rowan answered, his voice low. "You know that I feel the same?"

"I know ... I know ..." she whispered back and she ran her hand over his hot dry skin and they lapsed back into silence and stillness for who knows how long.

* * *

"Your skin is starting to feel cool. Lets go in. All that's left is the flute. Let's go in before it stops so that we can pretend that this night never ended," Rowan murmured running his hands over her cool arms then passing her her clothes.

They dressed and wove back through the trees as the lone flute played its wistful melody. She spied Yuka, sitting by the remains of the fire, her instrument raised gracefully to her lips. When they reached their door Rhiannon looked down at the moon on the ocean. She could see so clearly and it was impossible to miss the two black heads emerging from the water. Cole and Nimue. Their white shoulders showing above the waves, arms around one another. She looked away, into Rowan's eyes, his beautiful face. "My love," she whispered.

"Come. Let's go to bed." He opened the door and smiled A fire had been built in their hearth and the room was warm and welcoming. "We can get the leaves out of our hair in the morning."

Chapter 20

Rowan had been telling the truth when he said that everyone would sleep until noon the day after the full moon. The stronghold was quiet, so quiet. Completely free of bustle. The feeling of sleeping until she woke of her own accord, and then of lying there, knowing that there was nowhere pressing that anyone expected her to be, left her feeling free and light. It was the first time that Rhiannon had had the luxury of watching Rowan sleep. She picked leaves from his hair for a moment or two then lay her head back down and just gazed at him. His profile. The angle of his cheekbones. His refined nose. She'd never seen him asleep before but, like all things, it didn't last and almost as if the weight of her gaze had told him it was day, he opened his eyes and smiled. "I love waking up with you," he said stretching, then picking bits of twig and cedar needles out of her hair.

Breakfast was to be found waiting for them on the table in the sitting room. Rowan brought the tray to the bed and they lounged there, eating the hot rolls and butter, goat brie, dried figs and walnuts, then lingering over a pot of tea. Nothing was ever planned for the day following a full moon, if it could be avoided, and there was nothing to stop them from simply lying there all day. The feeling was incredible. Not to be taken for granted. They stayed were they were with no plans. Sometime in the afternoon the steward's wife called through the door, "I'm leaving a tray on the table. Come get it at your leisure." There was bread, some kind of hummus-like spread, apples, and an avocado.

Rhiannon gasped, "Oh my goodness! An avocado! I thought I'd never have another."

Rowan laughed, "They are delicious. I've only ever had them when I'm here. Lugh's people head pretty far south when they trade and usually, once a year, if we're lucky, they make it back with some ripe avocados."

Rhiannon cut into it. It was ripe straight through, soft and buttery. They ate, lounged, and watched the stained glass change as the day passed. Late afternoon she sighed contentedly, "I want to lie here and never leave, but at the same time, I want to go for a walk, see the sky, breathe the outdoors."

"Come on then. We can sneak out and turn ourselves invisible if anyone sees us. Immature in the extreme I know, but today is ours. I don't care how ridiculous we have to be to keep it that way," Rowan grinned.

Rhiannon rose and walked up to the wardrobe. While she had been aware that it had been filling, over the last two days, with beautiful new clothes, she hadn't had the presence of mind to look them over much, and after sifting through the dresses that were far too fine to simply go for a walk in, she selected a plain, long, leaf green wool dress that crossed over and tied at the back and then wrapped herself in a heavy wool shawl woven with indigo, olive green and pink paisleys on a sage green background. It should have been hideous, but was instead actually quite pretty in a casual feminine sort of way. Rowan dressed quickly from a stash of clothing that was in a tallboy on the opposite wall and they left the room through the stained glass doors.

They walked along the beach under the blue sky watching the ocean. Rhiannon had to admit that, despite the fact that it meant the end of gardening season, she loved autumn. It was the deep breath before winter. Life's brilliant bang before retreating into a long cold sleep. She watched the waves as they walked in silence. Cold saltwater. The ocean tang. The smell of seaweed. She looked at Rowan for a moment. His eyes were focused on the forests of the opposite shore. Dense, green and yellow. "Brown eyes, or blue? What do you think? What colour will her eyes be?" His voice was wistful, far away and dreamy, as he thought of the future and its possibilities.

"Brown," Rhiannon said positively. "Like yours. But," she stopped for a moment losing focus on her speech, "She'll be small and fair skinned, like me, with long dark hair."

The image in Rhiannon's mind was as strong as it could possibly be. It had a truth to it that was beyond mere fancy. A small girl who looked about nine, but Rhiannon knew was probably closer to thirteen. Her small curved feminine mouth was cherry red and her skin glowed against the backdrop of her wavy molasses hair. And her eyes? Dark and wild, just like her father's. "Look," Rhiannon said, and held on to Rowan's hands willing him to see what she could see. "Close your eyes," she whispered.

They stayed there seeing that image together, holding on to one another, as the salt breeze played with their hair and autumn crawled incrementally, fractionally, closer to winter. Was time crawling, or was it flowing through their hands with terrible speed? Rhiannon leaned into Rowan's chest and wrapped her arms around him and he put his arms around her, as if by holding on tightly enough they could slow the hands of time.

They walked further down the beach seeing no one, saying nothing, not needing to speak, when they heard the sound of swords crashing and the odd yell. It wasn't fighting. It was practice. They kept walking, maintaining their pace, not hurrying, until they could see the practice field. Cole and Nimue could be seen sitting on a bench, arms circled around the other's waist. Brian was standing, leaning on his sword in obvious exhaustion. Thaylum was standing upright, watching raptly, every move, every detail of the two combatants. By the look of things they had been at it a while. Nessa's shirt was plastered to her upper body with sweat, and she was getting slow, every movement laboured. Raphael on the other hand looked as fresh as if he had just woken from a perfect night's sleep. Rhiannon had seen Nessa spar with Rowan and Leif. She was nimble and extremely fast, and although she was quite slender and not of the body type to build bulky muscle, she could hold her own against Rowan for longer than one would have expected her to. Rhiannon had become aware at one point that the fact that Leif and Rowan were willing to fight her with naked blades, instead of the wooden practice swords that they reserved for Gareth, said quite a lot about their confidence in her abilities. She was probably a better fighter than most men. But now her breath was coming in great ragged gasps and she was just barely dancing out from under the giant angel's attacks. She parried, her slimmer lighter blade flashed as she got out of range, then she threw down her sword and shouted, "Enough!"

Thaylum picked up her sword and propped it against the bench next to her where she had collapsed, head between her knees, thick red braid hanging down. He obviously hadn't had a go at the angel yet and looked towards the giant creature with curiosity. Raphael pulled energy to himself, drawing from the surrounding trees much as a dryad would, then beckoned to Thaylum who drew his blade. He signalled to Raphael that he was ready, and it began. At first it didn't seem to Rhiannon that much was happening. They circled for a minute and Rowan whispered to her, "Thaylum is not easy to predict. He's very patient and often wins simply by exhausting his opponent then surprising them, although on the field he's more a combination of brute force and prudence. He doesn't waste energy."

Thaylum was big and strong, a little shorter and a little broader than Leif. Rhiannon watched, looking for the things that Rowan had pointed out as Raphael attacked and Thaylum deflected. He wasn't fast, and he wasn't elegant, but his timing was immaculate and not a movement was wasted. "Do you mind if we move closer?" Rowan asked her. "Professional curiosity has gotten the better of me and I'd like to watch this."

"I don't mind. I'd like to sit with Nimue for a while. Lets go up." And they wandered up the gradual incline to where the others were.

Brian noticed them first and Rhiannon raised her hand and shook her head as soon as she realized that he was going to bow and greet her formally. He smiled and nodded instead and came to stand by them.

"He's already been through Cole and I, but that sister of yours gave him grief for a while, until he figured out her weak points."

Rhiannon looked over at Thaylum and Raphael. The angel used his wings for balance yet kept them clear of the blades in what was obviously a well practised posture.

"Yeah, Nessa fights dirty. It makes up for her lack of mass," Rowan commented dryly. Then turned his attention back to the match.

If swordplay could be steady and metric then this was, and Rhiannon could see Thaylum reserving himself, and measuring. She sat down on the bench between Nimue and Nessa and her younger sister's small hand twined itself in her own. Two small hands that had been apart for so long, and in that moment, watching the steady progress of practised fighting, they held on tightly. Rhiannon could see Raphael using, almost effortlessly, Thaylum's own strengths against him. Some men are brilliant because they are born that way, but others still, are brilliant because they strive to be. They may not be the fastest or the strongest. They may not have the quickest wit or the flashiest style but they have determination, and the sense to build on their weaknesses and find strengths in unusual places.

Thaylum, the youngest son of a farmer with four older sons, was one of the latter. According to Nessa, who was sitting straight now and whispering to Rhiannon, sparring with him was a bit like sparring with a stone wall. But against the Angel, his strength, his stamina, his patience, and his impenetrable defence would erode eventually. Thaylum had been steadily defending, no flashy attacks, only a perfectly timed series of blocks, when out of no where, he attacked. Again, nothing dazzling, but it was precise and behind it lay all of the strength that he had been so carefully and prudently conserving. It surprised Raphael, everyone there could see, and Raphael himself seemed pleased to have been surprised, but he reacted so quickly at the same time that all of Thaylum's careful planning had been in vain, and the next attack would be in vain as well, and the one after that, and eventually the steady onslaught of the storm would take down the wall. Another three minutes, another five, not as many as ten, and Thaylum was pushed to his limits. He was beaded in sweat just maintaining his defence and he *had* attempted another attack but Raphael had seen it coming this time and grinned. The Angel appeared to be slowing somewhat, but not enough to level the playing field, and finally after one final attempt to break through Raphael's equally impenetrable defences, Thaylum danced back and declared gasping, "I yield, I yield," and placing his hands on his knees he bent and gasped for more air. Raphael was standing calmly, and Rowan was looking at him.

"Rowan is the only person I've ever seen fight like that," Nessa whispered in Rhiannon's ear.

"Are they *very* evenly matched do you think?" Rhiannon asked in return.

"Closer than Rowan and Leif. They'd have to fight for me to know which was the superior swordsman though. Raphael's style is different."

As much as she had felt tossed about and battered by the world she had turned her back on, this world, Rowan's world, had its harsh realities, and she could never lie and tell some-one that the look Raphael and Rowan were exchanging didn't bother her, that the idea that they were practising to put themselves in this position in actuality, with real people who were intending to kill them—kill or be killed—didn't make her feel like she was screaming with gut clenching terror inside. But Rowan and Raphael *were* looking at each other and a silent conversation was taking place about an Angel who'd spent half his life loving a girl, and the half breed Fairy who'd stepped in and taken his place. It was a complex conversation of acceptance and loss, anger and guilt, helplessness and love. They both turned and looked at Rhiannon, and Raphael's look was open for all to see. Love, and a heavy self loathing for letting the opportunity for it slip away, and in Rowan's face, when she looked, there was an apology, because even today, somehow, that old sadness had gotten hold of them. Rowan and Raphael looked back at one another and without words agreed, "What's done is done, but we'll have it out this once, and then have done with it for good."

Rowan approached Cole, "Would you lend me your sword?" he asked casually.

Cole rose quickly and passed Rowan his blade which was the same same basic, standard issue as Rowan's. Rhiannon glanced at the swords of the others and was astonished to see that nearly all were more ornate than the one Rowan normally carried. Rhiannon looked at him. His hair was loose, and in the Fay clothing he wore, he looked more Fairy than Human.

His grip on the sword hilt was a very natural thing, uncon-scious. He didn't need to think about it now that it was in his hand. He knelt before her and Rhiannon reached out and stroked his cheeks and hair, and kissed him.

"I'm sorry. I can't help this. I want to see if I can best him. I know that it's childish," Rowan said, locking his dark eyes on hers.

"It's alright. I understand." And even if it did make her feel like crying, though she knew that with the measure of skill they both possessed, they would not hurt each other, she did understand. She understood that there was a tension between Rowan and Raphael that would be there until one of them proved that he was the better somehow. For Rowan, that he truly did deserve Rhiannon, or for Raphael, that at least he could best Rowan with a sword, even if he hadn't gotten the girl. She also understood that for Rowan it ran a little deeper, for even though he despised war, and Rhiannon knew that killing tore him apart inside, what he could do with a sword was a gift, and there was a passion to it.

"Here," she said, taking out the little moonstone earring from one ear. "A long time ago in the other world, Knights competed in tournaments against one another for money, prizes and glory, and if a lady favoured a certain knight she would give him a token of her esteem to take with him into the arena to bring him luck." She deftly pressed the post of the earring through the fabric of Rowan's collar and slid the backing on. "There."

She pressed the collar back down and ran her hands over his chest. Her mouth quirked and she shook her head. Rowan kissed her forehead, stood and strode to the centre of the hard packed dirt square. All eyes were on the two men, and despite being only a small group, the tension amongst them was palpable. For the others Rhiannon knew that it was the question of whether Raphael would indeed be able to take on

Rowan, who had remained until that day, undefeated. Would their not particularly big Captain be any match for the seemingly inexhaustible seven foot tall Angel? Rhiannon admitted to herself that she was curious about that, but the strange and uncomfortable thoughts and feelings came from the image of the two men facing each other, and the reality that image forced on her; she may have felt that she was worthless in that other world, and the knowledge of Rowan's love may have helped her realize that she wasn't, but two others, *two* other remarkable men had loved her, and failed to tell her, and had, in turn, hurt her with it. *I don't need a man's love to tell me I'm of worth*, she told herself angrily, but in some distant craggy and desolate part of her memory, a mocking voice jeered and echoed, "Thumbelina!" at her. And now two of the three men who loved her stood before her looking at one another, poised to attack, just for practise, just to hone their skills. But behind that in the undercurrent, it was Rhiannon they fought for. A useless fight for a fate that was already decided. It made her cringe. She could see the anger and the hurt in Raphael's eyes, not a desire to kill, but a wish to make Rowan disappear. She could watch the thought like she could read words on a page, and it was chased by Raphael's knowledge that losing Rowan would break Rhiannon's heart, and that was unbearable to him. So he would slake his crimson and gold anger now, in the only way he could. Wings raised, sword ready, the denim and leather clad angel focused his golden eyes, and his anger, on Rowan. And Rowan? Rowan, perversely enough, smiled. An elegant, wicked, smile touched with a mirth that goaded the younger man to attack.

It was a glorious attack of speed and daring, but the thing that Raphael couldn't possibly understand about Rowan was that having a sword in his hand was more than profession or duty, it wasn't fighting or the intent to kill. It was the glory of a challenge and his blood sang with it. He was alive with it and with a single-minded devotion that he usually reserved for dancing or loving, he threw himself into a counter attack that sent Raphael reeling in astonishment. The Angel staggered. It wasn't much of a stagger. More a slight falter by lower standards, and Raphael's reaction was so immediate that the only real consequence was that he knew now that he couldn't take his own superiority for granted. He turned to face Rowan again and the battle began in earnest.

Rhiannon watched and as she watched, the thing that she was unaware of was that the others were watching her as her eyes flitted back and forth, following the two men. What they saw was a terrible beautiful serenity, unconsciously built to hide what she did not know she could not hide. Love, fear, hurt, understanding. *How could she be so serene and yet wear all of these emotions so openly?* they wondered, and why did their hearts ache so badly for her? And *their* eyes flitted back and forth between the tiny Queen and the two men fighting before her. *Her* eyes never left the two men sparring, practising, although they, and the small crowd that had gathered now, all knew that it was more than that. The only sign that she felt any of the tension that had the others holding their breath, were the white knuckles of the hand that held her sister's. But she watched and, while she was vaguely aware of Nessa's sudden indrawn breaths on her one side, and Nimue on her other turning and pressing her face into Cole's shoulder, she never looked away, not once, as Rowan and Raphael fought. And it *was* dazzling, intense, brutal, as their swords connected again and again but neither quite gained the upper hand. Rowan's speed compensated for his lack of size, and it was obvious that Raphael hadn't expected Rowan to be as strong as he was. Rowan was significantly more experienced and knew how to compensate when fighting someone taller, but on the flip side of that, Raphael was faster than anyone that tall had any right to be, and he'd been fighting elves since he was fourteen. So Rowan attacked again and Raphael fended him off desperately, then found an opening, forcing Rowan to twist and dance back, but just as it looked as if Raphael would win, that his renewed attack would be fast enough, that he would catch Rowan before his guard was back up, like a flash Rowan would block and force Raphael stumbling back and Rowan would attack again. Back and forth like an extremely violent pendulum on a terrible clock they went, and Rhiannon's heart pounded until the sound was almost as bad as the crashing swords. Back and forth, gradually slower. How long had she sat there? Would they ever stop? But it was still daylight. Then Raphael attacked with so much impossible speed that he had the upper hand, Rowan twisted, leapt, it was a near thing and as impossibly fast as Raphael's attack had been Rhiannon saw it, a tiny opening. Rowan knew that it was there and he ducked, lunged, twisted and in a fraction of a second Raphael was on his knees, and Rowan's sword was at his throat.

Chapter 21

Rowan withdrew Cole's blade and extended his hand to the kneeling Angel. Raphael reached out tentatively and took it, allowing Rowan to help him rise and they stood breathing hard in the deafening silence that surrounded them. "If you were five years older ... had five more years of experience, I wouldn't have been able to do that," Rowan admitted gasping. "You leave yourself open just a little on the left."

Raphael nodded, breathing too hard to reply.

"I've seldom fought someone so close to my equal," Rowan continued, screwing up his face as he fought to regain his breath. "That was ... very challenging."

Raphael found his voice, "I've never been pushed to the limit like that either. That was ..." he stopped to breathe and shook his head in disbelief at how completely winded he was, "Something else altogether."

They stood, breathing for another moment or two. Rhiannon still had the sound of metal on metal clanging about in her head and though her heart was somewhat quieter now, the release of tension when the fighting had stopped had left her feeling lightheaded, exposed, and fragile. She hadn't realized that her father was there until she felt his hand on her shoulder. She reached her own hand up and placed it on his in appreciation, but she still couldn't take her eyes off of Rowan and Raphael.

"I know that what I'm about to ask of you is unfair, but we are living in a time when everything is difficult and hurtful on some level," Rowan said to the Angel, then looked down for a moment hesitating to go forward with a request that would indeed be very heavy. He looked back at Raphael who no longer had any anger burning in his eyes, only sadness. "Would you continue as her guardian? Will you keep Rhiannon safe for me? I don't trust anyone else to be able to do it as effectively as you've already proven you can." He levelled his eyes on Raphael and waited. Rowan's face looked hard for a moment but Rhiannon knew, and Raphael did too, that it was only because he was holding back tears, because Rowan himself wouldn't be there, *couldn't* stay by her side, to keep her safe himself.

"Of course. Always. You can trust me, absolutely ..." the angel's face worked for a moment before he continued, "but I won't be able to stop loving her."

"I know ... I know. That's why it hurts so much," Rowan said, voice heavy.

Raphael nodded and walked away alone and Rowan turned to Rhiannon.

Everyone else, the some fifty Fay that had gathered to watch and their more immediate family and friends, were left with the sense that staying would be an invasion, and turned their backs and wandered off. Rowan walked to Rhiannon and knelt before her once more, but this time he buried his face in her lap and they stayed like that and she stroked his hair as the golden sun disappeared behind the trees.

* * *

Once darkness had fallen and the world was hidden in a cloak of black velvet, Rowan lifted his head, "This doesn't seem to be a very good time for us. Does it." He repeated what he'd said to her their first night together.

"Love didn't give us a choice, but even if it had," Rhiannon asked softly, "Would you give this up?"

"No. Not for the sun, the moon, and all the stars. Not for a moment," he said holding her face in his hands and kissing her.

"Good. Because neither would I," she answered back. "And I think that Nimue is right over there waiting for us with a lantern so we should stop kissing and go to her."

Rowan chuckled and rose to his feet, taking Rhiannon's hands in his own and drawing her up with him. They walked to where Nimue was indeed standing holding a magenta blown glass lantern and waiting for them. Cole stood with her, and as they approached he drew away from her slightly although they still held hands. "Here," Rowan said returning the sword to Cole. "It's a good sword that. Good balance. Thank you for lending it to me."

Rhiannon found Cole's reaction adorable. She couldn't help smiling as he took the sword back reverently from the captain he idolized and said, "Never again will anyone hear me bemoan my plain sword. I will carry this sword until the day I die."

Rowan laughed, tossing his head back. "I'm guessing that fight is going to leave an impression that'll stick around for a while?"

"Yes Sir. I don't think there's any doubt about that," Cole said smiling.

"In fact the entire stronghold is buzzing with it, so my father has arranged for dinner in his rooms. Just a small group of us so that we don't have to listen to all of the gossip," Nimue added.

"Oh, thank the stars. I couldn't handle dinner in the dinning hall tonight!" Rhiannon breathed in relief.

And they wandered in for dinner and sat around a table of friends and family. Lugh had even made sure that Raphael was

there with them at the table and, although he was very subdued he was not, it seemed, so torn apart that he wasn't fit for
company. They said goodbye that night to Gwydion and Nessa
who would be departing for the city early the next morning by
the main road disguised as an old clerk and his grand-
daughter. He had convinced Nessa to come and work as a spy
for him instead of joining the army as, a beautiful young
woman with a sword was a terrible thing to waste in his mind.
Not to suggest that spying would be safer than the army. He
simply meant that as a female she could do things and get
places that a man couldn't. The fact that she could and would
kill if necessary made her more valuable as a spy, so she'd
agreed to it. Rhiannon hugged Nessa and Nessa raised a wry
eyebrow, "Don't let them push you around. Remember, you're
the boss."

"Easier said than done Nessa," Rhiannon replied.

"I know," Nessa sighed. "Take care of Rowan, I know he
doesn't need it but ..." She blinked. "And try not to cry too
much," Nessa tacked on at the end, then embraced Rowan
and left the room. The others wasted no time in retiring for
the night as it would be an early morning and soon enough
Rhiannon found herself behind closed doors once more.

* * *

In a night gown sitting cross-legged on the bed Rhiannon
placed her hands on either side of her head and pressed.
"Why does it have to be this way Rowan? I don't feel like
the kind of person who has all this *history* leading up to me.
What am I supposed to do about Raphael? You saw the way he
looked at me at dinner? We should have stayed in this afternoon. I wish I hadn't had to watch you fight him."

Rowan looked at her, "You know that I had to fight him. It
wasn't only personal and it would have happened sooner or
later. I'm in a position of authority and I have a reputation to

maintain. If I hadn't been able to best Raphael it may have lessened me in the eyes of some. I had to fight him and win. I couldn't afford to lose or appear to be afraid to try. Not right now."

Rhiannon nodded but then looked up at Rowan, "Make it all go away Rowan, for twenty minutes, half an hour? Please? Just block it all out for me. I need you."

Rowan put his arms around her and kissed her.

* * *

As they lay there drifting off Rowan said to her, "You're going to have to talk to him ... To your Angel. He needs some kindness from you. You can't take your anger at your situation out on him. I see you doing it in small ways. His heart's broken Rhiannon. It's different for he and I to show animosity towards one another. As shallow as it sounds, we're male. We try to kill each other and then have done with it. But even if he's relinquished the anger that he felt towards me ..." Rowan sighed, "Sometimes anger is the quickest to burn away, but love lasts forever. Love doesn't die. It would be a little easier for him, if you would be kind to him."

Rhiannon nodded in the dark.

* * *

It wasn't the noise outside that woke her as she lay there in the warm darkness and tried to figure out why she was awake. What was nagging at her? *Aw cripes*, she rolled over in frustration. *I have to pee.* She lay there for a few more minutes before admitting that she wouldn't be able to ignore it and go back to sleep. She told herself, for future reference, that she needed to remember to drink a big glass of water *before* dinner *not* right before bed, as her bladder was obviously, *already* losing space. She tiptoed to the bathroom and it was only as she was returning that she heard the sounds from outside

Nothing frightening, or maybe they *were* frightening sounds, just not frightening in the typical sense. There *was* something that Rhiannon found frightening about what Raphael felt for her though, and the sound of his almost stifled sobs coming from the other side of the stained glass doors. She wouldn't be able to sleep now that she could hear him, and guilt was burning in her breast because Rowan had been right about what she was doing. Taking her anger out on Raphael. In the formal courtesy she showed him. In her reluctance to meet his eyes. She was being passive aggressive, which she'd never done to anyone before. But anger was easier.

She'd lain awake thinking about it and recognizing that he couldn't have revealed himself to her. He couldn't have remained her detached guardian if he'd been climbing in her window to spend time with her instead. It was a completely different circumstance from what had happened with Evan, and Raphael didn't deserve her anger. She bit her lip and slipped on some shoes, pulled on a sweater over her nightgown and wrapped herself in a shawl. She listened to Rowan's breath for a moment but he was breathing deeply and slowly, fast asleep. She kissed his brow lightly then slipped out through the doors. The moon was bright over head, still nearly full. Had it truly been only the other night that she had danced with Rowan under that moon? She leaned her forehead against the cold glass for a moment, reluctant to turn and face the angel who was breathing raggedly and standing on the grass below the patio. She could hear him looking at her. *Would more time make this easier, or would it just waste time?* She wondered, then turned. Down the stone stairs, across the grass. "Let's walk down to the water's edge," she said to Raphael when she reached him, and he followed her down to the beach where they stood silently in the still cold night.

"I don't know if I can do this Raphael," she said, watching her feet as the waves nearly met her toes.

"Do what?" he asked, subdued.

"Be strong and kind and brave, all of the time. I feel stretched thin."

Raphael was silent for a moment before speaking, "I've let you down in more ways than I understand, haven't I?"

She shook her head and took his hand, drawing him over to a log where she sat. He took a seat next to her. "No you haven't. You haven't let me down at all. This just ..." she took a deep breath. "This just sucks ... and it hurts, that's all." She looked up at him.

Raphael chuckled softly by her side, "That's definitely one way of putting it." But then his face fell, "I'm sorry for making things more ... difficult. I'm not good at hiding my feelings."

Rhiannon looked up at his face. He truly was very beautiful and somehow the sadness just made him more so. "Does it hurt more or less to know that I would have loved you back if things had played out differently?" she asked gently.

"Hard to say right now. Bit of both I think."

"Should I have kept that to myself?" she wondered out loud. She had no real frame of reference for this situation and questioned everything she said and did.

He looked down at her and his face worked for a moment but then settled into a sad smile, "No. I would rather know." He leaned towards her and kissed the top of her head. "Crap you're short. I really have to lean down a ways. I guess I am a bit too tall for you," he said in a gallant attempt at flippancy.

They sat in silence, looking out at the moonlit ocean and when a breeze picked up Raphael shifted closer to her and raised a wing, sheltering her there. "I know that this will sound terribly lame. It feels a bit lame to me too, but do you think that we could try being friends? It's an uncomfortable and rather horrible cliche, I know, not a consolation prize at all. But it would be easier for me to know that we were trying to be friends, you know, if you're going to keep hanging around outside my window? We haven't had some tortured and demented teenaged love affair to get in the way of that. You never know. It could work?" she looked at him hopefully as they sat together.

The corners of his mouth gave a minute twitch but he spoke heavily, "I'll think it over. But right now, not to sound bossy, you should go in. Come on, I'll walk you to your door." He rose and held out his hands to help her up but let go of her as soon as she was standing. They walked back across the grass and up the stone stairs to her door.

"Goodnight Raphael."

"Goodnight Rhiannon."

She turned towards the door then turned back to Raphael. "Raphael?" she called and he turned back to her. "Here," she said taking out her other earring and giving it to him.

He took it but said, "Are you sure? This is all you have left of *him*? He loved you, you know."

Rhiannon sighed realizing that Raphael must have been sitting in the willow tree at her old home eighteen months ago, the evening Evan had given her the little earrings as a birthday gift, and had seen the things she'd been blind to. "Don't bring up Evan tonight Raph, not now. Just take the damned earring."

Raphael took the tiny earring reverently, smiling a little, "Thank you."

"Goodnight Raphael," she smiled, then turned back to the door.

"Goodnight."

She closed the door behind her. Rowan had lit a candle and was sitting on the edge of the bed. "I was just going to come looking for you."

"I was outside talking to Raphael. You were sleeping so soundly, I didn't want to wake you," she said, kicking off her shoes and shivering as she bundled herself back into bed.

"How did it go?" Rowan asked.

Rhiannon looked up at the gossamer canopy asking herself the exact same question. "He confuses me Rowan. Would you just please hold me until I go back to sleep?" she asked, shaking, mostly, but not entirely, from the cold. And Rowan blew out the candle, put his arms around her, and they slept.

Chapter 22

Rhiannon stood on the beach as the mist coalesced around them. She looked down at the sand beneath her feet. The tracks she and Raphael had left only hours ago were gone now and her father, two Water Nymphs, and the Nixie called Lyla were standing next to the readied barge with their eyes closed, ankle deep in the ocean willing a dense cold fog, that filled the inlet, into existence. Rhiannon tried to shake off the heavy queasy exhaustion she was experiencing. She'd woken that morning feeling sick to her stomach but she'd attributed it in part to her disrupted night and the crushing guilt she felt. It improved once she'd eaten breakfast, but as she'd dressed in the riding clothes that were, typical of most things made by the Fay, functional yet very fine, she had exclaimed, as she'd drawn the fitted vest's laces tight, "Oh! Goodness! My breasts hurt!" And had continued dressing with more care. Rowan had grinned at her before rushing off to make sure that the preparations for their journey were going according to his standards and had met her on the beach only moments ago, leading Strawberry, his big black war horse, and a pack horse loaded with supplies with him. Both horses had survived the run in at the Grove. They waited until Lugh had deemed the fog dense enough before leading the horses onto the barge. Rhiannon turned to Lugh. She smiled, which was difficult in its way.

"I wish that your mother and I hadn't been so naive. I have lived the past over in my mind at least one thousand times this last week, finding all of the things that we did wrong. I wish that we could have spared you all of this upheaval," he said.

"I keep struggling against the past ... Wishing that I could unmake it." Rhiannon shook her head to clear the tears that were threatening. "There is nothing that can be done. The past will drown us if we let it. There is nothing to do now but push ahead. It's the only thing that makes sense now."

"That is very true." Lugh agreed, and he looked out into the fog for a moment before returning to himself. "Everything will be ready when you return. Delegates from the other strongholds are arriving. Everything is in motion now. If the Angels have hearts beating in their chests, then I know that they will hear you."

Rhiannon put her arms around Lugh and stood in his embrace for a moment, wishing that his arms felt like Gavin's and feeling guilty for it. Lugh wasn't the father who had raised her. "I will see you," she said to him, then turned and stepped onto the barge with the others. She watched as the beach disappeared into the fog. The entire stronghold had turned up to see them off. She raised her hand in farewell and the last thing that the onlookers saw as the fog swallowed the barge was one small fairy looking back at them with the weight of the world on her shoulders.

Rowan touched her hand and she jumped, turned, and seeing that it was him melted into his chest. "What's wrong my love?" he asked with concern in his eyes, placing his hands in her hair and stroking her cheeks with his thumbs.

"Everything. Nothing. I don't know." She looked towards Raphael who was standing at the front of the barge talking with Thaylum and Hans, who had apparently survived Lyla. The fog muffled their voices and she couldn't make out their words.

But Rowan understood her look and said quietly, "Someone like Raphael is bound to bring up some pretty conflicted feelings. It's what he is. I don't mean in terms of him being angelic, I mean his personality. The force of him. I don't blame you for feeling conflicted."

Rhiannon breathed out as if she had been holding her breath since waking that morning. "I love you Rowan. I love you so so much. I told him that, had things been different, I would have loved him, and I meant it. But life played out so that I met you first, and I don't regret it. You're my match, and all of those confused things that I feel about Raphael are there, but as long as you know that I love you and we can always talk, it's fine."

Rowan smiled, "So if I asked you again, 'what's wrong?' what would you say?"

"Oh, other than the impending revolution, the war, and the sad Angel outside my bedroom window," she smiled and kissed him, "Everything is perfect. Let's enjoy this boat ride."

Rowan laughed as they sat down together on a bench across from Cole and Nimue who were huddled close, singing low sweet love songs together.

When they reached the north shore of the inlet they set out on horseback. Thaylum, Cole, Hans, Lyla, and Nimue would accompany them as far as Thaylum's house. They would turn back, taking Thaylum's wife and children back to the stronghold with them, after which Thaylum, Cole, and Hans would ride back to the Capital with Brian before the day was out. Rowan, Rhiannon, and Raphael would continue up into the mountains accompanied by Yuka, Merlin's Shadow, an adorably ugly Urisk who looked like a cross between a chimp and a goat—and who was called David, of all things— and a Gwillion archer by the name of Aledwen. A mountain fairy, Aledwen was strange and harsh and attractive all at once. Her skin was like translucent smokey quartz, and her eyes the colour of shale. Her hair was glossy black like obsidian and was pulled back severely, revealing the shaved and tattooed sides of her head. Rowan told her that Aledwen was the best and fastest archer that he knew. They were also being accompanied by a sumptuously, decadently, seductively beautiful, golden haired Glaistig called Bonnie, but she didn't speak and she disappeared into the forest almost as soon as the barge met the shore and silently shadowed them as they progressed.

Once they left the shore and were clear of the fog, the sun shone. The leaves were all brilliant yellow now with occasional splashes of red against the dark green backdrop of the cedars, arbutus, and fir. Rhiannon could almost believe that they were simply on a pleasant ride through the woods on their way to a picnic, and that feeling was amplified when, in slightly less than an hour, they reached the little stone cottage in the woods where Thaylum lived with his wife and children when he wasn't with the army. It was a sweet little cottage built partially into the mountainside. Its slate roof was covered in moss and there were wind chimes in the surrounding trees. It made Rhiannon think of Snow-White and Rose-Red or East of the Sun West of the Moon. A little cottage at the beginning of a fairy tale. As they approached Thaylum dismounted and called out, "Feather! Peony! Quinn! I'm home!"

The two dirty but happy, healthy, children who were playing out front looked up, and at the sight of Thaylum, came running and screaming. Thaylum got down on his knees and they crashed into his arms in pure delight. He kissed their golden heads, smiling, then stood as his wife came skipping down the path with equal enthusiasm if not quite so much noise, and she and Thaylum stood, wrapped up in one another, oblivious to the world for several moments before he loosened his hold and turned to make introductions.

Rhiannon could see immediately why Thaylum's wife was called White Feather. Her hair was the palest blond Rhiannon had ever seen and with the perfect white pearlescent skin and the glistening white wing like nimbus that danced behind her, she did indeed resemble a white feather. She smiled sweetly. A smile that easily reached her electric blue eyes and spread across her ruby lips. She was quite possibly the loveliest creature Rhiannon had ever set eyes on. Rowan had told her that morning that White Feather was actually her cousin on her great grandmother's side. Thaylum's family were obviously not accustomed to strangers and even White Feather was almost trying to hide behind her husband. "This," Thaylum said prying a little girl with pale pink cheeks, strawberry blond curls and deep blue eyes, off his leg, "Is Peony. And this little dandelion," he said, lifting a smaller boy with a puff of blond hair, "Is Quinn."

He introduced White Feather to anyone who she didn't already know, leaving Rhiannon to the last at which point he told her, "This is Rowan's wife Rhiannon. She is the oldest acknowledged child of King Lugh and Queen Sulamith."

Rhiannon watched White Feather's face. The ethereal Sylph's eyes had been fixed in fascination on Raphael but as Thaylum's words trickled through she changed her focus and stared, all too aware of the implications of a Human Fay queen and the changes it would bring. A long overdue revolution. Relative freedom. No more hiding in the forest out of fear that someone would think her children abominations.

White Feather came forward and gave a smooth, graceful curtsy.

"Oh, please don't. This is your home," Rhiannon said taking White feather's hands and pulling her up.

"You're ..." White Feather started. "Half human. Like my children ..." There was hope and longing in her voice.

"We've come to take you and the kids back to the strong-hold," Thaylum told her.

White Feather looked stunned, off balance, as she stood blinking rapidly.

Rhiannon spoke, "The Fay kingdom is supportive of ending the taboo and uniting with the humans. I think that they have been more aware of the degree to which Human Fay relations have proliferated over the years and, what with the Fay predilection for ..." she smiled. "I have to find a politically correct, positive way of putting this, I can't say 'breaking the rules and stirring up trouble', so shall we go for 'embracing change and moving forward'?" She raised her eyebrows questioningly. "My father has asked Thaylum to bring you home, at least until things are safer. He has made sure that any Humans who are tied to Fay partners are welcome in the strongholds. It's Fay law now."

Rhiannon turned away, giving White Feather space. She, personally, found it difficult to receive emotionally charged news when all eyes were on her, and there was quite a crowd of them, comparatively speaking, standing now in White Feather's yard. Rhiannon walked to where Rowan stood and waited quietly for things to move on. After a few moments she heard White Feather telling Thaylum, "I'm glad you're home. Three nights ago a small band of elves made camp not far from here. I put a glamour over the cottage and kept the children in. I sat up all night in the kitchen with a bow and a large stack of arrows. I don't like feeling afraid in my own home. I am very glad that you're here."

Peony and Quinn had overcome their shyness and discovered Raphael, who now had a child on each arm and was bringing his wings up so that they were hidden in feathery cave from which giggles issued.

"We have to leave soon love," Thaylum said to White Feather.

"I just finished the week's baking and there is a big pot of mushroom and wild rice soup on the stove. Do you think that we have time to eat it before we leave so that it doesn't go to waste?"

Thaylum looked at Rowan questioningly.

"Fine, but we need to make it quick."

Rhiannon went with Nimue and Cole to the kitchen to slice bread and find dishes. She noticed that the two of them barely let more than a few feet of space grow between them, and that close enough to touch, seemed to be the preference. In another two hours Cole would ride away and Nimue would be left behind. They were making the most of the time left. Rhiannon knew first hand that this was a hard time to fall in love with someone. White Feather hurriedly packed clothes and fussed at the idea of Rhiannon working in her kitchen. Outside the others worked at boarding up the windows and loading Feather's preciously gathered sacks of wild mushrooms onto a pack horse. Within twenty minutes they were gathered around a rough table outside, eating what turned out to be a serendipitously welcome mid morning meal. The hot delicious soup and dense, hearty, fresh bread with lots of nuts baked into it eased Rhiannon's nausea and left her feeling stronger.

"I hope that you don't mind forest food?" Feather asked Rhiannon and Rowan shyly as they ate.

"Don't worry about those two," Thaylum reassured his wife half jokingly. "They're as Fay as it comes with regards to food and even Cole here is half Selkie so the only flesh you'll catch him eating is fish."

"Thaylum's right. Food doesn't get better than this," Rhiannon said as she wiped out the bottom of her bowl with the crust of her bread.

The sun shone through the trees as they ate in the little clearing, and from a certain perspective Rhiannon envied

Thaylum and White Feather their quiet life in the woods. The few minutes of camaraderie, conversation, and good food were somehow magical, but it was over all too soon. They washed the dishes, shut up the cottage and parted ways. It was the end of a very short era. Rhiannon looked back over her shoulder as they rode away from the clearing and Nimue was looking back from her seat behind Cole on his grey. They would never be together under those circumstances again. She could see in her sister's eyes, the same feeling of being trapped in a current pulling them irrevocably towards a fate that neither was sure she wanted.

Chapter 23

The going was easy on the first day of their journey into the mountains and it was a pleasant ride. Merlin's Shadow, David, and Aledwen melted into the rocks and forests and travelled on foot, silently and invisibly. Raphael would walk with them until his feet got sore, and then fly ahead and wait at a vantage point. Rhiannon had thought that perhaps it would look strange or unnatural to see the angel fly but it didn't at all. He would run at it, down hill if he could, kick off and fly. As simple as that. It was amazing, and yet he made it seem the most natural thing in the world. It didn't look awkward at all. Otherwise it was just herself, Rowan, and Yuka on horse back. Yuka rode a small palomino but even she would get down every few hours, take off her silk riding clothes, shift into the form of a small fleet fox, and dash off into the woods. She would return and dress herself, always leaving her feet bare, and remount. Rhiannon knew that if it weren't for her, they would all be going on foot but as it was, sitting and riding gave her a good opportunity to ask the dozens of questions that were always swimming around in her head. She picked their brains. Yuka, being just as amenable to questions, answered many and, being from across the Western Sea, as they called the Pacific ocean, she often had a less biased perspective on the situation. Rhiannon had asked why she thought that the taboo lingered like it did and Yuka's answer surprised her.

"There were never any Angels on the Islands I come from, and any distinction between the Human and Fay populations has long since faded away. It happened there even before the time of the Plague Wars and so, there was never anything to fuss over. No taboo. But when the ships that visited from the mainland brought traders who had been to the west, they told stories of the plague and of stonings and other barbaric attacks on the Fay at the hands of the Humans. The Humans were dying though, and the Fay were not only untouched by the plague, but they were unable to heal it and that, in and of itself, would be enough to create animosity."

"That and the elves and their fear forms and lies," Rowan said bitterly.

Rhiannon looked at him sharply. "In the other world the stories about the Fay are often very ambivalent or downright nasty and while the Fay themselves don't always mean to cause trouble, the stories don't always end well for the Humans. Are you saying that there are stories like that here? I mean, so far I haven't met a Fairy that I've found truly fright-ening, but in the other world, some of the stories tell of Sylvan girls killing men in the woods and of the Leanansidhe drinking human blood. No one here mentions Anthropophagi or the Lorelei or Boggarts."

"Anthropophagi?" Yuka repeated questioningly.

"Headless cannibal Fairy thingy," Rhiannon explained as briefly as she could.

Yuka wrinkled her dainty nose in distaste. "There were no elves to tell tales back home."

"What do the elves say? What lies?" Rhiannon asked.

"They started as the humans were leaving the old country. First the stories. Gwydion told me about them. Stories much like what you mentioned. Tales that made the Humans think twice before wandering the woods alone. Lies that made them believe that the Fay had turned. There was one story that they spread that told of how, while the plague killed humans, it had brought insanity to the Fay. There were also stories of creatures that killed or drank blood and what with the plague closing in and the pressure to flee, many believed the stories. Then came the fear forms."

"What do you mean by 'Fear Forms'?" Rhiannon asked.

"The elves can't use them on us, but any human without a drop of Fay blood is susceptible to them. I'm not sure exactly what they see, but when the elves get into someone's head badly enough they sometimes drive them permanently insane. They have dreams about being eaten alive, monsters, drownings ..." Rowan was silent for a moment. "I've seen it happen. I've never told any one before but when I choose men for covert missions, I often choose the ones that I suspect have fay blood, even if they don't know it themselves."

"But surely the Humans know now that the stories aren't true, and that the elves are the ones responsible for the nightmares? I mean, the Fay have hospitals at the edges of their strongholds where anyone can go and all of the Humans know this. Do they *really* think that a Fairy midwife would *really* turn and drink a Human's blood after helping birth their children?" Rhiannon asked in indignation.

"No, they don't believe all that, but there is a lingering mistrust that is stronger in some families than in others. A belief that the Fay will always be dishonest or use trickery in their dealings, and people like Seamus make it worse. He perpetuates the lie, and while the majority of the population see him as a possible dictator, there are those who follow him because of those old erroneous fears. That and a lust for conflict," Rowan tacked on.

They rode on in silence until Rhiannon found another question bursting to get out. She turned to Yuka. "Why did you come here?" she asked, doubly curious now that she knew Yuka came from a part of the world that was quite stable.

Yuka smiled and laughed, "Chronic and inescapable wanderlust. It doesn't matter where I am I always want to go somewhere else, although I've been here for quite some time now. I think it's because things stay interesting here."

"Where else have you travelled?"

"Further west of my home. There are cultural differences but life is homogeneously Fay there as well. It was very beautiful, warm and exotic. I stayed for a while." She smiled again showing her pronounced canines, then slipped down from her horse and began stripping, bundling her clothes into a saddle bag as she walked along beside the horse. Then she was gone and a red fox was scampering off into the woods.

Rhiannon looked to Rowan. It was just the two of them now. They hadn't caught up to Raphael yet. She watched him for a minute or two as he rode ahead of her. He was graceful astride a horse. He sat easily, confidently, so used to being on horseback that the fact that he was didn't even seem to register. She looked at the horse. He was big glossy and black. Jet black, a black that almost ate the light. There wasn't even a speck of any other colour.

"So, does that horse have a name?" she called forward to him.

He looked back and smiled, "Snicker Doodle."

"Snicker Doodle?" Rhiannon repeated back lamely.

The trail widened again allowing them to ride side by side once more.

"Yeah. Like the spicy little biscuits," he said still smiling

"I know what they are. Strangely enough they exist in the other world too. But why on earth would you name a *war* horse Snicker Doodle?"

Rowan's smile deepened. She could see that he was enjoying himself. "When he was a colt he was a funny thing. All gangly, awkward and sweet natured, but he had some spirit too. Like a snicker doodle. Sweet, but just a little spicy. I had a time of it breaking and training him, but now we're good friends. Although," Rowan said with a note of caution in his voice. "I sometimes wonder if he hasn't got a little Kelpie in him or if maybe he's really a Phooka and he doesn't know it yet and one day he's going to realize, run wild on me and dump me in a bramble or a mire."

Rhiannon laughed.

* * *

Once they had caught up to Raphael they stopped for lunch. Yuka rejoined them. She didn't shift back to human shape immediately but rather lounged around in fox form while crunching down a squirrel carcass. Rhiannon tried not to watch as she ate her own bread and cheese. They continued on after they had eaten. Yuka and Raphael stayed with them. As they'd ridden Rhiannon had been paying attention to the forest. Trying to read it, to sense it and all that was in it. She wasn't sure if the things that she was picking up on were accurate, but she liked the feeling of being open to the forest around them. It was a feeling that she had always tried to shut out when she was younger and now it was one of the joys of her present, so she ran with it and left herself open like a satellite receiver. She looked into the forest. Let her gaze snake deep between the massive trunks and got perhaps a little lost there, then she found something that didn't belong. Something malignant, dark in a bad way. Sometimes darkness is beautiful. The quiet darkness of a safe warm room inviting you to sleep in a lover's arms is wonderful. This darkness was the opposite. This was a 'cold and alone forever' darkness. A cruel darkness. Rhiannon recoiled. "Something's wrong. That way," she pointed into the trees.

The others were alert immediately.

"Elves," Rowan said.

Yuka didn't stop to put her clothes in her saddle bag but shifted halfway between the saddle and the forest floor then dashed off into the forest. Raphael stooped and bundled the clothing into a saddle bag.

"Hide her," Raphael addressed Rowan. "It's our safest bet. Opening a doorway to the other world here might not be a good idea especially if the elves figure out where we've gone. It's too public on the other side. People could get hurt." Rhiannon was a little surprised at the authority in Raphael's voice, but what he said was true. She was afraid to open a door to the other world right now, knowing that a slip up using that much power could cause a miscarriage or that she could seriously hurt or kill herself, so Raphael would have to do it for her, and an angel and a fairy princess would draw a fair amount of attention appearing suddenly on very popular hiking trails. Add to that the fact that some of the elves could follow them through. She was just as safe here.

"Done," Rowan said instantly. "You can find us if we're hidden?"

Raphael nodded, drew his bow and strung it.

Rowan dismounted as David materialized at his elbow. "They are headed this way. Yuka and your grandfather are tailing them and will make sure that we hear them coming. Aledwen and Bonnie are ready. I will take the horses."

Rhiannon dismounted and David started walking away with the four horses. "Come love." Rowan took her hand and began leading her away from the path.

Rhiannon's heart thudded in her chest as they hurried through the forest. If she were alone she would be *so* dead. She would be helpless to do anything but hide, and alone she would be found. Found, and then what? Probably not actually dead. There were things that were worse than dead. This was what ran through her mind as she ran beside Rowan nimbly

jumping logs and branches as he pulled her along looking for
a place that he found suitable. He stopped short. "In here.
Quick," he said bundling her into a hollow next to a big rock
under some tree roots. There was a shadowy pit at the back
that she scrunched into. *Small has its uses after all.* She
thought as she pulled the hood of her cloak up and drew the
green wool around her.

"Do you know how to make yourself invisible?" he asked so
calmly, looking at her reassuringly from where he crouched
just outside the hollow.

Rhiannon shook her head, gulped and stared at him with
big eyes.

"It doesn't take a lot of power. Just a little. Can you use
your magic or are you too frightened?"

Rhiannon did some more brainless staring.

Rowan looked in the direction that the elves were approaching from, then turned back to her, "Look, it's going to
be fine. This isn't the same as the day by the grove, but it'll be
even *more* fine if you're completely hidden. Take my hand, do
whatever it is that you do to find the magic."

The touch of his hand and the strange opposite feeling of
his very male way of accessing power were catalytic. Holding
on to what was important she accessed just a little magic of
her own. "Okay now what?" she whispered.

"Close your eyes."

She closed her eyes and a feeling stole over her that was
like being wrapped in a blanket.

"Do you feel that?"

Rhiannon nodded.

"You need to answer me verbally. I can't see you," he said
gently.

Rhiannon opened her eyes and realized that she was invisible and so was Rowan but she could still feel his hand.
"Yes I feel it."

"Okay. I'm going to let go of your hand. Hold on to the feeling."

He let go and she kept the feeling of the blanket around her.

Rowan reappeared briefly and said to her, "Stay hidden and absolutely silent. I won't leave you. You won't see me but I ll be close." Then he blinked out of sight.

Rhiannon concentrated on staying still and breathing slowly and quietly. She had to concentrate to remain invisible, so she focused on that too as she stared out the gap between the rocks and the roots. It didn't take her long to realize that she was wound tight like a spring watching out the gap wait-ing, and that was bad. She was afraid of using her magic incorrectly. She didn't want to lose her baby. The thought made her eyes water up so she closed them. It was a little better but she could feel the blankety feeling slipping. She took a deep breath and tried for the feeling she'd had when she'd been in the forest with her Grandmother and sister then brought the feeling of the warm blanket back. *Warm and safe. It's funny how those two things seem to go together,* she thought, curling up more tightly and burrowing more deeply into her hollow. The idea of people out there waiting to face danger on her account made her falter again, but she pulled herself together and imagined that the tree roots in which she hid were keeping her safe and restricted her mind to what Rowan had told her to do. Stay hidden. Eyes closed she rested her head on the side of the hollow and thought the word *Hidden.* She tasted it. Rolled it around in her mind. Distantly she heard a fox yipping and soon after that a bowstring release. It had a dream quality to it. As if she were separated from it. She heard arrows bury themselves in trees and more bowstrings releasing. She burrowed deeper. She heard arrows find live targets. Time lost definition. Swords met swords. There were shouts. *Oh, keep them safe. Keep them safe.* She breathed inwardly and soon it was silent. The silence stretched then contracted. She couldn't move. *Stay hidden.*

* * *

"Is that the last of them?" Rowan. He sounded distant. Muffled.

"I counted nineteen." Yuka.

"Raphael?" This was Rowan again.

"Yup. Nineteen. We got them all."

"Hey ..." It was Rowan. He spoke softly into the hollow, "Rhiannon ...? Are you there?" Concern seeping in.

He reached his hand into the hollow and Rhiannon who was still scrunched up with her eyes closed thinking *hidden* gave a short startled shriek when his hand bumped her leg and jolted out of her near trance. She sat blinking.

Rowan chuckled. "I can barely see you back there even when you're not invisible. You can come out. It's safe." He extended his hand.

Rhiannon unfolded herself and took Rowan's hand, ducking some roots as she emerged from the hollow still blinking. The others were standing around them. Merlin's Shadow still had his bow in his hands, and Bonnie and Aledwen could be seen a short way off gathering arrows. Raphael was cleaning his sword on the moss, and Yuka was standing there naked, in human form looking slightly nauseous.

"They're ... gone?" Rhiannon asked quietly.

"Well ... dead. But yes," Raphael answered her.

"How?" she whispered.

"We put a barrier around us, around you, and picked most of them off from a distance before they could pinpoint our location. By the time they came close enough to fight with swords there were only five of them left," Rowan said.

"Do you know what they were doing? Were they tracking us, or was it an accidental run in?"

"We don't know," Raphael admitted dissatisfied, sheathing his sword then checking his bow quickly before slinging it across his back.

Yuka, who was looking greener and greener suddenly said, "Excuse me," and shifted back into fox form. It wasn't a transformation like Rhiannon would have expected. It was more like changing channels on a television. One moment Coronation Street, Telly Tubbies the next. Yuka. Fox. The Fox braced then retched and vomited. There was a white ghastly thumb and forefinger in the stomach fluids along with half digested bits of squirrel. Rhiannon couldn't keep her lunch down after that sight and turned and retched as well.

* * *

She spent the fifteen minutes or so that it took to track down David and the horses telling Rowan repeatedly, "I'm fine. You don't need to carry me. You've seen how many cabbages I can lift. I'm not a wimp."

"I don't care," he'd respond. "You're not heavy. Just suck it up and let me fuss okay."

"But I'm fine, I just got woozy seeing the fingers," she'd say

And then he'd say, "Close your eyes there's another body on the left."

And she would somewhat sheepishly, but quite gratefully, bury her face in his neck until they were passed the corpses, because he was right, she didn't want to walk past the bodies.

* * *

They found David and rode till dusk was near. Raphael stopped them, "Just over the next rise there's a good place to make camp. It's sheltered and the ground is relatively flat."

Rowan set up one small oiled canvas tent and stretched a tarp above it while Yuka and Rhiannon looked for fire wood with Raphael. Then Yuka proceeded to build the fire and start a pot of rice cooking. Rhiannon sat on a stump and watched as the Fox Fairy added seaweed and dried mushrooms to another pot. Yuka also produced some tofu from a bag which she fried with some cabbage in something that almost tasted like teriyaki sauce. They ate as darkness fell and Rhiannon was glad to have a warm lump of sticky rice in her stomach as she drifted off in the tent. Rowan lay beside her and Yuka had changed back into a fox and curled up at their feet. She didn't think that she would sleep well, but she was out cold in a matter of seconds.

* * *

It was the musky animal smell that woke her. Rowan was gone but the fox was curled in a tight ball next to her. Rhiannon fought the urge to pet Yuka. Her ears looked so touchable. The sun was well up and Rhiannon could hear voices outside of the tent. She closed her eyes and tried to go back to sleep, if only for a few minutes, but the snippets of the conversation that Rowan and Raphael were having weren't making it easy. It was a vaguely embarrassing conversation about privacy. They obviously thought that she was still sleeping. Rhiannon thought over what she knew about Raphael and windows and wondered exactly what he'd said to Rowan to start this conversation. She knew Rowan wouldn't have started it.

"Well," Raphael mumbled, "It's a hard habit to break. I don't feel right at night if I don't at least check on her."

"Okay, fine. I'm not asking you to stop. I asked you to keep up your watch, I'm just saying that whatever you hear through our window ... just pretend you didn't. Just *don't* listen."

"Okay ..." Raphael said but then couldn't seem to resist asking, "But you're *sure* that she's not that mad at me?"

"She said those things before she'd had any time to think. She wouldn't have said them if she'd thought you were listening. She's not angry. Not at you. Not anymore." Rowan was exasperated.

Rhiannon scrambled out of the tent dislodging the sleeping fox in a desperate attempt to save Rowan.

"Good! You're up!" he smiled, looking relieved, and passed her a bowl of oatmeal.

They ate breakfast but Rhiannon felt like she was force feeding herself. She slipped away into the forest to relieve herself knowing that, even though she couldn't see them, Bonnie and Aledwen were there protecting her. She might never be truly alone ever again. It was a disconcerting thought.

* * *

Raphael estimated that they should reach the Angels' city by noon and it should have been a pleasant ride. Rhiannon couldn't tell if it was nerves—she'd always had a nervous stomach—or if it was morning sickness that was making it such a miserable ride. Her stomach wasn't normally quite *this* nervous and Strawberry's rocking motion was making it worse. The food she hadn't enjoyed that morning was churning in her stomach and going nowhere. She pulled her feet out of the stirrups and slipped off of Strawberry's back, crouched and retched. Rowan was down and beside her so quickly that she didn't realize he was there.

"What is it?" he asked, all concern.

Rhiannon didn't answer right away as she crouched waiting to see if she was going to vomit again. She didn't need this and she didn't want to say it out loud but she knew what it was for sure now. "Morning sickness," she muttered, still spitting.

Rowan winced. "We have really bad timing don't we."

Rhiannon chuckled at the ridiculousness of it as she wiped her mouth with the wet cloth Rowan passed her. "No, *we* have good timing. It's the rest of the world that's off. If there was no war, and no psycho uncle to deal with, we would be at home and it would be a perfect time to be laid up with morning sickness."

"Is that your way of telling me not to feel guilty?"

"It is. Let's get moving."

Rowan pulled her up behind him on Snicker Doodle. The war horse had a smoother gait than Strawberry and it was easier to to deal with the nausea when she didn't have to hold herself up or think about the reins. She rode for a while with her arms around Rowan's waist and her cheek resting on his back, eyes closed, but before long Raphael landed in front of them and told them that they would have to leave the horses as it got a little tricky up ahead. David and Bonnie stayed behind with the horses and the rest of them continued on foot. They passed through a couple of narrow rocky passages that the horses would not have been able to manage, before coming to a long stone staircase. Rhiannon found walking better than riding in terms of the nausea, but she had lost her breakfast and it had left her feeling lightheaded and as if her feet were made of lead. After a period of climbing stairs she had to stop. She sat, drank some water, ate some nuts and dried fruit, tried to stop her hands from shaking with fear at what they would find when they reached the city. Raphael was tight lipped on the subject but she got the impression that he was ashamed rather than worried. It didn't help. She was pretty sure that all the reassurances in the world wouldn't help now. She didn't know what she was going to say to the angels. She looked out over the bright autumn panorama below. *Stop putting it off. Just go. Get it over with,* she told herself as she got to her feet and, silently, they climbed the stone stairs into the mountains. The air was cold and the wind buffeted them. They had climbed for more than two hours before they reached the entrance to the city. A large outer courtyard, about the size of a schoolyard baseball field, opened up before them as they made it up the last few stairs. It seemed to be carved right out of the mountainside. At the far end was a gate, and in front of that gate was an angel.

Chapter 24

If Raphael was warm, open and perhaps, maybe, just a little bit quirky, then the angel who stood in front of the gates was the opposite. Cold, arrogant, and unimaginative. He watched the small group of Fay approach with a cynical jaded glower. The angel was every bit as good looking as Raphael, with indigo wings, grey eyes and black hair. He wore a blue grey tunic with brown pants and boots. The requisite long sword hung at his hip. He was taller than Raphael and looked like he was in his early twenties. Rhiannon watched his hard eyes flick from Raphael to herself to Rowan. There was suspicion and contempt in his eyes, but if he was surprised to see them he masked it well. Rhiannon approached him ahead of the others. Raphael had told them that morning at breakfast, that getting past the gates would either be a breeze or a challenge, depending on who was on guard. If it was Sarah she would let them right in, some of the older angels would take some convincing, but of the younger angels the only one that they had to worry about was Malik, and if Malik did indeed turn out to be the keeper of the gate, Raphael was pretty sure that they would not get by without a fight. He'd called Malik 'the anti-rebel'. "Malik sticks to the rules as his own private form of rebellion," Raphael had said shaking his head. "He isn't so bad underneath it all, but the four of us all feel pretty helpless, and clinging to all of the old dogmatic shit is Malik's way of coping."

"The four of you?" Yuka was quick to ask.

"There are only four of us, in my generation ... I'm the youngest. At present, it looks as if we will be the last."

Based on what Raphael had told them, Rhiannon was pretty sure that the angel before them now was Malik. When she was three feet away from him she stopped and curtsied then looked into the expressionless face and said to him, "My name is Rhiannon. I am the daughter of Queen Sulamith and King Lugh. I've come because I need your help. I wondered if you would be so kind as to let me pass so that I might speak to your people?" she asked politely if somewhat quietly, balked by the tall cold angel and the towering stone walls.

"None may pass," the angel said automatically.

"May I ask why not?" Rhiannon asked softly. "We've come a long way."

The angel said nothing.

"Come on Malik. Why don't you just admit that you don't know why your not letting her in," Raphael goaded.

"Shut up Raphael. Everyone knows that you're a misfit." Malik gave Raphael a hard glance, obviously unsurprised by Raphael's presence, even if he was surprised by the group of travellers.

"At least I'm not an automaton. At least I think for myself," Raphael responded.

This isn't going well. Rhiannon thought to herself and looked at Raphael as she said, "We didn't come here to fight. Please," she levelled a desperate pleading gaze at Malik hoping that 'pretty girl eyes' might soften him up. "We just want to talk. We don't want your magic, just your swords and your support. We wouldn't have come all this way if there wasn't a profound need. At least give me a chance."

"We are above you. There is no *reason* for us to help you. What happens to your people is of no concern to us."

"Not everyone believes that and you know it!" Raphael shouted in anger.

Malik glared at them. "Show me then. Show me that you are of some consequence." His eyes ran over the small group. He rolled his eyes at Raphael as his glance passed over the rebel angel, then he let his gaze rest on Rhiannon. "Little Fairy. I could crush you."

Rhiannon couldn't help but think that Malik spoke in the strangest tone, as if he was seeing her for the first time. Seeing how much smaller than him she was, that she was indeed little, and in her way, against him, really quite helpless. So many emotions passed over his face that it frightened her. She let him see that she was frightened in the hopes that it would at least cause him some discomfort. That it might bother him, on some level, to have frightened someone who he *could* so easily crush. There was a flicker of guilt and uncertainty in Malik's eyes but his words had had consequences and Rowan had stepped in front of her. She should have known that he wouldn't let her be threatened. Even Raphael now had a look of dangerous anger towards Malik in his eyes, but she knew that Raphael's hands were tied in this. If he fought Malik over this it would mean banishment or death for Raphael, and it was all the angel could do to keep his temper reined in and his hand off of his sword. But Rowan wasn't subject to their laws, so he said to Malik, "You have no cause to threaten her, but if you want consequences I can give them to you."

Rhiannon could see the confusion in Malik's eyes as he inspected Rowan and observed the anger that both he and Raphael now directed towards him, but all that the uncertainty did was push him back into the conviction that the old ways must somehow be right, and his face hardened again as he looked down at Rowan scornfully and said, "Fine. If you can overcome me, I will let you pass."

"No! We didn't come here to fight," Rhiannon cried out in alarm, even though Raphael had assured her that Rowan could

handle Malik ... even though she knew that Rowan was un-
afraid. Rowan drew her aside as she pursued her argument
"No my love. Please no. There has to be another way," She
pleaded, taking his hand in her own and holding it there.

Rowan shook his head sadly and stroked her cheek, "It is
the only way. It is the only language that this one understands."

"He's right Rhiannon," Raphael said quietly from where he
had come to stand beside them. "I would fight for you If I
could, but you know that I can't attack Malik."

Rhiannon could see that Rowan was right even if she didn't
want to admit it. She stepped forward and kissed him, noticing the earring pushed through his collar as she did. She
nodded, stepped back, and Raphael took her hand and led her
to the edge of the courtyard as Rowan turned to face Malik.
There was a semicircle of massive oaks growing around the
edge of the courtyard but even massive as they were, they
were dwarfed by the imposing stone walls. Aledwen, Merlin's
Shadow, and Yuka joined them by the side as Malik looked
from Rhiannon to Rowan with more confusion in his face
before he once more erected his wall of indifference.

Rowan walked to the centre of the courtyard, drew his
sword and said to Malik, "Have it your way. I'm ready." And
the angel was on him.

Rowan was out from under Malik's attack in a matter of
seconds and the angel was gripping his upper arm in shock
and anger. Rowan was both stronger and faster than Malik
had expected him to be. Rowan's face was hard as he held his
sword and waited patiently for Malik to renew his attack.
Rhiannon looked at the plain sword in Rowan's hands. It was a
funny thing, Rowan and swords, but he didn't really get
attached to them. She'd asked him about his sword one morning as they'd walked down to Gwydion's and he'd told her,
"It's a tool like a shovel or a pen. It works better if it's made

well, but even though the shovel that I use to dig potatoes works well, you don't see me getting attached to it or decorating it. I don't understand men who become attached to their swords."

Malik charged, alert now to Rowan's speed. Rowan raised his ordinary sword and met Malik's attack and though Malik gave it his all he was again deflected. Malik was glorious with his indigo wings poised and long sword flashing but Rowan was so light on his feet, so quick to defend and attack that, while if it came to a contest of brute strength Malik would probably win, Rowan's accuracy and skill were superior. It still bothered Rhiannon to watch, especially as they were not, as Rowan and Raphael had been only three short days earlier, taking care not to harm one another, but despite the heartache that it caused her, and the sick feeling in her stomach at the conflict, she had realized a few things watching this fight. One: when Rowan fought Leif, he was holding back. Two: While Malik was a practised fighter, he was not experienced. Not in real life combat. Not even like Raphael, fighting elves on the fly. Practice was all that Malik had ever done. And three: and this was probably the greatest example of Malik's inexperience and ignorance, he had challenged a Dryad to a dual in the centre of a ring of oak trees. The expression in the world she'd left behind would have been 'How stupid can you get.' And while watching this was still excruciating to her, she couldn't help being in awe of Rowan. They'd been at it now for nearly a half an hour and Rowan was dancing effortlessly out from under Malik's attacks and twisting the angel up in circles. He stepped in and attacked once again, nipping Malik's forearm with the tip of his blade. Malik was bleeding now from several small wounds and Rhiannon was pretty sure that Rowan was holding back just enough to keep from doing serious harm, while Malik was fighting for his life. Malik yelled in pain as Rowan slashed at his leg and a dark red patch seeped into the fabric of his breeches. Rhiannon was sure now that Rowan could end it any time he wanted, but he wasn't about to until he had made Malik understand that he wasn't dealing with a subspecies. In an act of desperation Malik leapt, pumping his wings. It wasn't honourable, but Rowan had pushed him to his limit. It was an attempt to gain the upper hand however he could, but no sooner had he lifted off, Rowan blinked out of sight. The angel had been pushed so far that he didn't have the energy to sustain flight and had no choice but to land, but where? He couldn't see Rowan anywhere. Within seconds of lifting off Malik was back on the ground looking around desperately. His sword flew from his hand and clattered against the nearest wall. Malik fell to his knees and shouted, "I yield!" As Rowan blinked back into view directly in front of Malik, his sword point at Malik's throat.

"You'll let us in?" Rowan asked.

Malik nodded. "I most humbly apologize for my behaviour. I see now that I was wrong," his voice shook as the words rushed out of his mouth.

Rowan withdrew his sword. "Stand," he said to Malik, not a request.

Malik stood, bleeding and unsteady.

"You're injured. Would you allow one of us to heal you?' Rowan asked.

"You can do that?" Malik asked incredulous.

"If you left the mountains every once in a while you would know this," Raphael interjected.

"Shut up Raph," Malik sighed, not in anger but simply in the tone of one with a severely injured pride whose world view has just been shattered.

"I don't think that I deserve it," Malik said to Rowan, then hung his head.

Rhiannon, who had been watching all of this from the sidelines, stepped forward. Her feet felt like lead. Her heart hurt.

This wasn't what she wanted to be. This wasn't what she wanted to do. She was only a little fairy. Nothing more. She didn't want to be a queen but the weight of what her future held pushed her forward like a current and she was helpless as she walked towards the angel who could crush her if he wanted to and said, "Please let me heal you?"

And more out of shock than permission he allowed her to take his hand. What he saw when he looked into her face as she gazed up at him, the small sweet face with dark blue eyes and the flashing opal, was the entirety of her pain. She gripped his hand not letting it go and she knew that what she was doing was cruel, but she let the worst parts of her life flash through her mind, maintaining the contact with his hand as she unloaded it into his brain. It tore her apart as she saw through his eyes, the newspaper clipping of her parent's burned out house, the way she'd yelled at Rowan after she'd learned who she truly was, Raphael on the beach, her father Lugh, the unhappiness she'd experienced in her childhood, the teasing, the bullying and now the constant fear that she wouldn't live out the year or that somehow she would lose the child she carried. And, worst of all, the fear that she felt for the people she loved who would have to fight, were fight-ing, for *her*. She held tightly to her life force and the little spark inside and she let him have these images and feelings as she healed him, then finally, before she let go of his hand she showed him the intensity of her hope and her desire for peace and freedom. She let go and staggered a little to the side, suddenly dizzy. Yuka took her arm and steadied her.

Rhiannon turned in shock and horror at what she'd just done. In her heart it felt like an atrocity. Now Malik would have to live with her experiences like they were his own, and she was pretty sure that he had his own issues to deal with. She had caused him pain but she'd wanted him to understand her and she hadn't known how else to do it. *But she had caused him pain.* She placed her hand over her mouth to stifle a sob then turned back to Malik who had a bruised look in his eyes. "I'm sorry, I'm so sorry," she said wiping ungracefully at her cheeks.

"Don't," Malik said to her. "Don't carry more sorrow on my account. I brought this on myself. It is my burden to bear. It is the price that I will pay for my pride."

"Stoic till the end. That's Malik," Raphael muttered under his breath.

Rhiannon swallowed and nodded then asked, "Will you take us now, to your people? I don't need to tell you that this is urgent."

"Yes. Come with me," Malik said quietly and lead them towards the gate.

"This one is your mate and champion?" he enquired, motioning towards Rowan.

"Yes. This is Rowan. He is my husband and the Captain of my army," she answered, and Rowan nodded to Malik as they walked.

"And you are the Queen of both the Human and Fay realms?"

"I am the rightful queen of the Human realm yes, but as my father still lives I am currently the heir to the Fay throne. The logistics of that may change if we succeed at what we hope to do."

Rhiannon introduced Malik to the others as they crossed the courtyard and passed through the gates. Malik turned and shoved a heavy lever so that a great grinding of gears could be heard within the stone walls and a solid and impassable grill came down on the outside of the gate.

"Are you going to leave the gate unguarded?" Raphael asked Malik incredulous.

Malik smiled ruefully, "No one has come to this gate in four hundred years except for *you*. You might be right Raphael.

Maybe it is time to start breaking the rules. I'm going to leave the gate unguarded. It's not like I'm leaving it unlocked and there's still a sentry up on the wall," Malik shrugged. "I feel like I'm going to be struck dead for doing it, but if I am I'll just blame you Raph."

"Uh yeah um, sure. No problem," Raphael accepted the blame for Malik's possible death uncertainly.

They were in what looked like an alcove with no exit, but Malik lead them to a hidden door that opened into a corridor. He threw another lever behind them and then lead the way along the corridor and out into a town square. It was obvious that no one had lived there in a long time except maybe a few ghosts. Gardens were barren, doors hung open like gaping black mouths starving for life and windows looked out at them like blind sightless eyes. It must have once been a beautiful city but now it was nearly dead. Rhiannon walked holding Rowan's hand and she could see him looking around and making the same observations she did. Raphael had been cagey about what to expect when they arrived in the angel's city and now Rhiannon understood that he was embarrassed.

"There used to be three thousand of us living here but now there are only forty-eight. We don't use this part of the city." He pressed his lips into a grim line.

"It's true. We are much diminished from what we were many generations ago," Malik agreed soberly. "We can't even heal people like you healed me anymore."

They walked in silence for a time, through the empty streets, before Raphael spoke again. "Long ago Humans and Fay used to come here. That's why we have streets, but some parts of the city only have landing pads."

Rhiannon looked around her. The city almost looked like pictures she had seen of ancient Greek ruins only much less ancient and not quite ruins. It seemed like a very sad place to live. It took nearly an hour but eventually they came to a part

of the city where people still lived. The buildings were maintained and the remains of summer could still be seen in the
garden plots. A few frowsy looking old angels sat in doorways
and gawked at the newcomers in amazement. They came to a
set of elegantly carved doors. "Raphael, you take them up to
the hall. I'll go find Nuriel," Malik said before making a short
quick run and lifting off.

The building that they were standing in front of looked like
a small very elegant Parthenon. All of the doors were wide
and high to accommodate wings. Raphael opened the doors
and ushered them in. Rhiannon felt like a Hobbit outside the
Shire in this place, built to accommodate people nearly two to
three feet taller than her. There was a spectacular marble
staircase leading up to a light filled chamber above with
vaulted ceilings. Raphael lead them up to the large room
where there was a long table surrounded by chairs with
benches along all of the walls.

Word had obviously spread that there were strangers in the
Angel's city and several tall dignified angels had come into
the hall to see what was happening. Within minutes the entire
Angel population was there including Malik, who was accompanied by an angel Rhiannon knew could only be Nuriel.
Malik and Nuriel arrived via french doors at the other end of
the room. Despite their small numbers, seeing the angels together in the flesh for the first time was an awe provoking
experience, and it was outside of any experience that
Rhiannon had ever dreamed of having. They were stern and
dignified but very beautiful. The women were serene and calm
and even the older angels had an ageless quality to them.
Rhiannon noticed however that there were no children anywhere. Raphael had been telling the truth. He was the youngest angel there. Rhiannon noticed a woman looking at her
with a strange intensity. She approached Rhiannon with a
look of tenderness and wonder, and Rhiannon realized that

this must be Sarah, Raphael's mother. She was overwhelm-
ingly beautiful with alabaster skin and glossy black hair that
fell around her in loose curls. Her cheeks were delicately
tinted a soft lavender pink, she had full soft pink lips and
incredible cheekbones. Her eyes were large dark violet pools
surrounded by thick long eyelashes and all of this was set
against the backdrop of her heavenly violet wings. The angel,
and that was what she was in every possible way, turned to
Raphael and asked, "Where have you been? I've been worried
sick. I've searched and searched for you." She put her arms
around her son who suddenly looked every bit a teenager.
Then she turned to Rhiannon, "I'm almost afraid to talk to
you," she whispered and then put her arms around Rhiannon
tightly. "I've wanted to do that so many times," she said,
wiping tears from her eyes. "When I saw that your house had
been burned I feared the worst. I thought that perhaps both
of you were dead."

There was a sudden hush and everyone turned towards the
end of the room where Nuriel stood. He was an enormous
angel with crimson wings and brown hair. He looked at
Rhiannon with arrogant hostility. Rhiannon approached him.
When in doubt curtsy, she thought to herself and sunk even
lower before the huge angel who towered over her by nearly
three feet.

"I am Nuriel. Malik tells me that you have something to ask
of us."

Rhiannon straightened. "My name is Rhiannon. I am the
rightful Queen of Nova Britannia and I have come to ask for
your help." Rhiannon wondered how she could stand so still
when she felt like her heart was beating hard enough to shake
the whole room.

"Our help in what?" Nuriel asked, still stone cold.

"We want to break the taboo." The moment the words were out of her mouth a hush came over the room that was more profound than anything Rhiannon had expected.

Nuriel's face flushed in anger. He looked down on the small queen who stood calmly in front of him. He would never know what that calm cost her. He looked her up and down noticing the fern pattern on her hand and her cobalt eyes. "What would one little fairy know about the taboo?" he spat at her contemptuously. "Do you think that you understand what you are meddling with?"

"I think that I understand it better than you ever possibly could," she said to him equally cold.

"How so?"

"I am the daughter of the *Fay* king and the *Human* queen. I think that I am clear evidence that the taboo is nonsense and I am not the only one." She softened her voice, "Help us please. Come amongst us once again. Help us fight the elves. If we can't bring the Humans and the Fay together we will be annihilated. Would it be such an evil thing to come down from your mountain even for a short time and lend us your support?"

"You understand so little," Nuriel said in a clipped tone.

"I understand that without a united Nova Britannia we don't stand a chance against Seamus' army. I understand that if the Fay maintain their position of neutrality and the Humans won't accept an alliance that my uncle *will* succeed and we might as well hand *everything* over to the elves right now. I understand that if this happens my life will be very short!" She took a deep breath. "We know that the Angels started the taboo but we don't know why. If you won't support this we *might* have a chance at succeeding, but if you *will* support this, if you *will* come down from the mountains and show the people that you support an end to the taboo then I know that the revolution that my parents started by conceiving me will succeed."

"You don't understand," Nuriel said again but he was beginning to deflate in the face of Rhiannon's stubborn passion.

"What don't I understand?!" Rhiannon exploded at him so that he flinched, which was a strange sight, the massive angel shrinking from the tiny queen. Rhiannon watched his face closely as he flushed again then, she only saw it for a second before it was pushed aside, there was an expression of discomfiture or maybe even an expression of ... shame?

"We will not leave the mountains." Nuriel's voice was flat and dull. He'd tried to make it sound final.

Rhiannon decided that it was time to take a risk. She risked alienating Nuriel further but if she was right about her suspicion, it would pay off. "The Humans in the world I grew up in kill each other over their differences. What could be worse than that? What are you hiding from us. What dirty little secret have you been keeping up in these mountains for all of these centuries?" She spoke softly keeping her eyes on his beautiful stern face. "We would hate you if we knew, so you've let it fester here ..." She paused then started to cry exhausted overwhelmed tears that she couldn't do anything about. "Look at you. There is nothing left of you but a handful of rag-tag Angels who can barely do magic. What are you so ashamed of?" Nuriel's face softened at the sight of her tears and Rhiannon knew that Rowan had been right when he'd told her that all she needed to do was to be brave and be herself.

"Tell her, Father."

It was Raphael who finally spoke and Rhiannon realized how very brave *he* must be to make the stand that he had all of his life if Nuriel, the leader of the angels, was his father. She kept her face passive not letting Nuriel see that she hadn't known he was Raphael's father.

"I've seen more of this world and more of the other worlds than any angel here. I know that everything she's saying is right and our fear of their hatred isn't a good enough reason for us to keep this from them anymore. They deserve to know the truth. They deserve to know how we've failed them."

Dead silence.

"TELL HER!" Raphael yelled, then paused to give Nuriel a chance to speak, "If you won't, I will." His voice was low, challenging his father.

"Then let it be so," Nuriel spoke quietly. In defeat.

Chapter 25

"Let's sit. It's a long story," Raphael motioned to the table as he took a seat at the head. Seats were taken and Rhiannon found herself sitting next to Raphael and across from Nuriel.

"I'm not sure where to start except to tell you why we let the taboo become what it is today and why it is that we retreated from the world." He looked around at everyone, already feeling the impact of what he was about to say, "It was the angels who let the elves into our world."

Rhiannon looked around at the faces of the Angels, downcast, remorseful and then at the faces of her Fay company. They looked ... bitter.

Raphael started again, "Many centuries ago, long before any of us were born, before the Plague Wars even, Angels, Humans, and Fay lived together in relative peace. It was not uncommon for us to intermarry. In fact a few years ago when I was rummaging around in the basement of the library I came across a very old journal that contained an account of an angel, his human wife, and their children. When a Human and an Angel come together their children are Fairy," Raphael looked up. "I was intrigued to say the least. From what I read this was common and acceptable practice, but about 1600 years ago there came an angel called Asbeel. He loved a human woman called Hannah who was very beautiful but she didn't care for him. She loved another. Asbeel became angry and jealous. He kidnapped and raped her. No angel had ever done such a thing before. It was not unheard of in a Human male, but not an Angel. They were ashamed. Asbeel was found and imprisoned and Hannah was cared for by the Angels in secret. They didn't want anyone to find out what had been done to her. Hannah had become pregnant but when the child was born she died. Despite the fact that the Angels had the power to heal, there was nothing that they could do for her. The child was given to a Human family to raise but something was wrong with it. It was evil. It was an elf, and from that time forward elves have spread throughout this world more rapidly than could be explained by the appearance of one single elf, but it was Asbeel's act that allowed it to start." Raphael sighed and mussed his hair.

"After a few hundred years the elves had become a problem and the Angels had begun a slow retreat from the world. We did everything that we could to stop the elves, including giving magic to the Human leaders of the old empire. Instead of using it to fight the elves, they used it to fight each other, and it was the start of the plague wars. The plague wars isolated the Humans from the Fay, as the Fay were immune, but their power to heal had no effect on the illness. They began living in the magically guarded strongholds that you live in today to keep out elves and plague victims. By this point in history the Angels could see what was happening and they encouraged the separation of the Angels, Humans and Fairies, thinking that perhaps it would help us stop the spread of the elves, or at least we could figure out where they were coming from. The plague situation became so severe we had to act, so we blasted everything. Not even the magic that we gave the Emperors survived and after that we retreated into our mountain cities for good. We never told anyone where the elves had come from but we are the descendants of Asbeel's people and we felt that it was our burden to bear. We lost most of our magic after the plague wars and as we diminish, the elves grow in strength."

It was a hollow moment for Rhiannon and Rowan, finally knowing why they had lived the way they had and why their lives had been what they had. All of the secrecy, growing up never knowing what they were and finding out the hard way. All because of pride. Rhiannon thought of all that her parents had had to go through. The death of her birth mother. The burning of her adoptive parents. Screw the elves. It was the Angels with their damned pride that had started all of this. Rhiannon turned to Nuriel, her voice barely under control, "You've always assumed that you knew best, haven't you." She didn't mean it as a question but her next words were, "Have you ever considered that it might be your toxic secret that has let the elves proliferate?"

Nuriel hung his head.

Raphael looked at Rhiannon for a long moment. "Please don't hate me?" he pleaded.

She looked into his eyes. "Never. I could never hate you Raphael," she managed.

Then Raphael turned to his mother Sarah, "Tell them Rhiannon's story," he asked her. "It's a perfect example of how upholding the decisions of our ancestors will only cause more pain."

Chapter 26

Rhiannon would not, at that moment, have been Raphael, Sarah, or Nuriel for all the worlds. It was not a pleasant feeling. Nuriel's hurt at being so completely excluded from what was obviously the focus of his son's life, and his anger at Sarah, his estranged mate, for raising Raphael the way she had, were evident in the Angel's eyes. Raphael, with his own rebellious spirit, was trapped in the middle and wracked with guilt at having chosen sides. And then there was Sarah. All of the secrets she had kept for so many years, and all of the sorrow that she had had to swallow alone as the result of her hidden rebellion were there on the table. Only Raphael had shared her burden, and now her secrets were out. The angels turned and looked at her, shocked at the full extent of her rebellion. She held her hands over her face for a moment, overwhelmed to be placed on the spot. She removed her hands and looked around the room for a moment. Her lip quivered and she tried to speak. "I didn't mean ..." her voice broke and she stopped and swallowed, pressed her lips together, then started over.

"I didn't mean to hurt anybody. I wanted to tell you so many times." She looked at Nuriel and it was a strange look that spoke volumes. Anger, regret, longing. Nuriel had never come close enough to admitting that the angels might be wrong for her to ever have dared to share her secret with him.

Sarah told them about her night flying, her curiosity, and the meeting between herself and Rhiannon's mother

Sulamith. She explained to them Sulamith's plight and told them of the friendship that grew between them. "She was my best friend, and later she was my lover. She was the only person who understood the rebellious feelings that I had and what it was like to carry a child who had *every* likelihood of living a complicated, unhappy, lonely, life. She understood my guilt. And we were both guilty. I wondered so many times what my son would have in his life to *live* for. This," she motioned vaguely to the dead city around them, "Is not a life. Rebellion was the only thing that I had to offer him. I couldn't promise him that he would grow up and have someone to hold at night, or that he would have his own children some day. I couldn't promise him anything but *this* pathetic existence. But I could share my secrets with him, and then at least his life would have some purpose." Sarah went on to describe Sulamith and the abuse that she had suffered over the years at the hands of Rhiannon's uncle, Sulamith's own brother. Then, how she had felt landing one night on the tower roof to find Sulamith gone, never to return. She was silent for several minutes before picking up again. "After Sulamith died, Raphael and Rhiannon were all that I had left. Raphael and I kept Rhiannon safe as well as we could. There were times when we had to take turns guarding her house around the clock but more recently, up until seven weeks ago, things have been relatively quiet. When Raphael didn't check in I flew to Rhiannon's house in the other world. It had been burned and, because I couldn't find Raphael, I feared that they had both perished in the fire. I do not know what happened after that."

Yuka spoke at this point, "I believe that I am informed enough to share the rest of the tale with these people, if that is what you would prefer?" She glanced from Raphael to Rhiannon and Rowan.

"Yes please do," Raphael said to Yuka and she proceeded to fill in the blanks.

Rhiannon blocked out Yuka's words. She was still lost in Sarah's story. It had been one more disturbing angle of the tale that inevitably lead back to her. It didn't hurt any less. It was another layer. Another pair of sad eyes. To hear of Sarah flying to her mother at night, bringing news of the daughter she had been forced to abandon, that they had been lovers. This angel probably knew her mother better than anyone living. The mother Rhiannon would never know. Whose arms she would never feel. To hear Sarah tell of her mother's tears was yet another new and painful way to hurt. Rhiannon looked at Malik and then turned away from her own cruelty. She placed her hands over her belly as if to try to hold on to her own child, as yet, she knew, just a little bundle of cells, but still, just to comfort that little spirit.

When Yuka was finished there was another long silence, but eventually Nuriel looked up and spoke, "The time of the angels is over. We do not know better. I am your humble servant. I will not speak for the rest. You are free to do as you choose. If you seek leadership amongst us look to my son." Then he directed his next words to Rhiannon, "I for one will do whatever you need of me. I am weary of feeling useless."

"Thank you," was all that Rhiannon had the strength for. Nausea was once again getting the better of her and she needed to lie down, at least for a little while.

Rowan came to her rescue. Always the hero. "Is there a place where Rhiannon can rest, and perhaps eat? I realize that there is much to talk about and little time, however it will be a waste if she passes out."

"Yes of course," Sarah said, rising from her seat. "Come with me. My house is close by. I will fix you something to eat. We've all forgotten that you've had to travel here the hard way."

Sarah's house wasn't far but Rhiannon's stomach didn't make it, and she knelt at the edge of the street over the gutter. Rowan picked her up and carried her the rest of the way. She let her head rest on his shoulder and half closed her eyes. The house was like a city town house, with a small kitchen and living room on the ground floor, and two bedrooms upstairs. Following Sarah up, Rowan carried her and laid her down on a bed next to a large, winged, tabby cat where she let her eyes close the rest of the way and fell immediately into oblivion.

* * *

She wasn't sure how long she had slept or what it was that woke her. She suspected that it was the sunlight around the edges of the curtains on the west facing windows rather than the large warm rumbling mass curled against her stomach and chest. Something told her that the rumbling mass had been there for the entire nap. Rhiannon opened her eyes slowly. Sarah was just coming in with a tray. She placed it on the bedside table and pulled a chair over. Rhiannon pulled herself up to a sitting position, dislodging the big cat who ruffled his wings and flicked his ears as he found another prime spot to curl up pressed against Rhiannon's thigh. Rhiannon ran her hand along his back following his spine between his wings and he rumbled even louder.

"That's Grimble. He's the last of his kind too," Sarah said, reaching for a thick folded blanket and placing it on Rhiannon's lap. "Here, the bowl's hot." She placed a bowl of hot steaming, what smelled like potato celery, soup on the blanket and passed Rhiannon a spoon. "Hot soup was one of the few things I kept down when I was pregnant with Raphael."

Rhiannon had to smile at the image of this beautiful angel with morning sickness. Rhiannon ate, grateful that the nausea had abated and grateful for plain hot food. "Have I been asleep long?"

"No, just long enough for me to prepare the food. You just needed a rest. It's normal and I'm guessing that rest is something you've not had the luxury of. Do you feel well enough to go back to the meeting hall?"

"I suppose I do," Rhiannon smiled. "Although I'm not sure that I *want* to. I'd rather stay here with Grimble." She scratched the cat's ears so that he turned his broad head and leaned into her hand.

"I must apologize for Nuriel. He has always believed that our ancestors were right, and I must apologize for myself as well for I have never had the courage to tell him of the things that I have seen and done. I knew in my heart that our ancestors were wrong but, I ... well ... I have no excuse. I told myself that everything I did for your mother absolved me of guilt, but my secret drove Nuriel and I apart and the more I tried to change him the more rigid he became. Because of the way I raised Raphael a rift grew between him and his father. I see now how wrong I was. Can you forgive me?" Sarah's lush violet eyes were full of regret.

Rhiannon kept her voice soft, "I keep telling this to people. There is nothing to forgive. Just promise me, no more secrets."

Sarah nodded.

* * *

In the meeting hall the Angels were animated in a way that they had never been in their lives. Action was something that they had always been denied. They had lived their lives and gone about their days in the same routine for many generations and they had not been unhappy lives except for the last generation ... and that is what they were, the last. As Raphael had said, there were only four angels under twenty-five and only one female amongst them, there had always been unrest. Malik had reacted by clinging to the old ways, Raphael was the rebel. Mikhail, who was between Raphael and Malik in age loved Arariel, the only female, but she had shunned him and retreated from everything. She felt it would be unfair to raise children who would grow up alone with no one to love. That was if she was even able to have children, as so many of the angels in the generation before her's had been unable. For these four angels in particular, what was happening now was like the beginning of a new life.

Rhiannon was shocked by how changed they seemed when she entered the room. Rowan had returned to the meeting hall ahead of her and she smiled at him as she walked in and sat quietly beside him. "I like it when you smile," he whispered in her ear and then searched for her hand under the table. It was such a small thing, but a wonderful thing to Rhiannon. Then Rowan told her more loudly, "It was wise of you to insist on bringing Yuka, by the way. She's a brilliant facilitator. Everything has been more or less decided with very little trauma. We can go home tomorrow and have a day to recuperate before we leave for the King's city. The angels will come. The younger ones anyway."

The sense of anticipation in the room was palpable. The angels seemed as if they had been sitting quietly in the mountains, dormant, just waiting for a catalyst to spur them into action, and now they were all intensity and purpose. They were speaking excitedly about the things that they would do out in the world or, and this was from the older ones, how wonderful it would be to have people in the city again. To see new faces and share stories and knowledge. Nuriel approached Rhiannon and she stood. He spoke tentatively, "This will be the end of our secret. Do you think the world will hate us so very much for it?"

Rhiannon spoke gently, "You are coming into the world again, with the purpose of making things right. There will be too much wonder at that for hatred, I hope."

Nuriel nodded silently.

"*Have* you ever considered that perhaps it was your secret that allowed the elves to spread? Did the angels never think it was that which has kept the elves strong all this time? There is power in naming things. Perhaps admitting that your ancestors made mistakes, perhaps telling this story will weaken the elves."

"I don't know," Nuriel admitted, "though both Sarah and Raphael have tried to convince me of it. I was always taught that the creation of the elves was our burden to bear and that it was not to be shared." He paused. "I don't know what to think now, but for the first time in my life I am confused." He smiled almost imperceptibly, "Perhaps it is a good thing, although I must admit that I am not used to it."

Chapter 27

Sixteen Angels in total agreed to come down from the mountains with them and when they appeared through the mist on the barge late the following night after having travelled all day, the Fairies of Lugh's stronghold stared at them in the torchlight, fascinated. After the journey into the mountains the familiarity of the stronghold was comforting and it was a homecoming of sorts. Rhiannon was very glad to see her father, sister, and grandmother, who greeted both herself and Rowan with hugs and the Fay community at large seemed to have accepted her as one of their own. Even Stone Keeper, who had seemed to Rhiannon so stern at first, greeted her with a merry wizened smile and a warm embrace. The stronghold thronged with talk of how their changeling princess had coaxed the Angels out of the mountains. There was a huge banquet held the evening after they returned in honour of the Angels, and it was then that the Angels shared their secret. It was a surreal evening that encapsulated so many different emotions, but after Raphael had finished telling his tale, Lugh stood and said to all of the sombre confused listeners, "Now let us relegate this tale to the past. It can have no power over us there. Let us welcome the future, and show these serious Angels how to have a good time as only the Fay know how." He smiled his elegant smile and raised his glass high, "To unity, to peace, and to freedom!"

It seemed to Rhiannon that in a matter of seconds the entire hall had erupted into a wild Fay party with music, dancing and all manner of Fay antics, making her believe every strange story that she had ever heard about fairies in her entire life. There is *nothing* in the world quite like a drunk wood sprite in action.

After a long sleep and a bath, a day had been spent by Rowan, with Yuka, Lugh, Yori (the commander of the Fay army), and Raphael, poring over maps and reading correspondences from the city, writing letters and sending instructions to Gwydion that would be taken, with great speed and stealth, to let the old druid know that it was time. When she wasn't being held in place by Nimue, Morgana and two or three frantic seamstresses, trying on new dresses and being stuck with pins, Rhiannon hung over their shoulders intent on understanding what was going on. She tried not to drive them crazy but she felt obligated to understand. Then, in what felt like significantly less than two nights and a single day, what felt more like moments, it was time to leave for the King's City.

Rhiannon woke early in the morning and began dressing with the aid of Nimue, Morgana, and two attendants. After carefully placing the opal circlet on her brow they caught up the top half of her hair and secured the braided coils with a glittering net of cut quartz, dark amethyst, moonstone and seed pearl beads, so that while it was elegant, sparkling and sophisticated, it still showed off the decadent length as the ash waves draped over her shoulder. Her father had given her a new pair of earrings, opal teardrops, and she carefully clasped the sapphire and pearl necklace around her neck. Nothing had been spared when it came to the dress that she would wear into the city. It was the finest gossamer silk, so soft that it felt like the petals of a wild rose, in a delicate colour that was neither mauve, lavender, nor pink, but some elusive in between shade that drew the eye, made Rhiannon's pale skin glow and brought out the soft pink in her cheeks. The heavy damask underskirt and train of the dress, along with the princess neckline and tightly fitted bodice, were lavishly yet delicately embroidered with gold leaves and stitched with seed pearls. Over the dress went a morning glory blue velvet cloak lined with violet silk, and last of all, tiny blue embroidered slippers. Rhiannon looked down at her small hands. The fluttering cuffs of the dress had been cut in such a way that the fern pattern on her hand and arm, which at this point was more than just ferns, was exposed. It seemed that every time she used her magic in some significant way she acquired a new flower or plant on her skin. Forget-me-nots after that first night with Rowan, a couple of little violets from her afternoon in the woods with Morgana and Nimue, tiny little star-like chickweed blossoms after the full moon, a single wild sweet pea when she'd shown Rowan the image of their child on the beach, a clump of winter ghostberries from when she'd hidden in the tree roots, and blood red bitter uva ursi berries after she'd healed Malik. It told a story and they wanted the people of the city to see it. She continued looking at her hands. At the simple band that Rowan had given to her, and the heartsease ring that her father had given to her mother years before, then she looked up into the mirror in front of her. Faery Queen. Those were the only words for the young woman who looked back at Rhiannon. Made of mist and flowers, except for the cherry lips and glowing eyes. But deep inside she still didn't feel like a queen and she knew that she never would. She was doing what she had to, and she was terrified.

Rowan came for her. He was in uniform. Rhiannon balked for a moment seeing him like that and resisted the tide that was pulling her further into the strange and twisted tale that she was so inextricably tangled in. He read her look like a page from a story, took her face in his hands and looked deep into her eyes. "Love," he said. "This isn't us. This isn't you and it isn't me either. I'm just a farmer and you're just a pretty girl who likes cabbages. We're just two halfbreed fairies who love each other and this will all be over someday ... . Somehow, I'll always be with you, even if I'm not beside you. Alright?"

Did it make it more bearable to know that Rowan felt the same? No not really. But there was no way in hell that Rhiannon would let him be as brave as he was, and not try to be brave too ... for him. "Alright," she nodded and took a deep steadying breath. "I love you. I always will," she told him. He kissed her and she wondered if his kisses would ever stop feeling like fireworks. She put her hands around his wrists to stop the world from spinning. "Let's go," she whispered when the kiss ended and she looked into Rowan's dark eyes for a moment longer. "Forward is the only place we can go now.'

They walked through her Father's empty halls hand in hand and left through the great carved doors that lead to the main courtyard and out onto the open expanse of the cobble mosaic that was made from black and white stones and formed a tree of life. The entire stronghold was there to see them off and cheers from hundreds of voices went up around them as they walked across the courtyard. A sparkling host of two thousand Fay knights stood to attention in a formation that stretched down the broad path, further than Rhiannon could see. Lugh stood near the horses waiting to say goodbye to his oldest daughter. Morgana and Yuka were already mounted and waiting. Raphael, Malik, and six other armed angels stood ready. Nimue stood with Lugh and those of the Fay council members who were remaining behind. Rowan lead her to her father. "I don't dare embrace you for fear of dis-arranging you."

But he didn't have the words more than half way out before she had thrown her arms around him. He put his arms around her and held on, for he had only just found her and now she was leaving, stepping out into a dangerous world that he had meant to make safe for her before he had lost the dream that *was* her. She stepped back and looked into Lugh's handsome, charming, elegant face. He smiled and there was a trace of the sardonic cool manner that Rhiannon was sure he used to cover up what he was really feeling. "You've completely destroyed my reputation as a self contained monarch," he said and then sighed. "I've wanted you to know that Rhiannon was the name that I asked your mother to give you. You don't know what it meant to me when I found out that you existed and your mother hadn't hated me so much, after everything, that she wouldn't call you Rhiannon."

Lugh reached out and ran a finger down her cheek and Rhiannon could see that it was time for her to turn away. She looked into Nimue's face, so like her own, and she knew instantly that her sister was up to something, but she pretended not to notice, said goodbye and kissed Nimue's soft cheek, then winked and gave her a barely perceptible smile.

"We shouldn't delay any longer my Love," Rowan said softly.

They turned towards the waiting horses and as if on cue the unicorn, the very same unicorn who had helped Rhiannon in the forest the night she feared Rowan was dying, stepped out of the trees and, with a grace that was almost painful to watch, it walked to Rhiannon and gently nuzzled her cheek.

"My friend," Rhiannon breathed in astonishment and curtsied low before the unicorn, then straightened and placed her hands on the unicorn's velvet neck. "Thank you. Oh, thank you."

Rhiannon could hear whispers of astonishment from the crowd around her. She knew that the belief, in both the world she had come from and this one, was that a unicorn would only let a virgin touch it. Rhiannon closed her eyes for a moment and felt the unicorn's warm hide as the awe struck whispers continued to ripple through the crowd. What was happening was unheard of and no one could be unmoved by this gesture on the part of the unicorn, but as if to outdo even itself, the unicorn stooped. It wished her to ride on its back. "You want to carry me?" Rhiannon asked with so much feeling in her voice. The unicorn bowed more deeply and Rowan knelt beside her and offered his hands to boost her up. She stepped lightly into his clasped hands and, without an awkward movement, arranged herself on the back of the unicorn. Cheers even louder than before erupted from the crowd and the cherry trees that surrounded the courtyard burst into bloom and showered them with white petals. Rhiannon laughed and looked at Rowan from where she sat on the back of the magnificent unicorn. It would become the symbol of her reign, both the unicorn that would carry her to the city, and the moon on her brow, and for years to come little girls would look at their mothers at bedtime and ask, "Mummy, tell me about the changeling princess and the unicorn?"

But in that moment there was hope. "I think that it's going to work," Rhiannon said to Rowan smiling. "I think we're going to make it."

He smiled back at her, "I think so too."

Part Three

Just Krista

Chapter 1

The rest of the story is too personal for me to tell as if I were writing about someone else. I keep trying but I can't seem to get the words to sit right on the page. Maybe it's because the person who I became during that period is closer to who I am now. I don't know, but I can't distance myself from her anymore. She is me, so I will just have to tell the story from my heart, and I do not think that my heart will ever forget the day that we rode to the King's City. I have been told that it was a sight to behold. The awe that the Humans of the city felt at seeing Angels for the first time, the beauty of the Sylph and Dryad knights on their black and white horses, and the wood and water Nymphs, with their slim blades and long braids down their backs, were often spoken of in the weeks and months after the unification of Nova Britannia. As was the discomfort the people felt at being confronted with the wilder chaos loving Fay such as the Glaistig, the Phookas and the Gwyllion. There were hosts of other Fay as well who were much like me. Fay, but not distinct to one type. Or, Fay ... but perhaps a little Human. All were clad in shining armour with polished weapons and shields. From a certain perspective it was, while very awe inspiring, also terrifying.

I was terrified. My heart pounded so hard I felt as if I were being shaken to pieces. Mine was a sparrow's heart that longed to fly away, that beat too hard and fast for its tiny body, when what I needed was a brave heart, a lion heart, a dragon heart. I could hear the echoes of the stamp, stamp, stamp, from the marching feet behind me and my heart pounded along with it, filling me with a panic that I thought might kill me.

Of course the people talked of this too, but it wasn't my terror that they saw and they will never know that I felt it. What they saw at the head of the Fay army was the Captain of the King's army, their hero, surrounded by angels, and at his side rode a girl on a unicorn. To this day it makes me squirm and sweat with discomfort when I think of the things that the people said about me, but I'm telling you the whole story so ... I suppose I ought to tell. They didn't see a terrified eighteen year old high school drop out. They saw a vision of serenity and peace, hope and beauty. They saw an ethereal woman child on the back of a unicorn, a creature believed to be too pure to carry lowly mortals, but there I sat as Gwydion's spies whispered through the crowds that I was the wife of the man who rode beside me on his big black charger, and pregnant with his child. There I sat, my face still and pale, in a gossamer gown the colour of wild aster blossoms, and a Fay circlet set with a glowing moon upon my brow. Anyone could imagine how it looked from the outside. Even in a world that knows that unicorns and fairies are real, it isn't everyday that a unicorn wanders the city streets carrying a pregnant Fairy princess on its back, surrounded by tall, vivid beautiful angels at the head of an army. The people of Nova Britannia saw this as a sign that peace was coming, and that I would bring it to them.

No pressure there huh?

An envoy had been sent to the King's castle ahead of the Fay army to advise my brother Liam of the 'gift' that King Lugh was sending, and as we made our way towards the bridge that lead to the almost Island where the castle sat, a contingent of the King's Army rode down to meet us. It was strangely comforting to see Leif and Thaylum at the head of the well regimented row of soldiers. I made eye contact with Leif for a brief moment and he gave me a barely perceptible nod, then got down from his horse and saluted Rowan. It all felt so stiff, so formal and alien to me. I was trying to adjust my world view to include my current reality, and struggling against it at the same time. The idea that I would rule here crashed violently against the knowledge that in another world, I was no more than an uneducated, knocked up teenager. I was caught in something of an identity crisis. There was a division in my mind and I was almost choking as I tried to swallow the thought of myself as the queen of this place. It had been so easy to accept Rowan's proposal to me, and accept the role that I would have played as his wife in that in-between life when I was his and before I knew who I was, but to be Queen ...? I watched as the King's castle loomed into view ahead of us. The King's Castle. That was it. That was what they called it. Not Camelot, Caer Sidi, or Caer Dathyl. Not Caer Paravel, or Cader Sedat, but I suppose that it didn't matter what it was called, it was still the heart of the journey. The place that lay in wait.

We crossed the bridge and the road disappeared under us at an alarming rate as we made our way toward the looming gates. I looked up to see a tall golden haired figure flanked by two archers watching from the ramparts above the portcullis, yellow and red banners behind them flapping briskly against the blue sky. A welcoming party in fine clothing stood outside of the gates watching our approach with astounded faces, and then the Fay army was falling into ranks and awaiting instruction. Rowan dismounted and a squire hurried to take the reins of his horse, then he turned to me and lifted me down from the unicorn's back. I think he saw then, for just a moment, how very frightened I was, because he left his hands on my waist, steadying me, and he flashed me an impetuous grin before turning serious again. I turned, once I had my balance, and pressed my cheek against the unicorn's for just a moment then kissed his muzzle, I'm pretty sure it was a him, and told him, "Thank you my friend," and then took a step back. The unicorn reared and whinnied then cantered off into the trees. I turned back to Rowan and he offered me his arm, which I took. Very conscious of moving properly in the dress, I stepped around the train so that it wouldn't tangle then gave it a twitch to straighten it out and tried to think tall thoughts as we approached the gates of the castle. It was more like a stereotypical medieval English castle than Fiannasmere was. With grey stone walls, banners flying, and tall stone turrets, it was very stiff and proper. The castle stands on what would be Stanley Park and it is by the water's edge at the northmost tip of the almost island. For the most part the surrounding land-scape was still wild and beautiful, there were towering cedars and a few oaks that had come as acorns from the old country, but there in front of the castle were elegant formal gardens with benches and carved archways reminiscent of the carv-ings that I'd seen in pictures of old Norwegian churches. It was all very impressive but somehow, despite the garden, not very welcoming.

The gates were opened and the portcullis was raised as the Angels and the King's Men arranged themselves around Rowan and I. I will admit that, while I knew that we were walking into what could potentially have been a very danger-ous situation, I did feel a hair safer with Rowan, Leif, Thaylum, Raphael, and Malik all there with swords buckled on as we walked through those gates. The huge courtyard on the other side of the gates was lined with trees dressed in red for autumn and court officials and tall elegant ladies in ornate gowns—although their gowns had none of the delicate other-ness of the one that I wore. A man hurried towards us, the chancellor, I realized. I was concentrating so hard on my poise and composure that I barely heard his words though, some sort of greeting I assumed, and I simply smiled and nodded as he lead us to a dais where a young man, tall with burnished hair and bright blue eyes—the figure I had seen up on the ramparts—stood. Liam, my brother. Rowan had already told me much about Liam but it still gave me a jolt to see the half-brother who apparently took almost entirely after our mother. He was quite decadently handsome. As handsome as my father Lugh. If my mother had been as beautiful as her son, then it was no wonder Lugh had loved her at first sight, but perhaps the most striking quality, even more so than that beauty, was the complete openness, and goodness, and desire to do right, evident in his eyes. I knew just looking at him that he was someone who would never knowingly do me harm. Liam smiled as he stepped down from the dais and embraced Rowan, speaking to him as an equal, "You've talked the Angels out of the mountains and the Fay out of the forests! How did you do this Rowan?" Liam was obviously in awe.

"It wasn't me," Rowan said.

Liam had been so busy taking in the Angels that he hadn't given me more than a passing glance. I was just a girl on Rowan's arm in a pretty dress, and Liam was a King with bigger things on his mind than his Captain's new wife. The gossip from the city was only just making its way to the castle. Although he had seen me ride up on the back of a unicorn, at that moment, he hadn't any reason to give me anything more than a cursory inspection, but as Rowan took my hand and drew me forward Liam's eyes rested on my face.

"Liam, I would like to introduce you to my wife, Rhiannon."

Rowan didn't say any more than that. He didn't need to. It was the way he said it ... I don't know if I can adequately describe the gravity and meaning he managed to convey in that one sentence, or the quality of force in him. From just his posture and his tone of voice it was apparent that Rowan had complete control over the situation. It was no wonder that he had climbed as high as he had in life. Rowan had a force to him that was undeniable, and Liam understood immediately that Rowan was telling him something of great significance. Something more than simply, "This is my wife."

Liam looked at me more sharply now, regarding me seriously. I let my eyes meet his and I blinked twice slowly then extended my hand toward my half brother. He took it and I smiled. It was as much a smile as I could manage but I knew that it would mean something to him. I knew that someone else had smiled at him that way, giving him as much as she could. He would have simply bowed over my hand but recognition flared in his eyes and instead he sank to his knees and pressed my hand to his forehead. "Lady," he whispered. That was all.

He knelt for several heartbeats before I said to him, "Come. Do stand. Please?"

Liam stood and took one more long look at me before turning abruptly to the chancellor, "Double the Guard and have my private meeting chamber and dining room prepared immediately." Then he faced Rowan and said under his breath, "You had better explain."

Rowan pitched his voice low but there was an edge to it, "You will have noticed that certain members of your court are ... conveniently absent, and that I have men loyal to me posted at intervals throughout the courtyard. There are two thousand Fay knights outside of this gate that will tear this castle apart stone by stone if *anything* happens to her, and as we speak her history and true identity are being spread throughout the city streets. I am *not* threatening you, but you need to understand that we have a certain amount of control over this situation."

Liam looked back at Rowan, dead serious, "Then come," he said. "There is much that we must sort out. Bring whoever you trust most."

I couldn't believe that Liam had only just turned seventeen.

Rowan gave several orders that I didn't have the where-with-all to fully register and that I couldn't quite hear over my heart, but then Cole materialized at his elbow. "I think that we have a stow away in the Fay ranks. You know who. Find her and bring her to us. I'd check the infantry first."

"Yes sir," Cole said and was away, then I was being whisked down long grey corridors. Leif and Thaylum in front of us and Raphael and Malik taking the rear and Rowan holding my hand tightly as Liam lead the way.

* * *

Now, it had always seemed improbable to me that it should have been possible to make the court safe, especially in so short a time. From what I'd learned of it, it could be a fractious place, but I had only been in that world a matter of weeks. I had no idea how extensive Gwydion's knowledge of the court was or how deep his network of spies went. For that matter it hadn't entirely dawned on me at first that Rowan had his own devoted inner circle that included more than a few spies in various households and different departments of the government and, what with the long term friendship that he had maintained with my father, he had his Fay connections as well. I was naive and I didn't understand how far blackmail, a few subtle leaks of information and a couple of rumours could go.

Within two days Gwydion's handy work had seen the heads of two of the thirteen most powerful families arrested for treason, a third had been placed under house arrest for suspected treason and three other families had suddenly left the court for their home estates. One of these families met with 'misfortune' on the road. A bundle of letters was intercepted and planted. They were filled with information that connected two lieutenants and one second lieutenant in the King's Army to the Exiled Prince. The men were placed in the dungeons and an investigation was started. Thaylum and Cole started rumours within the army. One that an alliance with the Fay was inevitable, and a second opposite rumour that the Crown would not tolerate Fay interlopers, and then for three days Leif, Brian, Cole, and Thaylum sat back and listened to the talk. Some of the men were striped of their rank and sent away for speaking treasonous words, others were arrested. One hundred and fifty questionables were grouped together and sent to a garrison Five leagues to the south of the city on a routine make work task to keep potential troublemakers out of the city on our arrival day.

I won't claim that they didn't have to kill people to make this happen, in fact I was told after the fact that five Glaistig assassins made certain that required absences were observed. But all of this was enacted like a carefully performed dance, like a clockwork that had been set in place for years but only just finally activated. Leif told me, after the fact, that the entire procedure had been like walking through a burning house in which you felt the flames licking your clothes and the roof would cave in on your head at any moment. The Human court was in a state of upheaval and uncertainty when we arrived. Liam was not in a position, with an enemy force gathering on the horizon, to send away a fighting force of two thousand potential allies, and those who would have opposed a Fay alliance were conveniently gone. It was as safe as it was going to get and as we walked quickly through the castle my story was being spread through the city streets like a wild fire. There was no way that it could be covered up. The streets thronged with talk of 'Queen Sulamith's lost child', 'The rightful Queen!' and how I'd brought the angels and the Fay army with me. The common people of the city knew who I was before Liam did. If anything happened to me now he'd have a bloody riot on his hands. I didn't think that this was a fair position to be putting my brother in, but this was about creating a world that I and others like me could live in.

* * *

It felt like an eternity before we were behind closed doors. Even once we reached Liam's private chambers Rowan had Leif and Malik enter and search them first to make sure that the rooms were safe and empty, but almost the moment the door was closed Liam turned to me, "I know that you're my mother's daughter, and I'm guessing that you're older than me, but other than that I'm in the dark so would somebody *please* enlighten me?" He was tense and very, very serious.

"Let's wait until everyone is here," Rowan said.

"Would you at least tell me who her father is?"

Liam directed the question at Rowan, but I answered. "King Lugh," I said simply.

Liam looked like he had been punched in the gut. "There are some people who really wouldn't like to hear that, but they are conveniently absent, *Rowan*." Liam looked at him sharply, "How long have you been planning this?"

"Mmm, about eleven days," Rowan said it casually as if he were telling Liam how long it takes to sprout pea plants.

"Fuck ... FUCK! Eleven days! Do you know how little I get done in eleven days!" Liam wasn't angry just deeply unsettled.

I found it interesting how irreverent he was for a supposed monarch.

Soon those we had been waiting for were assembled. Not a large group, just Gwydion, Yuka, Nuriel, Rowan's grandmother Caitlin—the head of the Human council—,the chancellor, Finn a conservative man who was none the less above reproach, a couple of other well trusted court officials who I didn't have the attention span at the time to really take note of, and then after a few more minutes of waiting, Nimue and Cole. Nimue, who *had* stowed away, looked sheepish as she sat down at the table and removed her helmet, but too pleased at being back with Cole to be truly embarrassed by her behaviour. Leif, Raphael and Malik were standing guard at the two doors and the window. We were seated around a small table. Rowan turned to Nimue and, with a pointed look and a gently sarcastic tone asked, "Since you are here," he paused for emphasis, "Would you mind filling our kind hosts in on the situation?"

Nimue could be impetuous, but she had also been raised as the heir to the Fay throne and was used to behaving properly when the occasion called for it. And so, Nimue told the story.

Chapter 2

The next two days felt like one endless council meeting. On the inside I was stretched thin and battling constant nausea, but all that anyone said about me was that I was sweet and gentle and so well spoken. So capable of seeing the most reasonable course of action and so patient and generous. I didn't deserve such high praise. Most of the time I felt like screaming, but at the end of those two days Liam announced publicly that he was abdicating the throne in favour of the rightful heir, and that a united Human Fay Nova Britannia was in the near future. But in the meantime, an army was marching on us.

The night before the Nova Britannian army was to depart to intercept my uncle's forces, there was a knock on the door to the very lavish state rooms that Rowan and I had been given. I had been asked if I wanted the rooms that had been my mother's but I felt a revulsion at that idea. I smiled politely and told them, "No thank you." Not to suggest that I liked the rooms that we *were* in. They were too fussy. I mean, I'm female, I like pretty things, yes, but the rooms felt stifling at first. Rowan and I had shut ourselves in the bedroom. I was wearing one of the 'too nice to sleep in' night gowns that had come with me from my father's home and a blue dressing gown, and Rowan still wore breeches and a linen shirt. We were sitting together on a settee next to the fire not speaking, for what was there to speak of? He was riding away in the morning, and all of the initial relief that we had felt at the success of our revolution was gone. War was coming, and this was it. All we could do was hold one another close for a few short hours, and then try to get some sleep. We were sitting quietly when the knock came and I heard Raphael in the other room answer the door. Raphael had a bed in the outer chamber and the window to the bedroom overlooked the ocean from high above. Only a fairy or an angel would have had any hope of reaching it undetected. Rowan and I waited, wondering who it could be when Raphael knocked, "Are you decent?" his voice came through the door.

"We are," Rowan called.

Raphael stuck his head in, "It's your brother."

I rose curious as to whether he meant Leif or Liam, and Rowan followed me as I walked out into the sitting room. Liam stood there holding a box in his hands and looking uncertain. It was a strange thing dealing with the different reactions that people had towards me. Especially those who were close to me. Rowan had never shown me anything but unhesitating love, and Nimue in her own exuberant unconditional way was the same, she simply gloried in having a sister and I will admit, that I did too. Leif, once he decided that resenting me was counter-productive, treated me like a little sister, like he did Fenna. I got a bizarre combination of affection and lectures from him. Raphael ... well, that was just plain old complicated, still is. And Lugh always looked at me with so much loss in his eyes that he kept me at arms length. But Liam? In those early days I hadn't had much time to spend with him in an unofficial capacity, and in an official capacity he was always very deferential towards me, very supportive. Although I knew that they both felt guilty for their feelings, I also knew that both he and Nimue felt relief that I was taking on the burdens that they had had to carry, though not because I wanted to but because I had no choice. I could see

the guilt and sympathy in Liam's eyes and I could see that he
wanted to help me, but there was also a timidity, an uncertainty to him, as if he were unsure if I needed or wanted
his help. And now he stood before me looking very shy, holding a small wooden box in his hands. He looked at me standing there in my nightgown, my hair loose, the jewellery,
except for my rings, removed, and then he said, astonished,
"Wow, you look like a little girl in your night gown." And then
he gave Rowan a funny look.

I couldn't help it. I snorted then laughed at the idea that
Rowan was attracted to me because I looked like a little girl.

Rowan smiled patiently, rolled his eyes, shook his head,
and then said in a good natured tone, "What do you want
Liam?"

Liam glanced at Raphael, then Rowan, before looking back
at me. "I know that this might not be a good time, but what
with the chaos of the last few days, I haven't had a chance to
show you these. If I don't do it now I ..." he broke off.

I knew what the rest of the words were going to be. He was
going to say, "I might never have a chance." Now that Liam
was no longer King he had more freedom, and he had chosen
to join the military. He was going away to fight in the morning
too. "Have a seat." I motioned to the small, round, ornate,
table surrounded by heavily carved, velvet cushioned chairs
and took a seat myself.

Liam, Rowan, and Raphael sat. Liam looked down at the
box in his hands. He sighed then looked at me again and said
cryptically, "The resemblance is stronger when you're like
this." Then he paused again before starting to explain, "In a
manner of speaking, I've known about you for nearly five
years now. Since shortly after my mother died. That was a
rotten time for me. I was angry. Angry that she was dead.
Angry that I was alone. Angry that I was King. I went up to her
old rooms to see if I would feel closer to her there, but they

were so empty without her that I only felt angrier. I was young." He rolled his eyes. "I mean younger than I am now. I'm not trying to justify what I did I'm just saying that at twelve I wasn't old enough to get a grip on my feelings and control myself. I completely ransacked her room. I smashed everything that I could get my hands on, absolutely to pieces. I didn't leave anything in the room intact, and I'd be com-pletely ashamed of myself, if I hadn't found these. I didn't feel so bad for myself after I found them because I knew that somehow, I wasn't really alone." He opened the box and lifted out a stack of photographs. "I was very worked up at the time and I cried myself to sleep on the floor in the mess I'd made. When I woke, these were right in front of me in the shards of a porcelain ornament that had always been in the corner. I couldn't even remember what it had been before I'd smashed it but these ..." He sighed and fingered the pictures. "I'd never seen images like these before. They're so real. It's as if they were made by magic. I sat in the rubble and gathered them all up and looked at them for hours. I've always kept them secret. I figured that there was a reason that my mother had kept them a secret. I was fascinated by them." Liam pushed the photographs over to me. "They're of you, mostly. I knew that you must be my older sister. I figured that you must have been taken away from my mother and that was why she was so sad sometimes. I don't know how she got them."

He looked at me and was silent as I slowly flipped through the stack of photos. I'd looked at about six of them when I turned to Raphael and asked him, "Would you mind finding Leif for me?"

Raphael nodded understanding, and headed for the door.

The photos had come from my home and had, obviously, come from my parent's camera. They were typical family pictures. One parent behind the camera, the other holding, or playing with, a child. There were fifteen photos total. One for each year that my mother had lived after my birth plus two others. One that I remembered taking of my parents myself. I remembered holding up the camera and pressing the button. They hadn't known I had the camera in my hands. It was the spring I'd turned thirteen. We'd gone to the beach for the day and they were looking at each other. I remembered thinking that I hoped when I was older that I would love somebody like that, and that they would love me back. Funny thing was, that while I remembered taking the picture, I never remembered seeing it. And there was one other picture too, of later that summer, the beginning of my garden. I'd gotten my dad to help me put in a small pond and I'd grown a water garden. Fairy moss and water lilies surrounded by irises, hostas, venusta, and ferns. It was at the centre of a little grassy lawn which I'd then surrounded with white and blue flowers. Roses, borage, more irises. I'd tried to make it enchanted. Eventually I *had* made it enchanted.

I slowly looked at each picture, myself at three asleep in Fionnuala's arms, at four riding high on Gavin's shoulder's, a bright smile on my face and my hair a tangled mop of loose blond curls. It had been one of my favourite things, riding on my dad's shoulders. I was always pestering him for it, "Daddy, lift me high up!" I would say. It wasn't until I was eight or so that he'd finally told me "no", although gently and with a smile at which point he'd admitted, "Yer mum says I carry you around too much and If I don't stop you'll never get used to walking on your own feet." I always remember thinking that it was funny that somehow my Mum was the boss of my big strong Dad. That s how I thought of it when I was eight any-way. There was a picture of the three of us sitting on a blanket having a picnic when I was twelve. I remember Fionnuala giving the camera to a passerby to take the picture.

I was lost in the past, sitting at a table in another world. I felt like a mess but I also felt like I wasn't allowed or entitled to feel that way. So I tried to keep it in, or I did until Raphael returned with Leif following behind looking worried. Raphael hadn't told Leif why I wanted him. I looked up as they took seats and I pushed the little stack of pictures over to Leif. "Liam had these. I thought you might like to see what they looked like before ..." I didn't need to finish the sentence.

It was a hard thing showing the pictures to Leif. He flipped through the pictures silently without saying a word. When he came to the one of just his parents, looking at one another in the sunset on the beach, he stopped and looked at it for a long time. His face worked. "Could I uh ..." his deep voice came out rough. "Could I keep this?" He looked at me.

"They're Liam's," I whispered.

"Yeah ... Yeah, I forgot, they were your parents too. Stupid of me. Of course you can have it," Liam said to Leif.

Leif nodded and swept his sleeve roughly across his eyes then got up to leave pressing the photo to his chest. "Thanks," his voice came out rough again, then he headed for the door.

"Leif," I said rising from my chair and he turned. I padded quickly towards him and got caught up in a gigantic bear hug that lifted me right of the floor as he buried his face in my hair for a moment and nearly squeezed the life out of me. Then he put me down rumpled my hair and left.

I went back to the table and thumped down in my seat. I looked at Rowan who smiled understanding and reached out and stroked my cheek.

"If I could have this one," Liam took the picture of me alone in my garden out of the stack, "then you can have the rest. They said your house was burnt down right? These are all that would be left."

I nodded and got too choked up to answer. Liam reached out and held my hand for a short moment then sighed, "I'm going to go and *pretend* to sleep now, cause the Trees and the Sea know I have enough on my mind to lie sleepless for the rest of my life. One question though. How did my mother get these?" He looked at Raphael.

"I used to sneak into Rhiannon's house through the attic window and pinch the photos from the envelopes of new pictures before Fionnuala had a chance to put them into albums. The older ones I had to steal from the albums. Sarah gave me a hard time for breaking into your house," he looked at me apologetically, "But the pictures made Sulamith so happy that she let me get away with it. Did you find the lock of her hair I got?" Raphael asked Liam.

Liam, in answer, pushed over the box and there in the bottom was a slightly golden, brownish blondish loop of hair tied with a piece of blue ribbon. By the colour, I must have been about thirteen. Raphael smiled. "That took some doing," he winked at me. "But it made her so happy." He smiled. It was a happy sad, memory laden, love filled smile. Only Raphael could make a smile so complicated.

Liam said goodnight and Rowan and I went back to our room. I'm pretty sure that we *all* pretended to sleep that night.

Chapter 3

The army of Nova Britannia, both Fay and Human forces, had been mobilized and every bodily sound man over the age of seventeen had been drafted into the army and given a sword. Rowan wasn't happy about the draft and he had his reasons, but the council voted on it and even as Queen I didn't have the power to undo the decision. Rowan did the best he could by leaving the men least skilled in battle behind to guard the castle so that they wouldn't be slaughtered on the battle field. I watched Rowan address the army in the hour before they left, as I stood on the ramparts above them. He didn't say much but by then he didn't need to. Everyone knew the story. In those few days since our ride to the city it had been repeated so many times I'm sure even the walls had come to understand it. It was all that anyone talked of. They knew Rowan's part in it and he was even more well loved for it than before. He had already been, to them, a man who loved his home and family enough to go above and beyond in his fight for peace, but who now loved the strange girl he'd found in the forest and made his wife, so much that he would do even more. He would help her finish the revolution she'd been conceived to start, and expose his Fay blood and wear it like a badge of honour. It turned out that nearly a third of the Human army had at least some Fay blood, and that another sixth or so were somehow connected to the Fay. Those who had been living hidden lives breathed a sigh of relief. Not that I'm saying everything was perfectly easy as these things took place, they weren't, but the Fay were glad to stop hiding and the humans were so generally appreciative to have allies that for the time being differences were overlooked and those who had been loyal to Queen Sulamith would abide by her wishes.

The rows upon rows of armed soldiers stood in wait on that overcast morning. Sometimes I would see their faces turn up towards me where I stood with Raphael, Nimue, the chancellor and other members of the court in the cold damp wind. Rowan, astride his big black war horse, bellowed at the army, "Whatever was different between us four days ago doesn't exist anymore! Lets show this pretend prince and the scum who would follow him what we're made of!"

The roar that went up from that army was so loud that I could feel it with my fingertips, then I stood and watched as they filed away from me. My brothers. My friends. My husband. Rowan sat for several minutes looking up at me before kicking Snicker Doodle into a trot and taking his place at the head of the army. I stayed there quiet, still, completely motionless as my heart was caught in a crushing grip in my chest. I felt Nimue's fingers close around mine and as the wind blew colder and harder I remember Raphael stepping forward and sheltering us with his wings. It happened several times that year and each time was the same.

That first battle was a victory for us but only by a very narrow margin. Cole didn't come home. Mikail and Nuriel often served as messengers, taking turns flying by night, back to the city. I remember Nuriel kneeling in front of my black haired sister, as she stood there in her nightgown, I remember him telling her gently that her love was gone. I spent many hours sitting with Nimue as she cried in my arms, trying not to think too hard about what she was going through. There were endless council meetings and it didn't take them long to figure out how much I hated bickering. I wished so much for

Fenna. I missed her but the roads had gotten far too dangerous for her to be able to come to me. I had Morgana, Sarah,
Nimue, Yuka, and Arariel with me which was truly a blessing
as the Ladies of the court could be a little like popular girls at
a high school. Fenna and Nessa were so unaffected and
natural. It didn't take me long to realize that the other rich
families in Nova Britannia didn't raise their daughters the
same way. Some of the things that Rowan had said to me
when we'd been getting to know each other made more sense
now, especially his comments about rich men's pampered
daughters. Although not all of the court ladies were like that.
Ingrid and Heather were truly sweet and without calculation
or venom. Their openness and curiosity lead them to form
friendships and attachments in the non-Human camp almost
from the start. Ingrid was teaching me how to sew and how to
play the harp and Heather, another one of those six foot tall
stunning Celtic redheads, had formed an almost immediate
attachment with Mikail. Mikail's wings and hair were blue
black, his long lashed eyes like deep pools and his skin was
deep bronze. You can imagine what he looked like next to a
milky skinned redhead. They were very beautiful together. I
tried not to stare. But the other ladies ...? Well let's just say
that I while I seemed perfectly able to handle council meetings and cranky politicians, I was sometimes taken aback by
how ill equipped I was to handle catty gossiping women, and
oh how the gossip did fly. They were curious about me and I
understood that. I understood that they *would* talk about me.
I was new, and I was mysterious, and I was the *Queen*. But
there was one thing that topped off the awkward factor, and
that was the fact that Rowan was *mine*, and he was devoted to
me.

I remember one night early in our time together, lying in
bed completely blissed out, looking at him, his eyes holding
mine with their warm dark fire. His hair loose, dark, making

shadows on his beautiful face as he smiled at me trying to lure me in.

"You're not as new to this as I am, are you?" I asked him and his smile turned just a little bit sheepish and he laughed.

"Not quite," he chuckled. "It's a little bit embarrassing actually." And he told me about life in the King's Castle and the '*ladies*' there. "It's not entirely that they mean to be the way they are, but there is a lot of competition amongst those families and they place pressure on their daughters to make good matches. I'm from a good family, I'm the Captain of the Army, my grandmother is the head of the council and apparently I'm not too hard on the eyes. I constitute a good catch and sometimes, if a girl thinks she has a chance with someone she'll take a risk and sneak into his bed at night in the hopes that once a man has had a taste of what she has to offer, that he'll ask her to be his." Rowan looked a bit uncomfortable but told me anyway, "I was never quite sure how to deal with it. Sometimes it's hard to resist a soft body and warm arms. It depended on the girl. If I knew she had been pressured into it by her parents I would send her away as nicely as I could, and usually with a bee in her ear about waiting for someone she actually cared about. But if it was a girl with a reputation," he made a face then asked me, "Do you know what I mean by that?" I nodded. "Then I figured that as long as I made it clear, before anything happened, that she shouldn't expect any promises or commitments from me, that it was her choice whether to stay or go. Sometimes they stayed," he shrugged, "but they were the ones turning up in *my* bed. It wasn't the other way around. And a handful of one night stands hardly constitutes real experience."

"Did you ever get anyone ..." I trailed off not entirely sure I wanted to know.

"Pregnant?" Rowan finished.

I nodded.

"Not that I know of. Although I obviously can't say for sure. I always tried to pull out, which I know isn't sure fire, but the girls ... they planned these things. They would never pick a day during their fertile phase to try sneaking into someone's bed. It's one thing to risk your heart or your honour, but risking a pregnancy? No." Rowan shook his head again.

"So if you could have had any girl, then why me?" I asked him. I was smiling. I was just playing, hoping he would say something dashing and try to lure me in again.

He was lying there propped up on one elbow, eyes twinkling merrily. "It's because you make me look tall," he said flippantly.

I put my hand on his chest and shoved him and he laughed as he let himself fall back onto the pillow. But then he looked over at me, ran the backs of his fingers down my cheek and his expression softened. "It's because I love you," he told me and I melted completely. No luring necessary. I was his.

But ... the *Ladies*? They could really get under my skin especially with all of the men away for weeks at a time fighting to protect *us*. I would pace the corridors alone, save for Raphael who loathed my habit. I paced, nauseous, worried, my hands moving restlessly over the small curve of my belly and I would pass a sitting room. I could hear them gossiping. I know that it comforted them. It was normal for them, but it wasn't my way.

One afternoon as I passed an alcove, walking softly, soundlessly down the hall, Raphael leaning against the end of the corridor, my grumpy resigned protector, I could hear two women speaking to each other. It was a hushed relaxed conversation. They spoke easily, as if confident that no one was there to hear them, and if it wasn't for my obsessive hall walking, there wouldn't have been.

"What do you suppose she has that I don't?" It was Bridget. Rowan had warned me about her. She was pretty enough, with a perfect Barbie doll body and nice skin, but years earlier, Rowan had learned the hard way to stay away from her, or more accurately, to keep her away from his bed.

"I don't know why you're even bothering to compare yourself to her," Heidi. Less vicious, insipid as hell. "You're her polar opposite. He obviously has a taste for ... well ... women who aren't like you," she said lamely.

I leaned against the wall outside the drawn curtains and listened. I picked up a *bad* habit of eavesdropping, living in that castle. Raphael, curious as to what had caught my attention, tiptoed towards me and I raised a finger to my lips.

"She's a strange, quiet, little, *creature.*" These words could be spoken in such a way that the described could come across as sweet, quirky and endearing, but the way Bridget spoke the words was as if she had just found something creepy under a log.

Heidi said, "I know what you mean. I can't imagine what he sees in her, and after you gave yourself to him he really should have asked you. Do you suppose he asked her because of her position?"

"Don't be silly," Bridget snapped. "We've all heard the story. He had no idea she was the queen and neither did she."

"Oh, well then," Heidi again. "At least you'd already lost your virginity to someone else. It's not as if you wasted it on Rowan."

Raphael and I exchanged looks.

There was a disgruntled silence from the other side of the curtains before Bridget gave an explosive sigh and said, "I wonder if *she* was a virgin?" The tone was absolutely snarky.

This was where I lost my inhibitions and, driven by irritation and a desire to put Bridget in her place, I opened the curtains and said with a bright smile, "Just to set the record straight, one; I was a virgin. Two; Rowan likes to be the pursuer, *not* the pursued. And three; *I* make him look tall."

I said all of this as smugly as I could to the shocked, gaping, dismayed, five foot ten inch tall Bridget, then I walked away smiling, thankful for probably only the second time in my life to be only five feet tall. The icing on the cake was Raphael doubled over laughing as I walked away then following after me staggering and gasping as he held his sides. I didn't have any problems with Bridget after that.

Life on the whole though, was grim. I think that at first, Raphael felt that he was missing out somehow by not leaving to fight with the rest of the army, and that his remaining behind as my bodyguard would be seen as cowardice. That was until the first assassination attempt. The castle was well guarded and not just by the drafted men who Rowan had left behind but by several Glaistig and by the barrier, similar to what was used to keep the strongholds hidden, but an elf managed to slip through by slitting the throat of one of the Dryads who had been maintaining the barrier, then creeping slowly through the castle. Getting past Raphael was hopeless though. He has elf radar. He said he can feel them coming. There were a couple more attempts that had Raphael on edge and gave me trouble sleeping, but once the enemy drew the conclusion that getting to me would take significantly more resources than a single assassin, they laid off. Raphael, though, was glad he'd stayed behind. Despite that, Raphael and I had a strange relationship. It could be uneasy and we drove each other a little crazy sometimes. If Raphael and I had ever had a time that was ours, it wouldn't have lasted. We would have been like Italian lovers. Always fighting, always yelling, and throwing each other's clothes out the window. It would have been beautiful and passionate, and the love would always be there, but the relationship would have crumbled. We could both see it and it made life easier in a way.

Rowan was gone from mid October until just before the winter solstice. While we had won the first round it was not a decisive win and my Darling Uncle—this was Liam's name for him and he said it with such bitterness and venom that it was hard not to adopt the term—saw that our win was not as decisive as it could have been and changed his strategy, bringing in illegally sourced weapons from the other world and switching to guerrilla tactics. Rowan withdrew our forces and adapted quickly—although not as quickly as he thought he should have—and while we took a blow we managed, by a thread, to maintain the upper hand. We had an advantage by then and that was magic. I was right in the end, about the Angels' secret. It *was* the source of the elves magic and from the time the secret was told onward the elves began a gradual decline. In a matter of weeks they were no more magical than lumps of rock. Now they were simply men with black hearts. No more enchanted weapons, no more charms to drive the men they were fighting insane. No more swarms of spell cast bees on the battle field, but now they had guns and bombs and they were nearly as bad. Luckily they were unable to procure enough weapons to outfit their entire army and without the ability to cross the threshold between the worlds they would eventually run out, but still ... It left me more terrified for Rowan than ever. Magic, he could handle. He was unbeatable with a sword, but bullets? He'd taken one before. If the elves had gotten a chance to enchant the weapons before their power had faded they would be twice as deadly. We didn't know then if the elves prior enchantments would fade with their abilities gone.

At the end of November after one of our spies, Nessa of all people, delivered a crucial piece of information, we were able to land a major blow; find and destroy their cache of weapons *and* take out their base of operations. We used one of their own bombs to do it by enlisting the help of a munitions expert that Flanagan found for us in the other world. Malik had to fly it in and Nessa was supposed to be there to help him plant it before they got out together, but something went wrong with that part of the plan. We don't know what happened and we never will. They never made it to the rendezvous point, but the bomb went off.

Rowan came back to the city along with most of the army. Seamus' army was scattered and a storm had hit that was unlike anything that Nova Britannia had ever experienced before. The temperature must have dropped to nearly minus ten degrees Celsius and feet of snow fell. The winds were so high that even the angels couldn't fly. *No one* could fight in that weather. It had never before been so cold in those parts. I waited, holding my breath as my stomach tied itself in knots.

It was terribly cold the day the army returned. I couldn't see them through the heavily falling snow from my vantage point up on the ramparts, and I remember driving Raphael crazy as I ran down and up the stairs from the ramparts to the courtyard and back again as their estimated time of arrival drew near. Suddenly a shadow was emerging through the blind of snow flakes as the army rode up and Rowan was outside the gates giving orders to the exhausted soldiers. I headed for the stairs and ran down to the courtyard, but the doors weren't opening yet, so back up I ran again. I was frantic. I think that all of the people watching must have questioned my sanity as Raphael once again followed me up the stairs complaining. "For a pregnant girl who vomits at least twice a day you sure do have a lot of energy. Can't you just wait in the courtyard?"

"I can't, Raphael. I just want him to be here *now* and I *can't* stay still." I reached the ledge of the ramparts, looked down, saw that the gates were being opened, and turned again and ran down the long spiral staircase. I remember the colour of the silk and velvet dress I wore. It was red. Like cherries, like blood against the snow that was falling. I ran out into the courtyard and kept going through the gates dropping the heavy wool shawl I'd had pulled around me. My slippers were wet and my fingers cold. The wind lifted and whipped my hair. The sun was setting, resting on the horizon briefly, and shining below the clouds, turning the heavily falling snow gold and turning the world, for the briefest moment, into a beautiful place once more as I ran to Rowan. He was passing the reins of his horse to a squire and he turned and saw me just before I reached him. It's a profound thing to see some-one else's need and love for you in their eyes, to see their relief at having you back written in their look, and reflecting back at you, your own need, love and relief. He held me so tightly as the sun slipped away. I could feel his armour digging into me and feel the prickle of his unshaven jaw against my brow, but to be close to him ... to be in his arms ... I cried out, loudly, the fear and worry that I'd been holding in, and he stroked my hair and kissed my face as if no one was watching. "My love, my love," he whispered. Then becoming aware of the world again, and that it held more than simply love and relief he said, "Lets go in, you must be freezing."

Chapter 4

For the most part I always felt extremely guilty about the indulgences that my position allowed for, and I rarely took advantage of the castle's willing and highly competent staff. I rarely had someone help me dress or clean my rooms. I usually did it myself. I sometimes had meals sent to my rooms for Raphael and I, if it was late, or if I was feeling sick, but I felt guilty enough about everything else. I felt guilty that Nimue was suffering and that people were dying. I felt guilty that there wasn't more that I could do. I felt guilty that Rowan was out there fighting ... but right then he was back with me, so as we walked across the courtyard and in through the great doors, I looked to the Chancellor and the Head Steward, "Have a hot bath brought up to our rooms immediately, and dinner. Nothing fancy. Bread, cheese, dried fruit, hard boiled eggs, stew, and I know I don't need to say this but, no meat. Make sure no one bothers us until tomorrow midday unless it's an emergency, and I want breakfast brought up, but not too early."

I think that it was the most I'd said all in one go, to Wilhelm, the head steward, since my arrival and he blinked at me and said, "Certainly My Lady. Right away." And then hurried away to make sure it was done.

I briefly hugged Liam and told him that I would see him the next day and told him to say the same to Leif if he saw him, and then I took Rowan's hand and we left the busy courtyard for the quiet peace of a candlelit room and closed doors. *You can feel guilty tomorrow,* I told myself.

Rowan didn't say much to me as I undid the buckles on his armour and tossed it in a pile for the attendants, who were filling the bath, to take away with them when they left. It was hard in a way. Rowan and I had known each other for about three and a half months by then, but we'd been apart more than we'd been together. There were things that had happened during that time apart. Battles, losing Nessa, Malik and Cole, my fights with the council. I wanted to shelter Rowan. Let him be away from all of that, but I wasn't sure what to say to him. I was pregnant with his baby, but I didn't know what to say? It wasn't an uneasy silence though, so I decided to let it be. Rowan threw his filthy clothes onto the pile and then sank into the tubful of hot water. I watched him fill his hands with water and pour it over his face, rubbing with his hands as if to clean it of more than just dirt. I turned to the wardrobe and swapped the red dress for a comfortable night gown then lay down on the foot of the bed curled on my side with my head propped on my hand. Rowan sank deeper into the water and then sank right under rubbing his face and head still. He emerged dripping and looked at me. Nothing more. He just rested there and looked at me for a long time then he smiled, "Pass me the soap and the razor, would you? Now that I'm all the way warm and my mind finally believes that my body is sleeping next to yours tonight, all I want is to be clean, shaved and dry."

I smiled and got up and passed him the tray with all of the toiletries on it. I pushed up my sleeves up and told him, "Here, lean forward and I'll scrub your back."

There were scars, *new* scars, on his back, and while I let my fingers linger over them briefly, wishing that I could erase them, I didn't ask how he had gotten them because I knew now that it wasn't that he didn't want to share with me, it was that when he was with me, the ugliness of war was something that he wanted to leave behind him and forget. So I wouldn't remind him. Not just then.

The tubful of dirty water was removed and food was brought up by Wilhelm himself. I took the tray from him and thanked him which was, I knew, not what the kings and queens before me would have done. They would have sat by and watched as he placed it on a table and set everything out, but I wasn't like that. I'm still not.

"Pwyll is in the hall. If you should need anything else just send for me," Wilhelm said in his efficient tone.

"Thank you, I will," I said as I pushed the door closed with my foot, then turned and brought the tray over to the bed so that we could eat and lounge.

"You know exactly what I need and want, don't you?" Rowan said looking at me appreciatively.

"For everyone to go away and let us be?" I smiled.

"Yes." He smiled back at me so that everything felt right in my heart.

"Are we going to have to pay for this with the council to-morrow? Are they waiting with baited breath for a report so that they can argue over how best to proceed?" he asked, and I'm sure that he asked so that he would know whether or not he would have to be mentally prepared for it.

"No. We met today shortly before you returned, and I did schedule a short meeting tomorrow before dinner just to keep them happy, but we've had steady communication through Nuriel and Mikail, and anything else can be discussed once you and the rest of the army have had a chance to sleep, eat, and see their families if they can. I had to push the issue home pretty hard but the fact is, that at this juncture, the weather is our friend, and we can afford a night to let every-one catch their breath." I didn't tell him that I'd had to yell and scream at some of the more obstinate, conservative, council members that my sister-in-law and a close friend had just been blown up, and that if they wanted sanity from me that I needed a break and that since we couldn't see more than four metres out from the castle anyway, that this seemed the night for it.

Rowan nodded, understanding that we could drop any talk of the council or duty or obligation and instead looked around the room, "It looks much better in here. What did you do?'

Ever since arriving at the castle I'd felt overwhelmed and overstimulated and after a few short weeks I realized that the castle was so heavily over-decorated that it felt cluttered and it was actually making me more anxious. The sheer volume of daybeds, settees, portraits, occasional chairs, tapestries, bureaus and every other imaginable type of furniture or decoration was quite beyond comprehending. Everything was heavily carved, excessively ornate, and, gloomily reminiscent of the Gothic revival and Jacobethan styles. It would have been kind of fun in a romanticized medieval sort of way if it weren't so *very* over the top.

I looked around the room. The castle would never have the airy golden feel of Rowan's family home, but at least now you could actually see some of the truly beautiful woodwork and tapestries with all the excess removed.

"I got rid of half the furniture," I told Rowan. "In fact I had nearly a full third of the furniture in the entire castle removed and given to less fortunate families in the city. It was a good thing too because the temperature was dropping and with all the men and many of the single women gone, those left behind have been pushed to the point of burning their own furniture for warmth. Their houses aren't built to handle this cold and there were children and old people with no beds to sleep in and not enough blankets."

Rowan was quiet for a moment. "The furniture is better off where it will get used. If old Queen Freya were alive to see it she would have some kind of internal rupture. What did my grandmother say?" he asked me with a smile as if he were expecting to be entertained by my answer.

"Caitlin backed me all the way on that one, and she's been laughing for the last three days. Ever since the furniture was moved out. She keeps making jokes about the most convoluted use of tax dollars she's ever seen, and every time I ask her to explain she laughs so hard that I can't get a coherent answer out of her."

Rowan laughed. "Freya was often criticized for, how shall we say it," he paused finding the right words, "Confusing her own comforts and desires with the needs of the people. She's the one responsible for the over-furnished castle. Of course it all came from taxes, so the fact that you've given all of the excess furniture to the poor, so that they can use their old furniture for fire wood, is a very convoluted use of tax dollars. My grandmother never did like Freya."

"Freya was *my* Grandmother wasn't she?"

"You're nothing like her, trust me," Rowan said, then, "More bread?"

"Mmm," I nodded. "More stew too," I said, grateful to finally be relaxed enough to eat a little more than usual without having my poor stomach twist into knots of anxiety and send me scurrying. It was normal for me to have a nervous stomach, but being pregnant was putting it over the top. We ate and talked, sticking to superficial topics, but when the food was gone and we had fed the fire, turned out the lamps, and lit a candle or two on the bedside table, it wasn't as easy. Not that it should have been. Awful things were happening.

The window in its pane shuddered as the gale force winds battered the castle walls. Rowan had just lifted the blankets to climb into bed next to me, but put them back down and walked over to the window and opened it then wedged a towel in between the window and the outer shutters so that the rattling stopped. He came back to the bed and lay down and I moved so that I could rest my head on his shoulder. He circled his arms around me and I buried my face against him and breathed. I'd never felt so much relief in my life as I did that night at having Rowan back, but I hadn't realized until he ran his hand down my abdomen so that it came to rest on the hard little curve between my hip bones that he had still been worrying. He let out a long breath, "Oh Rhiannon. You don't know how much I've hated leaving you here. When you came to me outside of the gates you were like a vision in that red dress with the snow and your hair swirling around you. More beautiful than any angel to me. But when you were in my arms and you cried I thought … I thought that perhaps you'd lost the baby and I've been afraid to ask you how you are for fear of upsetting you. But you're alright … You're alright."

I started to cry again for no good reason, but told him, "I'm fine, I'm fine. There's nothing wrong with me. Morgana says I'm perfectly healthy and that being sick as much as I am is a sign of a healthy baby. I just missed you so much."

"It's foolish of me I know, but every time I sent Nuriel or Mikail back to the castle I asked them to bring me word of you, and every time they came back they told me the same. That you were fine. There was a part of me that feared they only told me that you were fine so I wouldn't worry and let it distract me."

He held me tightly for a moment and then moved his hand back to my belly.

"I'm fine Rowan, I really am. Morgana told me that in a few more weeks I should be able to feel the baby moving. If … If you have to go away again, I'll write to you. I'm messy and stilted when I write in your script, but I'll write to you every day and tell you everything. I promise."

He nodded and looked at me in the candlelight. Gently brushed a few stray tears off of my cheeks and then sighed, "I love you."

"I love you too," I said and nestled in closer, liking the way relaxed muscles were so warm and comfortable to curl up against, and the fact that Rowan wasn't lacking in muscles. But since we were moving into painful territory I asked him, "How are you?"

"Now that I'm here," Rowan sighed, "I'm ... fine. Better anyway. I ... wish this were over."

I wasn't going to push him to tell me more than that, but I needed to know, "How is Leif?"

"Not well," Rowan said bluntly. "Not that I've pushed him, and I won't what with the words that have passed between us on the subject of love over the last year, but he won't speak to me beyond essentials. As far as I could find out he isn't speaking to anyone. Leif is very stubborn. He'll deal with Nessa's death in his own way, even if it kills him."

It was another hard thing. It left a lump in my throat and renewed the ache in my chest that had been there ever since news of the explosion had been brought to us. Nessa's death wasn't an easy one, because if Leif *had* made his relationship with her official she would probably have been at home and about as pregnant as I was by then, not fighting. But Leif didn't love her enough to want that with her anymore, not enough to be sure he wanted to tie himself to her. Or was it that he truly felt it would be unfair to her to commit to her when he had every likelihood of riding away and then being killed in battle? But Nessa was stubborn too, and had been an exceptional spy. What she had done in finding the enemy weapons cache and then helping Malik into the compound with the bomb may well have been the tipping point in allowing us to win the war. I couldn't regret what she and Malik had done, I could only regret that they were dead, and I knew that

Rowan felt the same way that I did. I couldn't imagine how Leif was feeling.

It made me think though. It made me imagine what would have been, how life would have turned out, if I had been too afraid of being hurt to have accepted Rowan's proposal that autumn evening. Too afraid of falling completely and then losing him, to have said yes. But I couldn't deny that I had already fallen completely by then. If I had said no, and he had died, I would have been left with nothing but regret. Even then, I knew that I would have spent the rest of my life wondering what it would have been like to be his, and have him be mine. I tightened my grip on him. "Let's not talk anymore," I said.

Rowan, in reply, kissed me. I wasn't so pregnant that we couldn't make love, so we did. And then we slept.

Chapter 5

The bad weather held up for another three weeks. I couldn't help wonder if the weather was as bad on the other side of the curtain, in that other world that had claimed so much of my life, and if so what the weather man on the television had to say about it. I relished that storm. That biting wind and flying snow that kept my love close to me. It was a strange and beautiful bubble in time. The future was too uncertain and the past too painful to talk about, so we lived in the moment as much as two people just starting out and expecting a baby in the middle of a war could.

I remember waking up with Rowan on that first morning after his return. His smile. The warmth of him. The fact that what he always said to me was true. There *was* something about waking up together that made everything that was painful in our lives just a little bit easier to bear. I woke feeling Rowan's strong arms circle around me, and the worry that I'd woken with every morning since he had left, melted away and with it half of the nausea. For a brief time, things were as they should be. I rolled over and smiled. I stretched and sank further into Rowan's arms and dozed until a knock came from the sitting room letting us know that a tray of food awaited us. We ignored it for a few minutes, then lounged over breakfast. Once we were fed and ready to contemplate rising Rowan smiled and said, "Humour me and put the red dress back on, if it isn't dirty. I want to look at you and imagine you coming to me in the snow over and over again."

"Alright. I think it's clean enough. You were pretty grimy yesterday when I hugged you, but I think that all of the dirt was so frozen onto you that it didn't really come off onto me,' I said, looking over the dress then slipping it on and unbraiding my hair. I sat down at the dressing table and brushed my hair out, making my brush strokes outwards and away from the dress so that I wouldn't snag it. Rowan took the brush from me. I looked at his reflection in the mirror as he stood behind me running the brush over the ripples of my hair. The dark circles that had been around his eyes the night before were almost gone now, but I could still see the toll that the last two months had taken on him. I could see that the fighting was eating away at him. "It seems such a small thing, but at least I can get the tangles out of your hair," he said, almost a whisper. And I sat until he was satisfied with the job he had done, then I stood and put my arms around him because I couldn't bear the look on his face.

"Rowan? What's wrong?" I asked.

"I'm just tired, that's all. Five years this war has been dragging on, and now we are closer than ever to ending it, and being so close is just making me feel how profoundly I want it to end. Especially when I'm here with you."

"Shh ..." I whispered and stroked his hair as he buried his face in my neck. I couldn't think of anything better to say. What could I say? I wanted to stop his tears and take away all of the hurt that a man who was faceless to me was inflicting on us, but I was helpless to do anything about that. What does a little gardener fairy do against an army? Nothing. I'm good at growing things. Plants. Flowers. Babies apparently. So I took his hand and said, "Come. I want to show you something." I lead him over to the fire and pulled him down on the settee next to me. I picked up the little trunk that sat on the floor by my feet and opened it. "This is where I keep all of the things I've been collecting. Ingrid has been teaching me how to sew and embroider." I took out a tiny linen baby dress that I'd finished, and a bonnet, and showed him the one I was still working on. "Finn found these amongst my mother's old things." I pulled out a tiny silver spoon that had the first letter of Liam's name engraved on it. "She must have fed Liam with this," I said, "And I think this must have been hers." It was a tiny string of coral beads with a little gold heart engraved with the symbol for the "S" sound. "Ingrid made these." I passed him the knitted booties. "And Sarah made this," another baby dress. Soft blue cotton. "And I keep these here too," I said, pulling out several wooden objects. Rowan smiled in recognition as soon as he saw them.

Each time Nuriel or Mikail had flown to the castle, Rowan had sent with them a little carved something. The first was a rattle made of three interconnected wooden rings carved out of a single piece of wood. "This must have taken you a long time. I'm always taking it out to look at, and this," I took out a carving of a seal. It was sweet, simple, and sleek and it jingled when you shook it. "I've been half tempted to carry this one around with me but most of the court thinks I'm eccentric already. How did you get the bell inside?"

Rowan chuckled and took the smooth little seal from me and shook it. His eyes twinkled. "Fairy magic," he said. "I found the bell in the road and when we made camp that night I found a small very old tree that was near the end of its life. I woke it from its sleep and I told it that I wanted its wood to make a toy for my child. The tree agreed and asked me if there was anything that it could do for me and so I asked if it could grow itself around the bell, so the tree used the last of its life force to grow around the bell and then died. So I cut the part that had the bell inside it and whittled away at it until it found a shape." He shook the seal so that it jingled.

There were little bowls carved to look like flowers, like buttercups, with scalloped edges that formed the overlapping petals, and seven little swallows swooping and diving.

"I'll ask Wilhelm for some oil, beeswax and some pumice and I can finish some of these ... tonight maybe. The swallows," he put the seal back in the box and picked up one of the little birds. "I'll plant little hooks in the backs and we can hang them from ribbons over the cradle so they swoop and dive." He smiled.

I smiled.

We sat for an hour like that before I finally, reluctantly, said, "I usually visit Nimue for a little while in the morning I don't want to upset her by not showing up when she's expecting me."

Rowan sighed. Nimue was one of the subjects that we had been avoiding. Cole had been dead now for five weeks. I didn't know the details of his death but Rowan told me. "You saw the scars on my back right? I mean the new ones."

"I did," I answered quietly.

"It was shrapnel. From a grenade. Cole was with me when the bastard threw it at us. He took the brunt of the explosion. I was with him when he died. He had something that he wanted me to tell her."

I nodded. "Do you want to come with me to see her?"

"How is she?" he asked in a cautious tone. "Will seeing you and I together upset her? If she's recovering I don't want to drag her back down by talking about Cole. Not if she's trying to move on."

I wasn't sure exactly what to say or how to tell Rowan about Nimue. I'm not a doctor, obviously, but Nimue seemed to me to be experiencing more than just grief. I questioned her sanity. "I don't think that it will upset her," I told him. "But she's not herself. She's manic one moment and practically catatonic the next. It might help. It might snap her out of it."

"Do you think it will make things worse?" he asked me.

My heart turned to lead in my chest as I thought of my sister. I loved her. I had never thought of what it would be like to have siblings before. I hadn't expected to love Nimue as much as I did and I hurt so much watching her suffer. Rowan could see all of this in my look and repeated his question.

"*Do* you think that it will make it worse?"

"I'm not sure that it can get worse," I whispered.

Chapter 6

I led Rowan down the hall to Nimue's room and opened the door as slowly and quietly as I could. I peeked my head around the door. Nimue was curled up in a tight ball sitting in the window seat looking out at the swirling snow. She might as well have been watching a television that wasn't turned on. Morgana, who was sitting by the fire and knitting a baby blanket, looked up and smiled. She and Nimue hadn't come out the day before to watch the army return. Morgana selcom left Nimue's side and I couldn't blame Nimue for not wanting to watch other people's loved ones ride home. Not when she knew Cole wasn't coming. I couldn't keep the memories at bay as I closed the door softly behind Rowan and I, and I stood for a moment, hearing the sound of Cole and Nimue singing together, seeing Cole's sweet face and his goofy grin. Hearing Rowan say, as we'd taken the barge across the water at the beginning of our journey to the angels, "That kid can incite riots with his voice. Back when I was a Lieutenant and he had just been assigned to my regiment as a new recruit he would take out his accordion and play in the evenings. He would get everyone so riled up that I had to give him strict orders. Love songs and lullabies. That was it, and even then." Rowan had smiled and shaken his head. "He's got a lot of magic tied up in his music."

And now there was nothing. No more music. Nimue told me that she felt as if her voice had died too. "Cole and I, we only knew each other for two weeks. We never talked about forever. There was no understanding between us." By *under-standing* I knew she meant that they hadn't promised themselves to one another in the sense that Rowan and I had. "Maybe that would have come later," she'd continued, "But I can't hear his music anymore and these cold stone walls don't sing like the trees do, I feel like my voice is dead, Rhiannon. Maybe my voice is dead?" and then she had gone wild on me, looking at me with frightened eyes and I'd had to take her hands in mine and hold her still with all of my strength to keep her from hurting herself.

I shook myself free from the memories and turned to Rowan who was looking at me uncertainly. I crossed the room to Nimue and sat next to her silently for a few moments before whispering, "It falls so heavily doesn't it?"

Without showing any other sign that she had heard me she nodded but kept on watching and then after a few minutes she turned and gave me one of her distracted delayed responses, "Rhiannon?" She smiled, but it wasn't a comforting smile and I could sense almost immediately that she was going to turn manic on me. I had, after weeks of this, developed a sense for her moods. I saw Morgana out of the corner of my eye put aside her knitting and watch. I put my hand on Nimue's. It used to be that any time we touched, the magic in us would flare and coloured lights would dance around us, but not anymore. She pulled her hand back when the lights didn't come and stood, paced a short way towards the centre of the room then turned as if she had forgotten what she had gotten up for and pushed the heel of her hand into her forehead, then looked at me and said, "I do long for rain, I wonder ..." She spaced out again, walked to the wall and put her hand against it as if she were dizzy.

Her hair was a tangled mess so I followed her and took her hand again and asked her, "Nimue, can I brush your hair? I would like to. You can just sit and I'll get all of the tangles out?"

"But it doesn't matter. Nothing does," she said and then laughed as her face was clouded by that strange vacant hysteria.

I looked at Rowan who was clearly shaken. It was like I had said. It was more than grief that plagued her.

"Nimue?" I took her face in my hands. "Nimue, sweetheart. Please look at me."

Her eyes focused on my face and she stopped laughing and put her arms around me resting her head on my shoulder and I put my arms around her. "Rhiannon I can't *keep* myself. I can't *find* myself. Everything is flying around in my head." It was the first time in days that the voice that had come out of her mouth sounded present, and as painful as the words that had come from her mouth were, it was preferable to her inane babbling and fluttering.

I waited for her to loosen her grip on me and then I led her over to the bed and sat, pulling her down so that we sat facing one another. "Nimue, maybe you're looking for the wrong girl. Your life isn't the same as it was before you met Cole. These things change you. You can't keep the girl you were. She's gone, but you're still in there, you're just different now. Maybe you need to stop searching. Stop *trying* to hold on."

Nimue nodded and sat on the bed rocking back and forth, but there was a heaviness in her eyes, a presence that was less frightening than the desperate laughter and pacing had been.

"It will rain again. The world will turn green again. Things will grow, but everything is always changing. Even us." I looked at her, weighing whether or not I should ask Rowan further into the room. He was still standing in the shadow of the entrance. I looked to Morgana who was sitting forward now, looking pensive with her hand over her mouth. I raised my eyebrows asking the question silently and she gave a single nod.

"Rowan's here," I said softly, and watched her reaction, wondering if these few moments of lucidity were all I was going to get, but she nodded, still looking heavy. I motioned for him to come.

He walked over and with his typical fluid grace, knelt on the floor beside us, and looked into Nimue's face, "Hey little sister. How are you?"

Nimue's face twitched, her lip quivered and she shrugged awkwardly, "I'm ... here, um ... I suppose," and then, still rocking, she nodded as if to confirm to herself that it was indeed the answer that she wanted to give.

"This is a big strange castle isn't it? My home is much nicer than this. So is the stronghold," Rowan said to her.

Nimue looked at him as if she were actually processing what he'd said. She nodded.

"Cole never liked it here either. Always called it 'A ridiculous pile o' rocks by the sea'," Rowan told her.

Nimue smiled, closed her eyes and tipped her head to the side. She stayed like that for a moment before saying, "He did, I remember. When I got here and he found me hiding out in the Fay ranks. I threw my arms around him and he laughed and said, 'I can't believe you'd come all the way to this ridiculous pile o' rocks just to see me'."

"He wanted me to tell you something," Rowan said gently.

I tried not to listen as he told her the words that the boy she had loved had wanted her to hear as he lay dying in the dark. They weren't meant for my ears, but her fingers found mine so I held on to her hand as Rowan said to her, "He wanted you to know that his heart was at home when he was with you, and he died saying that he had known love, and that he was glad of it."

I looked at Rowan, wondering how many times over the years he'd had to do that, and if it got to him. I don't think that it's something I could have done so gently, and without choking up.

Nimue bit her lip and nodded. I could see tears gathering and pooling in her eyes before they dropped onto her lap and she nodded again and said, "I think I'm going to cry very loudly for a while. Do you mind leaving?" she asked Rowan.

He nodded and rose.

"Will you stay for a little?" she asked me.

"I will," I said. Then, to Rowan, "Have Wilhelm bring some lunch up for us would you? I'll be there in a little while."

He nodded and Morgana left with him.

It didn't take Nimue long to exhaust herself and she looked at me eventually and said, "Rhiannon I'm so tired."

"I know ... I know," I said to her, weary and nauseous myself. I did manage to get her hair brushed and braided before she fell asleep. The whole while Rowan's words echoed in my mind, "It seems such a small thing, but at least I can get the tangles out of your hair.'

Chapter 7

At the Council meeting that afternoon I sat and listened, not saying much. I'd been sick that afternoon and I felt lightheaded. It was a precarious situation as it was against the rules for the head of the council to be a relative of the monarch and Caitlin, being my husband's grandmother, was technically a relative. But we were in too much a state of upheaval for an election, so Caitlin had remained the head. She had to walk a fine line however, as the head of the council was meant as a check to ensure that the monarch kept the best interest of the kingdom at the forefront, just as the monarch was a check to the council head. The Fay council operated the same way and several members of the fay council had been added to the Human council. The problem was that Caitlin had her sympathies and since the union of the kingdom her sympathies, and her past, were out in the open. Not even her husband had known that Bronwen, Rowan's mother, was not his offspring. Bronwen looked just like Caitlin. You can see where this was going. Caitlin had to do a bit of a juggling act. She couldn't be seen as too much in favour of my way of doing things. If she thought anything I wanted done *too* radical for the old school council members, she would oppose me as a matter of form and sometimes it didn't matter how hard I talked. The matter would be handed to the council and a vote would be held, then it was out of my hands. I often wished that Gwydion hadn't left to study in the Angel's library up in the mountain city, as he had been perfectly adept at managing the old guard members of the Human court and making them think that even the most radical change was in line with their way of doing things. but he, along with all the other druids, had departed to go learn from the Angels. I understood the rationale; there may be information in the library that the Angels wouldn't realize was important as they had been so long removed from society, but I still wished the crafty, wily, old druid was with me to back me up.

But there was only one issue I had to put forward at the meeting that afternoon, and that was the draft. I wanted an end to it, but I had Rowan there to argue it for me that day. I had made it clear that after Rowan had delivered a full report on the war, we would deal with that one issue and then adjourn. Rowan had explained that between the weather, and the significant blow we had dealt my uncle's army, there was little we could do but wait out the storm and send out scouts, try to keep our ears to the ground.

"In the last four days I've lost nineteen men to hypothermia and another five have simply been lost to the storms. I can only assume that they have frozen to death after losing their way in the snow. From what I understand the people of the city are burning their furniture to keep warm. Right now the drafted men need to be with their families to help in the cold. A mother in a house alone with three small ones is going to have little opportunity to find more fuel to keep warm. There is *no* point in keeping men out in the freezing forests searching for an enemy that *we can't find,* to protect children who are freezing to death in their own homes. At this point you also need to realize that the drafted men simply don't have the skill to cope with the kind of attacks that we are dealing with, and the trained soldiers spend as much time protecting them as they do fighting. The drafted men may or may not have tipped the balance in that first battle. It's in the past now so there is little point in debating it, but at this point the enemy is like a cornered puma. Dangerous. We *are* beating them back but my men need to be able to concentrate on fighting not protecting."

"Do you think that you have the manpower to do this without the drafted men?" Lars, very human, very status quo, very plodding, asked. He was one of the ones who had pushed for the draft in the first place. According to Rowan Lars had never lifted a sword in his life yet fancied himself a tactician. His questions didn't even make any sense. He drove me crazy but I kept my mouth shut.

"Of the five thousand and thirty two men I took into battle in October, I've lost approximately one thousand and thirty. Six-hundred of those men were *drafted* men. I took eight hundred of them with us and left four hundred of the least battle ready behind. You think about those numbers and you tell *me* whether it's to any one's benefit that our master potters and weavers and glass blowers are the ones dying out there?" Rowan said, bristling aggressively. He'd opposed the draft from the start saying that it wasn't a guarantee that it would help and that it may even hinder. I'd backed him but Caitlin had been caught between a rock and a hard place on that one and it had gone to the council. The vote had just barely passed for an involuntary draft with the fay council members taking my side. There had been a lot of hostility over the issue.

I looked at Lars and raised my eyebrows in a silent serious, "I told you so." I had trusted Rowan's judgment on that one. There was a reason he had been made Captain. He knew.

"What are Seamus' numbers now?" Caitlin asked.

"We estimate that he's got about one thousand eight hundred followers left. The Brownridge family withdrew their support and took about three hundred men back to their estate with them. All he has left now are elves, bandits, hill tribes and other exiles. He's lost all of the legitimate political support that he had three months ago."

Caitlin nodded, "End the draft. Is there anything else that we need to discuss?"

"I have an idea that I would like to entertain," I piped up for the first time. I hadn't even realized that I was going to say it, but the faces around me were all so grey and tired. "The winter solstice is in three days. Are there any logistical difficulties involved in planning a feast?" I looked at Finn and smiled and there must have been something in my look that tipped him off because he smiled craftily back at me.

"A feast of ... *very great* proportions?" he questioned.

"Yes," I smiled.

I had gone over the larders with Wilhelm three weeks ago and I had been shocked at the excess.

"Does the castle really go through all of this food in a year? There are only eighty permanent residents?" I'd asked.

"No lady. We usually give the excess to the poor in the spring. That's how Freya always had it done and somehow in the nine years since her death it has never been changed."

"You give the leftovers to the poor in the *spring*! When the chickens have started to lay again and the dandelion greens are sweet and tender? I'm sure the flour is turning stale by then and the potatoes have gone soft. How much spoilage is there?" I was irate.

He gave me his answer and I blew a gasket. I knew that we had the resources to do more.

I looked across the council hall at Finn, "I want you to talk with Wilhelm and Ona," She was the head of the kitchen staff. "I'm sure you have a better idea than me what can be done, but I'm told that the great hall can accommodate some fifteen hundred people. I want to invite anyone from the city whose spirits would be uplifted by a feast and I want a feast *brought* to any families who need food or who are too downtrodden to have the spirit for festivities. Also, look over the furniture again. It still feels crowded in here to me." I looked at Reina. She lived in the city full time and she and her family were cloth merchants who had a good trade relationship with the Fay. She knew the city well and had helped make sure that the furniture had been fairly distributed where it was needed most. "Would you mind helping them?" I asked her.

"It would be my pleasure," Reina answered. I knew she meant it. She was one of the council members that I trusted. She was there out of a desire to make the world a better place with no other motives.

I looked around at the council in general, "Does anyone object?"

"No," Caitlin said firmly before anyone could speak.

There were a few disgruntled faces but no one became vocal so I figured that I had won.

* * *

The castle hummed for two days and I don't think that the kitchen staff slept. I didn't feel bad though because everyone was smiling for the first time in the two months since I had become Queen. Even Bridget, who usually avoided me, was smiling and curtsying to me in the halls as if I were a normal person. I wasn't expected to help set up tables or anything like that, it irked me in a sense, but I was busy as Wilhelm and Finn came at me with constant questions on what my preferences were, where I wanted this or that, what to decorate with, should someone organize games for the children. I tried to stay where they could find me but Rowan was with me and we were bent and determined to spend every possible moment together, so we wandered the halls together hand in hand and Raphael had some time off. Wilhelm came at me with the first real hitch and that was the lighting.

"I'm afraid the hall will not be quite as bright as I'd hoped. We have extra candelabras but no one seems to know where they were stored and ..."

"Where are the globes that my father sent?" I cut him off.

"The boxes of glass orbs?" he asked perplexed.

I'd forgotten that they were a Fay thing. They had them at Rowan's home because Lugh had given them to Rowan as a gift and Rowan knew how to light them but, at what everyone had adjusted to calling The Queen's Castle, they were un-known.

"Have the boxes taken to the hall and then find Yuka. She will be able to find someone to hang and light them. The hall will be bright enough," I told him.

* * *

The younger soldiers, Fay and Human, spent the day cart-ing hot meals together through the storm and into the city to the unsuspecting recipients, Rowan and I stood on the ramparts watching as they came back for another cart-load, their eyes full of laughter to be doing something that brought hope and joy instead of nightmares and death.

We dressed. Morgana fussed with my hair as she pinned it up in a net of pearls. I had left the circlet off, but that morn-ing, as he was about to head out to deliver meals, Liam tracked me down with a tooled leather box in his hands.

"So," he walked towards me purposefully. "Rumour has it that *you* are wearing a devastating cream silk jacquard dress tonight. I thought to myself, 'Hmm what goes with cream silk?' And then it struck me that I knew of the perfect thing, so I took the liberty of raiding the treasury for you." He placed the box in my hands, carefully lifted the clasp and pulled the hinged lid up, revealing ruby cabochons set in a lacy inter-connected network of gold huckleberry leaves. Necklace and earrings, stunning and perfect. I didn't quite gape but he could see that he had hit the nail on the head. He winked and gave me a cocky charming smile before sauntering off calling, "Save me a dance," over his shoulder.

I clasped the necklace around my throat and put in the earrings then checked the effect in the mirror. The dress was a simple empire waisted gown that had been made for me before I left the stronghold. The empire waist was a good thing though because suddenly my little body was showing the pregnancy and over those few days since Rowan had come back from the fighting my belly had seemed to grow rapidly into a gentle curve that was obvious even when I was dressed. The gown was lovely though. Classic, with cap sleeves and a graceful scoop neck that left ample skin showing and per-fectly suited the vivid ruby jewellery. If you looked carefully you could see that the pattern in the jacquard was that of stylized doves flying in circling groups of three, and the rubies were almost the same red as my mouth. Rowan came up behind me and put his arms around me, smiling. He smoothed the silk down over my belly with his hands and told me, "You know, I could just look at you all night. I'm not sure that I want to go down there and share you with other people." He grinned.

"Don't wrinkle her dress." Morgana tried to pinch Rowan and I laughed as he moved quickly away still grinning, too fast for her. "Leif is sitting with Nimue tonight but do you mind stopping quickly and saying goodnight to her before we go down? She would like, very much, to see your dress," Morgana told me. I could tell, as my Grandmother stood next to me looking exceptionally lovely herself in burgundy silk, that she too was enjoying the prospect of an elegant evening.

"Of course I don't mind," I said gently. "Finn doesn't want Rowan and I to arrive until all of the guests are seated anyway. He wants us to make a 'grand entrance'." I rolled my eyes.

I hadn't actually seen Leif since the army had returned. He was a very private person in some ways and, stubborn as he was, he would work through his issues in his own way, on his own. But I was touched that he would sit with my sister so that Morgana could go to the feast and get away from Nimue for a time, as none of what had happened had been easy for my grandmother either. Leif was leaving in the morning on a scouting mission and I knew that he wouldn't want to go to a feast. Not then. As we approached Nimue's room Rowan told me, "You go in, I'll wait here." And he leaned against the wall and crossed his ankles casually.

I knew that Leif found Rowan's presence difficult outside of their professional relationship. Leif could take orders from Rowan, but not comfort. So I pushed the door open and went in alone. Nimue had been subdued and distracted since the other morning but not self-destructive or manic. She'd been sleeping a lot, but when I entered she was up and sitting at the small table with Leif drinking tea and eating. They appeared to have been having a conversation but cut it short when I walked in. Nimue stood and gave a muted smile. "Oh, you look lovely," she said softly and kissed my cheek then returned to her chair.

I smiled back at her. It was still disturbing to see her like that but less so than the vacant/manic period had been. "I see they brought you some of the food. Is it any good?" I asked

"Yes it's nice," she answered mildly. "I'm not sure what we'll do with it all? Look how much they sent up."

The quantities were rather large, but I'd seen Leif eat.

Just as the thought crossed my mind Leif said to Nimue in his deep gruff voice, "Don't worry about it. This isn't a lot of food. Trust me."

I looked at Leif then. He looked back at me but his eyes flicked on and off of mine reluctant to maintain contact.

"Hey," I said.

"Hey." I got back, two octaves deeper and gravely as hell.

I reached out and gave his shoulder a shove. I barely budged him but it got me a shadow of a smile.

"I have to go. I'll see you in the morning," I said to Nimue and kissed the top of her head, nodded to Leif and then joined Rowan in the corridor.

The massive carved doors to the great hall were closed and my grandmother was waiting, holding the long detachable train to my dress. I let her tie it on and arrange it behind me. I felt vaguely ridiculous in those situations, with a full staff standing by so that Rowan and I could walk through a door. All for the spectacle of it. I had to put myself out of my own head for a moment and appreciate how a little girl would see it though. When I was eight years old I would have given anything to see a pretty fairy queen wander gracefully past, and so I nodded to the two squires who had been placed on door duty and the great entrance cracked wide, exposing us to the gathered people waiting eagerly for the feast to begin and marvelling at the fairy lights and the garlands of ivy, mistletoe, holly, and, up on the dais where traditionally the Queen and her Consort would have sat, the tall decorated tree.

I know what you're thinking. A Christmas Tree? And yes, I suppose it was, but it seemed fitting to me. It was the only part of the whole holiday that I liked in that other world, and Wilhelm had done an amazing job of decorating it. It was dazzling. I looked up at Rowan and smiled. He smiled back at me and offered me his arm and we walked in together, down to the table at the end of the hall that was nearest the tree, amid clapping, laughter, cheers and happy voices.

I had made sure that the seating was mixed so that rich families and poor, Fairies and Humans were forced to sit together and enjoy themselves as the meal was served, and they did. It was an evening to remember. It was magical. It was the best of two worlds coming together. There was music and dancing and as the night drew on the flickers of coloured lights danced along my arms to my fingertips and the fairy lights suspended from the ceiling continued to glow. I danced with Rowan and Liam, Raphael and Thaylum too—who I could tell missed his wife—and I did hear a little girl at one point in the evening say, "Look Mum. She's right there. She's sooo pretty." All of the women there were lovely in their best dresses. It was something that I had overlooked, but self absorbed Bridget, of all people, had seen to it that even the poorest girl had something beautiful to wear that evening, *and* keep if she wanted.

I spoke with people who I wouldn't otherwise have had a chance to meet. A sweet little old lady who had never imagined seeing the inside of the castle. A young soldier who had recently lost his leg to an explosion. I saw him wistfully watching the dancing but then his wife sat beside him and kissed his cheek. He motioned to the whirling couples but she shook her head smiled and clasped his arm tightly. I saw him smile at her with tears in his eyes. I could see that the people of Nova Britannia were real, not just a faceless mass of taxpayers. And they could see that I was real too. Liam said to me at one point, "Nothing like this has been done since before our grandmother's time. There have been balls with lords and ladies and powerful families but this is different. We have to make sure that this happens again next year. Amazing things are happening here tonight." He was excited. Everyone was. It was a respite from war, worry and cold. It brought back the memory of peace and happiness and with those things came hope.

"You're tired aren't you?" Rowan said to me as the revels continued and I began to droop.

"How can you tell?" I smiled.

"You're wilting."

"Is it that obvious?"

He answered me with a question, "Shall we slip away? Retire for the night and let the revels continue without us?"

"Yes. Lets."

And hand in hand we made our way surreptitiously around the edges of the magnificent great hall, behind the stone pillars, past the tapestries, and towards the great carved doors. Just as we made our escape we heard one of the squires who was theoretically on door duty but was now lounging against a pillar watching the festivities announce to his partner, "You know, when I find a wife, I don't care if she's beautiful. If she looks at me the way the Queen looks at the Captain, I'll be happy for the rest of my life."

As we hurried towards the long sweeping staircase under the dancing fairy-lights Rowan looked at me, "How's that for romance?"

It was romantic. It was like a fairytale.

Chapter 8

The days and weeks that followed were like a dream that neither Rowan nor I wanted to wake from. We spent those cold white days curled up by the fire or walking together in the formal gardens, sometimes just the two of us but often accompanied by Liam. Raphael, Sarah, and Arariel were always on the periphery with their long swords belted on, keeping watch as we strolled along the snowy paths. Past the holly bushes with their sharp leaves and bright red berries, through the hedges, around the carvings and standing stones we wandered, hand in hand, talking, often laughing. When it was just Rowan and I we would stop behind trees and steal kisses, and if Liam was with us he would keep us smiling with his entertaining banter and we would wander as the snow fell around us.

"I wonder what it would have been like to have grown up together?" Liam asked one afternoon as it was starting to warm up.

"I would have been a bossy and controlling older sister. You would have been the only thing in my life that I could have bossed around and I would have milked it for all it was worth."

Rowan snorted, "You don't like asking people to pass you the salt let alone telling them what to do."

"Yeah but Liam would have been more like a little doll. I would have known that he was the baby and that I was older, and it's his disposition too. I wouldn't have been able to get away with it with Nimue."

"No. She's right," Liam took my side. "I would have followed Rhiannon around and done what ever she said and, for all that Nimue is younger, I'll bet that if, through some strange turn of events we'd been raised together, all three of us, that Nimue would have been a little tyrant. She had so much spirit before ..." Liam trailed off and I could see in his eyes an odd admiration for my younger half sister followed by a struggle to keep his levity and not let thoughts of her present condition ruin our afternoon.

I idly lifted a clump of snow and formed it into a snowball patting it softly with my gloved hands then on a whim lobbed it at Liam who watched the snowball fly through the air with a look of disbelief on his face. It hit him square in the fore-head.

"That's not fair!" he laughed, scraping snow off his face and laughing. "You know I won't throw a snowball back at my tiny pregnant sister!"

Rowan laughed at Liam's expression so I lobbed a snowball at *him* too. He dodged and threw up a hand avoiding the worst of it as the loose snowball broke apart against his forearm, but I knew that Rowan wouldn't throw a snowball at me either. I thought I was safe but just as the thought crossed my mind a perfectly aimed soft wet snowball caught me in the shoulder so that it broke apart and splattered my face and neck. I shrieked as the snow slid down under my cloak against bare skin and Raphael roared laughter at me then turned and hid behind a wing as Liam and Rowan came to my defence and a barrage of snowballs sailed through the air towards him, catching Arariel in the crossfire. She shook chunks of snow out of her black ringlets and took Raphael's side. We were drenched, cold and tired from laughing by the time we went in and ate a private dinner in Liam's rooms.

* * *

News of Seamus and the elves trickled in but they were using the bad weather to their advantage too. Rowan knew that something was up and after three weeks of quiet he was uneasy. He would distract himself whittling teething rings and baby toys while I sat sewing, but as scouting party after scouting party came back with minimal news the tension mounted until the morning Leif rode back to the castle.

His face was red from days of exposure to the elements. He looked careworn and bedraggled but he had information, "They're hiding out on one of the Gulf Islands. Rumour has it they have a few ships and they're planning an attack on Fiannasmere. They want to draw us out."

The look on Leif's face as he delivered this news was agony. My heart constricted and I bit my lip as thoughts of Fenna's safety flew through my mind. I tried to conceal the fear and horror I felt at the thought of the place where I dreamed about living out my days and the people who lived there being harmed. The council chamber was silent as the various members sat in their seats pensive but, thankfully, not argumentative. "How much time have we got. Can we be there to stop it?" I asked.

"I caught an elf landing a small craft coming in off the Islands and I ... convinced him to share some details with me. If he's to be believed we have very little time. We should leave within the hour."

"It's either an ambush to persuade us to leave the Queen's Castle under-defended and ride out to protect Fiannasmere, or Seamus wants us to believe that it is." Rowan said immediately. "We need to be prepared for either situation."

No one argued with Rowan as he ordered Yori to gather all of the Dryads and Water Fay in the army and have them wait, ready to travel unseen, in the woods next to the castle. He looked at Raphael. "You've got the castle. Leif, Liam, do whatever he says." And Rowan was striding from the room.

Rowan was able to do this. Make a decision, make it quickly and have confidence in it. He was rarely wrong. I followed him out of the council hall scurrying to keep up with him. "Are you going to go?" I asked him.

"I have to. It's my home." So serious.

"I know, I just ... Make sure everyone is safe. Fenna, your mum, the boys. And then come back to me," I stammered.

"I will. I'll come back." He kissed me then strode away and I turned and went back to the council chamber.

Chapter 9

January through March I didn't see Rowan at all. He was gone. Fighting. I tried not to let it show just how much it bothered me, shook me, tore at my heart, to have him away. It wasn't as if I was the only one whose loved ones were away fighting, but the thing was that my 'Darling Uncle' knew that he couldn't win now, so instead he was just going to torture us from a distance. Even though he was faceless to me, it was personal. He'd hated my mother and he hated the fact that I was alive and well, and living up to every dream my mother had ever had for me, and he hated that despite his best effort to crush her, somehow, even in death, she was winning. So he was doing as much damage as he could. It was more along the lines of guerrilla terrorism. Hard to fight. Hard to predict, and I knew that he was doing it to make Rowan and I miserable, to deny us happiness. He was a psycho.

His attack on Fiannasmere proved that. Rowan arrived just in time to prevent the village being looted. Rowan's grand-father, Merlin's Shadow, had gotten Bronwen, Fenna, and Dunstan out just before the attack and taken them to the Broad River Stronghold, but the attack was brutal. The castle itself was quite stout and if they had seen it coming they would have been better able to defend themselves. Rowan's father was badly injured but survived, he had been a soldier in his youth, although in times of peace, but Rowan's Uncle, his cousin Lewis, and Gareth who had just turned sixteen didn't make it.

Like I said, Seamus was doing it to hurt us. He didn't care about winning anymore.

Rowan spent the following weeks trying in vain to isolate and destroy the exiled prince's army, and I had my long grey halls. I paced while Raphael begged me to stop. "Rhiannon stop this. Sit by the fire, rest. Go sit and sew with Sarah," he always called his mother by name, "or visit with Nimue." It was mid February. I'd been pacing for weeks.

I didn't want to think about Nimue so I asked Raphael a lame philosophical question instead. "Do you believe in fate?"

He gave me a 'You've got to be kidding me' look. "If it has somehow been predetermined that I am going to spend my days watching you walk up and down a blasted hallway, some-one's gonna have to pay!" his tone was caustic.

I ignored it and asked, "So you figure that if fate *is* prede-termined, that someone is in control?"

Raphael shook his head and snickered, "I think fate is the stupidest idea anyone has ever come up with and I find the idea of my life really disturbing when put in the context of fate. I mean honestly, I'm the last Angel. Although," he winced, "With the way my parents are going at it these days, that just might change." He sighed and pushed a hand through his golden hair and looked at me from the end of the hall where he was leaning against the wall with his ankles crossed. During the weeks that Rowan had been there to act as my body guard, Raphael had disappeared a few times and managed to find a pair of black leather pants and a long sleeved tight black shirt that showed off his muscles. "No one has control over our lives except for us. We're responsible for our actions and there is no one else to blame or to absolve us when things go wrong."

I gave a slight ironic smile at the idea of an atheist angel and wondered what someone from the other world would think of that.

Raphael gave me another *look,* "Don't tell me that you believe in fate?"

I shook my head vehemently, "No, I'm with you on that The idea that this was predetermined is completely insane."

I couldn't shake thoughts of Nimue though. Even asking Raphael stupid questions couldn't distract me from her that day. She wasn't well and, although there had been a breakthrough of sorts during the time that Rowan had been back, she was slipping away. She had no interest in living and had sunk into a deep depression, but it wasn't that simple either. She was a fairy trapped in a stone castle. She was used to having the natural world touchably close and almost feeding off of it. Morgana had admitted to me that if the roads hadn't been so dangerous that she would have taken Nimue home to the Stronghold. I knew what Nimue was experiencing. I'd felt it myself living in the other world. But why had I coped there? Then something occurred to me. "Come on," I said, pushed off the wall and starting for the stairwell.

"*Thank* you," I heard Raphael's dry irritated tone as he followed.

I was still pretty nimble despite the growing belly and I skipped down the stairs lightly with Raphael behind me calling, "Rhiannon slow down. If you fall on the stairs Rowan will kill me."

And me calling back, "I'm not going to fall Raph. I'm not clumsy. You know that."

I turned and passed through an archway and down the hall to my rooms with Raphael close behind and started rummaging around. I dug through trunks and finally found what I was looking for in the drawer in the bottom of an armoire. I pulled out the package and held it in my hands. Raphael looked at it curiously. He was oddly sensitive to anything from the other world and he was drawn to the plastic wrapped books that I held in my hands. *Plastic*, I thought. It felt strange under my fingers. Plastic had become alien to me. The packing tape was sticky and unnatural as I pulled it off of the plastic bag and took the books out of their wrappings. I held them, feeling their soothing weight in my hands before I spun on my heel in the direction of Nimue's room with Raphael trailing along behind.

"I'm going to read you a story," I told her. I didn't get much of a response. She spent most of her time staring out of the window lately. I opened the smaller of the two books. "Peter S. Beagle. The Last Unicorn." I read the title of the first novella in the volume knowing that I wouldn't have to translate. It was the Dryad blood. Apparently we all operate on a sort of tree frequency. I started reading, holding the book in my hands and walking up and down the length of the room.

After two chapters I stopped and looked up about to say to Raphael, "Would you ask someone to bring us some lunch?" but he was looking fixedly at Nimue. I shifted my gaze and met her eyes. She was sitting forward. "Keep reading. Please?" She spoke for the first time in three days so I kept reading. I wasn't quite sure that a story about an incompetent wizard, a red bull, the last unicorn in the world and the hero who gives his life to save her, was quite what Nimue needed, but she was enchanted by it. When I finished she looked at me with wide eyes and said, "So there *is* Magic in your world then?"

I smiled. "I lived there so I suppose that there must have been a little. I've heard about other Fay living there, but I think that we all stayed pretty much hidden in the woodwork."

"But the story?" she said, confused. "It feels true."

"It's a novella," I explained. "Just a story made up by a man to make us think, to make us cry, to entertain us or, I don't know ... to get us out of our own heads for a while ... Or maybe back into them."

"Well then, the person who wrote that story must have a kind of magic that I've never heard of before," Nimue said firmly.

And that was how we spent our days—Not that I could entirely give up my hall walking. I read to Nimue from the only two books that I had, and at night she slept beside me because my nightmares weren't quite so bad if I wasn't alone when I slept.

Chapter 10

At the end of March the army came back to rest and resupply. Rowan was worn down. We didn't have much time together but I sat in on the war councils just to be in the same room with him and we walked the walled gardens together. I'd sent him letters every day so he knew that I was 'well enough'. I remember sitting with him late on one of those in-between evenings. The baby was squirming inside of me and pushing actively against me from within. I took his hand and placed it on my belly. The baby had been kicking for weeks but that was the first time that I had been able to let Rowan feel it, that we had been able so share it. He smiled softly and placed his other hand on my belly and waited for more of the tiny movements. I had whispered later that night in the dark, softly so that no one else could possibly overhear me, "When all of this is over I will abdicate the throne and you and I and our wee sweet babe can run away together, and just be happy."

Rowan didn't answer but pulled me close and breathed into my hair, but the next morning when we woke he told me as he so often did when he had the chance, "You're my morning glory you know. Waking up with you is like stepping out into a new, warm, sunlit day and seeing them bloom. The blue and pink ones, the ones that bloom along the road that leads home."

I felt so guilty then, for my tears. I wanted to stay strong for him. He had enough on his shoulders.

Three days later, in the hour or two before he had to leave, we walked in the gardens where spring was making its first timid advances after the terrible winter. He put his arms around me and stroked my hair. "I hate this so much," he whispered. "I hate seeing you like this." He meant seeing me fall apart. "Will you promise me something?"

"What?" I asked.

"If I die, and my body is recovered ... Promise me that you won't look at it." He took my face in his hands. "*Promise me?* I can't bear the idea of you seeing me like that. That's not how I want you to remember me. I want you to remember me alive and loving you." He wiped the tears off my cheeks then whispered, "Promise me."

My voice cracked when I spoke. "I promise but please my love, please ... stop talking this way. I can't stand it."

He put his arms around me and held me for a half hour or so then he said, his voice steadier, "I must go. I should be back by tomorrow night." Then he kissed me and walked away and I went back to pacing my grey halls, my hands on my growing belly.

Chapter 11

Rowan returned late the next evening. He looked at me, calm and grim. "I ... We ... Need to speak with you." I nodded and followed him to a small council chamber. I knew immediately that whatever it was that needed to be discussed was heavy. All of the highest ranking most trusted officers were there. Yori, Brian, Thaylum, Liam, Fern, Mikail, and Nuriel. Gwydion, Caitlin and Yuka sat at one end of the table and to my surprise Nimue and my father Lugh were present as well. I hadn't seen my father since I'd left the Stronghold some months earlier. He smiled his sad, elegant, sardonic smile and nodded. I took a seat next to him. Rowan looked to Liam. "Would you do the honours?" he asked in a quiet serious tone.

Liam sighed but nodded. It seemed that it was often Liam who got to be the spokesperson for unfortunate facts. "Okay, so, as you know, what we have going here is some kind of ugly guerrilla attrition thing, and we're at a point where Darling Uncle just might win if we don't change our tactics, cause we can't fight what we can't catch and can't find. We have to place ourselves in a position to use his weaknesses against him, and he has them, but we need to draw him out into the open. We need some bait. Something that he won't be able to resist. We want to use you," he looked at me then changed his focus to my sister, "Or more specifically, we want to use Nimue disguised as you to lure him." Liam licked his lips and looked around the room before continuing. "Now, Rowan here hates this idea, even though it was his, but he says it's our best bet. We'll need to lay the plan carefully and we're pretty sure we can pull it off with minimal risks to Nimue. Seamus is nearly out of weapons and according to our intel the elves are pretty much useless now. They can't cross the boundary be-tween the worlds or perform any other works of magic. We just need to get them out into the open so that we can end this thing. Once and for all." He levelled his gaze at me once more. "What do you say?"

I looked to Nimue who spoke immediately, "They've al-ready asked me and I've already agreed to it."

I turned to Rowan who spoke reluctantly, "I told them that I wouldn't agree to it without telling you first. I do think that it's our best chance though, even if I hate it."

My stomach churned and my heart constricted but I nodded, "Do it then," I said. "End it."

* * *

I was in the last trimester of my pregnancy. I felt heavy, stretched taut, both physically and mentally. I didn't attend any of the war councils. It bothered Rowan and every other overprotective male in my life to see me there, so I kept to my rooms and my long grey hallways. Raph kept me up to date on everything that was happening. My Guardian Angel, he was almost always with me. Rowan didn't trust anyone else to be able to protect me, to make sure no one got to me somehow. The days dragged by and I hated every minute of it.

Plans were patiently and carefully laid, webs woven, traps set, forged letters 'lost', spies planted. All too soon the battle was being fought. It was loud enough for me to hear it from the castle. There was nothing for me to do because what does a little gardener Fairy do in a war? So I paced my halls, the cold grey stones almost comforting in the heat of the summer solstice.

* * *

A week before the summer solstice it had been announced that I had given birth to a daughter. I hadn't, but it was all a part of the plan. The section of the castle that I tended to keep to was cordoned off and no one save family and close friends were allowed in. I stayed quiet as I was in theory, lying in, although I wasn't showing any signs of going into labour yet. It was a strange time. In some respects I was relishing the privacy but I wasn't sleeping well. One part pregnancy, two parts pure anxiety. I woke one night from the same dream I'd been having since since I'd first come to Rowan's world. It was a shapeless formless dream of fear and sadness, nothing more, just feelings, but I woke with a cry and found Rowan curled protectively around my back. Nimue was asleep on a cot against the wall and Raphael was sitting in the window half asleep.

"It's alright, you're fine," Rowan whispered to me pulling me closer to him.

I was too uncomfortable to go back to sleep. The baby was kicking and squirming inside my tight sore belly. I had vivid red stretch marks that itched and burned. I could feel Rowan's hand resting there, feeling that little life in me as she kicked and rolled. I drifted off eventually and when I woke Rowan was still with me. The sun was only just rising, filling the sky with a gold, pink and soft blue glow, reminding me of another morning nine months earlier. Rowan had still been with me that morning too. He smiled at me as if he weren't about to ride away again. "My morning glory," he said to me. "You truly are."

I smiled back and kissed his mouth, his forehead, stroked his hair. And then he said to me. "Are we doing the right thing? Maybe we should have just run? Maybe I could have kept you safe that way."

"I don't know," I said to him. "I don't know the end of the story. But even if we had run instead of making a stand, could you have lived with yourself never knowing if we were safe and all the while knowing that a terrible war was being waged that we had the potential to end? As much as I hate it, this is about more than us ... And I don't think that we ever truly had a choice."

He put his arms around me and held me like he would never let me go, then slowly released me and looked at me with such an expression of helplessness in his eyes. "My love ..." he said.

"Must you?" I whispered.

"I have no choice. I must go."

He kissed my mouth, my belly, let his hand linger there for a moment, then he was gone and I felt like a giant dark pit had opened up inside of me.

* * *

The night before the Summer Solstice, I dreamt. At first I didn't realize that I was dreaming as I looked around the bright white room. The furniture was sturdy simple pine, and the linens on the bed upon which I sat cross legged were white as were the curtains that fluttered in the windows. Sunlight poured in as it dawned on me that they didn't have the chemical process for pure white linens in Rowan's world. The closest they could come was a rich cream. That was when I realized that I was holding something in my arms and I looked down at the newborn baby asleep there. Dark eyelashes against delicate pink cheeks. Little wisps of molasses coloured hair. She was so tiny ... so precious. I gazed at her astounded, and leaned back against the headboard of the dream bed. "Oh my little girl," I whispered and kissed her gently and breathed in her sweet baby smell. I wondered for a brief moment if I was dead but then decided that I didn't care and focused my attention back on the little bundle in my arms. I smoothed my thumb down her cheek and took her tiny hand so that her fingers automatically grasped the tip of my index finger. She bunched up her face and squirmed then gave a great baby sigh and relaxed again. She was wonderful.

A door that I hadn't realized was there opened and Rowan stepped into the dream looking confused until his eyes focused in on me and what, or, I should say, who, I was holding.

"Oh Rhiannon. Look at her," he breathed as he lowered himself, sitting opposite me on the bed and looked down into her little face. He was, like me, astounded.

"Here." I softly and gently transferred her into his arms. He took her and cradled her against his chest as she squirmed then settled and slowly peeped her dark little eyes open for a moment or two, looking up at him, before letting them close and going back to sleep. Rowan did as I had and gazed at her, put his lips to her downy little head, breathed her in. He touched her little hands and cheeks and tucked the woven blanket she was wrapped in around her, making sure she was safe and warm. He sat for a while like that, in quiet rapture, not speaking, lost in the beauty of the moment, for it was beautiful. After a time he looked up at me. He looked so young. Life was so new in that moment as we sat together with our baby. I looked down at her and leaned forward, kissed her again and turned my face, brushing my cheek gently against her downy head before looking back at him.

He looked into my face and smiled, placed a hand on my cheek. "I'll never regret the time I've had with you. I *need* you to know that. I wouldn't trade this or change the things we've done for anything. Not for all the worlds."

I took his face in my hands as he so often did mine, kissed him, and told him, "I love you. I could never regret you ... or this."

He blinked rapidly and then asked me, "Can we name her Sulamith?"

Strangely, we had never talked about names before that moment.

"Yes," I nodded unable to say more, then whispered, "Sulamith." And stroked her tiny brow lightly with the backs of my fingers.

"Rhiannon. I love you," he said, and then his face twisted and tears streamed down his cheeks. More tears than was fair for a father holding his child for the first time. "I have to go. The sun is rising," he said and his voice broke. He reluctantly placed Sulamith back in my arms, took my face in his hands and kissed me. "I wish this could be forever," he whispered, then rose.

And as the dream faded I woke with a cry. "Rowan!" I called out. But he wasn't there, and the Summer Solstice had arrived.

* * *

I stood next to Nimue as we looked into the mirror at one another and she slowly wove a glamour around herself, concentrating on my face and holding Raphael's hand, drawing on his reserves of magic. I think that when she was done maybe only Rowan would have been able to tell us apart. I placed my hands on my belly trying to ease the stretched, burning, taut feeling as Nimue walked to the bed and picked up the bundled cloth doll glamoured to look like a real baby. We didn't have anything to say to one another that hadn't already been said so Nimue kissed my cheek and looked to Raphael, "I will wait for you in the hall." She left Raphael and me alone.

Raphael took my hands in his and looked down at me then, feeling awkward, knelt, "You gonna be okay?"

"I don't know Raphael," I said and my shredded composure slipped further. I felt my eyes and nose start to run and my bottom lip quiver. I looked at him, realizing full force how much I had come to depend on him despite our strange cranky relationship. The idea of having my favourite body-guard away from me left me feeling stripped and vulnerable, but the queen wouldn't leave the castle without her favourite bodyguard, would she ... ? And I didn't trust anyone else to keep her safe. So Raphael had to go with Nimue.

They would leave together in a closed carriage so that all could see the queen step from the castle with her new baby in her arms and her guardian angel by her side, at which point they would ride to an undisclosed location where she would change carriages, but she would not really be in the new coach. She would drop the glamour, make herself invisible and slip out as Raphael would open a doorway to the other world and they would be left behind by the coach unknown to Seamus' spies who would be left with the impression that they had a perfect opportunity to both take the castle, and capture the queen.

"Nimue and I will be back by lunch time, you'll see. I won't let anything happen to her." He looked at me seriously, his golden eyes trying to will me to be calm.

"Come on Rhiannon, take a deep breath," he said to me as if I were a hysterical child, but oddly it helped.

I drew in a breath and nodded. Raphael put his arm around my back, kissed my forehead and the top of my head. "Lunch time. I promise," and he strode from the room.

* * *

I don't know how long I'd walked that hot summer solstice, wandering in a world of hope, fear, memories and long grey corridors, before I realized that I was having contractions. Sarah and Morgana had told me many times what to expect. I wasn't in a panic, she was my first baby, she wasn't likely to come quickly so I continued walking up and down and as the hours past and as the battle that was being waged somewhere outside got louder, the contractions grew stronger. When they started to get bad I would lean my elbows against the wall, look down at the floor and count the cracks.

It was Nimue who found me like this. She turned the corner to my chosen corridor, nodded at one of the many invisible Glaistig who had replaced Raphael for the morning, then turned and called over her shoulder, "It's alright. She's here."

Raphael appeared just behind her as she exclaimed, "Rhiannon!" paused then asked. "Are you ...?"

I looked up and nodded as the contraction passed. I looked behind her at Raphael who suddenly looked as if he would rather be somewhere else. I looked back to Nimue, "Walk with me."

"Alright, but let's at least go and walk in the hall outside your room."

We walked until my water broke but the contractions had gotten much harder and faster after that so Nimue helped me to my bed where I knelt, clinging to the foot board and bed post, as the pain had been unbearable when I'd tried to lie down. I was getting tired by then and in between contractions I would cry like a baby and ask for Rowan. Nimue had gone to fetch our grandmother and I felt a childlike relief to have her there as she shushed me and said, "Not much more now. Just a little longer."

Time must have passed I suppose, although it seemed meaningless, when suddenly Morgana said to me, "Listen Rhiannon ... Listen ..." just as a contraction had released me.

I was dazed. Spaced out. I looked at her confused. "I don't hear anything?" I said.

"The fighting's stopped," she whispered just as I was gripped by another contraction.

Then it wasn't much longer before everything changed. I felt it immediately. Suddenly the pain was gone replaced by an overwhelming urge to push. "She's coming," I gasped as a powerful contraction literally began to move my baby down and out of me. I pushed hard still clinging to the bed post and began to feel a burning ache as the widest part of her head made it through. I stopped to breathe before another contraction hit and I gave a final push then reached below me where I could feel the beginnings of a tiny shoulder emerging. I hooked my thumb under and pulled her the rest of the way into the world and, clutching her to my chest, let myself fall back exhausted onto the bed.

* * *

I had eyes for her only. She was amazing. I wiped the white vernix off of her face as she gave a hearty little bellow of life then began searching me with her face. "Rooting," Morgana called it. It took me a couple tries but I got her latched on and for a time all was right in my world. I vaguely remember pushing out the placenta. Morgana healed me as much as she could from within the walls of a stone castle, stopping the little trickle of blood that I otherwise would have had to put up with for a few days, and taking the edge off of the sting from the little skid mark that my little girl had left as she'd passed through me. I remember lying on Nimue's cot while she washed me with clean warm water and helped me into a fresh nightgown. My bedding had been replaced although I don't remember anyone doing it. I just gazed at my tiny precious child and marvelled at her. I looked into her dark eyes as she peered up at me and we made eye contact for the first time. I'd held her in my dream only that morning, but to have her in my arms again ... There was a rightness to it. She was my child.

I was lying on my side resting, still sore and exhausted but calm, looking into that little face as she slept tucked into the curve of my arm. Nimue was sitting on the bed behind me working industriously on the knots in my hair. "She reminds me of you," I said to my sister.

"That's because she looks like her mother, but she has her father's dark hair," Nimue said softly, which was true. Nimue and I are very much alike with the exception of her black and my ash hair. The differences in our faces are slight. But Nimue had said it, "Her father."

"Rowan … " I sighed. "Oh please … please … please come."

The battle was done and we'd had news of victory so I lay there as Nimue worked doggedly at my hair. I lay there with my baby and I loved … and I hoped … But I know that you know. I know that you've already figured it out. I haven't been able to keep it out of my voice, even though these are only words on a page. We heard footsteps in the hall. The clink of armour. My heart … *Oh my heart* … I know that you can tell. I know that I don't *need* to say it. It wasn't Rowan on the other side of the door. *Rowan* … even now … writing it. I know that I don't need to tell you. Rowan wasn't coming home. He wasn't coming back to me.

Chapter 12

Nimue and I looked up. Sarah and Morgana were on their feet, and the door opened. It was Leif. I had only to look at his face to know. I remember the sound as a single cry was torn from deep within me and it echoed as my heart shattered and everything that I'd been holding together so desperately for so long flew apart into a million tiny pieces. I clung to my baby with my arms, holding on and clutched inwardly at shards that cut me and hurt as I grabbed, trying to hold on to some semblance of *myself*. I wasn't crying, but tears poured down my face and I shook. I looked down at my baby then up into Leif's tortured face. "Tell me," I said, and if a sound could bleed the sound of my voice did, and Leif winced with the pain of it, but he nodded and then came to the side of my bed and knelt. He looked down at the baby in my arms. Rowan's child. I thought he might break then, but he didn't.

"We won," he said, but the words came from some dark hollow place. "Your uncle is dead. His army is dead, surrendered or scattered. You're ..." he blinked and swallowed, "safe."

Leif knelt there silent and unmoving for a time before he started to speak again and then he told me everything. "Rowan ..." Leif's voice cracked and he swallowed as he wiped tears with a gore crusted hand across his gore crusted cheek, then continued. "He ordered Liam and I not to tell you what he was going to do and we couldn't talk him out of it. No one else knew," he balled his fist up in frustration and hit his leg with it. "The plan worked perfectly. Seamus' Army appeared exactly where Rowan said they would and Lugh had a large contingent of water fay waiting under the surface to cut Seamus' men down as we forced them into the sea. It all happened according to plan. Rowan knew that Seamus, being the narcissistic, self preserving bastard he was, would run as soon as he realized he'd been had, so Rowan was ready. He didn't go alone. He took Bonnie and Aledwen with him as well as those two mean Glaistig twins. He took soldiers who would fight dirty if they had to and who wouldn't be afraid to use every Fay trick they knew to take Seamus down. I watched them follow Seamus away ... tracking him into the forest where they should have been able to ..." Leif stopped again and I could see him working inwardly trying to hold himself together. He let out a sound that was half cry half snarl like a hurt angry lion. The sound made the baby in my arms stir for a moment but I shushed her and waited for Leif to continue. He breathed heavily for a moment then forced onward. "I watched all through the battle, I waited to see him striding out of the woods free and confident like he was *supposed* to," Leif said the words angrily. "But he didn't. I followed him in as soon as the war was won. As soon as I could get away. I found Bonnie first, shot, bullet in her forehead, then the twins, bits of them anyway. I think Aledwen must have lasted a good while. She had nine arrows in her and about four bullet wounds. She must have got close because it was a dagger in her heart that killed her." Leif was silent again.

"Leif, just tell me about Rowan," I told him, not wanting to hear it but needing to.

"He shouldn'a done it! Everyone always said he was unbeatable but that wasn't quite true! He should of just let Seamus go but he's so bloody stubborn and he said he couldn't live knowing that he'd promised you that he'd never let your daughter be harmed. He said Seamus would just keep trying!" Leif yelled.

"Just tell me please Leif ... I need to know," I begged as tears flooded my eyes, my cheeks, my life.

Leif pressed his lips together, closed his eyes and nodded. "He was holding on by a thread when I found him. He was hurt badly Rhiannon. I asked him if I could take him to the healers but he said that he was too far gone, that he would only die faster if I moved him and that he wasn't quite ready to go." Leif stopped again, breathing hard. "Rowan looked up at me and smiled. Looked around with his eyes and said, 'It's beautiful the way the sun shines through the leaves isn't it?' I didn't know what to say to him Rhiannon. He's my brother but I didn't know what to say to him." Leif wiped his nose on the back of his hand.

Leif was suffering, tortured. I didn't know then, the words that had passed between Rowan and Leif ten months earlier, in the armoury at Fiannasmere. Those strange, almost pro-phetic words.

Leif continued in a sudden odd calm, "Rowan said then, he said, 'I did it. It's over. I killed him, and now I never have to do it again.' And then tears poured down his face all of a sudden and he started talking about you." Leif looked at me, meeting my eyes for a brief moment and then looking down once more. "He said, he said that he was sorry. He cried. He said you made him feel like his heart was free. He wanted me to tell you, he was really insistent, I had to repeat the message, his words were, 'I was with you in the dream, I saw, I wish it could be forever.' He asked me over and over, 'Tell Rhiannon I love her. Tell Rhiannon I love her.' It was as if he had a million things to say to you and the thought of only being able to choose a few was tying his tongue. He said, 'Tell my daughter, tell Rhiannon to tell her that ... I love her. Make sure she always knows that I love her.' Then he looked at me and said,

'Leif there's so much more but I haven't got time. I'm sorry about the things that went unsaid.' He took my hand. He squeezed it and then he was in too much pain to say more. He looked at me and whispered, 'I'm going now,' and ... that was it. That was the end." Leif let out a sound of strange animal grief and then fell silent.

I looked down at my baby ... At Rowan's baby, and wondered if they had even been in the world together for more than a few minutes or had Rowan died just as I was pushing her out? I think that Leif must have been thinking something along the same lines because he rose suddenly, went to the window and yelled so loudly and so long. It was a roar of anger and helplessness that went on and on and woke my wee babe who mewled for comfort. I pulled her to my breast, concentrating on caring for her, and let Leif's angry wounded cry count for me too. When he stopped and fell to his knees in the window casing I looked out over his head at the perfect azure sky then back down at the bundle in my arms. "Sulamith," I said out loud. "Rowan ... wanted me to call her Sulamith."

I didn't know it then. I wouldn't find out until six months later when Sheila would look at me and say, "Did you know the meaning of the name Sulamith when you gave it to her?"

I would shake my head and say, "No. It was my mother's name. I never even considered its meaning."

She would look at me and say, "It means 'Peace'."

And Sulamith was my peace. She was a refuge. A place where my broken heart could be free.

Chapter 13

Over the next six months I tried to do everything right, I tried to be good, starting with that day, that long summer day. The solstice. The longest day of the year. The longest day of my life.

I lay there recovering, silent tears rolling down my cheeks as Leif sat kneeling in the casement in his armour, covered in the gore of war. Time stopped moving and the sun stood still on the horizon. The stars pulled their curtains and the moon sank to the bottom of the sea. Liam came, his expression laced with sorrow and uncertainty. He was clean and dressed but his right arm was bound to his chest and he had cuts on his face. He approached Leif with a pronounced limp and a subdued tone. "You should go clean up. There's a new baby in here and you smell like a battle field."

Leif nodded, rose silently and strode from the room. Then Liam turned to me, and to Nimue who still sat on the bed next to me. "I don't know if this is the time, but waiting til tomorrow won't make this easier." He paused, looked down, back up and into my eyes then switched his gaze to Nimue, "Your father ... He was injured. He didn't make it."

Nimue put her hand to her mouth, stifling sobs. She sat for a moment but she must have sensed the rain coming because she ran from the room. I looked at my brother and begged him, "Please Liam. Follow her. Make sure she doesn't hurt herself." He looked at me with so much pain in his eyes, but nodded and turned to follow Nimue.

* * *

Af ter I'd recovered from Sulamith's birth I did what was expected of me but it was all mechanical. I was going through the motions of being alive. Liam helped me with everything. He'd held the position of monarch since he was very young and he knew the drill. He was very kind to me. Proclamations of peace were sent out and a holiday was declared, but it was summer in a largely agrarian society and fields needed planting and crops tending. Fighters went home to their families and with the exception of a small force to guard the castle much of the military was demobilized. Leif stayed away from me. Not to suggest that he went home. No. He spent his days hunting and eliminating what was left of Seamus' army. He wasn't alone in this pursuit. There were other young angry fighters, too damaged by the war to rest easy.

Morgana had to leave to manage the Fay Human political amalgamation within the strongholds. It should have, by all rights, been Nimue's responsibility, but she refused to leave my side. "No Gran I won't go back," she'd said. "The world is changing and I won't be bound by old laws. You can try to force me but I'll either run away or loose my mind. Rhiannon needs me more than the strongholds do. I'm staying here."

And she was right, I did need her. I was facing the final political amalgamation of the Human and Fay kingdoms and the joining of the two councils. It was messy and frustrating. Yuka was my right hand in this and Nimue's presence helped keep Fay members in line, as Liam's did the Humans. But for me it was awful. At least Nimue and Liam were willing to be my public face. I never had to face the people of the city. I didn't have it in me. I've never been that sort of person and after all that had passed ...? I've never been a political person either. Passionate yes. Political no. None of what was happening held any appeal. I couldn't help it. I felt as if everything around me was too sharp, too abrupt, and when I had to leave Sulamith in Sarah's arms to go sit and listen to people bicker I would loose my patience and force them to stop. I would stand over them until they had worked the problem out like grownups and then I would say, conscious of the tears that never had a chance to dry on my face, "I must go, my daughter needs me," and I would walk down long grey halls back to my baby so that I could feed her and care for her because I'm her mother and that's what mothers do.

I was constantly being offered a wet nurse but this became a bone of contention. I knew that the ladies of the court saw my insistence on nursing my own child as eccentric and the council thought that I needed to focus more on the tasks at hand. I felt so alone with people's eyes on me at all times and I couldn't do anything about the tears that fell all day down my face. When I looked around at the people I loved I could see the immediacy of their pain, both what they carried for themselves and the reflection of my own. Every time Nimue looked at me it twisted me up inside.

Liam would try to spend time with me but I would always ask him difficult questions like,

"Liam, who was your father?"

His face turned to stone.

"I'm sorry I didn't mean to pry."

"No. It's fine. People don't talk about it, that's all."

"Oh," I said quietly.

Liam was silent for a long moment, obviously weighing whether he wanted to tell me himself or if he wanted me to find out from someone else. He sighed long and heavy. "He was one of the Brownridge sons. Foisted on my mother to keep her out of trouble. She hated him. My conception was practically rape. Not like yours. I think Thaylum killed him in the battle just before the Brownridges withdrew their support from Seamus' army." A long silence followed.

Then on another afternoon as we were walking the ramparts together Liam told me, "When I was a little boy I used to walk up here with my mother and she would make up stories for me. I wish I could remember the stories."

"How did she die?" I asked.

"Aw Rhiannon. You don't want to know that. Didn't Rowan ever tell you?"

"No. He wouldn't. And it's not something people talk about."

Liam gave me a funny look. "Rowan *wouldn't* tell you?"

I nodded into the late autumn wind and adjusted my grip on Sulamith as we strolled along the ramparts.

Liam sighed, "Can't you just be content not knowing?"

"She was my mother too Liam. I have a right to know. And anyway, content doesn't exist anymore."

"Alright." Liam paused, "Seamus pushed her out her window after forcing her at knife point to write a suicide letter."

I looked up at the high tower where her rooms had been. "How come he didn't get away with it?"

"Rowan, of all people, caught him in the act, just as she lost her grip in the casement and fell. He was bringing her a letter from the then captain. Her guard was missing. He thought something was off so he broke down the door to her rooms. He attacked Seamus then and there but Rowan was only eighteen and Seamus was bigger meaner and faster. He almost killed Rowan. He thought he had, but the commotion was enough to bring the other guards running. Seamus ran and was eventually banished. Rowan always had issues about it after."

"It always comes back to Rowan doesn't it," I muttered at the stones under foot then looked up at my tall handsome brother, "I hate this place Liam. I hate it."

Raphael alone seemed to sense that I didn't want sympathy and that I was too close to the edge of an abyss to accept comfort, but as the weeks and months passed I could see that I was hurting him. I felt guilty all the time and though my tears fell, I could not cry. I did not weep. I couldn't cry with all of those curious eyes waiting to see if I would. I couldn't cry without shelter and since Rowan was gone I felt I didn't have any. How could I cry without Rowan there to help me stop? I dreamed of Rowan every night and woke again each day to find him gone. Each day I woke to find that I'd lost just a little more of myself as well.

About a week after my walk up on the ramparts with Liam, after a morning of tedious meetings, I had retreated gratefully to the quiet of my rooms and sat in a comfortable chair in the corner with Sulamith in my arms nursing hungrily. It didn't take long for her to drift off to sleep. She usually napped in the afternoon. It's hard for a baby with a full tummy to stay awake sometimes. I laid her on my bed—she always looked so tiny there—and sat watching her sleep. I felt right when I was with her. Not necessarily happy or even content, but not so jarringly wrong either. Nimue opened the door and entered quietly. At first she did as I was doing and sat baby gazing, but after a time she said my name. "Rhiannon?" Her voice and her expression were so loaded that I thought she was going to try to talk to me, but I saw it in her eyes. I saw her lose her nerve and instead of whatever it was that she was going to say she told me, "I can sit with her if you like, and you could go walk in the gardens or take a bath."

I didn't give it serious thought, but being outside did bring me a relief of sorts so even though I knew that it meant less time with my baby I decided that twenty minutes in the small private gardens just outside the rooms that Nimue had moved me to after the war had ended wouldn't be a bad thing. While no one else had any other demands, before something came up and I lost my chance. I nodded and said, "Um, I will maybe, go out for a few minutes. I'll stick to the gardens."

I slipped out through the french doors and into the early December rain. It was misty and cool but not cold. The grey fog made me feel sheltered and took away all of the sharp edges. The dead plants didn't jar me. It was a reflection of my inner landscape. Muted. Dull. It made no demands. It was dormant with no expectation of life or action. No growth. Nothing. I let my face relax and let down the walls that I kept erected around me. I was so, so tired. My feet carried me along the paths and I paid them no heed. I thought about Sulamith's little seal toy. She was old enough by then to grasp it and shake it and realize cause and effect. She shook, and it jingled. Rowan had carved it a year ago from a dying tree. Dying. The word played over in my head and my feet carried me on through that grey world. I lost all sense of life, of space, of time. Dying. I wasn't looking where I was going and my head was filled with one reverberating word. Dying. So it was no wonder that I walked right into Raphael. Without my walls erected the brightness of him seared me and I gave a cry that implied real pain. Raphael took my shoulders to keep me from falling.

I don't want to know what he saw in my face to make him look at me the way he did that afternoon, and in my unguarded state I couldn't handle his expression, but I couldn't look away either. I think he could see me for what I had become. A fresh river of tears spilled down my not quite dry face as I looked into Raphael's eyes and hated myself for hurting him, for the tears that were spilling down *his* face. We stood there for an amorphous expanding and contracting length of meaningless time, Raphael gripping my arms so hard

I knew it would leave bruises. When he spoke he cried my name. "Rhiannon ... What are you doing to yourself?" His voice was raw. "You can't keep this up ... Look at you. I can't find you when I look in your eyes anymore. If Rowan could see you like this it would break his heart. You're breaking *my* heart."

He shook me, not hard, just hard enough to provoke a response, "What the hell do you want me to do Raphael? I haven't got any fight left in me!" I almost shouted at him, and he kissed me.

He hadn't meant to kiss me as he gripped my arms even harder and lifted me to my toes. I hadn't meant to react. I hadn't meant to kiss him back, but I did. It was the only thing I'd reacted to other than Sulamith in months. It was crazy and furious. He was lifting me up to hold me against him and we were kissing each other brutally. I don't even remember anymore how we got to his room only that his bed was rumpled and unmade. I remember his skin and the way he looked at me. I'll never forget our one afternoon when we let that strange love of ours spread its wings. It was a freedom of sorts. A release that obliterated everything except for love and I loved Raphael too much to want to hurt him. I didn't want to break his heart. I couldn't *stand* the idea that I was breaking his heart and I would offer him the only comfort I could just as he was doing for me. Not that I'm saying that one hour-and-a-half with Raphael could, in and of itself, have solved anything. It couldn't. Raphael and I would never be happy together like that, not that happiness with him could have chased away my demons. Ours is a strange friendship. I'm not even sure that you could call it friendship. It's too painful in some ways. But in that hour-and-a-half he gave me space. Respite. A temporary release from my demons that brought me back to myself and as I lay there watching him rest, lying in the soft warm shelter of his brilliant wing, I was in the eye of the storm. My face was dry and, for the first time in months, I could see that Raphael was right. I was slowly dying and I had to make a decision. I lay there quietly and ran a finger down his cheek. He turned and opened his eyes, smiled softly at me. He took my hand and held it in his gently, looking at how much smaller than his it was, then brought his gaze back to my face.

"This ... us ..." he swallowed. "It's a one time deal. I know it is, but not being with you, like this, at least once in my life would have been a regret. If Rowan were still here I would never have crossed that line and it makes me feel conflicted that I did, but I can't help the way I feel."

I smiled a little and realized how seldom I did that for anyone other than Sulamith anymore, but it was classic Raphael. Always so open about how he felt. "We can't change the past," I told him. "Let's not feel guilty about the present. If this is a one time deal let's make the most of it because Sulamith never naps for more than two hours."

I watched as his beautiful wings arched above me one more time. I felt the kisses he rained down on my face and when we were finished, and he slept in earnest this time, I slid out from under his heavy arm and, shivering outside the warmth of his wings, I dressed hurriedly and crept surreptitiously back to my rooms.

Chapter 14

When I opened the door to my bed chamber Heather was sitting in the corner sewing. I briefly wondered where Nimue had gone but was relieved in a way that she wasn't there and I let the thought go. Sulamith was making little 'waking baby' grunts and starting to squirm. "Thank you. You can go," I said absently to Heather and she gathered her things and rose to go but hesitated briefly.

"You look tired. Shall I have your dinner sent to your rooms?" she asked without beating around the bush or attempting small talk, which I appreciated.

"Yes please Heather. And, thank you. I appreciate it."

Heather nodded and swept out as I lifted Sulamith and settled with her in my preferred chair so that she could nurse.

I had a feeling of disbelief in me. A feeling I'd only had when reading a story whose ending I didn't like, but I was awake and I could feel a truth in what I knew was going to happen next. It wasn't the ending I had hoped for so very much, but I'd realized that it wasn't an ending at all. It was a middle. *I'm still in the middle of the story*, I thought to myself, and I almost lost my nerve. *But this is how the story is going to go*, I told myself. *It doesn't matter if you believe it yet.* Sulamith was fussing in my arms so I lifted her to my shoulder for a moment, feeling her plump baby warmth. She gave a small burp and I offered her my other breast, where she settled in happily. I took a deep breath. I knew what I needed to do. I knew then, where I needed to go.

I ate my dinner and shared my sweet potatoes with Sulamith. It was the first time in weeks that eating had given me any satisfaction. I played with Sulamith, lying on the floor on a soft rug with her. She had just begun to be able to sit up on her own and this brought new games. Knocking over blocks, bunching up silk scarves with her little fists, shaking things to see if they jingled. She loved peek-a-boo. It was serendipitous that no one interrupted us and I was able to look through my things without interference. When she started to fuss and swipe her beautiful little hands at her face, I knew she was getting tired so I changed her and put her in warm clothes then rocked her and sang to her, paced with her, smoothing her back, and finally nursed her. Soon she was drifting off for the night.

Everything was quiet. I sat down at my desk and wrote a letter. It was clumsy and not particularly elegant, but it was passionate as I begged them not to follow me, to let me go, and let there be an end to the monarchy that was nothing more than a legacy of pain. I begged that they not pressure my brother and sister into taking on that mantle. It was over, and they all needed to see it. It could only bring more pain.

I signed the letter and sealed it then went to my wardrobe and took out my old pink dress, my jeans, and the old green sweater that Fionnuala had knitted me, and I slipped into my old clothes. My shoes had long since fallen apart so I pulled on Rowan's old riding boots. I still had my old shoulder bag as well and I put it over my head and across my body. I walked over to the table in the corner and opened the jewellery box that someone had put there for me. I took out the pearl necklace, the ring that Rowan had given me, and his ring. I would have preferred it to have been buried with him but it was taken off his body and given to me before he was taken back

to Fiannasmere to be buried. I placed these things along with
the heartsease ring, the ruby jewellery, and the opal earrings
in my bag. I placed the circlet in its box and the letter that I
had written on top of that, and then returned to the wardrobe
and took out a large shawl. I spread it on the bed and very
carefully chose what else to bring. A few outfits for Sulamith.
Enough diapers to get her through the next day. The little
collection of toys that Rowan had carved for her, and all of
the little keepsakes he had given me along the way. The blue
dress Nessa had made for me, and the pink dress I had worn
the night Rowan had asked me to be his. A night gown.
Fenna's old hairbrush. I could feel my heart swelling and
aching as I took out the things that I could hardly bear to look
at but couldn't bear to leave behind. Little pieces of the life
that I'd had with Rowan. I carefully wrapped them up in the
shawl and tied it so that I had a handle, then looked to my
wee sweet babe. I picked up a long length of cloth and spread
it out then lifted Sulamith in my arms shushing her and humming, then, as Sarah had taught me, I began wrapping the
length of cloth around us crossing and tying it in such a way
that it became a baby carrier in the style of the angels. Finally
I wrapped another shawl around us, picked up my luggage and
slipped out the door, stopping on my way to pick up the
circlet and the letter. I walked lightly down the hall to
Nimue's room, opening her door then closing it softly and,
searching inward for a moment, I willed the candles to light.

I was surprised but not displeased to see my brother there,
sleeping in the bed next to her, his arm around her as she
slept, her head upon his shoulder. One dark head, one golden.
I hadn't realized that they had grown close in that respect. I
won't say that seeing them like that, I didn't briefly consider
unwrapping my wee babe, leaving her with my brother and
sister, knowing she would be loved by them, and then running
down to the water's edge to take my own life. But as soon as

the thought rose my heart gave a terrible lurch at the idea of leaving my daughter. *No*, I thought, *If I have enough life in me to love this much, I have enough life in me to push forward just a little longer, and try to mend.*

I gently touched Nimue's shoulder, then put my fingers to her lips as she woke and turned to look at me. She gently moved Liam's arm and sat up, disregarding her nakedness.

"I couldn't leave without saying goodbye," I whispered.

"Where are you going?" she asked, dismay and heartache spreading across her face.

"I don't know." Tears were streaming down my face. "Away," I half sobbed out the word. I put my arm around her neck and held my cheek against hers as I sat next to her on the bed. "Tell Raphael ... Tell him thanks, for bringing me back to myself. Tell him that I'll always love him, no matter what." Then I pulled back and told her seriously, "You and Liam need to leave the castle tonight. Find Raphael if you can, and go. Give me twenty minutes or so head start then leave. Here," I said, and put the letter and the circlet in her hands. Liam started to stir and I didn't think I could handle his kind eyes at that moment so I rose quickly and opened the door. "Goodbye.' I looked at Nimue one last time, at her dark blue eyes staring out at me from her pale face and tousled black hair. I closed the door.

Chapter 15

I ran down the long grey corridors of the castle clutching Sulamith in my arms. Out, silently and invisibly, past the night guard, and down the slope through the trees to the water's edge where I was conceived. I stood there breathing hard and knowing, this time, exactly what I was doing. I opened a doorway to the other world and came through near the 'girl in a wet suit' statue at the northern tip of Stanley Park. I stood in the moonlight and looked out over the water at the girl on the rock. When I was little I always though she was a mermaid and in the soft light, I almost expected her to turn and look at me.

I walked down the paths and through the trees until I came to the bus loop where I sat and waited. It felt like a lifetime had passed since I had last waited for a bus and the alien familiar feeling was difficult to pin down but intense. It was neither frightening nor comforting but some oddly reassuring combination of the two that told me that I was alive. Sulamith stirred and murmured, so I stood and shushed her, rocking from foot to foot as I'd seen dozens of other mothers do. The bus pulled up. It read 19 Metrotown. I fished through my bag asking the driver if the fare was still two seventy five. The massive wad of cash was still there in my bag along with the bit of change left over from what I'd spent over a year earlier. I put a loonie and a toonie in the box, then took a seat about halfway back. I sat, stunned, as the bus passed through the city heading more or less directly east. I watched familiar sites

410

pass by in tear blurred neon technicolour as my two worlds crashed together with brutal force, and when I saw the street sign marked Victoria Drive I reached up quickly, pulled the cord for the bus stop, and then stepped out onto the grimy East Vancouver sidewalk.

'North' my feet said to me, and I let them have the lead. Sulamith began to fuss again so I undid the top few buttons of my dress and shifted her so that she could nurse. I walked along Victoria Drive. Past closed shop windows and all night Chinese groceries. I saw the Hungarian butcher shop that Fionnuala always went to for sausages and the vegetarian eatery where I used to have lunch with Evan. I turned automatically onto a side street and looked up at the naked December trees that lined it. I never thought I'd be back. *What happened to that life*? I asked myself, then started down the street and followed it to Sheila's house.

It was dark but I climbed the stairs and rang the bell anyway. I heard her before I saw the lights go on, then the porch light flicked on and the door opened. I could tell that I'd woken her.

"Sprite! Am I dreaming?" She stood in her nightgown looking bleary.

"No Sheila. It's really me." My voice sounded beaten down even to my ears.

She hustled me in, taking my luggage, then looked into my face. Something in me was slipping and I knew she could see it. "Kristabell, what is it?" She looked me over taking in my carefully clutched bundle.

"I was wondering if I could stay for a while ... and if I could," my voice broke, "have my job back."

"Kristabell, why! I thought ...?" Sheila asked dismayed.

It was the breaking point. Something snapped inside. I put my cheek against my baby's head and went down on my knees. "Rowan ..." I sobbed. "Rowan died. He's gone. I can't *live* that life without him! Oh Sheila. I miss him so much. I wasn't ready to loose him."

It was the first time I'd thought the words, let alone said them. Sheila was on the floor with her arms around me, then she untied the cloth that held Sulamith and lifted her from my arms and took her to another room so that the storm could break and I finally cried for Rowan, for my lost love. There, kneeling on the floor of Sheila's entrance way. I sobbed and it hurt so bad and I really did think that maybe I wouldn't be able to stop. Sometimes I thought it might kill me and I welcomed it because I hurt so bad. How could he die like that? How could we love each other *so* much and have this happen? He was supposed to be beside me and he wasn't and now I was ... what *was* I? I wanted his arms around me and I wanted him to tell me that it was okay, but he wasn't there and it wasn't okay. *I'm not okay. This hurts. This feels like it's going to hurt forever. I'm not okay. I'm not okay.* The thoughts ran through my head. *Your husband died. A true love. You're not supposed to be okay.* Suddenly It was Raphael's voice in my head as another torrent of sobs was pulled from my throat and I felt like I might vomit, but the Raphael voice in my head was right. I wasn't supposed to be okay.

I don't know how long I sat there sobbing on the floor of Sheila's front hall. Hours I think. I don't think that I fell asleep or passed out but at a certain point I realized that I had cried myself out for the time being. I felt drained and transparent. I lifted my head off of my forearms. I felt faded but my arms wanted my daughter so I went looking for Sheila. I found them in the living room. Sheila sitting in a rocking chair gazing raptly at my baby. "She's beautiful," Sheila spoke softly. "What's her name?"

"Sulamith. Rowan and I agreed before ..." I swallowed. "That we would name her that."

Sheila rose, passing a sleeping Sulamith to me and offered me the rocker.

"I'm going to make some tea," Sheila said as she walked from the room.

Chapter 16

S heila came back with a tray of tea things and poured out two cups. I sipped, careful not to spill any on Sulamith, although Sheila had doused mine with a healthy splash of milk so it wasn't hot. I'd forgotten black tea and its bizarre capacity to make things less bad. It couldn't change the world or undo the past but 'less bad' counted for something that night. Sheila sat in a fat plaid armchair with her cup and took a sip, letting the silence in the room settle comfortably into the corners before she said to me, "If you don't have it in you, that's alright, but if you feel like you can tell me, if you'd like to, I'd be honoured to hear your story."

"Are you sure?" I asked her. "It's very long, and very sad."

"I'm sure," she said.

So I told her everything, starting with the package of wildflower seeds I'd purchased with my own money when I was on the brink of my thirteenth birthday. I told her about Sulamith and Lugh, Gavin and Fionnuala. I told her about Gwydion, about Sarah, about my cruel psychopathic uncle and how he'd been inadvertently allowed so much power. I told Sheila about my brothers, about Nimue, Cole, and Raphael. I told her about the summer solstice, the day my daughter was born, and I told her about Rowan. I didn't leave anything out. Not even the personal bits because in a way some of those times were my happiest and I told her as much to remind *myself* that they had happened, as to share them with Sheila.

Fairies and Unicorns. Castles and knights. Black hearts and Heroes. It seemed unbelievable, impossible, that it was my life. Surely it was just a dark and beautiful nightmare studded with stars and monsters? A temporary lapse of reality, of reason, of sanity? But I held a baby in my arms, and the heart in my chest was broken. No mere dream could ever leave me like that.

When I finished Sheila sat there silent for a long time. She wiped her eyes without fuss and sat thinking before asking, "So what do I call you?"

"Let's settle on Krista," I said. "Rhiannon, well ... I think she died with Rowan. And Kristabell died in a house fire."

Sheila nodded. "And you're ... A fairy?"

I nodded and smiled then lifted my hand and let the opalescent nimbus flicker and dance along my fingertips then willed the lights to coalesce in my palm into a flaming soap bubble of colour. I watched for a moment, still fascinated on some level by my ability, before pulling the lights back into myself.

"Oh my god," Sheila whispered and then wiped her eyes again.

* * *

Sheila found me a spare toothbrush and settled me in the spare bedroom, tucking me in almost like I was a little girl. I didn't lay awake long as I gently moved Sulamith close and nestled into the bed. I didn't have the energy for more than fleeting half thoughts but, as sleep washed over me, I was grateful for the haven I had been able to run to.

* * *

Once Sheila was sure that Krista slept she hopped in her car and drove to the garden centre. She unlocked the back door, headed for the office and woke the computer. She

typed up a short message then printed it off. DUE TO A
FAMILY EMERGENCY WE WILL BE CLOSED FOR THE WEEK.
WE WILL REOPEN RESUMING REGULAR HOURS ON DEC.
20. SORRY FOR ANY INCONVENIENCE.

Sheila taped the paper to the inside of the customer entrance, double checking that she had faced the words out-
ward. She was tired and more than a little emotionally bowled
over. Posting a sign backwards was exactly the sort of thing
she did when she was preoccupied. She'd done it after the fire
that had taken Krista's parents. She wrote up a list of jobs
that she could have Tanya do while they were closed, then,
locking the staff door behind her, she drove home through
the late night traffic. She pulled up in front of her house,
stepped out of the car, hit the auto lock button then turned,
glancing down at the curb in the shadows of the street lamp
and walked towards her front gate.

She almost leaped out of her skin when the massive angel
stepped out of the shadows towards her. "Good God! That girl
trails angels in her wake!" Sheila burst out, throwing her hand
to her pounding heart. "You scared the living daylights out of
me," she scolded.

"Sorry." The angel shrugged sheepishly but then asked
immediately, "She's here then?"

"Yes, she's here," Sheila admitted.

The angel closed his eyes tightly and let out a shudder as
tears of relief escaped his closed lids. He wiped his face with
his hands then took a deep breath.

"It's Raphael right?" Sheila confirmed as much to have
something to say as anything else.

He nodded. He looked as tired as Krista had. He sighed
then admitted hesitantly, "I know she didn't want to be
followed. I ... I don't need to see her. Don't tell her I came. I
just needed to know that she's ... she ..."

"She's safe enough," Sheila told him. "She cried long and hard on my entrance way floor then told me everything she's been through. I won't tell you that she's okay, but she's here, with her baby, and she's alive."

The angel's face worked. He turned from her, placed his hand against a tree and buried his face in the corner of his elbow.

Sheila admired his beautiful variegated wings as he wept and shook her head in bewildered wonder. Fairies. Angels. She wouldn't be surprised to wake up and find a unicorn in her backyard.

The angel took another deep breath and faced Sheila. "She cried?" he asked. And she thought she could detect a lightness in him at the thought.

"She did," Sheila confirmed gently.

Raphael blinked back more tears of relief. "If it's okay with you, I'm gonna spend a few hours in your tree," Raphael nodded towards the cherry tree, "just for old times sake. I'll be gone by sunrise."

Sheila couldn't suppress a small chuckle, "Be my guest, it's all yours."

He was silent for a moment nodding thoughtfully, "If you ever need me, there's a tree next to the duck pond at Queen Elizabeth Park. A beech with a knot half way up and a little hollow about one of your arms length up from that. Leave me a message. I'll check it every full moon."

"Are the moons the same?" Sheila asked.

"They are," Raphael confirmed, as if he found comfort in the fact.

"I'd better be going in." Sheila headed towards her door, but had to turn for one more look at the beautiful angel.

"Thanks. You know ... For the tree." The angel jerked his head at the cherry tree again and gave her a complicated lop-sided grin.

Sheila chuckled and went in, set her alarm clock for six-thirty, put a reminder in her phone to call her employees about the schedule changes, and then went to bed.

Chapter 17

It was the long deep dreamless sleep of recovery. The kind of sleep that takes you after the ravages of a fever and allows you wake up clearheaded and assess the damage. I vaguely remember Sulamith waking me in the morning and moaning to her, "Oh Baby, Mama's so tired," as she patted my face and made the funny experimental 'neenle neenle' sound she'd been making of late. Then she went for my hair. "Ouch. No no Sulamith. That's my hair. Owie."

Then Sheila cracked the door, swept in, scooped up Sulamith and told me, "Sleep as long as you need. Don't worry about anything else or force yourself up because you feel obligated. Is she okay with pureed fruits and vegetables?"

"Mm hmm yeah," I mumbled, but I was already dropping back into that deep deep sleep.

I was somewhat aware of Sheila putting Sulamith back in the bed with me a couple of times but that was it until Sulamith woke me sometime in the wee hours of the next night fussing, and I shifted positions so that she could nurse, then I dropped back off. When I woke in earnest the sun was up and I was alone in the bed. I lay there taking stock. I thought about my night flight and panicked. *No. You don't need to worry about that. Think smaller. Think present not past,* I told myself and I calmed down. I was hungry, I had to pee, and my breasts felt full, meaning Sulamith was probably hungry too. I could cope with those things. I climbed out of bed feeling a bit weak, but not heavy, not tired. I brushed my hair and pulled my cardigan on over my nightgown, then padded down the hall to the bathroom. After I'd washed my hands I twisted my hair behind me and splashed my face, then tiptoed down to the kitchen.

Sheila sat at the table with a pot of tea and a plate of toast with peanut butter and banana. Sulamith was in an old, but sturdy and clean, wooden high chair, pounding on the tray exuberantly and squealing, reaching for the spoonful of mashed banana Sheila was holding. Sheila looked up at me and smiled, then turned to Sulamith who was getting desperate for that mouthful. Sheila inserted it and Sulamith went still, focused and intent as she worked down the mouthful of sweet mush. Sheila looked back at me, "Somebody *loves* bananas."

Sulamith started to squeal and pound again.

"Yes, yes it's coming," Sheila inserted another mouthful.

"She's never had bananas before," I couldn't help smiling as I sat down at the table and watched.

"Help yourself to the bread, there's sourdough rye and some kind of multi-grain cracked wheat." Sheila waved a hand towards the bags of bread on the counter next to the toaster.

I cut a thick slice of the sourdough rye and popped it in the old battered toaster, pressing down the lever and feeling that weird crackly feeling that I always felt when I used electric devices. I winced, half afraid of blowing the toaster, but it was alright. I came back to the table with my toast and reached for the almond butter and strawberry jam that Sheila had put out, poured myself a cup of tea, and ate watching the banana shenanigans. I finished my last bite of toast as Sheila was telling Sulamith, "All gone. See?" But Sulamith was still hungry.

"Here I'll take her. I'm going to start leaking if she doesn't nurse soon," I said to Sheila, and I moved my tea to the side table next to the loveseat at the far end of the kitchen. I took a few sheets of paper towel and folded them to tuck in my nightgown knowing by then that as soon as she latched onto one side and my milk let down, that the other side would leak too, and there was nothing more irritating than a wet patch on my clothes. I crossed my legs, settled with Sulamith lying in my lap and breathed a sigh of relief as the overfull sensation eased off.

Sheila had moved to the wicker armchair nearby and held her tea in her hands.

"How long did I sleep?" I asked her.

"Mmm," she tilted her head considering. "About thirty hours."

I nodded.

"Do I dare ask how you feel?" she asked, a mix of concern and caring in her voice and in her warm hazel eyes.

I looked back at Sheila, taking her in properly for the first time since I had returned. She was about five six, curvy, almost plump, with incredible fair olive skin that was blessed with a perfect sprinkling of freckles. She had dark brown hair that turned slightly auburn in the sun. It was greying at the temples but that didn't detract at all. If anything it made her shoulder length waves more elegant. She had all the best of her Scottish/Italian heritage.

I sighed eventually. "I feel ... lighter, but like a strong wind might blow me away. Conversely, I also feel more grounded. Probably the sleep. Thank you for that, by the way. I must have really needed it," I paused, "but everything that's happened? The past ...? I feel so angry, and so ... ripped off. I think I have a lot more crying to do over that. And the future?" I shook my head and blinked hard a few times. "I'm not even ready to think about that. Overall, I guess ... I guess I feel ... less bad."

Sheila was silent but she smiled. Not exactly a happy smile, but a caring smile. We sat quietly and finished our tea. Sheila puttered around the kitchen clearing away dishes and wiping up toast crumbs while I sat on the love seat with Sulamith who, with a full tummy, was ready to play. I tickled her neck and blew raspberries on her soft skin, then there was the eternally delightful peek-a-boo. I kissed and cuddled and marvelled at how happy she was. I had been under so much pressure and so often sad, worried, or scared during my pregnancy with her that I felt like it was some kind of miracle that she was such a happy baby. It was wonderful to spend the morning with her too. It was her best time, but because I had been expected to attend council meetings in the morning I had so often missed those hours.

"More tea?" Sheila asked, eyebrows raised.

"Yes please." I passed her my cup, which she filled from her old fat Brown Betty tea pot. Everything in Sheila's house was like that. Old and care worn but high quality. Shabby enough to be comfortable and never *un*comfortable. It was a bit of an old, quirky, hippie house that had received a few odd renovations to 'modernize' it in the sixties. Like the kitchen. It was decked out in chrome, harvest gold, and olive green with what Sheila always described as "wretchedly tacky" brown and mustard yellow ceramic floor tiles. I remembered the first time I'd ever been into that kitchen nearly four years earlier and she'd said dryly, "Whoever decorated this kitchen back in nineteen sixty-eight was truly living in the moment, but they did such a darn good job of it that I can't justify renovating. So I just go with the flow and run with it." She had filled it with sturdy wooden furniture that had a Scandinavian look to it, but not in an Ikea way. There were two wicker armchairs, and the loveseat, which was covered in wild 'Cotswolds go psychedelic' upholstery. I'd always loved Sheila's kitchen.

Sheila sat back down in the armchair with the tea, placing mine on the side table. She took a few sips then placed hers on the steamer trunk in front of the love seat. "So, I've closed the garden centre for the week and Tanya's able to go in every day and deal with the maintenance duties. I don't want you to worry about *anything* this week." Sheila gave me her best 'I mean business' look, "Rest as much as you need to. Sleep as much as you want. I'll do all the cooking and cleaning, you're only allowed to help if you're doing it for the fun of it. I don't want you worrying about the weeks and months to come. The future will take care of itself. At the end of February I *will* need you at the garden centre but I don't want you worrying about that either because you can bring Sulamith to work with you. When Evan was little I brought him in with me every day. It was never a problem. And as for you staying here, well, I love this house and I don't really want to sell it, but it's just me here, and it's too big for one person so you're welcome to stay as long as you need to." Sheila picked up her tea and sipped thoughtfully before turning back to me, "I think I've covered everything?"

She said it like a question but I couldn't answer because I was too busy wiping grateful tears off my cheeks.

Sheila smiled and placed a box of tissues beside me.

* * *

I did as I was told with a relief that brought forth the griev-ing that I should have been doing for the last six months. I mourned Rowan. I cried for the life we weren't going to live together, and being back in the world of my childhood brought back memories of my parents that had me realizing how little opportunity I'd had to truly register my loss of them. I did as Sheila told me and it was easy because she was my boss and because in this world I wasn't a queen. I think that sometimes I needed to be told what to do because I would get lost in the fog of grief and instructions gave me something to focus on. For that first week I slept whenever Sulamith did and rested and ate. I was, "frighteningly underweight," as Sheila put it, and she cooked constantly. I would wake from a nap with Sulamith and find a big pot of rice pudding sitting on the stove. Sheila would say, "Give me that baby and get yourself a bowl," and I would eat. I stopped feeling like I could be blown away by a strong breeze and I must have put enough weight back on to satisfy Sheila, because by the end of the week she slowed down on the cooking a little. I helped Sheila clean out her attic the afternoon before she reopened the garden centre. "I've been meaning to do this for years. I keep stuffing things up here without thinking and I know that I have things buried up here that you could use."

Sheila had been bringing items down all week. The high chair. A playpen. A box of old sleepers from the late seventies that had been Evan's. A toy box and toys. A little dresser just right for baby clothes. A cradle and a rocking horse. The best was the box of vintage seventies India cotton dresses, wrap-around skirts, and blouses. Sheila was too young to have been a true hippie, but she had definitely gone for the aesthetic back in nineteen seventy-seven. "I had this ridiculous fantasy that I would still fit into these after Evan was born," she told me, pulling a blue Gunne Sax dress out of the box. "The sleeves will be too long on you. Can you sew?"

* * *

I felt right living with Sheila. I had always felt a kinship to her. She was like the eccentric aunt that I had more in common with than my own mother. We have similar ways of doing things and we're both gardening nuts. I kept busy with Sulamith. A baby is good for that, she kept my hands busy, and I would fix dinner for Sheila and me on the days that Sheila was at the garden centre. I reattached the cuffs to the sleeves of the dresses and blouses I'd cut down. I did any kind of little task to keep myself sane and keep myself in the present. January and February passed. I had my quiet little routine. I slept whenever I got the chance. I would walk around Trout Lake a few times each afternoon with Sulamith in the wrap carrier and the motion always put her to sleep, so I would walk home and we would sleep. When we woke up I would pop her in the highchair with a tray full of finger food to entertain her while I started dinner. I kept the house tidy, had tea with another new mother who lived across the street (Sheila warned her that I was a little ... odd), and if I was feeling brave I would bundle Sulamith up and head out on the bus to search thrift stores for clothes and other useful necessities.

Mid February we readied Sheila's garden for spring. Getting my hands back into the dirt was like growing new skin over invisible wounds. It was thin and delicate. It could bruise or tear at the slightest touch but it was there and I could feel it. It was at this point that I decided I needed to deal with some of the practical aspects of living in a twenty-first century modern city. Like having I.D., a bank account, and a social insurance number, so Sheila took me downtown to see Flanagan. I'd been declared dead but Flanagan took care of everything, no questions asked, and a few weeks later I had a little stack of cards to put in my wallet and birth certificates for both Sulamith and I. Mine said simply Krista O'Reilly. Sheila told me then, "I never spent the money you gave me. I invested it. I wasn't sure what to do with it so I thought it was better off tucked away. I want to give it back to you."

I didn't need much then, and I still had some of the cash in my bag. Sheila had insisted that I didn't need to chip in for food or pay her rent, and what with the contributions from Sheila's attic all I'd really needed was clothing for Sulamith and me, and I'd bought a stack of cloth diapers and good covers for her. Cloth is what she was used too and I worried that disposables would give her a rash. I had what I needed for the time being so I asked Sheila, "Is it alright If we leave the money where it is for now?"

Chapter 18

At the end of February Sheila and I set things up at the Garden centre so that I would be able to take Sulamith to work with me. I had the most bizarre feeling walking back into Buds and Blossoms with Sulamith on my hip. It was one of the uncomfortable realities of my decision to go back to the world of my birth. Things are different here. The general expectation of young people is that they will finish high school, go to university, college, or trade school, party, travel—whatever—establish a career, and only *then,* settle down and contemplate having children. But birth control makes all of that possible. (Okay, I'll admit that abstinence does too, but that's *really* not my thing and I don't know many other young people who really go for it either.) At nineteen, recently returned, I didn't fit into that general expectation. I was, for all intents and purposes, an unwed, uneducated, heavily tattooed, teenaged mother, and don't ever let anyone tell you that there isn't a stigma in Canada against teenaged mothers. Some people view us as social pariah and automatically assume that it could only be the result of a gross lapse in judgment, or of wild behaviour, or poor parenting on the part of the girl's parents. I never tried to explain or defend myself, I just tried to set a good example and be a good mother. But I knew ahead of time that going back out into the public world might be hard sometimes.

The day before I went back to work, Sheila and I went out in the morning to buy a few baby gates, a second playpen, and a super saucer—Sulamith was crawling by then and I needed to be able to fence her in and occasionally immobilize her. We then headed to the garden centre to install the gates and clear a corner of the greenhouse. I'd picked my outfit carefully that morning, conscious of the fact that I was seeing Tanya for the first time in a year and a half, and meeting Brittany, the high school student who worked there after school and on Saturdays. I put on a knee length India cotton dress with an ethnic looking print in deep red, indigo, and brown, a keyhole neckline, and loose sleeves that gathered at the cuffs. I wore it over black leggings with Rowan's old boots—which looked like the trendiest thing in existence that year. I pulled a brown knitted zip-front hoodie over the dress and a cute blue denim jacket that I'd picked up at a thrift store over that and checked my reflection in the hall mirror. I combed my fingers through my newly cut bangs, pulled my hair over one shoulder and stared uncertainly. "You look smart. That dress suits you," Sheila commented as she bustled into the entrance and passed me Sulamith.

After we'd picked up the baby gear and were sitting in the car on the way to Cambie and 43rd Avenue Sheila gave me a heads up of sorts, "Tanya, of course, knows a bit of your background so I had to give her a little more on exactly how it was that you *didn't* die in the house fire. I gave her the cover story Flanagan suggested. You had to leave for your own safety yada yada, but Brittany is a different matter. She's the nicest kid in the world and a great dependable employee, but she does sometimes degrade into a tactless bimbo. If she chatters away at you too much and asks you things that you'd rather not talk about, just tell her that you don't talk about those things. She'll get it eventually."

And so I was back at my old job. Stopping in that first afternoon broke the ice. The garden centre was always quiet at that time of the year—no more than five or so customers around at the most—and walking into most social situations with an adorable baby on your hip, well, it sort of diffuses things. There was one customer browsing the one-of-a-kind birdbaths as Sheila introduced me to Brittany, and Tanya came wandering out of the stock room.

Brittany did show her tactless bimbo side for a few minutes with her, "OhmyGod, your baby is so cute. OhmyGod, where did you get those boots? Are those real tattoos?"

"Thanks ... um yeah, they're real, and my boots are from the cobbler on my husband's family estate," I told her, not being sure what to say about boots that she couldn't get at the mall, but in hindsight I should have lied and said "Value Village", because the first thing out of her mouth was, "Ohmygod, you're married?"

"No," I said softly.

"Oh," she said, confused. Then, "You're ... divorced ... ?"

"No ... I'm not divorced." I said and watched her think it through and then blanch to a shade of white only redheads are usually capable of. I was only a year and ten months older than her, but she was smarter than she made herself out to be and it didn't take her long to figure out that there was a big difference between our actual age gap and our experiential age gap and that I was in essence much older than her. In truth I think she was a little intimidated by me, which was a new and unusual sensation in this world.

Tanya smiled shyly at first and said simply, "Hi. It's good you're back." But after baby gates had been installed and Sheila was busy showing Brittany how to do inventory checks on the computer she said to me, eyeing Sulamith dubiously, "Look, I'm not going to apologize because, based on what Sheila told me about your last year or so, you've been through some shit. I guess I feel like an apology at this point would come across as really trite and self-centred on my part, when you probably don't even remember that day. But, the day you disappeared, I said things behind your back that I shouldn't have, and once words are out you can't take them back." she rolled her eyes at herself. "Anyway the reason I'm spouting platitudes at you is that I don't gossip anymore or let the people around me do it in my presence. I guess it's for largely selfish reasons, for instance, I don't ever want to feel as guilty as I did that day ever again, and people like you a whole lot better when you don't do it ... but, I just wanted you to know."

I nodded, "I do remember that day, and I appreciate what you're saying."

It was Tanya's turn to nod.

* * *

As spring approached the garden centre got busy. A summer staff needed to be hired. Seedlings needed to be started in the greenhouse. Seeds, specialty roses, plant pots, fertilizers, and more needed to be ordered. Work took my mind off of everything and Sulamith was happy and stimulated but not overwhelmed as I only went in four days a week. Brittany was great with her and would spend almost as much time as I did doing the watering with Sulamith tied to her back in a carrier. After a few weeks even Tanya had gotten comfortable enough with her that she asked me with so much dubious caution in her voice that I laughed, "Can I uh, hold your baby?"

"I don't know if she'll settle with you. She's in the throes of some pretty intense stranger anxiety. Brittany bribed her with a banana. But we can try. If I stand close she might tolerate you."

It was true about Sulamith and the stranger anxiety. The new situation might have been a part of what had brought it on, but she was also nine months old and according to the many books I was reading, it was normal for her age. She had gone from outrageously happy to see anyone, to coy, shy, and flirty. Sheila and Brittany were the only ones who could hold her except for me, but I was willing to give Tanya a try if she wanted.

"Uh ... Okay," Tanya nodded.

"She goes for the hair, and she's fast," I warned.

Tanya nodded again and braced herself as if she were waiting for a hurricane. I passed Sulamith over.

Sulamith looked at me, a little concerned, but tolerated the pass off. "Tanya wants to say 'Hi'," I told her. And stood right next to Tanya.

"This isn't that bad," Tanya said after a few minutes of gazing into Sulamith's dark eyes. "She's so soft, and she smells good. My boyfriend just finished his advanced bricklayer's apprenticeship and landed a pretty good job. He really wants kids but I'm not so sure. He didn't exactly give me an ultimatum, but he wants me to think it over. I'll be done my bachelor's degree in September. He wants us to try next spring ... Is it scary? Is it hard?"

I sighed, "I suppose the responsibility is daunting ... but scary? Men with guns are scary. Not babies. They're just lots of work."

Tanya nodded and fingered one of Sulamith's curls as Sulamith patted Tanya's forehead then tried to pull the drawstring out of her hoodie, "I guess perspective is everything." She was silent for another moment, "You totally don't have to answer this, but I don't have any friends outside of work who have kids to ask these questions. Why did you decide to have her, especially so young? I mean, you must be taking some flak for that."

I sighed again. A part of me wanted to take Tanya seriously and not answer, but I could see Tanya's mind working and I didn't want her to assume that I regretted what Rowan and I had done. Not if she was trying to make a decision about her own future. "When Sulamith's dad and I first met, the timing was perfect and we were so in love, but then certain facts about my past, things that I didn't know about, came to light and made life way more complicated, but we still wanted the dream. We didn't want to give up what we thought we'd have together and having children was a part of that. We both wanted her so much, and we were *so* in love." I bit my lip and brushed tears from my cheeks and Tanya, not being the sort of person to hug someone passed Sulamith back to me and stepped a bit away. I held my daughter with my eyes closed, feeling the ground beneath my feet and listening to the rain on the greenhouse roof.

When I opened my eyes Tanya was regarding me seriously. "I'm sorry, I shouldn't have asked," she said.

"No, it's okay. Answering wasn't as bad as I though it was going to be," I told her.

She nodded. "So, no regrets?"

"No regrets. Some days are really hard, but I always tell myself that I only need to make it till nightfall. I can face to-morrow later."

Chapter 19

I was sometimes taken aback by how much comfort I took at being back in the world that I thought I had rejected, and how the chaos that had once seemed unbearable to me was now a friend. Chaos and anonymity were a shelter of sorts. I felt so small here, like a child, but my insignificance in the madness of this world was like a mother's warm arms. I was, in a sense, free. I was still sad and broken, but maybe that would change. Maybe that was hope? Could hope survive the loss and hatred and despair that threatened to swallow me up every day? If love had survived, then maybe hope had too?

These were the thoughts that filled my mind and heart as the days and weeks passed and I slowly built a life for my daughter and myself. As time passed I began to realize just how deeply entwined we had become in Sheila's life, and she in ours. It was mid-summer, late in the evening after a long day of carting pots around, helping people select plants, and explaining for the umpteenth time what to do—or not do—about aphids. Sheila and I were sitting at the small table on the back porch eating dinner and watching Sulamith on the little patch of grass, reaching into the flower beds and pulling apart lavender flowers and daisies with her tiny fingers. She was wearing a simple little yellow dress I'd picked up at a thrift store, and a diaper. Her plump baby legs were bare in the grass and I could see it tickling her as she crawled towards another daisy to grasp it and pull with her clumsy yet elegant baby movements. Her face intent. Her little head, covered in wispy molasses coloured curls, bent over her work. When she had first started doing this I'd tried to stop her, but Sheila had said, "Oh she's fine, leave her to it. She's just learning her flowers."

Sheila and I had completely overhauled her back garden so that there were no toxic or prickly plants for us to worry about, and while I'd worried at first that Sulamith might get stung by a bee, she never did, so we watched her and enjoyed her antics as she would find yet another flower to pluck to pieces. Honestly, she wasn't in any danger of running out.

Sheila turned to me as we ate and asked, "Do you ever think about the future? Where you'd like to go? Where you'd like to be eventually?"

I made a face, pressed my lips together and scowled. It's the face I make when something comes up that I don't want to deal with. Sheila knows that face and she said hurriedly, "I'm not trying to pressure you, the opposite really. I don't want you to feel obligated to stay but, I wanted to tell you that ..." Sheila's face went soft and she looked out over the garden as Sulamith pulled down a borage plant, "I love you and your little girl as if you were my own flesh and blood. I know that I said that you could stay as long as you *needed* to, but I wanted you to know that you don't ever have to leave if you don't *want* to."

I think I started sobbing pretty uncontrollably at that moment. I didn't want or mean to, but I'd been worried about being away from Sheila and not just because she was helping me keep my act together, but because I love her too. In some ways, after all I'd been through, it was like I needed a mother and I felt like I was *home*.

I remember Sheila hugging me and stroking my hair, saying, "No no, I didn't mean to make you cry. Sh sh sh ..."

But after I finally settled down I told her, "I love you too Sheila."

After that it only took me a few days to decide what to do with the money my parents had left behind. I had often wondered if that brutal December storm that had hit Nova Britannia a year and a half earlier had been mirrored in this world, and it turned out that it had, and boy did it do a number on the garden centre. The worst part was that, through some loophole in Sheila's insurance, only a portion of the repairs had been covered and she had been forced to take out a small mortgage on the house.

"It's not a big deal," Sheila had told me. "It'll push back my retirement by a few years but it's not the end of the world.'

The term was up on the money that Sheila had saved for me so I used some of it to clear out the mortgage on the house and another chunk for some improvements to the greenhouse which left me with a small nest egg to tuck away. Sheila put my name with hers on the deed to the house, and made me a part owner of Buds and Blossoms.

* * *

And so the summer passed. I had my okay days. I had my bad days. Sulamith was my little light, the thing I held myself together for. To see her face each day and see her grow and change and hear her little voice as she would look at us and say, "Ma-ma? Shee-ya?"

I would watch her, transfixed, as she toyed with the idea of walking, and hold my breath thinking, *Is she going to do it? Is she going to step away from the chesterfield?* Her chubby tentative feet wobbling, then she'd smile, coy all of a sudden and change her mind. Then one day, I looked up from what I was doing and there she was, teetering towards me, a giant smile on her face. I got down on my knees and waited for her to make it to me and when she did she let herself fall into my arms and I held her and said to her, "Oh my girl! Look how far you walked!"

She was so proud of herself and I couldn't believe how sweet and wonderful she was but that night after she was asleep I cried harder than I had in a long time. Rowan would never see her walk. I couldn't even tell him about it.

Days passed. Flowers bloomed and faded. Sulamith's walking turned to running and Sheila and I were hard pressed to keep up to her. The busy buzz of summer mellowed to a sweet hum, and then, at the end of August something unexpected happened. Evan came home.

Chapter 20

Now, what of Evan? You might ask. Well, Sheila and I had something of an unspoken agreement not to talk about Evan, but Sheila was his mother and once upon a time he'd been my best friend. I was living in the house he'd been raised in and the house was rife with evidence of this. Photos, framed art projects from his childhood, the dent in the hall from a tumble down the stairs during his clumsy mid teens, and his room was the same as it had ever been, although cleaner without him in it. There were memories, and the most seemingly unrelated event could bring them up. I remember Sheila cutting my bangs.

A pregnancy interrupts the normal pattern of shedding and regrowth of hair and usually at approximately four months postpartum the pattern resumes. With a vengeance. By the time Sulamith was eight months old I was over the shedding and my hair had started to regrow, thickening back up and coming in a half shade darker, but I had all these wispy tendrils around my face that had begun to drift into my eyes. I couldn't get them into my pony tail, they wouldn't stay in clips, and they were driving me crazy, so one morning Sheila looked at me swiping madly at my hair and said, "Why don't you let me cut bangs. It would keep your hair out of your eyes."

I'd agreed without hesitation, and had been more than pleasantly surprised at the result. Sheila had looked at my face before hand and said, "What about bangs like Jane Birkin's in the 70's?"

"Jane Birkin?" I'd looked at her blankly.

Sheila typed the name into the search engine, pulled up images and then, careful not to let her laptop get too close to me, she turned it so that I could see. "Alright," I nodded. "Those are nice bangs."

"Okay go wash your hair and use lots of conditioner so that it's easy to comb," she told me and when I was back in the kitchen with wet hair she carefully combed it this way and that and then slowly snipped and clipped until she was satisfied, then blow dried my hair for me. I'd looked in the mirror surprised, both at how well bangs suited me, and at the perfect job Sheila had done. "I didn't know you could cut hair. This is amazing," I told her.

She smiled, pleased that I liked the job she had done and told me, "I shared a house with a group of girls when I was in university and one of them was attending beauty school. I got her to teach me to do hair and she said I had the knack for it. I always cut my own hair and even Evan lets me cut his, which is high praise indeed because I'm sure you remember how he is about his hair."

It was one off hand comment but it plunged us both into a past when Evan would say to me, "Hey. There's a Labyrinth/ Dark Crystal double feature playing at the Rio tomorrow night if you're interested?"

"I'm not doing anything," I'd reply.

"Bring a change of clothes to work with you and we can eat dinner with my mum, then get cleaned up and walk to the theatre from my house."

I would go home after work with Sheila and Evan. We'd eat in Sheila's kitchen and laugh over dinner then take turns showering. Clean and in a decent outfit, I would end up hanging out with Evan in his room for a while before it was time to leave. Obviously, with the obsessively platonic nature of my friendship with Evan, nothing ever happened up there, but I would sit on his bed looking through his books. That particular night, as we were going to see movies with art direction by Brian Froud, I'd taken Evan's copy of Faeries down and turned the pages. Evan was standing in front of the mirror messing with his hair. That was typical. He'd turned to me and said with a glint in his eye, "So, Brian Froud? Or Allan Lee?"

"Evan, you can't choose between Brian Froud and Allan Lee. It would be like choosing between strawberries and blackberries."

"That's easy, the obvious choice is strawberries. The seeds are smaller." He looked at me for a moment then turned back to the mirror and scowled at his reflection while rearranging his auburn locks again.

"Well yeah strawberries are wonderful, and they smell good, and they're *so* pretty, but you know when it's hot out like today and you head out to a lake or go for a walk down an alley where a big wild bramble has had a chance to take over, and you're not really expecting to, but you find handfuls of perfectly ripe, sweet, insanely juicy blackberries and you just stand there and eat them and they're hot from the sun."

Evan had turned again and was leaning against the dresser now. "Okay, okay. I concede defeat," he'd smiled. "In that context you can't choose between strawberries and black-berries. But since you've come up with this seriously over-thought berry analogy, I have to ask you, would Brian Froud be the blackberries or the strawberries."

I remember snorting laughter at him through my nose and smiling, "Come on let's just go to the theatre."

Evan had turned back to the mirror and given one last desperate attempt to make his hair look right, then followed me down the stairs.

Sometimes the memories of those days would hit, and most of the time I cold shouldered them, but that Sunday afternoon, sitting with Sheila in the kitchen with my freshly cut bangs I'd asked, "So ... How is Evan?" I'd felt weird asking, but then, I'd felt weird *not* asking too.

Sheila sighed a long resigned sigh and told me about Evan. "He's fine." She didn't say it like she meant it. "He finished his PhD and got married just before you came back." Then she sighed again, "But the thing about Evan is that he tries too hard to think with his head instead of listening to his heart. At times I think that he would be better off thinking with his cock because at least it would point him in the right direction sometimes," she said dryly and rolled her eyes. (For the record, Sheila can be crass sometimes.) She looked at me for a moment as if undecided whether to say more before she continued, "He never got over you. The day of the fire he called and told me he'd booked a flight home to try to make everything up to you. He'd been a real shit all year. He barely called. I think he was avoiding me because I'd *told* him that he was being a shit. He'd called once or twice, *drunk*, and asked about you before that, and then out of the blue, I had to tell him that you were dead, just as he'd finally come to his senses. He came home for a few days just after the fire ... but before I saw you, before I knew that you were alive. I'm sorry if it was the wrong decision, but I didn't know what to tell him, so he still believes that you're dead. You were living in another world as the wife of another man. I couldn't be sure he'd believe me if I told him. I thought that he might be better off believing that you were dead." She looked at me apologetically.

"It's alright." I shrugged, then asked, "What's his wife like?"

"Oh, on the surface she seems nice enough. I only saw her for a few days."

"But?" I prompted Sheila who grinned wickedly and said, "You knew I was holding that 'But' back didn't you?"

I smiled and she said, "But underneath the surface I think she's a *real* bitch. It won't last. I don't think he really loves her. He never got over *you*."

Sheila didn't tell Evan that I was alive and that I'd come back, and I was careful not to answer the phone if the display showed his number. If he had broken my heart three years earlier, I hadn't let myself recognize it. In all honesty I'd been young, innocent, extremely confused, and my feelings had been so hurt at the time, that even if I could have fallen for him before what he'd done and said, I was so angry at him that I certainly wasn't going to let myself recognize those feelings after, when I thought he was disgusted by *his* feelings for me. But knowing that he'd been about to come home and make things right? I didn't let myself think about it. I put the thoughts in a box and buried them behind the compost heap like a dead bird that died of a clean window. I wasn't ready to cope with feelings and I certainly wasn't prepared to see him, or for the way seeing him would make me feel.

But Sheila was right, and after five short months of unhappy marriage and a thick stack of divorce papers Evan came back to Vancouver with a PhD in Literature and a job waiting for him at a community college teaching Literature, Mythology, and Mythology in Literature. He moved back without telling his mother. He found an apartment and got settled before deciding that it was time to go to her and make amends, and when Evan climbed the stairs to his mother's house that hot August Sunday afternoon, he hadn't expected *me* to answer the door. But I did. Barefoot in a pair of torn jeans and a tank top, standing there with a baby on my hip and vine patterns spiralling up to my shoulder. I remember looking at him for a long time, Sulamith clapping her plump little hands against my shoulder and pulling my hair. I looked into his face, at his chiselled features, the now collar length auburn hair, his sensitive green eyes and his perfect, almost feminine mouth. He stood there staring at me then dropped the chocolates he'd been holding and just stood there a while longer before he spun on his heel and hurried away from the house to the car that was parked out front. He sat there in the driver's seat with his forehead on the steering wheel. I could see his shoulders heaving.

I tried not to react. I popped the baby gate in the doorway leaving the door open and put Sulamith down on the kitchen floor so that I could finish washing the lunch dishes. Evan came back after about ten minutes. I was sitting in the rocker with Sulamith by then, nursing her down for a nap. She was blinking slowly, sleepily. I put my finger to my lips and Evan sat down quietly on the chesterfield trying not to stare at me while I breastfed my baby. Worlds were colliding. Once her eyes had closed I stood with her and whispered, "I'll be right back." And I took her up to the room I shared with her and tucked her in, all the while wondering what I would say to Evan when I went back downstairs. Feeling the old hurt and anger pushing at me, I padded down the stairs. He was standing in the living room taking in the toys and the playpen and looking overwrought. I still didn't know what to say to him so I settled on, "Tea?"

"Uh ... Sure?" he answered lamely, with a shrug.

I walked to the kitchen and put the kettle on to boil, but I was already boiling over inside. I turned and looked at Evan who was standing there looking from me to the highchair and then back at me, with such an overfull expression in his eyes that I knew how much he must be feeling, but at that particular moment I was so angry with him that I didn't care about his feelings.

"'Bloody hell' Evan!?!" I yelled at him. "Those were the last words you *ever* spoke to me, 'Bloody Hell'! And now, after *three years* 'Uh ... Sure' is the best you can do!?" I was shaking and tears ran down my face. My lip quivered and I couldn't keep my hands still. The light bulb in the ceiling popped inside the globe and went out with a sound of glass tinkling within glass. Evan pulled out a chair, motioned for me to sit and then went about making the tea himself. He put the pot and the tea things on the table and then sat across from me.

"I was a fool Kristabell ..." he started.

"*Don't* call me Kristabell!" I snapped.

Evan looked like he had been slapped and I knew that I was being cruel but I'd been hurt and I was hurting still. I didn't have the strength at that moment; I didn't have it in me to be kind to him.

Evan swallowed then asked me softly, "What do you want me to call you?"

"Just Krista is fine. It's what you always used to call me."

He nodded and fidgeted with his mug for a moment then sighed, "Can you ever forgive me?"

"*Don't* ask me for that!" I exploded again. "I've been through *too much* and I don't have room in me for that! I don't *want* to forgive you!"

"Then what do you want?!" he shouted at me, then whispered, as his tears spilled down his cheeks, "I would do anything for *you*."

I fixed my eyes on his, "I want your friendship. I want you to make me feel normal again." And then I quoted, knowing that he would recognize the quote and understand, "Drown out my dreams, keep me from remembering whatever wants me to remember it."

He smiled then, the most profoundly sad smile, completely unable to keep further tears at bay or the emotion out of his voice, "Peter S. Beagle, The Last Unicorn. Amalthea to Prince Lir. That line always ... breaks my heart a little ..." he swallowed. "What *happened* to you Krista? I thought that you were dead." He pushed his hand through his hair and rubbed his face.

I gave him the heavily edited version, "I went away the day of the fire. Lets just say for now that," I shrugged. "I was in Ireland. I met someone there. His name was Rowan. We fell hard for each other. He asked me to be his wife. I agreed ... and then the past caught up with us. My natural parents played a dangerous game before I was born, and I got caught in the middle. Rowan ... died protecting me ... us. He died protecting us, the day our daughter was born," I told him this, and my voice tore itself to pieces on the shards of my heart and I shook myself as if to shake off an unwanted touch. "It's all over now. It's all in the past somewhere ... far away." I closed my eyes tightly and tried to steady my breath. We sat at the table silent for a long time, mentally, emotionally, digesting everything.

"Your baby," Evan eventually, tentatively ventured. "How old is she?"

"She's fourteen months old." I gave him a watery smile.

Evan must have sensed that it was easier for me to talk about her so he asked again, "What's her name?"

"Sulamith," I told him.

"Like the painter, Sulamith Wulfing," he said.

"Yeah," I nodded.

"She's walking and talking I guess?" he questioned further.

"Running and babbling is more like it," I said with a wry smile.

"How long have you been back?"

"Since December."

"And you live here?" He motioned to the house around us.

I nodded, "My parents are dead. I didn't have anywhere else to go." I pressed my lips together and took a deep breath, "Your wife is here with you?" I started to ask as I didn't know then, but I didn't get more than the first two words out before he cut me off shaking his head emphatically.

"That's over. We're divorced."

I nodded and we sat there in silence a while longer until Sheila came bustling in with the groceries looking completely shell shocked to see Evan and I sitting at the table together. "Oh my God! What are you doing here!" Sheila nearly screamed the words as Evan stood and hugged her.

"Eugénie asked for a divorce and I had a job offer from Langara so ... I decided to come home. But don't worry. I have my own place," he added casually, yet not casually.

* * *

Evan stayed for dinner that night and it was a difficult evening in a sense. Not awkward per se, and not bad, but I knew that he had some pretty massive issues around my death, and now suddenly I wasn't dead, but things could never be the same again either, and we couldn't pretend that they ever would. When Sulamith woke from her nap I brought her downstairs to meet Evan. At first she was shy and very cuddly, only wanting to sit with me and nurse, or cuddle with Sheila in the rocking chair, but once she had woken up all the way she became curious about this new person sitting in *her* house as if he belonged there. I watched with mixed feelings as he sat on the floor and began to build a tower with her blocks and then pushed it over and waited to see what she would do. She watched him suspiciously from Sheila's lap and gave a little "Uh-oh."

Evan smiled at her and did it again. She scowled at him. He started to build a third tower, starting with one block then another and another, but the fourth block he held out to her. I held my breath, wondering if she would go to him. She climbed out of Sheila's lap and walked over to him, taking the block away, clutching it in both hands and looking at Evan,

considering the situation before squatting down and placing
the block on the stack. She placed the block and then over
balanced as she tried to straighten up and she plunked down
on her little diapered butt and almost tumbled all the way
back, but Evan put out a hand, stopping the progress of her
tumble, then once she was firmly planted on her back side, he
gave her another block. She placed that one too, scowling and
concentrating on getting it lined up, but her co-ordination
wasn't as accurate this time, so Evan reached out and guided
her little fingers and the block was placed. By the end of
dinner he had her taking his hand and dragging him to her toy
box, or to her bean tee pees in the back garden and, yes, a one
year old can drag a big six foot three, one-hundred-and-ninety
pound man around, because he was helpless before her, and
even though he'd had to do the coaxing, it was *she* who had
him wrapped irrevocably around her little finger. But even
that hurt in a way, for me to see her go to him and pull at his
pant leg until he lifted her into his arms, to hold her there,
and look at her as if she were the most incredible thing he had
ever seen, and smile, because then he would turn to me, and
our eyes would meet, and he would see how much it hurt me
to see *him* hold her ... because *Rowan* would never hold her. I
would never see *Rowan* hold her again, and Evan could see
that sadness in my eyes.

Over dinner we stuck to safe topics of conversation. Evan's
new job, Sheila was thrilled for him. We talked about the
garden centre. Sheila told him that I was a part owner and
that seemed to please him. And of course we talked about
Sulamith. It's hard not to. Babies do have a way of monopoliz-
ing your life. As the evening drew on and Sulamith got tired
she returned to me, toddling to my feet wanting to be close.
Sheila was clearing the table and loading the dishwasher. I
lifted Sulamith into my lap and she burrowed her tired little
curly head into my shoulder and rubbed her eyes with chubby

fists as I held her close, and you could see that despite the walking and talking, that she was still very much a baby. Evan looked at us for several heartbeats then looked away for a moment and I saw his hand rise to his face before he looked back into my eyes. "Your daughter is adorable Krista," he told me in earnest, and then as if he were handing me stones that he had been carefully holding in his hands for those three years, he told me. "Krista ... I am still so ashamed of how I left things between us, and I've never stopped regretting it. You were my best friend and I know that I hurt you. I told you that I would do anything, and you said that you wanted my friendship. If that's what you want, you have it, irrevocably, but you were so angry ... if you want me to stay away ..."

I cut him off, "No Evan. I want your friendship. Irrevocably. Don't talk about going away again. It hurt badly enough the first time." And I knew I was going to cry, because as much as I still wanted to yell and scream at him I also wanted him back.

"I won't go, I won't," he said hurriedly, seeing my face. His green eyes met mine and he said again with utter conviction, "I won't go away again, I promise."

"Good. I'm holding you to it," I managed to say before rising with a droopy tired baby in my arms and saying, "I need to change Sulamith and put her to bed. I'll be back down in a while," and I headed upstairs and went about the beautifully absorbing task of putting Sulamith to bed.

* * *

When I was sure she slept, when her eyelashes rested on her cheeks, and her little mouth was completely relaxed and just a little slack, when her balled up fists had come just a little undone, I flipped on the baby monitor, then closed the bedroom door softly behind me, and the baby gate at the top of the stairs after that, and crept downstairs. I could hear

Sheila and Evan talking in the living room and I sat down on the stairs not really caring that I was eavesdropping. Sheila was telling Evan about Sulamith, "I love having her here Evan. She's the sweetest baby. So full of life and joy. She has me smiling everyday."

"Did you ever meet her father?" Evan asked Sheila.

Sheila sighed a heavy sigh, "Yes. Once."

"What was he like?" Evan asked.

"It's a little hard to say. His English wasn't good, and I only met him the once, but he was a handsome devil, I'll tell you that much. He was about your age, dark hair and eyes, like his daughter. He was a soldier which shocked me at first. I never figured Krista would go for a military type, but he was a bit of a renegade. He had a wildness to him that I think she liked. He was completely devoted to her. It hurts to think about the way they were together. They made a beautiful couple."

There was a silence before I heard anyone speak again. It was Sheila.

"You still have feelings for her, don't you," not asking. Confirming.

I didn't hear Evan's response but his answer was obvious from Sheila's reply.

"Well ... He'll be a tough act to follow," she said into the silence.

I leaned my head against the stairwell wall, feeling heavy, when Evan asked his mother, "How is she Mum, really? I don't dare ask her."

"Knowing will only make having her back harder, not easier."

"Tell me," he insisted.

Sheila sighed again, "She's ... Fragile, Evan. *Very, extremely*, fragile. Her life split into a million tiny little pieces and she's trying to pick them *all* back up again, she really is. Some days I think she's doing fine, but others ... I don't know. I still hear her crying on the stairs at night. Maybe she'll never be whole again." Sheila was silent for a moment before telling Evan "She has family elsewhere that she could be with, but I think that they are ... too much a part of what happened to her, and too much a reminder of everything she lost. She still has a long road ahead of her."

There was another long silence then I heard Evan say, "Look, I think I'd better go. Tell Krista ... tell her I'll be by later this week."

Chapter 21

The next two years were hard, but they were better too. The garden centre flourished. We were doing extremely well. Tanya married her boyfriend and they moved to the interior after jobs. We replaced her with another university student by the name of Selma. A law student this time. She was very serious and very organized but seemed, for whatever reason, very good at dealing with my and Sheila's quirks and eccentricities.

Evan, true to his word, came by the Friday evening following his return, leaning in the door frame looking pretty devastating in jeans, a blazer and a pair of good brown leather casual shoes. Nice shoes, not too stuffy, but not at all punk now. "So, rumour has it my mum is willing to babysit. There's a Ridley Scott double feature at the Rio tonight. Blade Runner and Legend. What do you say? Will you go with me?"

And I went. Even though I was nervous about leaving Sulamith for a whole four hours. Even though I thought that Legend, with all its unicorns, fairies, and swords, might hit a little too close to home. I went. I knew that it would hurt but I had to try, and I'd come to realize that some things were painful because it meant I was moving past them. Growing, so to speak. I cried walking home from the theatre with Evan that night, hoping that I wasn't weirding him out too much by refusing to explain what had gotten me going, but knowing that if he could handle the fallout from Legend, that he could probably handle a lot.

And he did. He arrived on the doorstep the following Saturday just before lunch. He ate with Sulamith and I, then we walked to the park for a good play. Sulamith adored him and he was wonderful with her. I couldn't help but notice that I didn't get dirty looks from the other mums at the park when Evan was with us. When she was tired we took her home and I put her down for her nap then headed downstairs. Sheila had just returned from the garden centre and Evan appeared to be saying goodbye but then he looked at me and said, "Coming?"

"Yes she's going," Sheila called down the hall as she bustled to the kitchen. "Sulamith's down for a nap that gives me more than enough time to shower and put my feet up, then I get her to myself for an hour or two. It's fine go," Sheila encouraged.

But I still wasn't exactly sure where I was going as I slipped my feet into sandals and followed Evan down the front stairs.

"I figure that it would be good if we stayed away from unicorns and swords," Evan said, opening the passenger door of his car for me then coming around to sit in the driver's seat. "It's only two-thirty in the afternoon. I figure we can catch a matinee."

He took me to see Harold and Maude at a little second run in a weird part of town. Despite the grim humour, and bitter sweet ending, I almost died laughing. It had been so long since I had felt like that. Years. Not since Evan had left. We walked along the seawall after the movie and Evan said to me, "It's so good to hear you laugh again."

We fell into a pattern that wasn't unlike our friendship before, and yet, it was completely unlike those days. No one mistook me for Evan's little sister anymore. I guess I'd grown an inch or two, but it was more than that. Having a baby changed my body, I have contours now where I used to be all straight lines and a little childish looking, and the grief changed me too. That and simply *being* older. I still look young but not like I did before. I could see the grief in Evan's face too and sometimes that was hard, but at the same time I knew it meant that on some level he understood me. He was always a gentleman though. He never touched me, like the old days. Which must have seemed strange to onlookers who generally assumed I was his girlfriend, especially if Sulamith was with us. I gradually came to understand why Evan would have held his feelings back from me when I was younger. Many a seventeen year old girl can make herself look twenty-one, but at seventeen the best I could do was *not* look twelve, otherwise I risked looking like a child prostitute. Evan was more relaxed around me now and I knew that a big part of it was that I looked older, and that I *was* older. He didn't have to worry anymore that someone would think he was a creep for hanging out with me. I was getting to know him better than I had before as a result. He was a steady person. Quiet and deep. Teaching suited him and he was enjoying the work he was doing. He'd shed the forced social gregariousness that had been left over from his popular days in high school. We didn't talk about the in between years. Not to say that it didn't come up occasionally.

I remember one Sunday afternoon late in September just over a year after Evan had come home. We'd driven out to Crescent Beach in Sheila's car, the four of us. Sulamith had run around like a little hurricane over the sand, her bare little feet prancing, giant smile plastered to her face. I'll never forget her at two. She wasn't terrible. She didn't have tantrums, but she was a force all her own. Keeping up with her was exhausting but the saving grace was that she was so busy that she would wear herself out and then sleep, good, long, and hard. That day she had crashed on the blanket and fallen asleep at around two-thirty in the afternoon. Not too late for a nap. Good timing on the whole. It meant she wouldn't fall asleep in the car on the way home, and I'd have her to bed on time (she was in the process of giving up her naps). I sat next to her on the blanket, smoothing her hair back from her brow and taking in the changes. Her face was looking less and less baby and more like mine each day, with the exception of her eyes, which were getting darker and more fiery, and her hair, which had grown almost to her shoulders in silky molasses curls. I shifted, letting her head down gently off of my lap and onto my bunched up sweater. "I need a walk," I turned to Sheila knowing that Evan would just as happily stay on the blanket with Sulamith. "Want to come?"

Sheila looked up from her book blankly at me, "What, come where?"

"For a walk."

"Oh no, this is the first book I've had a chance to pick up since mid-April." She looked at Evan, "Evan go walk with her, I'm staying right here with my book."

We walked on wet sand that stretched forever, jean cuffs rolled, feet bare. I remember borrowing Evan's old Common-wealth Games swim team hoodie and rolling the cuffs. It was huge on me. Evan looked back at the blanket that was shrink-ing in the distance. "Where do you suppose she gets all that energy?" he asked.

I sighed, "I wish I could ask Fionnuala what I was like at that age. It wouldn't surprise me if she got it from Rowan though. He was pretty energetic."

"I don't know," Evan said. "I remember you at sixteen. You could be downright hyper. I remember you climbing the cherry tree in the front yard like you had electricity running through you. I still have the picture."

"Maybe all two-year-olds are like that," I said.

"Not a chance. By the time I split from Eugénie the only thing I liked about her was her family. She came from a big French Canadian family, eight older brothers and sisters. She had *sixteen* nieces and nephews and at the time *five* of them were two. They were all different. One threw tantrums but was placid the rest of the time. Another was hyper but easy to get along with."

"It's weird to picture you in that situation, so far away from here," I said squinting into the sun at him, "married to a lawyer, of all things."

"Mm ... It was a part of a different life. I was trying to hide from things that I shouldn't have been hiding from. It was just another distraction in a long stream of distractions," he looked down and kicked at the sand. "It was difficult for me to adjust to the idea of all that you've been through too," he said to me.

"A different life," I mulled the words over knowing that I had expressed the same thought more than once. "Is this a different life now then? Or is it a continuation from before?"

"This?" he looked around for a moment. There was a strange expression in his eyes. Almost happiness. "This is different. Neither of us is the same as we were, whether we're better for it or worse I can't say, but we've both changed in fundamental ways. And now, here we are, both of us, alive. So I suppose this is life. We're certainly not dead."

I watched his face as he focused on some point out in the distance.

"No. We aren't dead are we," I said.

He smiled then pointed, "See that abandoned beach ball way out there."

I nodded.

"I'll race you?"

I smiled. "I bet I can beat you," I said, then took off.

I heard Evan laugh as his feet pounded the sand behind me.

* * *

Winter was quiet. Wet, brown and green. The still hours passed and I found myself restless sometimes. Restlessness was alien, a shadow of a memory. It took me a long time to recognize the feeling and realize that it was boredom. I started raiding the book shelf in Evan's old room, picking up stories that I'd read years before. Or I would sit in the living room listening to Sheila's records. Kate Bush, Peter Gabriel, The Cockatoo Twins, old Sarah McLachlan. I listened to music again and read stories and felt the strange feelings that came along with them. Other people's feelings. Maybe I would start thinking about my own feelings again someday. For the most part I still had a habit of pushing feelings away like unwanted shadows, but that was getting harder. Sometimes in the evening when the restlessness struck while I was worn out from the day, but not yet ready to sleep, I wouldn't quite know what to do with myself. I would pace as Sheila poured over seed catalogues. Often Evan would have come to the house after he finished teaching for the day and had dinner with us, but on one particular evening he hadn't. Sulamith was fast asleep and I couldn't settle. I found myself walking to the phone, dialling, holding the receiver to my ear thinking, *Please pick up, Please* ... It rang once, then a second time. "Hello?"

"Evan?" I didn't usually call Evan.

"Krista? Is everything alright?"

"Um, yeah I just, well I wanted to ... see you. I mean, are you free? Do you have an hour?"

"Yeah. I'm just leaving the pool." He was on his cell. "I can swing by and get you if you want. I need some dinner. I guess you've eaten, but do you want to have a coffee or desert with me?"

"That would be great," I told him feeling a relief that I tried not to let myself register.

* * *

Somewhere between two and three Sulamith changed from a chubby baby to a trim little pixy. A proper little girl speaking full sentences and driving me crazy with her constant chatter. Sometimes she reminded me of Nimue and sometimes she looked at me with her father's eyes. I don't know exactly what it was she saw back then, but she would put her arms around my neck and say, "Is okay Mummy, is okay," and I'd hold her like I'd never let her go. She made me smile every day with the pictures she'd paint and all of her little pressed flower projects. And she liked to collect treasures. Pretty stones, snail shells, beach glass, feathers. She had covered every window-sill in the house with them and we could always hear her happy little voice chattering away, forever traipsing after some-one, whether it be me Sheila, Evan, Brittany or Selma, asking, "Why?" Sheila gloried in it and it made me glad that it brought her so much happiness.

January days fell by, bringing a miserable February in their wake. Rain and sleet every day. The temperature oscillating from minus one to plus one, so that there was always a layer of melting ice on everything and it was as if life was trying to imitate the weather. My ladies were dying. I know that out of context that doesn't make any sense. What I mean by it is, my ladies at the garden centre. It was Evan who had started call-ing them that, one day years ago when Mrs. Wong had come in looking for heritage sweet peas.

Tanya, who had been new at the time, was trying to help her, but Evan had said to Tanya, "Oh, that's one of Krista's ladies. Go find her and tell her Mrs. Wong is here."

Tanya had come in search of me and had announced in her dry dubious tone, "Uh, Evan says one of your 'Ladies' is here, a Mrs. Wong. He said I should find you."

"I'll be right there," I'd said, chuckling inwardly as I brushed dirt off my legs and rose from in front of the planter garden I was building.

Later when I'd sent Mrs. Wong happily on her way with six packages of sweet peas, I'd asked Evan, "So they're *my* ladies are they?"

"Yes. They are," he'd said smiling, his tone definite. "I've counted seven of them since I got home in May. They're all the same in that they have an old world romantic sensibility, and I think that you appeal to that sensibility. They've been coming to buy plants here as long as I can remember, but ever since *you* started working here, they wander in looking for you so that they can tell you about their peonies and how lovely they look when it's 'Just a little cloudy.' And you get this dreamy look on your face and sigh happily then say, 'I *do* love peonies, they're such gentle flowers.'" he imitated, almost but not quite making fun of me. "And then your lady will say, 'Yes! I've *always* thought that about Peonies.' and smile at you as if they've found a kindred spirit."

I'd looked at Evan and squinted, "Are you teasing me?" I'd asked him self-consciously.

"No," He'd smiled gently. "It amuses me, but on the whole I think that it's really sweet."

But from that day forward, everybody at the garden centre called them 'Kristabell's Ladies' and I'll admit that I always thought they were kind of special. They had all lived through at least one of the world wars and remembered a time that was simpler in its way. They weren't shocked by the fact that I hadn't finished high school, as many of them hadn't either. It wasn't the done thing in their day. I felt quite comfortable around them and rarely felt judged. They would come in and we would talk flowers or vegetables, whatever their preference, (Mrs. Jones liked peonies but the staunch and practical Ms. Ashcroft was a vegetable fanatic.) If I admitted to them that I thought that my garden was the best on a hot afternoon after a hard rain when I could walk the soil barefoot and feel how warm and alive it was they always agreed. For these ladies life was winding down, and gardening was one of the few pleasures they had left as friends and husbands were passing away. Their grandchildren lived busy fast-paced lives, and they liked it that I would slow down and listen.

It was hard when, after a year and a half away, I had come back to find that Mrs. Wong had passed away, (she'd been ninety-five), Mrs. McLeod was in a home for Alzheimer's patients, and Ms. Ashcroft had moved back east to care for her ailing older sister. But my favourite of the ladies, Mrs. Larson, or Audrey as she insisted I call her, was still around. My first day back Sheila had told me, "I hope you don't mind but I called Audrey and let her know that you've come back and that you're starting work today. She told me that she would ask her daughter to bring her in."

And sure enough at two o'clock that afternoon, as I was dusting shelves and sweeping, with a then only eight month old Sulamith on my back in a carrier, Audrey had arrived. Her arthritis had put her in a wheelchair and her youngest daughter Caroline, who was about Sheila's age, was pushing her along. Even though she was physically diminished, I could see it in her face that she was still the same. Still the sharp, elegant, wistful Audrey I'd known before.

I smiled and walked to meet them and lead them over to a portion of the retail space where there were garden benches and statues. I sat, easing Sulamith off my back and around to my hip then finally settling her on my lap and said to Audrey, once her daughter had her safely parked, "It's so good to see you, how have you been?"

"Stiff, and bored. My hips have decided to revolt. My body has betrayed me," she smiled ruefully. "My eyes, ears, and mind seem to be staying afloat though." Audrey had married a Canadian soldier shortly after WWII and come back to Canada with him. She always had an elegant way of speaking even though her English accent was faded. She smiled again.

"I suppose I shouldn't complain at my age. I do miss my garden though. But enough about me. Tell me about you and about this charming little creature." She smiled at Sulamith who had been doing her coy flirty thing; smiling and then burying her face against me. "We all thought you were dead. How did this come to be?"

I sighed. I didn't like telling people what had happened. It had a strange and improbable ring to it and I didn't like the way people looked at me once they knew, even though I left out the parts about Fairies and other worlds. "I wasn't in the house the night of the fire," I said softly. "I, had to leave. It was to do with my biological parents and it's ... complicated. The city wasn't safe for me. Someone with some connections in the police faked my death so that it looked like I had died in the fire too. I went someplace far away, and I met someone there." I was silent as I collected the oomph I would need to say the next part. "He was a soldier ..."

I didn't get any further. Audrey stopped me, taking my free hand in her soft frail one, "No, I think I know. You needn't say more. It can wait for a quiet afternoon and a cup of tea." She looked at the smiling bundle in my arms glancing at the tangled botanical design etched into the skin of my right hand as she looked Sulamith over. "Sometimes the best things come from the worst situations."

The next Sunday afternoon, taking Sulamith with me, I went to the care home that Audrey's daughter had moved her to for tea. It became a regular thing. Once or twice a month I would go, usually bringing some little potted plant with me. Violets, an Elephant Ear Begonia, or some exotic lacy ferns and Audrey and I would talk. She would tell me about her girlhood in England, her married years in Canada, her children. She had lived a long life, and a good life, full of ups and downs and I found it comforting to hear about those ups and downs and the resiliency of her spirit. She told me about her first child and the tears she'd shed. The baby was stillborn. "I had waited so long to meet him, to look into his eyes and know him, see him grow and become," she said, and even though I could see that old loss in her eyes there was light there too. "My husband was so kind to me during that time. It was just a year after we'd married. I never would have seen that kindness or the depth of his love for me if I hadn't lost that baby. He was a very reserved man in some ways, but those months that we mourned together are full of precious memories, and I had four healthy babies after that."

Visits with Audrey were a part of the landscape of my life. Sulamith was used to our trips to the rest home where Audrey lived. She loved all of the attention she got there and I felt good that she had a wide variety of people in her life. Mrs. Jones, Agnes, had moved into the same home. I would drink tea with them, and we often talked flowers or I listened to them reminisce about the past and before I left I would always take their hands in mine and use what magic I could to ease their aches and pains. I did it as I said goodbye, trying to mask it as normal human warmth, but Audrey always squinted at me as if she suspected there was something I wasn't telling her. For two years I did this, but she never questioned me.

Agnes faded first. I brought her Peonies at the end of January. Imported from a hot house of course, but they were her favourites, and the next week when I went in she was gone. "She died in her sleep. Just drifted off," Audrey told me. "I hope I go like that, no fuss, no waiting around."

But the damp, cold weather in the middle of cold and flu season was a bad combination. Pneumonia. It was slow and there wasn't anything I could do but make her comfortable. No magic in the world could let her live forever and I could see that she didn't want to. I visited her every day, often seeing her children or grandchildren in passing. Sometimes she was so sleepy that she didn't seem to notice that anyone was there, but one afternoon she was clear and lucid. She looked at me and smiled. "Krista. I was dreaming about you."

"What did you dream?" I asked.

"That's the irritating part. I can't remember," she scowled petulantly, but looked me over thoughtfully and sighed. "I'm going to tell you something that I've never told my children, not even my husband knew the whole story, not that there was much to it, but I find myself thinking about it every time I see you lately."

I nodded. "I'm listening," I said, and rested my hand on hers.

"Alright," she said as firmly as an invalid could muster. "When I was seventeen I lived in London with my family in a nice middle class neighbourhood. We had lived on that street for generations. My father was a solicitor. Nice tidy little life. On that street lived another family, and they had a son three years older than me. We grew up together and I think that I was about eleven when I realized that I loved him. It was all very innocent of course, but we knew that it was inevitable. One day we would grow up, fall in love properly, and get married," she paused. "It never happened. The war came. I stood in front of our house by the wrought iron gate and said goodbye to him. His name was Tom. He was in his R.A.F uniform and he looked very handsome. He took my hand and told me that when the war was over he was going to buy me a ring that glittered, and ask me to marry him. He gave me a little nosegay of violets. His words still ring in my ears, 'Will you wait for me?' I told him 'yes'." She stopped and looked out into an imaginary distance or the invisible past. "My sister and I were sent out to family in the country during The Blitz. I received a few letters from him but after a time I had no word. The war ended and I went back to London. All that remained of our house was the wrought iron gate. It had been bombed. I stood next to my mother and sister and stared and stared. I could hear crying and I looked down the street to Tom's house. His mother was standing in front of their gate holding an envelope." Audrey shook her head. "His plane was shot down. The world we had known as children was gone. I had to figure out what to do with my life. All because some lunatic wanted a war." Audrey was struck by a feeble coughing fit. "There. I've said it. Now someone will remember that I loved him, after I'm gone."

She stopped speaking and her eyes closed.

* * *

The next day I was in the greenhouse with Brittany and Sulamith, cleaning. It was a job that took about a week. Cleaning under trays, sweeping, mopping, scrubbing, scraping hardened-on dirt off of display shelves and tables. Exhausting, but in a good way. "Krista?" I heard Sheila's voice call from the doorway. I looked up and she motioned to me. I walked down to the end of the greenhouse towards her. "Caroline Larson is here. She's in the office waiting." Sheila looked at me with concern because we both knew that there was only one reason why Caroline would come mid-afternoon like that and ask to see me in private. I opened the office door and she looked up. Her eyes were red but she gave me a wan smile, "I guess you know why I'm here."

I nodded.

"She passed away late last night. I was with her." Caroline looked down at a small box in her lap, "She wanted you to have these things. I'm not sure what's in it, she tied it up a few weeks ago and asked me to set it aside for you, and last night in a moment of lucidity she asked me to write something down and give it to you. It doesn't make sense to me, but I'm sure she meant something by it."

Caroline gave me the box and the envelope and said goodbye, leaving me to my thoughts.

* * *

That night I sat alone in the living room with the box and the envelope still unopened, puzzling over why Audrey had left her story with me. Or maybe not so much puzzling—I knew why—as trying to push it away, and puzzling over how to do that. But I couldn't. Try as I·might, I couldn't push it away. I reached out and opened the envelope. On the botanically themed stationary was written;

Krista,

Don't forget the love you've had. Just because it's gone doesn't mean it's not precious. But don't ignore the love that looks you in the face every day. I know you're a smart girl. Stop fooling yourself.

Your Everlasting Friend,

Audrey

P.S. I always knew there were fairies at the bottom of the garden."

I opened the box and carefully emptied the contents onto the coffee table. Letters. Very old. Hand written. Four of them. A photograph of a young girl and an older boy on a garden swing, and an old gardening manual from the late nineteen forties. Some old-fashioned handkerchiefs with A.L. embroidered on them, and her watch. I ignored the watch and flipped through the gardening manual, being gentle with the old paper. I couldn't help but imagine her flipping through it on a rainy Vancouver winter day, dreaming about gladiolas. On the inside of the front cover was written, "Flowers for your birthday, Love Paul, Dec. 4 1948."

Paul was her husband. I fingered the neat masculine writing then closed the book and picked up the letters. I slid the first one out of its envelope.

Audrey,

I don't have much time to write but wanted to send you a note to let you know I'm doing well while I had the chance. When I think of you it's like I'm home. I keep your picture with me always. Will write longer next time.

Love, Tom

I opened the next one.

Audrey,

Wish I were with you. Your memory is like a light in my dark heart. I hate thinking of home being bombed when I'm high in the sky dropping bombs on other people's homes. Every time I think of Dresden I choke on my tears. I don't want to write to you like this, but you're the only person I know who understands me.

I love you, Tom

That last one must have escaped the sensors. I thought, as I slipped it into its envelope. And picked up the third of the four letters.

Audrey,

I bought a ring today and I wanted to surprise you but I'm just too happy to wait. It has a ruby at its centre and two little diamonds on either side and every time I picture it on your pretty hand I feel like I'm going to burst into song which would be extremely unfortunate for those within hearing range. Will keep it next to my heart until I can put it on your hand myself.

Love you always, Tom

I brushed angrily at the tears on my cheeks and reached for the last envelope. It was different and had no post mark but instead across the envelope, in a different hand, was written:

To the girl with the sad eyes,

I see you from my hospital bed every day. I'm lucky to have a bed by the window. There are all kinds of things to see. The chap I share a room with is blind now, so I suppose I'm lucky about that too. But that's beside the point. I know how ir-

regular this is, and I know that were I up and able, I probably
wouldn't have the courage to run after you and ask you
what's wrong. I'm shy that way, but seen as this is the second
week in a row that I've watched you pass each morning, and
seen as how I'm going to have to ask the nurse to run after
you with this letter, I figured I'd give it a shot.

I wish that I knew how to make you smile because you look
like your heart is broken and it makes me wish I could fix it. I
wish I could leave flowers on the side walk for you so that I
could look out my window and see you smile, because I bet
you've got the prettiest smile in the world.

Paul Larson, Room 401.

I was sitting on the floor with my back against the chesterfield and my knees pulled up. I slid the letter back into the
envelope and put it back in the box with the book and the
other letters, then my fingers hovered hesitantly over the
watch. I sighed and then picked it up. It was Audrey's watch.
That was all. It was a ladies watch. The kind you pin to your
shirt. It wasn't fancy, maybe an inch across, sterling silver
with some minimal scroll work. The portion with the pin was
likewise simple and no fuss with just a little scroll work. It was
quite old. Wind up, no battery. I'd seen Audrey wear it so
many times. I ran my fingers over the case, finding the little
notch to flip it open and gently lifted the cover. There was the
ivory watch face. Small but practical. Simple and easy to read.
And then there on the inside of the lid, was a little glass piece,
and underneath that was a violet. It was old and faded, but
unmistakably a violet. I summoned up a little magic and
watched as the colour bloomed in the old petals under the
glass. I looked up at the clock on the wall. It was late but not
that late. I wound the watch and set it.

I knew what Audrey was telling me and I won't pretend
that her death didn't send me into a tailspin of confusion,
because how could I live with Rowan's memory every day?

And if I admitted to myself that Evan was much more than a friend to me, what did I do then? What if it didn't work out? She'd been through as much hardship as me and yet, she had been whole, and at peace at the end, but maybe I wasn't that brave? Maybe I wasn't as strong? Memories and feelings pushed and shoved at me and I covered my face in a vain attempt to hide from them. I got up off the floor, went to the phone and dialled Evan's number, scolding myself for needing him even as I kicked myself for not talking about this with Audrey while she was still alive. Then Evan picked up.

"Evan? Are you sleeping?"

"No I'm up. What's going on?"

"Audrey died last night."

"Oh, Krista. Why didn't you tell me at dinner?"

"I haven't told Sulamith yet," I started sniffling as my voice grew thick. "I'm not sure what to tell her. I'll tell her tomorrow I guess ... I just ... I don't know."

"Look, I'm grabbing my keys right now. I'll be over in five. We'll go out. It's Friday night. I don't need to be coherent tomorrow. We can just drive around all night or whatever."

"Okay ... Evan?"

"Yeah?"

"Thanks."

Chapter 22

I ran up to Sheila's room and was relieved to see a light shining under her door. I knocked, "Sheila?"

"Come in?"

I opened the door and stuck my head in.

"Hey you," she said from bed where she sat with her laptop wearing Calvin and Hobbs pajamas. I could see the concern and sympathy in her eyes as she asked me, "What's up? Are you okay?"

I smiled an uncertain teary smile, "Probably. Evan's coming by to pick me up. I need to get out for a while. Can you keep an ear open for Sulamith? She's been sleeping straight through the night lately but I still feel paranoid that she'll wake and be upset if I'm not here."

"Sure. Go get me the baby monitor."

I flipped on the monitor by my bed where Sulamith slept, and put its partner on Sheila's night stand.

"See you in the morning," I said, gently closing her door behind me, and then the baby gate at the top of the stairs after that. I pulled on a jacket and stepped out into the freezing night air locking the door behind me, then down the stairs, through the gate, and into Evan's car.

"Where to?" he asked, looking at me.

He held my gaze and I looked back at him seeing what Audrey wanted me to see, there in his green eyes. I looked away. "Anywhere."

He nodded, flipped on my seat warmer, turned on some music and just drove. We watched the city lights slide by in silence for a long time, not saying anything, and after about an hour I asked, "How do you want to die Evan?"

He gave a small ironic laugh and shook his head slightly as he shifted and took a curve on Marine drive, "I'm still working on how to *live*." He was silent for a minute thinking, then sighed, "I suppose that I would like to die with fewer regrets, or at least knowing that I'd done what I could to make up for them. You?"

"I don't know. I feel guilty for being alive sometimes. And then I feel guilty for wasting time feeling guilty instead of living. Which is ... you know, stupid. There are some things that I'm trying to wrap my brain around but, Audrey didn't have the easiest life in the world. Her life was deeply affected by WWII but she picked up and moved on I ..." I sighed. "I hope that at the end, I'm like her."

"Have you figured out what to tell Sulamith?" he asked.

"I'll tell her that Audrey died but that she had a long life that was full of love so even though we'll miss her it's okay. Does that sound alright?" I asked Evan.

"Yeah. That sounds fine. I think she'll understand. She's pretty perceptive for two and three quarters."

I sighed again.

"Hey, I keep forgetting that you're over nineteen," Evan said to me. "I could use a drink let's swing by the pub near my place and we can toast Audrey."

"Sounds good."

* * *

"To dying well," Evan raised his glass.

"To dying well." I lightly tapped the neck of my cider bottle against his glass.

"I've never lost anyone that I was close to, except for you." Evan looked at me and I felt at ease under his gaze as he spoke. "I can't tell you how much the way I believed you had died bothered me. It still bothers me knowing that your parents were in the house that night ... Even though your dad hated me," Evan raised his eyebrow ruefully.

"I know," I shook my head. "It took me a year to stop feeling sick to my stomach every time I thought about it. But if it makes it any easier, they always knew that something like that might happen someday. I didn't know that until after but ..." I shrugged, at a loss for words and still reluctant to tell Evan the more improbable aspects of my past. But thinking back I realized there were things I could share. "For the record, my dad didn't hate you," I told him.

"Could have fooled me. I hated picking you up at your house. He'd stand there looking at me and even though I'm pretty sure that I was eye to eye with him I always felt about six inches shorter. And the look he'd give me ..." Evan shuddered.

I couldn't help laughing, "I'd never thought about him from your perspective, but I guess he would have been pretty intimidating." I shook my head thinking about the way my dad had stood by the door looking like a giant, eyes narrowed as I would join Evan on the landing of the front porch. "He asked me about you once or twice but I just looked at him like he was crazy and told him, 'Trust me Dad, Evan is just a friend.' I don't know if he believed me but I think that he would have been suspicious of any guy coming to the house to see me. Truth is he probably would have hated Rowan even more because Rowan always made his intentions so damn obvious, and Raphael would have put him through the roof" I looked at my cider telling myself to slow down before it loosened my tongue to a point I'd regret and hoped that Evan would let Raphael's name slide.

"Raphael?" Evan fixed me with a look.

No such luck.

"Who's Raphael?" Evan asked, all amused curiosity.

I thought about it. I didn't have to tell him that Raph was an angel. It wasn't as if Evan avoided all mention of people he'd been romantically involved with and he had a long string of ex-girlfriends.

"Former lover," I told Evan, because ex-boyfriend wasn't the word.

"Really?" Evan's eyebrows went up.

"Really," I confirmed nodding. "I think your mum met him once."

"What's he like?"

"Charming, oddball, devastatingly good looking, completely infuriating." I took a sip of my drink. "He drove me insane but we had good chemistry."

"Before or after Rowan?"

"That's messy and complicated." I tried to brush it off.

"Now I'm *really* curious."

I tilted my head thinking about it, "I suppose in a way there was some overlap. I was never unfaithful to Rowan, but I couldn't deny that Raphael had a way of getting under my skin, and Rowan knew that. Raph and I spent an afternoon together after Rowan was gone. I think that it was his way of reminding me that I wasn't dead. Typical complicated Raphael," I shrugged. "Audrey was trying to give me the same message but I get scared whenever I think about living my life more loudly. I'm still standing on the edge of a cold lake trying to work up the guts to jump in, worried that I'll sink."

"You're not the only one guilty of that," Evan said shifting his glass back and forth on the table from one seam in the wood to another.

"So how's teaching?" I changed the subject.

"It's fine, actually," Evan answered me, relieved for the change as well. "There's a rumour flying that I'm being considered for a promotion, so all is well. I'm enjoying it and I m not apprehensive before giving lectures anymore. I always wondered what I would do after I had my PhD. I remember you teasing me about it every time I tried to get you to go back to school. I wasn't sure I could picture myself teaching full-time so it's a relief in a sense, to be where I am."

I smiled, "You used to get so mad at me. What was it I said?"

Evan grinned remembering every word, "I would say, 'Krista won't you please consider going back to school.' and you'd give me a scathing look and say, 'Why, so I can get a job working for your mum at the garden centre? Grade twelve would be about as useful to me as a PhD in Literature'," Evan laughed, "I don't know why it seems so funny now but I was pretty uptight back then. And I don't think that there would be any point in you finishing grade twelve *now* because even if you did decide to go to university, you're almost old enough to go as a mature student."

"I wouldn't want to commit to something like that until Sulamith was older anyway," I said.

* * *

It was a good night. We talked and drank, said some things that needed to be said without crossing that boundary into the issues that we both seemed to be avoiding. I would look at him sometimes and I could see that he loved me, and I couldn't believe that I hadn't recognized it years earlier, but Evan never presumed too much. The nonphysical closeness remained and a part of me wondered if he would ever follow through on his feelings for me. Another part of me wondered if he had given up on that, but I always remembered what Sheila had said when I'd asked about him, "He never got over you."

And he hadn't had a girlfriend in years now. In any case, Evan had held his feelings for me back before, and I wasn't sure that I was ready for someone else's feelings. I was still trying not to be afraid of my own. That night after we had left the pub and Evan had walked me home he said to me, "Call me tomorrow if you need a breather. I can take Sulamith to the Aquarium for an hour or two."

"Yeah, thanks I might ..."

He looked at me for a moment, the street lamp catching the angle of his cheekbone, then said, "Goodnight."

"Goodnight," I said, and watched him walk away, pulling the collar up on his grey wool coat and adjusting his scarf against the chill. But as I turned and opened the gate and hurried into the house I had this disappointed feeling. I should have kissed Evan goodnight.

Chapter 23

Spring was busy like always and I let myself get caught up in it. Evan and I had moved on to something that more closely resembled dating, but the things that were being left unsaid were like elephants in the room. Evan showed up early one morning late in May, the morning of my birthday, with a wrapped package in his hands. It was an original edition of Undine. I knew, odds were, that Evan hadn't found this one by chance at a flee market. It was a calculated gift. I stood in front of him on the porch in my nightgown clutching it to my chest as he looked at me. I could see that ache in his eyes and emotion in his handsome face. "Thank you. My old one burned," I managed to say as he looked into my eyes.

"Krista ..." he said, and then—looking like he might cry, looking like he had that day in the potting shed—he'd said, "Happy birthday." Then he turned and headed for his car.

* * *

Sheila always takes me in stride and back then it was a good thing. I remember that birthday, running past her, up the stairs in tears, still clutching the book to my chest and running to Evan's room where he still slept occasionally, closing the door behind me and laying myself down where his smell lingered slightly. Soap, chlorinated swimming pool, clean water, clover. That was his smell.

I remember Sulamith's first birthday too. The Summer Solstice. I was a mess and Sheila, at first, hadn't understood why until I had somehow managed to remind her that it was also the anniversary of Rowan's death. Sheila took Sulamith out with her, telling me, "I'll make sure she has a good day," then left me to my tears and took Sulamith for ice cream. That's how the next year went too, and, in theory, the one after that. Sulamith's third birthday.

Sulamith and Sheila had a whole day of pleasures planned. Granville Island, a movie, and a fancy dinner out at the Old Spaghetti Factory. Sulamith was ready to go, wearing a pretty dress I'd made for her over the winter, specially for her birthday. She was so exited that I kept checking to see if her feet were touching the floor. I hugged her, "You have a wonderful day Pixie." I kissed her soft cheek and breathed in her smell. She looked up and it was like a tidal wave crashed over me. Rowan looking at me. His eyes, *looking* at me, merry, wild, full of life, but I couldn't quite get the rest of his face. I made a sound.

"Are you alright?" Sheila looked at me, her eyebrows knit.

I shrugged, "You'd better go."

Sheila gave me a 'look', "Are you sure?"

"I don't know but Sulamith's so exited. I don't want her to be disappointed. Go."

Sheila took Sulamith's hand, "Come on Sweet Pea, let's go get in the car," she said, and I watched them head down the front steps and climb in. Sheila looked back at me again as she opened the driver's side door. It took a few minutes as she buckled Sulamith into her car seat. I saw Sheila take out her cell phone, but then they finally pulled away.

In theory it was getting easier for me to keep it together day to day by then, and my goal was to be with Sulamith on her fourth birthday, but that day three years after Rowan had died I was as lost as I'd been the day that I'd run from the Fay world. I curled up in a ball on the chesterfield, paralysed by that look in Sulamith's eyes and all of the memories that I had been pushing away came pressing in, but they were faded, and I wanted Rowan. I sat there wishing ... Wishing that he could come to me ... Hold me ... Wipe away my tears, but knowing that he never would, and his face was starting to blur just a little bit in my mind. It was like I was losing him all over again, and it hurt.

I didn't hear Evan come in but heard the click of the door closing behind him. I looked up, for a split second worried that Sheila and Sulamith had returned and not wanting Sulamith to see me falling apart. I wasn't expecting Evan. He should have been at the college teaching. I scrambled to my feet trying desperately to stop crying, to just *stop*, but I couldn't. I tried to turn, to leave the room, but my legs wouldn't listen and he was standing in front of me as I cried and tried to say god knows what to him.

He looked at me and said, "Tell me what you need," and I could see in his eyes the desire to do whatever it was that I needed him to do to help me.

"Hold me," I gasped. "Please just hold me. I can't ... keep this in ... but I don't want to be alone."

In three quick steps he was there with his arms around me for the first time ever. He carried me to the chesterfield and held me tightly as I shook and he kept on holding me until I was still and quiet.

"I know how you feel, you know?" he said eventually, stroking my hair. "I still cry like this for you."

I looked up into his face, seeing the tears on his cheeks and deep emotion in his eyes, "You do?"

Evan nodded.

"I feel like I'm losing him Evan. I don't have any pictures of him. His face is blurring in my mind. I've spent all this time trying to learn how to live without him and now that I can stand thinking about him, he's slipping away!"

I was lying across Evan's lap. He had one arm around my waist and the other under my head on the arm of the chesterfield as I looked up into his face. "Then tell *me* about him. Bring him back with your words," he said.

I laid there a while longer not wanting, quite yet, to leave whatever it was that I had found there in Evan's arms, but also thinking over what he'd said. "Alright, but not here."

"Okay," he said. "I'm just going to call my mum and give her an update."

I went upstairs and put on an indigo India cotton summer dress that I had bought but never wore. It reminded me of that other world, that other life. I slipped it over my head, brushed out my hair and looked in the mirror seeing the things that I had been trying to ignore for the last three years. I walked over to my dresser and took out the heartsease ring and slipped it onto my right hand looking at the ferns and flowers etched into my skin. People always thought they were tattoos. I kept long sleeves and gloves on at the garden centre. I took out the sapphire and pearl necklace, clasping it around my neck and letting myself see the way it matched my eyes as I had the night Bronwen had given it to me, the night Rowan asked me to be his. I took the long chain out as well. The one that I had once worn around my neck with only one ring on it, but that now held two rings. I didn't know what to do with the rings. They'd felt displaced ever since Rowan had died, but they were a part of the story, so I tucked them in my pocket, then pinned Audrey's watch to my dress, put in the opal earrings, and went downstairs. Evan looked at me for a moment, the dress, the carefully brushed hair, the jewels. I carried myself differently when I wore them. I knew that. "You're beautiful," he said as I reached the bottom steps. He held out his hand to me for the first time, and I took it feeling the complete rightness of his fingers closing around mine, and looking into his eyes I watched as that simple touch registered. It was magic.

"Where do you want to go?" he asked me once we were sitting in his car.

"Deer Lake," I told him.

He drove east, into Burnaby and parked near the vintage carousel.

"We should take Sulamith there sometime," he remarked casually as we got out of the car and looked to where we could see the painted horses whirling.

I took his hand as he came around to me and we began walking slowly down to the lake shore.

"I want to tell you everything," I told him. "I want you to understand me completely. But this isn't an easy story, and it's going to hurt, and I'm sorry."

"Krista, nothing is going to hurt as much as the day I lost you. After two years of having you back, I think that I can safely tell you that. I told you that I would do anything for you. I meant it. You can tell me and you don't need to apologize."

I squeezed his hand and tried to smile. I looked up at the hill diagonally across the lake from us. "It's hard to believe that it's been nearly five years since the day you walked out on me. That was hard for me to take. I didn't know what to do. I was so hurt. I tried not to be, I tried to forget you, but for months my heart sank every morning when there was no letter from you waiting in the post. And I *waited* for it. I *dreamed* about what it might say. Maybe you would beg for my forgiveness, beg to have my friendship back, or tell me that you had been an idiot. Sometimes, I even dreamt that you might write and tell me that you loved me. I was angry with myself for not writing to you and letting you have it, telling you what a complete ass you'd been not to stay and talk to me, but I thought that you were disgusted by the way you felt, and I didn't know how to handle that. I was *only* seventeen, and I was completely inexperienced. Suddenly I felt … worthless, and *so* alone moving through the world without some tie to you. Not even a letter. I used to get beaten up at school, and put in lockers. You were the first friend I ever had, but I was afraid to tell you that, in case you wouldn't like me any more." I looked up at Evan, wanting him to know that I wasn't telling him to hurt him, but because I needed him to understand, and I could see the guilt and anguish in his eyes but I could also see that he understood, and that it was okay, so I continued, "By the time a year had passed I was seriously depressed. I was having a hard time and everyone but your mother seemed to be rejecting me. You hadn't come home, and even my own parents would have conversations about how strange I was when they thought I wasn't listening. There was so much that I didn't know, but on top of everything, I had this feeling building in me all the time that scared the crap out of me because I felt that whatever was happening to me would set me apart from the rest of the world even further. It felt like this fiery pressure and … flowing cool green lightness was pushing at me, inside." I placed my hand over my sternum. "Sometimes I wanted to follow it, but mostly it scared me. I though I was going crazy. Then I had a bad day at work and your mum could see that I was too shaken to stay, so she sent me home. I went home to try to get a grip and once I was calm I went for a walk in the woods at the base of Queen Elizabeth Park. That's when it happened. I … I'm not sure how to carry on telling you with words. It would probably be easier if I just showed you."

I looked again, up at the hill across the lake. I felt Evan's smooth hand in mine. An academic's hand, not a swordsman's, but no less comforting for it. "This is going to be weird," I told him, then reached inside and, pulling magic, I opened a door and pulled us through. "There it is," I said, pointing to the beautiful castle on the hill. "That's where it all started. That's where he took me after he found me in the woods."

I could see Fenna and Dunstan on the beach further down the lake shore. Fenna turned and looked at me. Our eyes met. I wanted to run to her but I couldn't. I raised my hand, reaching out to her, then opened the door again and stepped back pulling Evan with me and disappearing from Fenna's sight.

"What the hell was that?! How did you do that?" Evan gaped at me as the world he knew rematerialized around us.

"Magic. You see, the first time I did that, I didn't know that *I'd* done it. I was *so* unhappy and I wanted to escape and I couldn't hold the magic in anymore, so without even knowing it, I took myself away, to another world."

I lead him to the trees and found a grassy place to sit. "One minute I was wandering the paths at the edge of the park and the next I was standing in dense old growth forest with a knight in dirty bloodstained armour charging towards me on a big black war horse. It was Rowan. That was the *first* time he saved my life."

And so I'd started the story. Sometimes I used words, sometimes I took Evan's hands and showed him the images in my mind and sometimes I would let the magic flow and conjure images that we could watch like we would a movie screen, and sometimes I could see Rowan's face as clearly as the day I'd met him. I showed Evan everything. Falling in love with Rowan, the Fay, the angels, the unicorn, my brothers and sister, and while I told my story the trees around us lost their leaves in a torrent of red and gold then budded anew. I came to the part of the story when Leif came to me on the Summer Solstice covered in the blood and gore of war and, as I held my newborn babe in my arms, told me that Rowan was dead, and gave Rowan's message to me, "Tell Rhiannon ..."

I told Evan of my six months in that world without Rowan. Trying to stay true to my station, trying to stay strong, then Raphael's bed and arms, and my decision. How I'd written my letter begging them to let the monarchy die, to let it stop with me, to let me be the last queen and let it end, and then my night flight. The night I let Rhiannon die.

It was the summer solstice and I could feel the energy all around us as we sat on the grass in the sun. Life, magic, my own, Evan's, the trees surrounding us. I let the trees burst into flower. Some of them weren't even flowering trees. A little boy was watching us from a distance. I raised my hand and smiled. He turned and ran back to his parents. I looked into Evan's face. There were tears of grief, joy, and amazement. We sat face to face and a lock of Evan's hair that was always falling forward, and that I was always fighting an urge to fix, fell into his face and I reached up and pushed it back. He looked into my eyes and I felt myself falling for *his* beautiful green eyes. "I never imagined that so much had happened to you," he said softly. "I don't think that I would have been as strong as you."

"I'm not strong Evan. It nearly killed me."

He nodded, swallowed, looked down. Suddenly a strong breeze swept by and the petals on the trees started to fall around us swirling in a summer scented hurricane of pink and white until the trees were just green again and we were sitting under a blanket of petals.

"I don't know what else to say," Evan said to me.

"Neither do I," I told him as another strong breeze picked up all of the petals and blew them out over the lake where they fluttered for a moment, like a million tiny butterflies, then disappeared under the water. I stood and Evan followed me as I headed for the boardwalk that lead around the lake. We walked silently. Evan took my hand again and I marvelled at the feeling. That was where my hand belonged. The sun shone down and the leaves rushed and rustled in the hot summer breeze.

"Tell me your story," I asked him.

"It's not nearly as interesting and it doesn't have any special effects," he told me.

"I want to hear it," I persisted.

"Okay … Well. I guess I'd better start with my mother then. In case you didn't already know," he said dryly, "she was pretty wild when she was young. Lots of escapades. Lots of lovers. Lots of fun. Then one day she met my father. She said that it was the best three weeks of her life. He was a sailor on leave and she knew from the start that he'd be gone at the end of it, but what she didn't know, until about three weeks *after* he'd gone, was that he'd left her a little something to remember him by. She settled down quickly. Her parents helped her open the nursery. She's always been good with plants and it did well from the start. She bought the house and she's been, on the whole, a pretty good mother."

"Your father was a sailor?" I questioned.

"Mm hm, why?"

"It just explains a lot."

"Explains what?"

"I'll tell you later, keep going."

He shrugged. "So you know, my early life was pretty good but in my teens I started searching for something that I couldn't quite put my finger on, but I found it in three places; in the water, I hate being away from it for too long, and in stories. In books. I couldn't get enough of them. It was enough of an obsession that I followed it into adult life and majored in literature once I'd reached university. And I found it in you, I found what I was looking for in you. I was just about to start my master's degree when I met you." Evan stopped and looked at me for a moment. "I didn't know what to make of you. You were this strange self-contained little woman child.

The way I felt for you didn't really sink in at first. You were ... well ... How to put this ..." he said awkwardly.

"I know, I know," I said gently, interrupting him again. "I looked like a twelve year old."

Evan smiled, "I missed you that winter after we met though. I thought about you every day. I still have all of the letters that you sent me. It wasn't until I found that copy of Undine at the flee market that I realized *just* how much I was looking forward to seeing you again. When I came home that summer it slowly sank in that I was in love with you." He took a deep breath and his expression changed. I could see the regret in his eyes. "I felt very conflicted," he said. "The difference between seventeen and twenty-three isn't really so vast, but you did look quite young. I was always conscious of it when we were out together. Afraid that someone would get the wrong idea. It was almost a relief when people assumed that I was your older brother, because then it would be perfectly natural for you to be in my company, even though you looked ten years younger than me. I had to continually remind myself that I wasn't attracted to thirteen year old girls, only to you, but at the same time I felt continually more uncomfortable with the fact that I *was, very* attracted to you. I decided that I should wait until you were eighteen to tell you how I felt, which was hard, but I thought that maybe at eighteen you would look a little older, and that maybe the six year age gap wouldn't feel so big to me. You don't know how angry I was with myself when I couldn't keep my hands off of you." Evan's voice shook a little and he paused breathing with forced evenness for a moment. "But I didn't wait, and you were standing there on that step ladder with little bits of peat moss in your hair looking right into my eyes and batting your lashes at me. I still remember the light, the way the reflection of the sun in the doorway made your skin so bright. The way your mouth was open just a little, your lips ... I couldn't help it, I just wanted to kiss you. It was an automatic response and kissing you felt like nothing else ... the feel of you ... I don't know. It was magic, but you weren't kissing me back, so I pulled away and you looked *so* young, and *so* confused and I knew that I should have waited, or that I should have asked. I was going to explain myself to you then and there, but I found myself thinking, *Shit Evan, you just fucked that up royally.*" He sighed.

"I was *never* disgusted by my feelings for you. Confused, yes, certainly, but the only thing that I was *ever* disgusted by, was *myself* for my complete lack of restraint and for destroying our friendship. And when you overheard me arguing with my mother in the office, that was just my insecurities coming through, but stepping out the door and seeing your face? Oh god Krista. All I could think, was to get as far away from you as fast as I could before I hurt you even more, and I didn't believe that I deserved your forgiveness. In hindsight I knew that I couldn't handle the idea that you might reject me, so I ran like a coward. If I had thought things through, if I had listened to my mother—who absolutely took your side by the way—I would have stayed and told you how I felt and tried to take the hurt away, but I was stuck in a bad place, and I screwed up." He was silent for a few moments. "I did all kinds of stupid things to try to forget you that year, and the fact that I don't have any illegitimate children or horrible diseases or serious addiction problems to show for it is nothing short of miraculous. When I was drunk enough I wrote you letters, beautiful love letters, and I dreamt about mailing them but never had the nerve. I got kicked off the swim team. I still can't believe that I kept my grades up during that period. When spring came I was too ashamed of my behaviour to face you, but that was a horrible excruciating summer. When it ended and the semester started I realized that I needed to see you, at least, just to tell you that I was sorry, so I booked a

plane ticket for the Thanksgiving long weekend and called my
mother to tell her that I was coming home but ..." Evan turned
and looked at me again, still holding my hand. "When my
mother answered the phone that night she was distraught and
she didn't want to say it. I had to drag the words out of her. I
can still remember the way she said 'Molotov cocktails',
'house fire', and 'dead'. I came home for a few days and asked
her then, how you'd been before the fire. She said that you'd
been dwindling. She said that it was like your pilot light was
flickering. I flew back to Montreal, tried to ignore how I was
feeling and plunged into my studies. I didn't really cry for you
at first. I focused on my thesis and met Eugénie. That was a
disaster. We both got married for the wrong reasons. I didn't
want to be alone because when I was alone I had to face the
things that I was hiding from, and I thought that she could
keep me from missing you. She thought I could fix her life.
Like a husband and a ring were the accessories that she
needed for everything to *look* perfect on the outside. I
finished my PhD and the day I handed in my thesis I started
to cry. I couldn't stop. Eugénie couldn't handle it. She was
angry and when I told her why I couldn't leave the house, why
I was falling apart, she looked at me and said. 'You mean all of
'*this*' is over some twinkie you kissed once?'"

Evan shook his head bitterly, "I walked out on her and she
sent me divorce papers. Then I came home. And you were
here." He sat down on a bench and rubbed his hands over his
face. I sat next to him and looked out over the lake. "I thought
that I was finally clear," he told me. "I'd cried my tears, I'd
made my mistakes and I was making peace with the past.
Time to move on ... and then there you were. More beautiful
than ever, not looking *one bit* like a thirteen year old, with a
baby on your hip and all of this sadness in your eyes. My
mother said that getting you back might be harder than losing
you was. For the first few months I drank a lot more than I

should have, and swam lap after lap just so that I could feel numb. I'm not going to say that the last two years have been easy. They haven't, in fact they've been bloody hard. But they've been good too, and the cliche stands. Nobody ever said that life was going to be easy."

Evan was silent again and I sat there beside him looking around at how ordinary everything seemed on the surface, but knowing that just below the surface, nothing was ord_- nary. I slipped my hand back into Evan's and listened as he started to speak again, "Krista, I know that you've been through worse than any pain I've caused you, but I'm still sorry. I'm so sorry for what I did to you that summer. I'm not going to make the same mistake I made five years ago. I won't throw myself at you, but ..." He blinked back tears and I could hear the ache in his voice as he told me, "I'm still in love with you. The day I came home you quoted The Last Unicorn to me. 'Drown out my dreams, keep me from remembering what- ever wants me to remember it,' and I couldn't help but hope, that if I did everything right, that if I proved to you that you could count on me, that maybe I had reason to hope that you would love me too, because Amalthea loved Lir in the end. Please. If there's even a small chance that you might love me, tell me. If there's a chance that I could make you love me would you let me try? Because I know that I'm never going to stop loving you."

His face was wet. I didn't know what to say to him. I wasn't sure I could answer him so I blurted out the first words that came to my lips which were, "Take me home Evan," and I started walking quickly back to the car. Evan followed. I knew that I should say something to him. He wasn't holding my hand anymore and it felt empty. I could see him battling his emotions, trying to keep them from me. I knew that I should reach out to him but it was like that day in the potting shed. I felt young and confused and unsure of what to do. We drove back to the house in silence and my throat felt so tight and my eyes burned with tears. When Evan pulled up in front of the house I just sat there. He got out of the car and came around to my side. He opened my door and took my hand, drawing me out of the car. "I need you to throw me a line Krista. I'm drowning. I don't know what to do."

I stood there thinking about how I'd felt that August when he'd shut me out of his life. Had I been in denial all those years? Had I hidden, even from myself, that I *had* loved him? Had I been so naive? And if I let myself love him now, really, fully, *love* him, could I bear it if I lost him?

I couldn't speak so I took his hand and pulled him towards the house. I fumbled for my keys but he had his in hand so he unlocked the door. It was early afternoon. Sheila and Sulamith wouldn't be home for hours yet. I took his hand again and pulled him up the stairs to my room and closed the door behind us. I looked up at him. He was bewildered. I pulled my dress up over my head, tossing it on a chair. I stepped up on my toes, reached up behind his head so that I could pull him down and kiss him, and for several long intense minutes we just kissed before Evan pulled back and looked at me, stunned and incredulous, "Krista, are you sure?" he asked.

I shook my head. "No," I spoke through quivering lips, "but if I don't do this now I'm going to lose my courage, and I can't go on like this. Are you sure?" I whispered back to him.

"Yes," he paused, "but you've got to understand that this can't be a one time thing. I can't do that. You take me to your bed, and you're stuck with me until I die." He was looking into my eyes and he was absolutely serious. I don't think I'd ever seen him so intense.

That lock of auburn hair was hanging in his face again, so I reached up and pushed it back. "Even if things are horribly awkward and I cry?" I said, still nearly a whisper.

"You're stuck with me," he repeated. "We'll just keep trying until we get it right."

"Do you promise?" I whispered again and tried to keep from shaking.

"I promise."

"I ... I strongly suspect that I love you," I whispered as his arms went around me lifting me off the floor and he started kissing me again in earnest and ... It wasn't awkward.

* * *

We lay there in each other's arms that afternoon whispering amazed and inconsequential things to one another.

"Your skin is almost as pale as mine."

"I love the way you smell. Like wisteria ... and honey-suckle."

"Your eyes are beautiful. They're so green."

"Your mouth is perfect."

"This is right."

"It is, isn't it."

* * *

As the day drew on we reluctantly drew our clothes back on, all too aware that Sheila and Sulamith would be home at some point, and we wandered down to the kitchen. We fixed dinner for two and sat close to one another eating with candles lit. I didn't hide my fayness from Evan and he was delighted when the candles seemed to light themselves. I didn't stop the flickers of coloured light from dancing around me. Evan seemed to bring them out.

Sheila and Sulamith came home at around seven-thirty and they were both tuckered out. It was good timing. I'd had a long conversation with Sulamith a week earlier about how she was getting big enough for her own bed in her own room. I wasn't sure how *I* felt about that, it was the end of her babyhood and it made me a little weepy and sentimental to see her growing so fast, but *she* was ready and excited. Over the week Sheila and I had made up Evan's old room for her, taking her out to choose new curtains and a bed spread. We moved his old things out, stashing everything but his books in the attic (I'd moved his books to my room). We re-painted the toy box and moved her toys into her new room. I hung the little carved swallows that Rowan had made for her over her bed and arranged her treasures on her windowsills. Feeling just a little like life was moving too fast for me that night, I tucked her into her very own big girl bed for the very first time. "Did you have a good birthday Sweet Pea?" I asked her.

I got a very serious, very sleepy nod. "Will you come next year Mummy?"

"I will baby."

"Do you promise?"

I smiled, "I promise. I love you Sulamith."

"I love you Mummy. Gnigh," she yawned, then mumbled, "Liked the brown bunny better ..." She pulled the brown plush rabbit that she had chosen at the kid's market close and turned as her eyes fell closed. I kissed her forehead and watched her for a moment before I headed down to the back porch where Evan was sitting with Sheila.

"That was quick," Sheila said looking up at me as I walked out onto the porch.

"I think she was too tired to stay awake for more than a minute. She dropped off mid sentence like a little rock," I said, sitting down on the wicker love seat next to Evan and leaning into him. Without thinking his arm came around me and pulled me in that little bit closer.

The look we got from Sheila was absolutely hilarious. Evan was, obviously, comfortable in his mother's house. He'd grown up there. It was home. Him wandering around barefoot with his shirt tails untucked was nothing new, but Sheila hadn't been upstairs yet where Evan's blazer, socks, and belt were still draped over the chair in my room. She gaped for several seconds before exclaiming loudly, "Oh, my god! Is that *physical contact* I detect? Why didn't you say!?" She looked at Evan.

"What was I *supposed* to say? You've been home for all of ten minutes. Now you know," Evan shrugged as a smile tugged the corners of his mouth.

"*What*, exactly, do I know?" Sheila grinned her wicked curiosity and I blushed for the first time in nearly four years then turned and pressed my cheek against Evan's shoulder fighting an urge to giggle. Evan, for his part, blushed too and snickered into my hair as he kissed my head.

"So you told him?" She looked at me pointedly. "*Everything*?" she stressed the word. "I don't have to make weird excuses to him when you blow up the light bulbs anymore?" she added.

I laughed softly, and maybe a little sadly, "Yes ... I told him everything ... I didn't leave anything out this time."

Sheila nodded and sat lost in her own thoughts for a moment when I told her, "Thank you Sheila. For everything. For putting up with me. For all your help. For calling Evan. You always seem to know what I need. It's like ..." I hesitated, "It's like magic."

"Sprite," she said. "You don't ever need to thank me. I'd do it all again, and, credit where due, while I *did* call Evan this morning, I didn't have to ask him to come. He was already on his way." Sheila stood, "And that little girl of yours has worn me right out. I'm going to bed and I hope that I drop off like a rock too because we've got that order of David Austen Roses coming in tomorrow at six A.M. and we need to be in to meet the truck." She closed the porch door behind her and I heard the creak of the banister as she headed upstairs.

I turned and looked at Evan questioningly. He was looking back at me, a complicated smile— certainly worthy of Raphael—playing around his mouth and eyes. "I know that Sulamith's birthday is hard for you. I made sure that I would have the day free weeks ago, and emailed my students the lecture notes yesterday. You've seemed, delicate, and ... in a flux ever since Audrey died. I just wanted to make sure that I was here ... If you needed me."

"I do need you Evan," I said to him and rested my head against him, enjoying the contact, enjoying the fact that it was *Evan* that I was sitting with on that quiet summer evening.

Eventually he told me with a sigh, "I've got to go. I have a few papers to mark and I need to revise my lecture for Thursday."

I was silent for a moment; he'd told me only a few short hours ago that he was never going to stop loving me, that I was stuck with him. "Will I see you tomorrow?"

I turned and looked into his face and his mouth quirked and he nodded, "Definitely." Then he kissed me and said to me, "If someone had told me this morning, that my day would end like this, I wouldn't have believed them. I can't quite get over the idea that there *is* magic in this world after all. I searched and searched. I thought that it only existed in stories, but here I am sitting on the porch with the last Fairy queen, and she just happens to be the girl that I love." Evan looked down for a moment and sighed, then he gave me a conflicted and reluctant, but satisfied, smile, "I should be going."

He got up off of the wicker love seat. I heard him go upstairs to retrieve his things from my room and, I'm sure, to take a peek at Sulamith. I followed him and met him at the door just as he was coming back down. He bent and removed a wrapped package from a bag that he'd brought in that morning, and that I'd been too preoccupied to notice. "Give this to Sulamith when she wakes up. Tell her it's from me." He placed the present on the hall table.

"I love you," I whispered standing on tiptoe and reaching around his neck.

He gave me a dazzling bone melting smile and kissed me, "I'd live the last five years all over, just to hear you say you love me again."

"You don't have to. I love you Evan."

He smiled, kissed me again and told me, "I love you." Then he was off.

I climbed the stairs and stood in the hall for a moment looking at my bed. It was really very rumpled. Just then Sheila emerged from the bathroom with a towel on her head and stood next to me wondering what I was staring at so intently. She looked at the bed then at me, eyebrows raised. I turned bright pink.

* * *

When I crawled into bed I lay there alone for the first time since Sulamith's birth, and I thought of Rowan. I remembered his smile, the way he would wait for me to wake in the morning, watching my face. I remembered dancing with him, laughing as he swung me around, and the way he would put his hands on either side of my face and look into my eyes. I remembered, perfectly, his face and his wild dark eyes, and all of this I remembered without feeling that I would drown in my tears. There *were* tears, there always would be, but at least now they were sweet as well as bitter, and I had Evan to thank for it. For helping me hold on to Rowan, for finding the lost pieces of my heart, and mending some of the cracks.

Evan is, in his way, every bit as much my hero as Rowan.

Chapter 24

I *am* the last Fairy Queen. Evan was right about that. It wasn't something that I had planned on confirming, but you know what they say about plans. Evan hadn't planned on moving in with us right away either. "I still have over a month left on my lease. We don't need to hurry," he'd said when I'd brought it up one evening at his place, then he told me, "I *want* to move in ... more than anything, but it'll be a big adjustment for you and Sulamith. I'll start moving my things in over the next few weeks and spend a few nights so that Sulamith has some time to get used to the idea of me being there full time."

He hadn't wanted to rush us, but it was Sulamith who forced the issue.

She had become friends with Sophie, the little girl across the street. I had a casual friendship with Sophie's mother Tammy, and I was comfortable with the situation, but as Sulamith was making her little three year old way in the world, she was figuring things out. I could see it happening right in front of my eyes. She was becoming very much her own little person, and one night about three days after her birthday, as we all sat around the table eating dinner, Sulamith, after having spent the afternoon with Sophie, looked up and said very seriously in her halting little three year old voice, "Mummy, did you know ... that udder little girls daddies ... stay wit dem, *all* de time?" She look a deep breath.

"Why does Eban,"she had trouble with her Vs, "Hab to go away, ebry night? I don't want him to."

It was like she was looking straight into my heart with her round dark eyes, and it was a beautiful heart-achy moment. Evan was sitting next to her and the look on his face was priceless. I don't think that he really knew up until that moment how much he meant to her, and he melted. I could see a little panic and worry over how to handle the situation there too, but I trusted Evan. From the very beginning he had made an enormous effort to get to know Sulamith and to connect with her, and not just because she was my daughter, but as a person in her own right. Even when she was only one year old. He would carry her high on his shoulder, take her to the park, build blocks with her on the floor. He bought us yearly memberships to the Vancouver Aquarium and he'd show up with his car on drizzly Sunday afternoons, just as I thought I would go crazy trapped inside with a two year old. He'd walk in the door, scoop Sulamith up in his arms, and say "Hey Pilly Wiggin. Want to go see the fish?" Then he'd look over his shoulder at me and say, "Coming?"

And almost as soon as Evan figured she could sit still and listen he started reading to her. Beatrix Potter, Kenneth Grahame, and Cecily Mary Barker (her fairy books not her religious works). Always beautiful first editions. Even when he took me out without her, he would show up at the house an hour in advance mostly just to play for a while. He was always very conscious of the fact that I was a mother and that I couldn't just run out the door because I was off work, so if he wanted to see me it meant including Sulamith, often gearing the activity towards her, and he ate dinner with us almost every night too. So really, it was no wonder, that when push came to shove, and Sulamith started to make sense of the world, in her little heart and mind, Evan was her father, and she was sitting there waiting for an answer. I left it up to him.

He knew I wanted him to move in, and I was too choked up with happy/sad feelings to talk anyway. Sheila was grinning from ear to ear. He turned to Sulamith and asked her tentatively, "Do *you* want me to stay?"

She nodded very solemnly.

He turned to me, asking silently with his eyes.

I nodded too, a little less solemnly.

"Okay," Evan said turning back to Sulamith, "I'll stay." And he did.

Sulamith was so excited that as soon as we finished eating, she insisted Evan drive with her to his apartment and pack enough of his belongings to get by until the weekend and it couldn't have been more than a week before we had the bulk of his things, mostly just clothes, a fish tank, and books, (lots of books) moved to the house and settled into place.

That first night, after Sulamith had been put to bed and was fast asleep, and the house was quiet, I sat on the edge of the bed flipping through a seed catalogue in my nightgown. I marked my page and set it aside then picked up a novel instead and eased back onto the pillows. I read a page, but then set it aside as well and watched Evan's back as he sat at the desk by the window marking the last few papers in his stack. He sat up and put the pen in the pen cup and stretched, then rubbed his eyes. He turned and smiled a tired smile then stood and came over to the bed. He watched me watch him and sat at the foot of the bed, placed his hand on my foot. His touch was like a hot breeze, a current, a connection. Had we known it would be that way and had it scared us? Is that why our arms had never brushed in the movie theatres five years ago? Or were we scared that it wouldn't be like this?

"What's on your mind?" Evan asked me levelling me with his green eyed gaze.

"That day in the potting shed. Do you think of it often?"

Evan gave a gently bitter chuckle, "More often than is good for me. You?"

I shrugged, "For years I pushed it away because of how badly I wanted you when I imagined that things had been different. I wasn't sure if the feeling was real, or if it had only come about because it had been unbelievable to me, before that moment, that you could have those kinds of feelings for me ... and then I believed that you didn't *want* to have them. I tried to kill the memory, to smother it, to push it into the darkest corner of my mind ..." I hesitated, "If you had it to do over and you were standing in the potting shed right now, looking at me being naive and confused at you, what would you say?"

Evan looked down and away from my eyes, then back to my face. I waited for the answer.

"I had the words in my mind that day. At that very moment even, and I've spoken them over and over to you these last years, even when you were dead to me. I was going to say ..." he looked away again then back into my eyes. He sighed, "I was going to say, 'Krista ... I've fallen in love with you and I seem to have lost my head. I'm sorry. I didn't mean to surprise you like that.' What you said back to me in my imagination depended on a variety of things. How much I was hating myself, how drunk I was ..." Evan pulled a face, "or how horny ... Sometimes you slapped me. Sometimes you fell into my arms. Sometimes you kissed me."

I felt momentarily guilty for bringing it up, but I *had* brought it up and the truth was that I'd had my own short lived fantasies before I'd decided that thinking about it was just going to hurt me more. "When I think back to that day ... If you'd said that to me? I think I would have reached out to you," I moved close enough to him to reach him with my hands. About the distance he had been from me that day. "When things are intense, when I'm overwhelmed, it's hard for me to speak. I think I would have reached out and touched you, like this," and I reached out my hand and ran my fingertips from his cheekbone to his jaw then let my hand rest on his chest where his heart was beating. "Would that have been enough? Would that have told you that I was open to your love, even if I *was* naive and confused?" I looked at him with my hand on his heart as that hot feeling of tears welling bloomed in my eyes.

He placed his hand over mine. "It would have been more than enough," he said to me and I collapsed into his arms. Much later, when we were still and the night was quiet and dark and the air that came through the window was something approaching cool, I asked Evan, "Did you keep all of those drunken love letters that you wrote to me but never sent?"

I looked up from where I was lying partially draped over him.

"Here. Move." He sat up and rummaged around in the vintage steamer trunk that he'd used as a coffee table in his apartment. He passed me a thick stack of envelopes. "There are seventy-three."

"Can I read them?"

"I wrote them for you. I want you to read them."

I opened the first envelope and read, then the next, and the one after. Evan relaxed back and watched me, running a hand along the bare skin of my back every so often. After the fifteenth letter I looked up at Evan incredulous, "Evan, these aren't just love letters, they're poems. This is poetry. They're beautiful ... I ... I can't quite believe that you wrote them for *me*. I didn't know that you saw me that way."

He smiled ruefully, "I do see you that way." He looked away and made another face, the sort of face one makes in the throes of a self deprecating thought, but then he turned back to me, "Do you remember what I said about hoping to die with fewer regrets or at least knowing that I'd done what I could to make up for them?"

I nodded.

"I'm going to make up for my regrets, and I'm going to try to stop over-thinking things." He passed me a small worn red velvet box. "I bought this just before you disappeared, the week that I'd decided to come home and try to talk to you. I've had it for years now but I haven't been impulsive enough to give it to you and just ask you to marry me, even though I've been sure for a long time now."

"Evan ... ?" I looked at him feeling weirdly insecure but strangely hopeful. "Are you proposing to me?"

"Yes. You're my best friend and we have more than enough chemistry to last a lifetime. I *want* you *and* I love you. When I'm with you and that little girl of yours I feel like we're a family, and I want that to be real. I'm going to stop doing what I *think* is right and start doing what I *feel* is right. I'm asking you to marry me."

The ring box tumbled to the floor unheeded as I tumbled back into his arms.

Sometime in the wee hours, after hours more of making love and talking, I realized that I'd inadvertently done something ... something that I didn't know that I could do, although when I thought it over I shouldn't have been that surprised. "Evan?"

"Mmm, Hmm," he sighed content and sleepy.

"Would it be a big problem for you if I were pregnant?"

"I ... told you. I had a vasectomy years ago I ... that ... shouldn't be ..." he looked at me. "Are you trying to tell me something?"

"I think that I might have magically overridden it. I'm ... pretty sure that I'm pregnant."

Evan gave me a look, a look that was pleased and content and just a little bit wry. He kissed the top of my head. "You're a fertility fairy, aren't you?"

"Guilty as charged," I gave a contented sigh and sank back into his arms.

Chapter 25

Three weeks later Evan and I got married in the backyard. We would have gone to city hall but it turned out that in Vancouver they don't do that anymore. I think that the whole event confused Sulamith to no end but she was happy to bake a cake and put on a pretty dress. Sheila was floating. She worried about Evan and I in her way and it was a relief to her, after years of watching us, that we had finally figured out that we were supposed to be together properly and permanently. I found myself looking down at the little vintage engagement ring on my finger. Evan told me that he would get me a nicer flashier one if I wanted—now that he wasn't a poor university student anymore—but I didn't want a flashier ring. This one meant more to me. I could sense his stored up dreams in this little ring.

About two days after that dreamy weekend, after the dinner dishes had been dealt with and Sulamith was in bed, Sheila sat down at the kitchen table with a thick manila envelope and waved me over, "Put on a pot of tea then come look this over with me Krista."

I put the pot and two cups on the table. "What is that? It looks very formal," I commented as I poured out the tea.

"Somebody has made us an offer on the garden centre," Sheila didn't move to empty the envelope and she didn't say any more.

"How much are they offering?" I asked. "Would it be enough for you to retire?"

"It would be enough for me to retire, for us to put Sulamith through university—if she wants to go—, and for you and Evan to go on a honeymoon. It's a very good offer."

"Do you still want to retire?" I asked Sheila.

"Yeah. I'll admit that I do. I just want to play grandma to Sulamith and get back to enjoying my own garden. Maybe I could get a part time job at a bookstore for fun."

Sheila pulled the papers out of the envelope and pushed them across the table to me. "They won't do as well without a garden fairy working there, but it's still a solid business."

I read over the document and almost fell off my chair when I saw the amount of the offer. I smiled, "Let's do it then. Let's sell. It would be good timing. Sulamith's going to need more time with her grandma next year in any case."

Sheila gave me a shrewd look, "What are you trying to tell me? Were you thinking about doing something different next year?"

"Not so much different, just ... more," I said, teasing Sheila a bit, making her curious.

She gave me an impatient puzzled look and motioned me to get on with it.

"We're gonna have a baby boy in March ..."

I didn't get to finish my sentence. Sheila leapt up screaming and did a funny dance. She made so much noise that Evan, who'd been prepping a lecture upstairs, came hurrying down the stairs looking concerned, "What's going on? Did a rat get in the kitchen again?" He looked around the kitchen for a suspect rodent.

Sheila didn't answer. She just kept laughing and shrieking like a teenaged girl at a Beatles concert and eventually even Sulamith, sleepy and disoriented, bumped down the stairs and padded into the kitchen, "What's de matter? Is dere a rat?" she mumbled, rubbing her eyes and dragging her bunny by the ear.

"Oh goodness Pixy. I didn't mean to wake you. Your Mum just gave me a surprise that's all. Come on I'll tuck you back in."

Sheila scooped Sulamith up and carried her up the stairs beaming. As they disappeared up the stairs Sulamith asked, "Did my mum say 'Boo' very loudly?"

Sheila chuckled, "Gosh you're a sweet girl. We'll tell you in the morning."

Evan gave me a questioning look, "No rat?" he asked.

"No rat," I smiled. "I hope you weren't hoping to be the one to tell her but ... it came up, and I let drop that I'm pregnant."

Evan laughed, "No. I don't mind. It was worth it actually, just to hear the commotion."

Chapter 26

It happened just four days later. Sulamith was asleep, Sheila was at the garden centre clearing out the office, and it was one of those long, hot, still, summer evenings that you can feel clinging to your skin. It was Friday night and neither Evan nor I had anywhere to be the next day, so we were sitting in the grass in the back garden, enjoying the quiet, the warm air and the night scented blossoms, just talking and making-out a little, when something caught our eyes high in the oak tree at the back of the lot. Then we heard the leaves rustle and something started to flash in the last rays of the setting sun. Crimson and gold. Then a voice, a rich resonant voice, "Aw shit! Crap-olla."

Evan looked at me and whispered, "Crapolla?"

I shook my head and said one word, "Raphael."

We sat and waited to see if the angel would come out of the tree on his own but after a few minutes, he was still up there. "Does he think that we don't know he's there?" Evan asked me in a low voice.

"This is Raphael we're talking about. He can be ... a bit ... different. Who knows what's going through his mind," I said.

"Raph?" I called out. "We know you're up there. You're molting all over the yard." I turned to Evan and whispered, "He really hates it when I tell him he's molting."

And sure enough, Raphael came crashing to the ground.

I'll be honest. I wasn't prepared to see Raphael. Telling Evan about the things that had happened to me had been hard enough, but there was something so immediate about Raphael—there still is, there always will be—and that day it brought the past too close for comfort, and I couldn't help but remember that the last time I'd seen Raphael I had been naked and in his arms. Seeing him also sent a shot of apprehension through me because there was always a chance that Raphael was there because he thought that Sulamith and I needed protection, and that thought set my heart pounding. But if he was only curious … ? I'd asked to be left alone, but did I have a right to keep him away? I had just started to feel like the collection of broken pieces I'd been gathering up for the past three years would fit together to make a whole and functioning heart. I had them all in one place, and I could see where they fit, but having Raphael there in front of me opened parts of me that I'd thought were gone, not just closed off.

"I'm not molting. You *know* that. Angels don't *molt*," he said with a toss of his head that was oddly calculated, yet nonchalant.

Evan and I stood. I looked Raphael up and down. He was wearing factory distressed dark blue jeans, a pair of skater sneakers, and a T-shirt with 'These aren't the droids you're looking for' written across the front. His golden hair was a little on the long side, but tousled to angelic perfection. His face, like mine, was older now, refined, with layers of history in his eyes, and, as always, a longsword hung at his side. "Well if you're not here to molt, what are you doing? I asked not to be followed," I said to him.

"Rhiannon?" he said, sounding uncertain and maybe a little hurt, and my old name on his lips carried with it the echoes of another life.

Our eyes met and I endured his golden gaze for a moment before looking down, but that didn't feel right either, so I looked back into his eyes, "Just ... Call me Krista, okay. I don't go by ... *that name* ... anymore," I said softly to him. I held his gaze and this time it was he who looked away, turning to Evan, and I watched as Raphael sized him up. Evan to his credit stood straight and didn't look away. "Raph, I think you remember Evan. Evan, this is Raphael," I said into the heavy summer night.

"Water Fay," Raphael commented. "Reminds me of Lugh."

"I guess he is a little like Lugh," I said, irked by the comparison to my father and added, "But only superficially. Underneath they're completely different."

I could see Evan's irritation as well as he stood next to me. He took my hand then said to Raphael, "We still don't know why you're here." His tone wasn't hostile, just serious.

Raphael sighed, "Fenna ... She went to visit her parents a few weeks ago and she saw you, by the lake. She was so upset. She just wanted me to see if you were alright. I caved and told her I'd check on you. We've all ... missed you. Nobody blamed you for leaving after everything that happened. It's just that for some of us, we have a sore spot in our hearts around the place where you used to be. I don't want to be shut out anymore. I just ... need to know how you are."

He looked directly into my eyes again and I could see that old strange love there still, and I couldn't deny my own love for him. I turned and buried my face against Evan's chest for a moment and let the steadiness of his heartbeat remind me that I was safe now. I felt his hands on my back silently reassuring me, then I relented and turned back to Raphael, "I'm getting better. Every day I'm a little less fragile. I'm not all the way there, but I'm beginning to feel like maybe someday I might be. There are some things that I'm not really prepared to face yet, but sometimes I *think* about facing them, and it isn't so hard."

Raphael nodded, "It's just, good to see your face and ... hear your voice." A tear trickled down his cheek.

"Oh Raphael!" I breathed, and flung my arms around him and his massive arms and wings closed around me and he pressed his mouth to the top of my head. We stayed like that for several heartbeats before I pulled away. He loosened his grip and I turned and ran into the house to try to catch my breath and get my composure back. I'd gotten to a point where, if I could keep from crying then I didn't have to try to stop, and stopping was still so much harder. I took a few deep breaths and pressed the heels of my hands into my eyes. I was standing near the screen door and I heard Evan say to Raphael, "I'll just give her a couple of minutes."

"It's fine. Just let her be. It's okay if she doesn't come back out," Raphael answered.

I peeked around the door frame and looked at Evan and Raph standing there talking and the scene would have almost have looked normal if it weren't for Raphael's wings. Strange, but I was pretty sure that they were wearing the same jeans, although Evan's feet were bare and he was was wearing a good celadon linen button up shirt that was hanging unbuttoned and untucked in the heat, showing his lean swimmer's muscles, which completely changed the look. He wasn't *that* much shorter than Raphael, but I was used to Evan being the tallest person in the room. Raphael, for all his quirkiness, was pretty easy company, as long as I wasn't there setting him off, and while there was definitely a 'worlds colliding' feel to the image of Evan and Raph standing there chatting comfortably in the garden, it made it easier to go back out. I smoothed my hands over the old red India cotton sundress that used to be Sheila's then headed back out.

Evan looked at me, concerned, "You okay?" he asked, rubbing the back of my arm.

I looked up at him, smiled hesitantly and took his hand. "I think so," I said, then took a deep breath and asked Raphael, "Tell me, since you're here ... How is everybody?"

I wasn't sure that I wanted to know, or maybe I was afraid of what I might hear, or that hearing might hurt. But it was like going to see Legend that day with Evan two years ago. I had to try.

Raphael's beautiful face softened as he looked at me and he motioned to the porch, "Let's sit," he said and lowered himself into a slouchy wicker chair. He tucked his feet up and neatly ordered his wings with an unconscious grace that had always fascinated me. I sat on the loveseat next to Evan, looked at Raphael, and waited for his answer. I must have looked pretty worried because he said, in the most reassuring tone I'd ever heard from him, "It's all okay. Honestly. Everybody is fine. There's *nothing* happening that you need to worry about."

I smiled and nodded, not feeling very sure of myself but appreciating his reassurance all the same.

He sighed, "After the war ended I don't think that anyone realized as fully as they should have how much things still needed to change but, when you walked out on us it sent a huge message." I watched Raphael's face as his mind fell back in time those two and a half years, to the night I ran away. Emotions flitted across his face. He looked at me for a moment before going on and he smiled a smile that was both sad and amused, wry and self-deprecating. "Leaving was the best thing you could have done," he said shaking his head. "Even at the time I knew it but ... that night when Nimue snuck into my room through the window, shook me awake and told me you had run, was probably one of the hardest nights of my life. Definitely up there with believing you had died in the house fire. Nimue, Liam and I left that night and went to Gwydion's house in the city. We didn't know where else to go, or exactly what to do. Neither Nimue or Liam wanted the burden of monarch. They had committed themselves to one another and, without you there, they were the obvious next in line. Together they would have had the support of the people. They were the children of the revolutionaries who had conceived *you*. It would have been fitting in a way, but they had grown up with the pressure of knowing that some day they would be forced to live lives of obligation and responsibility and they didn't want it for themselves. Liam had already had a taste of it, and Nimue was already pregnant and she certainly didn't want it for their child, so their only real choice was to head up another revolution. It was wise of you to leave that letter with her, and the circlet. The morning after you left she stood on a platform in the centre of the market square in the city, with Liam there beside her, and me as her body guard, holding your circlet in her hand, and she read your letter out to the people and told them how much your wishes meant to her. There were riots. Liam and Nimue escaped to Fiannasmere. We did everything we could to uphold your wishes and eventually things turned around. Even the most staunch traditionalists couldn't look at what had happened to your life and see the validity of maintaining a royal family. It's meant changes, mostly good, but change can be hard too ..." Raphael shrugged. "But closer to home, Thaylum ended up running in the election. He's the head of the new council. He and White Feather have two more children. Brian is Captain of the army. My parents patched things up, had another baby. She'll be the last though. For a year after things settled down I flew. I searched for leagues and asked the people I encountered on my journey if they had seen any angels," he shook his head with finality. "The angels are gone." He flexed his wings as if the thought made him uncomfortable. "But interestingly, so are the humans. I couldn't find any full blooded humans anywhere outside of Nova Britannia. So I flew home but I couldn't settle anywhere. The place is rife with bad memories. I spent some time with Liam and Nimue at Fiannasmere, they live there permanently and they're very happy there, but I got bored. I was pretty restless and I ended up at the Broad River stronghold." Raphael stopped abruptly and gave me a conflicted look then blushed.

I had never seen Raphael blush before but I'd heard, earlier, the tone in his voice when he'd explained what he was doing in my garden. I'd heard the name he'd spoken and the softness in his voice when he'd spoken it. "Fenna." He wouldn't risk *my* anger for just anyone, but if he'd fallen in love ...? If someone who he couldn't say no to had asked him to find out how I was ... ? I put two and two together so fast that I had Raphael blushing even harder. "That's where you met Fenna isn't it? You're in love with her aren't you," I said smiling.

He smiled and looked up and away from my face and, trying to quell the urge to grin like a complete idiot, he chuckled lightly, shook his head with a look of sheepish pride on his face and turned an even deeper shade of pink. "Yeah ... I met Fenna. She was there doing an apprenticeship with the healers," he said finally, looking back into my eyes and I smiled at him again. "Magically speaking she was a bit of a late bloomer but nowadays she's as fay as you are." He was silent for a few heartbeats, "I finally understand how you must feel. She's my wife. I would never betray her, I love her like I never imagined I would love anyone, and I know now why you would have found Rowan so completely irresistible, Fenna is a lot like him. But at the same time, I still love you. I always will, but I don't feel all that grief and conflict over it anymore. And, just so you know, you look amazing," he tagged on with an irrepressible grin then winked at Evan.

I shook my head then asked, "What about Leif?"

"He's doing ... Better. We don't see a whole lot of him, but when we do he seems like he's getting clear of things."

I nodded. I hadn't been sure what sort of news Raphael would have had for me of Leif and I'd been half afraid to hear.

Raphael continued, "He was one of the loudest to defend your right to be left alone and he's gonna be pretty pissed off with me when I tell him I came here. I think that he understood best in some ways that you ... *needed* to be away from us."

I nodded slowly before commenting, "*You're* obviously still comfortable here."

"Yeah," Raphael chuckled. "I can't really hang out in this world much unless I'm at a costume party but I still like to visit now and again."

Then a look of impatience flitted across his face, "But enough about me. What have you been doing with yourself these last two and a half years?"

I sighed, "Not much really. I helped Sheila run the garden centre. We sold it recently. I take care of Sulamith ... I ..." I faltered then took a breath and said what I meant. "I was falling apart when I left your world. I felt ... no, I didn't *feel*. My life *was*, shattered. There were pieces everywhere. So I suppose I've been mending for the last two and a half years. I need time and space and love and patience to do that, and I have those things here." I leaned into Evan's side as I spoke and held onto his hand more tightly. "No magic in the world can give them to me."

Raphael nodded and was silent for a moment before asking, "What about Sulamith? How is she?"

"She's," I smiled and paused trying to find words that were adequate. "Oh, I don't know ... She's wonderful. She's sleeping right now but if you're quiet I can take you up and you can have a peek at her."

"Yeah, I want to see her," Raph nodded.

So I took him up stairs and cracked her door open so that the light fell on her face and you could see her dark curls and her smooth, still baby perfect cheek and brow. Raphael gazed at her for several minutes before we headed down to the kitchen where Evan had put on a pot of tea. Sitting at the table I pushed one of the most recent photo albums that Sheila had put together over to Raphael and he flipped through it, seeing little snapshots of our life. He stopped and stayed at a picture of Sulamith, fingering the image lightly and gazing softly at it. "She's a beautiful little girl," he said. The picture was of Sulamith with a watering can at the nursery smiling in rubber boots and mud pants, her hair in wispy little curls around her face and her dark eyes sparkling. "She's perfect," Raphael went on. "I can see so much of both you and Rowan there, and her eyes, it's like he's looking out through her eyes."

"Raphael ... don't," I said placing my hand on his arm. I didn't want him to push me past that point that could be difficult for me to come back from.

He nodded and stopped. He looked at me silently weighing what to say next. Eventually he sighed, "I'm going to go, but ... I want you to know, if you ever decide to come back, even just for a day, we all meet at the castle in the city on the winter solstice. Everyone is there and we made a pact to keep it going. It was Liam's idea. If you ever want to come ... you could bring your family ..." he trailed off.

"I ... I'll think it over. I really can't make any promises. The idea of being back there still ..." I shook my head unable to go on.

Raphael stood. He bent and kissed the top of my head, headed for the back door and out into the garden. I followed as far as the doorway and raised my hand. He turned and raised his hand in return and I could see that it hurt him to leave, and then he winked out of sight.

Chapter 27

I stood in the doorway and placed my hand on the wood frame, trying to let the feel of the paint under my fingers eclipse everything else, but failing. Evan had followed me to the door. He'd been quiet during most of the encounter with Raphael, not saying much beyond what was required for the sake of manners, but now he took my hand and turned me to face him. "Oh no," he said softly, his eyebrows drawing together in concern. "No no," he whispered, then, "Shh, shh, shh. Don't cry."

He gathered me up in his arms for a time then carried me up the stairs. He wiped away my tears and held me until I was calm, then made love to me until I'd almost forgotten that I'd been sad. We lay there in the dark with the window open, Evan running his fingers along the bare skin over my spine.

"He's something else ... Your angel," Evan told me.

I smiled in the dark, "You sound like Rowan when you say that. Rowan always used to tell me that Raphael was 'my angel'."

* * *

I was in the front garden with Sulamith the next morning taking the dead heads off the rose bushes and pulling weeds from the border. Puttering around really, and breathing in the garden. Letting the plants, trees and sun recharge me, so to speak. I was relishing the long stretch of days, months, and years I had ahead of me to really figure myself out. It was warm but not hot, with a light cloud cover. I love days like that because the light from the sun is diffuse and it makes the plants and flowers look like they're glowing. It lends a surreal quality to everything. I would smile and laugh every time Sulamith crept into the plants again to pop out and try to make me jump, her face glowing, happy and bright in the frame of her dark hair. Evan came out onto the porch and sat on the steps with his mug of tea and another one for me. It's an almost tactile memory. The clingy feel of the moist morning air on my skin, the hot mug in my hands, thyme ground cover under my bare feet releasing its sent. I sat next to Evan on the steps and leaned against his shoulder as Sulamith called out, "Mummy look! A banana slug! He's a bery handsome slug. We could call him Herman!"

I could hear Evan chuckling under his breath, doing his best not to let Sulamith hear him as she removed 'Herman' from the flower bed and off to the slug garden (the wild patch next to the shed), all the while talking to the slug.

"Who's she talking to?" Sheila asked coming out onto the porch, then heading down the steps and starting her own half conscious perusal of the garden, pulling a weed here and plucking a dead blossom there.

"Herman the banana slug," Evan said smiling.

"That girl," Sheila smiled, shaking her head.

"That's what you get when you raise a little girl in a house with a garden fairy and a hippie," Evan said chuckling.

"You don't think that it has anything to do with all the Beatrix Potter and Wind In the Willows you read her?" I asked him, raising an eyebrow.

"There's probably a chance," Evan admitted, still smiling.

Chapter 28

These were very domestic years. Our baby boy arrived in the early spring. Toby was the name that we finally settled on. He was a plump, mellow, wonderful baby. So obviously Evan's with his copper tinged hair. We all enjoyed him so much and Sulamith was so happy to have a sibling. She asked every day, "Mummy, when will he be old enough to play with me?" and it seemed like no time until he was crawling and then walking after her. In the moments between chasing kids and doing laundry I learned how to knit and make soap. I made ointments and balms and maintained a little table at the farmer's market that was held every weekend by the lake. I encouraged Evan to edit the love letters that he had written me and submit them to a publisher. In this day and age no one gets famous off of poetry, but for a literature teacher it was a very big deal, and it meant a lot to both of us. He was eventually promoted to the head of his department at the college and then a year later he secured a very good position at one of the universities. For our first anniversary Evan bought me a writing desk and reams of good quality writing paper and a box of good pens.

They were sweet years filled with love and purpose. Neither Evan nor I could take that time for granted. The only major trauma of those years took place the day Sulamith discovered that Evan wasn't her biological father, but even that was a cloud with a silver lining.

Now, I've never really had friends in the world where I live now. There was Evan, but that's more than friendship now. I think of Sheila as a mother, and Audrey was almost like a grandmother so really, when it boils right down to it I have more family than friends. I haven't had many close relationships with the people of this world, except for Tammy.

Left to my own devices I'm not sure that I would have ever become friends with Tammy, we're very different, but when I came back to this world and moved in with Sheila, Tammy and her husband Brent had just bought the house across the street, and moved in with their six month old baby girl. Tammy saw this as a sign that she and I were meant to be friends, and god was she persistent—I think that Sheila encouraged her. I was still an emotional train wreck back then, but she would show up on Sheila's doorstep and say brightly, "Coffee's on." Standing there looking at me with her big brown eyes and Sophie on her hip. I was usually so dazed that I would just follow her back to her place and politely sip coffee while she prattled away to me about the renovations they were planning for the house. I understood how she felt though. There *is* something quite wonderful about spending your days with a tiny baby. They are magical creatures, but it can be very wearing too and I think that for her it was nice to have someone who understood that close by to say, "That s a nice shade of green," or, "Skylights would be great there."

I think that Sheila must have told Tammy just enough about me that Tammy didn't seem to expect too much, but the real saving grace in the relationship is that Tammy and I are very similar mothers. We were then and we still are. For different reasons of course. Tammy, raised by an alcoholic father and a depressed chain smoking mother, wanted for Sophie everything that she herself had been denied. Security, warm arms around her, a healthy home, to wake up in the night safe and snug not cold and lonely. She had studied to become a chartered accountant—she's very good—then married the most emotionally stable, good natured, guy she could find. I on the other hand wanted for Sulamith what my parents had given me. I had slept in my parent's bed until I was four and even after that if I woke, cold or scared in the night, I would pad into their room, snuggle down between them, and let their warmth lull me back to sleep. Of course I wanted that feeling of love and safety for Sulamith and Toby.

So Tammy and I would sit around at her place breastfeeding and talking about the best way to wash cloth diapers. It was good for me. It got me out of my own head and Tammy, nine years older than me, never saw my age as a drawback, unlike some of the mothers at the playground who always seemed to give me wide berth. As the girls got older the relationship evolved. Tammy started working again and she could, for the most part, work from home with Sophie there, but she needed a day a week free to see clients so I arranged my schedule so that one day a week Sophie could come spend the day with Sulamith and I, and Sulamith in return would spend a day with Tammy and Sophie. I was fine with this. Sophie was sweet and easy to have around, and Sulamith spent her day in Tammy's warm, comfortable, safe, house eating organic applesauce and homemade cookies. It gave Tammy a day to see to business and it gave me a blessed peaceful day alone. Sulamith was right across the street and Tammy knew how paranoid I could be. She would leave her living room curtains open so that I could see them if I looked across, and I had a baby monitor with a good range that I could turn on any time I felt worried. In some ways my friendship with Tammy was very close, but it really did centre around our daughters. It was interesting to see how exposure to a different family was affecting Sulamith. The influences were all good. They gave her a different perspective. She would come home to me saying things like, "Dere was a sale on bananas at Super Store so Tammy made lots of banana bread," and I would send Sophie home telling Tammy things like, "Shhh, if you listen, you can hear the roses growing."

Tammy always says that if Sophie grows up to have an imagination, that she'll give me all the credit. Sophie and Sulamith were then, and still are best friends. They rarely fight, but one day early spring, a four and-a-bit years after we'd first met, Tammy brought Sulamith home to me in tears. Destitute, inconsolable, tears.

Of course we were on our feet in an instant as Sulamith stood there sobbing, tears running down her cheeks. It wasn't as if she didn't cry sometimes. She was a child. Children cry. They skin their knees, they make confusing upsetting mistakes, they have all kinds of reasons to cry and Sulamith was no different. Usually a hug and a kiss and a little talk was all that she needed to set things right, but this time I could tell that it was worse. I'd never seen her so upset and my heart lurched. Tammy and Sophie were in the doorway behind her and Tammy looked nearly as upset as Sulamith as she said to us, her voice laden with remorse, "I'm so sorry. It's all my fault. Sophie told Sulamith that Evan's not her dad. It really is my fault. Brent and I were just talking, we thought Sophie was sleeping. I didn't know she'd overheard."

My instinct was to rush to Sulamith and put my arms around her, hold her to me, and try to make everything okay, but Evan got there first. He scooped her up so that her head was resting on his shoulder, turned to me and said in a calm voice and with an expression of absolute conviction and re-assurance on his face, "It's okay. I've got this," and he turned and headed up the stairs with Sulamith in his arms still crying like her little heart was broken.

I turned to Tammy who again began to stammer apologies. I motioned her to come in and said to Sophie, who had big confused tears dripping down her face as well, "It's okay Soph, you didn't do anything wrong. Why don't you go play with Sulamith's toys for a few minutes while I talk to your mum?" She nodded and headed over to the toy box in the corner. I looked at Tammy and sat down on the chesterfield beside her, deftly sliding Toby from my hip to my lap. I could tell that Tammy wanted to explain so I let her.

"I really wouldn't ever have said anything about this in front of Sophie." Tammy started, "Brent and I were just talking while we were getting ready for bed last night. Sophie had been in bed for about an hour, I thought she was sleeping and Brent can be a bit clueless sometimes. He said, 'It's nice that Krista and Evan got back together. They seem happy.' then I told him, 'They've been friends for a long time but it's only been romantic for the last couple years.' and Brent's response was, 'Oh, I thought that Sulamith was his and that they'd broken up?' and then I told him, 'No, Krista was with someone else back then. Evan isn't Sulamith's father.' and Brent said, 'Oh. Shows what I know.' and that was it. We weren't trying to be mean or gossipy. I would never have said that in front of Sophie, and then today out of the blue Sophie blurted it out while they were playing."

"It's okay," I told her. "It really is. I should have talked to Sulamith about this sooner. The truth is that I haven't been sure how to tell her about her biological father. Losing him was hard and Evan has been a part of her life since she was so little that she doesn't really remember a time without him. Talking about it isn't easy even now, and I don't want to upset her or confuse her even more by crying in front of her." But I was strangely very calm at that moment.

Tammy nodded then told me, "You know, when I first met you, you seemed like the slightest bump would shatter you. I can't believe how much you've changed."

"You and Sophie have always made me feel very safe and welcome. It's gone a long way to helping me feel like I'm not going to shatter."

* * *

Sheila came home just as I was saying goodbye to Tammy and I asked her if she could keep tabs on Toby for a bit as I left them together then crept quietly up the stairs. I could hear Evan's voice. For the record, Evan has a great voice. It's expressive and flexible, a perfect teacher's voice. A perfect bedtime story voice. A perfect voice to hear when you feel down, and I could hear him sitting with Sulamith, talking to her and setting everything right. I sat there on the stairs and let his voice work its magic on me too.

"Shh, shh, shh. I'm not going anywhere."

Then tiny little hiccupy sobs.

"Sophie was confused. I'm your dad, and I'd never leave I love you far too much to ever want to be away from you." Then, "Shh, shh, shh," again and, "I love you, I would never leave."

I could hear her little sobs gradually slowing down, then Evan asked her, "Do you know what makes me your dad?"

I could make out her squeaky hiccupy little,"Uh-uh," and picture her shaking her head and looking at Evan with wide curious eyes.

"It's because I love you, and I love your mum, and everything about both of you. And I want to be here for you and do all of those things that dads do, like taking you to the aquarium, tucking you in at night, reading to you, and kissing your owies better. But do you know something? Something that makes you kind of special?"

"No, what?" went Sulamith's tiny five-year-old voice.

"You have *two* dads."

"I do?"

"Mm hm. Remember when your mum explained to you how she and I love each other so much that a baby started growing inside her?"

"Mm hm," went the little voice.

"Well, a long time ago when your mum was a bit younger than she is now, I was very much in love with her, but I was confused too, like Sophie was today, and I made a big mistake. I did, and said, something that hurt her feelings very badly and then I went away, and she met someone new. Someone who was very kind to her and who loved her very very much, and they loved each other so much that they made you," Evan paused for a moment. "But the world wasn't a very safe place for your mum back then and she was pregnant with you, so your father set out to make the world safe for you. Because that's how much he loved you, even though he'd never met you. He *did it* too. He made the world over so that you don't need to worry, and you and your mum are safe and sound, but something sad happened."

"What happened?" asked Sulamith.

"He was badly hurt and he died before he could come home to you."

"Like Audrey died?"

"Yes, like Audrey."

"Oh," she said, but there was a little edge of sadness in her voice.

"Do you know what his name was?" Evan asked her.

"Uh-uh, no."

"Rowan."

"Like my brother's middle name?"

"That's right."

"Is that why my Mum is sad sometimes?"

"Yes it is," Evan answered in a heavy voice. Then he said to her, "But you don't need to be sad. Your other dad, Rowan, he wouldn't want you to be. He did what he did so that you could grow up happy." Then Evan asked her, "Do you remember how I told you that I made a mistake a long time ago?"

"Mm hm."

"Well, do you remember what I said to you about mistakes when you put your fingers on the stove top after your mum said, 'Be careful, don't touch, it's hot it will burn you.' and it was very hot and it burned you and you cried?"

"Mm hm."

"Well, when I made my mistake and I hurt your mum's feelings, *my* mum, your Sheila, told me, she said, 'Evan your making a big mistake. Tell her you're sorry,' but I didn't listen and I went away and boy did it hurt. Even worse than your fingers. I cried for a long time. And you won't touch the hot stove again will you?"

"No."

"Well I learned from my mistake too and I won't ever leave your mum again. I love everything about her and everything that she loves, and that means you too. I want to stay with you and make sure that the the things that your other dad did to make you safe and sound don't go to waste. I'm never going to leave. I promise."

"Dad?" went the little voice.

"Mm hm?"

"I love you too."

I sat on the stairs and listened to Evan talk to Sulamith until her little world made sense again and she felt safe and secure, and when they were quiet I peeked my head over the top stair to look into her room. Evan was sitting on her bed with his long legs stretched out and his back against the headboard with Sulamith perched sideways on his lap, her head against his chest. I crept back downstairs to sit in the living room with Sheila, feeling like my heart was going to burst.

"Sulamith sure was upset when I came home. What happened? Is she alright?" Sheila asked from the rocker.

"Sophie told her that Evan isn't her father," I sighed. "Sheila, I've never seen her so upset but Evan is up there with her, putting her world back together for her even better than it was before and telling her all of the things that I've been too scared or confused to tell her ... I don't deserve him Sheila. I don't deserve you."

Sheila looked down at Toby, sitting in her lap playing with the seal toy that Rowan had carved for Sulamith years before, "You know, when I was younger I used to wonder why I could never attract a man who would stay, and why Evan was the only child I ever conceived. I was too busy being wild back then," she admitted in a wry tone. "I wasn't always careful. But at some point in my mid-thirties I accepted that *this* was my life and that it wasn't half bad, and when you showed up on my doorstep four and a half years ago I realized that if I'd had those things, a husband, more children, that I wouldn't have been in a position to do for you what I've been able to do, and I would have been disappointed. I would have regretted it. I'm happy Krista. So happy. This is how I want my life to be."

"It is so strange isn't it? How life plays out," I said, then smiled. "I'm going to go start dinner."

* * *

By the time Sheila joined me in the kitchen I had pizza dough kneaded and rising in the corner and a pile of chopped mushrooms growing on the cutting board.

"Somebody is feeling tired and cuddly," she said, gently passing the heavy toddler into my arms. I settled with him on the love seat at the end of the kitchen, the one that Rowan had sat me on and comforted me on in another life. Evan walked in a few minutes later looking emotionally full. Love struck, sleepy, bewildered, all of those things and more. He sat down next to me and played with a little foot for a moment, then took my free hand and turned to me, smiling a soft smile that made me heartachy in a good way, and said. "She's sleeping." Then, "She thought that if I wasn't her dad that it meant I would leave. I love her so much Krista, I thought my heart was going to break when she came in crying like that," he said to me then got up, opened the fridge, took out the mozzarella and got down the cheese grater.

* * *

I didn't talk to Sulamith about Rowan very often, but every year on her birthday I told her that he loved her. It seemed to be enough. Sometimes I felt like I was betraying him by not sharing more with her, but I also knew that he wouldn't want sadness hanging over her head either, and since she was such a happy child I let the past be.

Chapter 29

Between Sheila and I the garden ran riot ... just like the kids. They are very much their own people. From birth Toby had my talent for frying electronics and Sulamith was so quirky and stubborn that we decided to avoid entirely the whole topic of school. I know that it's screwy logic, but Evan figured that if we just didn't send them to school then he couldn't feel rankled if they dropped out. It worked out for us. Sulamith was a voracious reader from the start and, though her education might have been balanced a little too far towards poetry and art, by the time she was fifteen she had found a goldsmith willing to teach her the trade. She set up a workshop in the garage and was selling her own jewellery designs on her online shop by the time she was seventeen. Toby on the other hand is determined to do his PhD in marine biology. I remember sitting on the beach when he was about nine and commenting to Evan that, between him and my father, Toby had more water flowing through his veins than blood. We can't go on vacation without him somehow managing the situation to ensure that we go someplace with good surfing. He started doing community college courses when he was thirteen because he had already finished the biology twelve curriculum.

And Evan and I? It is true that some things just keep getting better. But I think of Rowan often. You can't love someone and not carry it with you for the rest of your life. In the morning Evan nearly always wakes at some obscene hour to go the the pool and swim. He kisses my sleepy head just before he leaves and as I wake on my own I let myself remember Rowan for a moment or two, and how that moment, just as you realize you are awake, was the moment that he had wanted to share with me for the rest of his life. That moment will always be his.

* * *

S ulamith didn't come out and ask me about the past until just after her eighteenth birthday. She grew into such a pretty girl. She let her hair grow long in dark glossy spirals. She's petite but not so tiny as me, and she always smiles and she always looks like she's up to something. But at eighteen suddenly she was pensive. Her impulsivity was dimmed. She sighed long complicated sighs an moped for perhaps the first time in her life. Something was bothering her and I couldn't put it down to too much Lana Del Rey. It was raining that day and she wandered, unwilling to settle on a task, read a book, or go hang out with Sophie. I watched her climb the stairs and heard the creak of her feet on the boards as she made her way up to the attic. I finished washing the carrots and green beans that I had brought in from the garden for dinner and then climbed the stairs after her. I knocked on the door to her attic bedroom. She had decorated it with William Morris wallpaper and old carved oak furniture. A face looked out from a pattern of carved oak leaves on her dresser. She was sitting on her bed looking out into the branches of the cherry tree outside her window. She was dressed in short jean shorts and a black spaghetti strap tank-top. She looked so gloomy.

"Hey," I sat down on the end of her bed and tucked my feet under me.

"Hey," she said back, without enthusiasm. Then looked at me for a few minutes as if she were seeing me as not 'just

Mum', but as a person separate from herself. "Mum, why do you have all of those tattoos?" she asked.

I pressed my lips together and looked down my right arm. There were morning glories blooming over my bicep and shoulder from the day I'd told Evan what had happened to me while we'd been apart, and little strawberry blossoms that had appeared the night I'd conceived Toby. "I guess I have them because they mark me as different."

"I feel ... different," she murmured and a tear dropped down her cheek. "How is it that you've managed to be different and yet, have a life and fall in love and all that?"

"It hasn't always been easy," I admitted.

"Tell me about it?" She looked at me. "Why did you leave Dad and get knocked up with me?"

"I didn't leave him. He left me," I told her. I hadn't realized that all that time she'd interpreted things that way. "I left Vancouver after he was already gone. He was afraid of doing the wrong thing with me. He thought that I was too young. He was afraid to admit that he was in love with me. We were young and foolish. But I don't regret meeting Rowan, your father, and ... *he* loved me *because* I'm different." I took a deep breath, "I haven't shared this with you, and I'll be honest and tell you that I don't have a concrete reason for having held it back. I've just been going on instinct and I just want you to be happy ... except that I can see that lately, you aren't happy. I don't know if this will make you happy, but you are certainly old enough to know. *I* was eighteen when I found out."

"Found out what?" Sulamith looked at me with interest.

"Hold out your hand," I told her, and I reached out and let my magic flare so that the rainbow flickers travelled along my skin and called to the amber and gold magic that I'd been able to sense building in Sulamith over the last year.

Her fingers shook and her lip quivered as the amber lights sparked and leapt from her skin and little golden stars glowed in her hair.

"Look," I motioned and turned my head to look at her in the mirror of her dresser. She turned to look at the reflection, her dark eyes opening wide, then looked back at me, watching the flickers of magic that I was drawing out of her. I knew that she could feel it. I knew exactly what she was feeling.

"What the hell Mum?" she whispered, incredulous.

"When I was seventeen your Dad kissed me, and then worried that he had made a mistake. He left and I was angry and hurt and depressed. I left Vancouver. I left this world and went back to the one I came from. The world that *you* came from. I'm not human in the way that the people of this world think of it. Neither is Evan's father. I think, when I look back, that might have been a part of why we had such a hard time making it work in this world. I didn't plan on leaving ..." I reached out my hand and wrapped my fingers around hers and let her see my memory of meeting her biological father for the first time. Of waking up in his arms on horseback. Just a flash ... a taste. "Do ... do you want to know everything?" I asked her.

"Will knowing change me? Will it, you know ... be a 'life altering experience'?" she asked with a 'jaded teenager' roll of her eyes.

"Probably. Maybe not. I don't know ..." I shrugged. "I think that ... I might be ready for you to know and, in any case," I smiled at her, "I think that you can handle it. But I'll warn you, it's sad."

"I always knew it would be sad. But ... I'm not a kid any-more. Would you tell me?"

I nodded. "Yeah." I reached out and caught her fingers again. "Words aren't always enough. This is the only way I

know how to tell you now. Close your eyes," I told her, and I
let the memories flow.

I realized, as I relived my life through my daughter's eyes,
that I had managed to hold on to the beauty of what I had
experienced, and let go of so much of the ugliness. The hard,
dark, feelings were still there, woven into the tapestry of my
story, but they only served to make the brilliant moments
that much more brilliant. All of those beautiful moments were
gathered in one place, like the shards of my heart, until they
made a perfect whole.

It took only moments, that wild magic. Only moments to
share a lifetime, and Sulamith looked back at me stunned
when I withdrew my hand from hers. She took a long shuddering breath and wiped her cheeks with the backs of her
hands. She was quiet for a long time and I sat with her and we
watched the rain fall on the top of the cherry tree. "When I
was nine I woke in the night and I thought that I heard something. I assumed that it was you or Dad so I went downstairs.
There was an angel in the dining room looking at our photographs. He was wearing jeans and a leather vest ... and sneakers. He smiled and said, 'Hey Sulamith. This is just a dream.
Go back to bed okay sweetie?' So I just went back to bed. I've
thought that it was a dream all these years. But it wasn't, was
it?"

"No. It wasn't a dream. Raph has been sneaking in here to
steal pictures for your grandmother for years now. I catch him
sometimes too."

"You had *sex* with him?" she gave me a look.

I chuckled but didn't blush, "Yes, but he's married to your
aunt now so we can leave that in the past."

She nodded and then another batch of tears spilled over
her cheeks, "You really loved my ... Rowan ... my other dad.
You guys were like ... Epic."

"Love *is* epic. And I've been lucky. I've gotten to love some pretty amazing people ... like you."

"I always thought that you were just a runaway teenaged mom."

"Nobody is ever only and entirely *one* thing."

She nodded and looked down at her hands, gave a little half sob, half laugh of surprise at the little forget-me-nots scattered around the wrist of the hand I had been holding.

"Why have you stayed away from the other world? It looked so beautiful there," she looked back up at me.

"I know. It *is* beautiful, but without Rowan it just seemed so pale."

"But this world is terrible. I mean, have you watched the news lately?" she asked me in anguished confusion.

"I know. I know what you're getting at, but somehow in this world, where I have to struggle to see the beauty in life, it seems so much more important to try. Do you want to see it? The other world?"

Sulamith shook her head, "I don't know. I think that I need some time to ... let this sink in properly. This is too huge for my head." She placed her hands on her head and then began to cry in earnest. I put my arms around her and held her until she stopped and she was, for just a few minutes and for perhaps the last time in her life, my little girl.

"Mum?" she said eventually. "I love you."

"I love you too. Are you going to be okay?"

"Yeah." She sat up and stretched. "Yeah, but you have to take me outside and teach me how to use magic properly, 'cause if I'm different ... I'm just gonna run with it."

She smiled a small smile and I knew that she would be okay.

"Sure. Lets go now. And you have lots of time to think it over, but if you want to see where you were born I can take you on the winter solstice."

She nodded, "I'll think it over. Let's go outside."

Chapter 30

Sulamith didn't talk much over the next few months, about anything really. She dove into books and the rest of the time she was out in her workshop. She spent a couple of days at a gem show and then was in her workshop ten hours a day. "What's with Sulamith?" Toby asked me on a grey day in mid October. "I can't get her to hang out with me. She's turned into crabby hermit girl."

I looked up at Toby. He was growing so fast and at fourteen he had already hit the six foot mark. He'd been raiding his dad's boxes of old clothes. I'd have to tell him the history of the decrepit Pixies concert t-shirt that he was wearing. He'd get a kick out of it. I sighed, "You need someone to hang out with?"

"Well I just got Guardians of the Galaxy on blue ray and I can't get the machine to work ... But Sulamith always used to stay and watch movies with me even if she wasn't that interested. She said that she would be in to turn it on for me in twenty minutes, but that was over a half-an-hour ago. She's just totally forgotten. And even when she remembers she won't stay and watch movies with me anymore," Toby grumbled.

"Well, I know that I'm not as cool as Sulamith, but if we can get your Grandma to turn on the movie for us, I'll watch it with you."

Toby grinned, "I'll go get Grandma," and he bounded up the stairs with the combined volume and enthusiasm that only a six foot tall fourteen-year-old boy can manage.

* * *

"Ya know when you keep eating the popcorn even though you have lots of little popcorn bits stuck in your teeth and you don't actually want anymore popcorn but you're too lazy to go upstairs and floss anyway so you just eat more pop-corn 'cause it's not like it could get worse?" Toby asked after the credits had rolled.

I moved the popcorn out of his reach.

"Thank you," he said, then, "So what's up with Sulamith anyway?"

"I offered to take her to see her biological father's family and my extended family in December. I think that she feels a bit ... disconnected from the world lately."

Toby nodded, "I thought your family was all dead or some-thing mysterious like that?"

"My grandmother and my half siblings are still alive."

"So, have I got like ... cousins and shit?"

I raised an eyebrow at him, "Interesting turn of phrase Toby, but yes, you do have cousins."

"Can I come too?"

"Do you want to?"

"Fuck yeah! I mean ... That would be nice."

"I'd like it if you came," I told him.

"Then count me in."

"We won't leave without you," I smiled.

"Mum?" He fixed me with a serious look, "Is it your side of the family that fries computers and shi ... I mean, stuff?"

"I'm not completely sure, but I think so. Why?"

"Are we like, Star-Lord ... or something?"

I chuckled at the mental image, but I knew what he was getting at. His friends had gotten tired of his, 'Bet you I can fry your Iphone' trick fast. "We're not aliens sweetie, but ... yeah."

Toby nodded for a few thoughtful moments. "Cool," was what he said, but his tone wasn't flippant. He got up off the couch and headed up the stairs, then stopped and turned to me with a puzzled look, "So Mum I'm guessing that you *know* that Angel who raids my DVD collection and always insists that I'm dreaming?"

"Yeah that's Raphael." I shook my head, "I'll tell him that you know he's real the next time I see him."

"Thanks," Toby smiled, ran the rest of the way up the stairs and closed his bedroom door. Within moments thundering bass lines shuddered through the floor.

* * *

I hadn't actually gotten an answer from Sulamith as to whether she wanted to go, but about four weeks later she found me in my room. It was mid-morning. Evan was at the university, Toby at a course, and Sheila was in the back yard digging around in the dirt.

Sulamith looked skittish for a moment, like she'd bolt if I made any sudden movements, and then like that her posture changed and she took my jewellery box and sat with it cross-legged in the middle of my bed. This was an old habit of hers. It started when she was six and I had an unusual collection of jewellery.

"When I was little I used to take it for granted that all mothers had jewellery like this. It's only over the last few years that I've sort of wondered where it came from some-times." She lifted out the ruby set that Liam had given me and stared at it entranced.

"I have a dress that goes beautifully with that set if you'd like to try it on."

She looked at me like I was crazy—or a big dork—for a moment, and then she looked frightened. She looked back at the necklace. "Okay," came her timid reply.

"I'll be right back," I told her.

I'd had the dresses that I'd brought back with me specially packed by cleaners and Raphael had eventually brought me a couple more he'd thought that I would have rather kept. There were four in total. I opened the boxes with some hangers handy, and one by one hung the dresses so that Sulamith could see them. She fingered the cream silk dress and the red dress that had been one of Rowan's favourites. She smiled at the pink dress that I had worn the night Rowan had asked me to be his. "This one is like a Disney princess dress."

"I know. It screams Cinderella doesn't it?"

She smiled and nodded.

She walked back to the cream coloured dress, "This is the one that you wore with the rubies?"

"Yeah. My brother Liam gave me the rubies to go with it."

"If I try this dress on will you put on the dark blue dress?"

"Alright," I smiled and moved the other dresses to the closet.

We tied each other's laces and I clasped the rubies around her throat as she held her hair. She looked like a princess. "Would this be too fancy to wear on the winter solstice?" she asked as she stared into my mirror at her reflection.

"No, not at all, and I think that those rubies want to belong to you now."

Her hand rose to her throat and I wondered what she was thinking but I didn't ask.

"Will you wear that dress?" she asked me of the blue dress I was wearing.

"Sure. Are you telling me that you want to go?"

She nodded, "I made you something. Here put your sapphire necklace on." She rummaged in the pocket of the hoodie that was lying crumpled on my bed and pulled out a small velvet bag. "I was worried that I wouldn't be able to match the sapphires," she told me as she passed me the bag.

I pulled the drawstring loose and emptied the contents of the bag into my hand. She had made earrings to match the necklace Bronwen had given me so many years earlier. They were the perfect accompaniment. Every detail. "Sulamith, these are incredible! I can't believe how good you are at this. These would cost thousands in a jewellery store! I wouldn't be able to tell that they hadn't been made with the necklace as a set." I fastened the earrings and kept turning from the mirror and catching Sulamith's eyes. I could tell that she was pleased with herself. She was almost bouncing on the bed.

"Ever since the summer it's been like the stones and the metal are whispering to me and telling me what to do. Maybe later today I can show you some of the other pieces I've made?"

"I would like that. Can Toby come too? He's been missing you lately."

Sulamith looked troubled for a moment, "Does he know ...?"

"Not quite as much as you do," I paused then told her, "He thinks we're like Star-Lord only, not aliens. But he seems good with it so far."

Sulamith gave a snort of amusement, "I think that I'll have to sit down and watch that movie with him. I feel bad. I know he's been a bit lonely. I'll make it up to him ... and I won't tell him anything that I don't think you would," she added.

I smiled, maybe a little sadly, "I knew that you would be sensible if I showed you everything. Do you think that it was too much? Did I make a mistake?"

"No. Don't think that for a second Mum."

I took her hand.

* * *

When I came downstairs later that day Sulamith and Toby were on the couch watching Guardians of the Galaxy. Sulamith had a huge smile plastered across her face.

Chapter 31

Sheila had declined my offer to bring her with us, but Toby wouldn't let her stay behind. "No way Grandma. You gotta come too."

"That's alright Tobes, I'd just be a fifth wheel."

"Mum tell her that's not true!"

"Oh she knows how I feel about it," I commented and gave Sheila a look that told her that I knew exactly who would win.

Sheila looked to Sulamith for help and Sulamith just told her, "I'm not getting involved. Toby talked me into going to a *monster truck rally* with him last week. Do you really think that I can help you?"

"Toby really, I don't know these people. I don't want to be seen as an interloper."

"Grandma, you are the coolest grandma on the face of the earth. *Nobody* will mind, and you've already met some of these people anyway. I bet they *want* to see you."

After an hour and a half of Toby following her around the house she caved.

* * *

Although there had never been any question of whether Evan would go with us, I knew that for him it was perhaps a more daunting prospect. Would they compare him to Rowan? I hoped that they wouldn't. I hoped that they understood that after Rowan, any man that I became involved with would have been held to a very high standard and, as far as I was concerned, Evan met that standard. But the night before the winter solstice Evan said to me, "Look, I don't want you to think that I spend a lot of time dwelling on this, but I want you to know that ... if there is any such thing as an afterlife ... I would understand if you chose Rowan."

He looked into my eyes and I could see that he meant it and I could see just how much he must love me if he would give me up so that I could be happy with someone else. But I could never be truly happy without *him*, and I was furious. Not with him, but with myself for not making him understand just how much he meant to me sooner. "Evan Taylor. If there is any such bleeding ridiculous thing as an afterlife that forces me to choose between you and Rowan, then when I get to the gates I will stamp my foot and argue until they change the rules, and don't you *dare* believe that I can't do it! You and Rowan will just have to learn to share! I *love you* dammit!"

Evan looked so startled. He just stood there caught in the moment.

"So kiss me already!" I cried.

After fifteen years it's good to know that we still want to tear each other's clothes off sometimes

Chapter 32

I was walking along a path through the trees, dappled in sunlight. The air was warm and it tickled the bare skin of my arms and legs. I quickened my pace and looked ahead. I could see a little house in the woods, just down the slope and around the bend. Like a little house at the heart of a story. A place that lay in wait. I could feel morning coming, that undercurrent of wakefulness, and I pushed it aside and skipped lightly down the path and into the clearing. Rowan straightened, looked up at me and I danced into his arms as he caught me up laughing. I woke to the sound of his laughter.

* * *

Toby and Sulamith were fighting over the bathroom and I was glad that I'd gotten in there before either of them were awake. "Sulamith! You've been in there for over an hour. I need to shower too!" He started pounding on the door.

"Tobeeey! Stop it. That's not going to make me go faster it's just going to make noise! I'm trying to be fast but I have three feet of hair and I want it to look nice!" came Sulamith's shrill irritation, blessedly muffled by the bathroom door.

"Yeah well, someone ought to institute a hair tax!" Toby yelled.

"We do seem to have teenagers don't we?" Evan muttered as he adjusted his tie in the dresser mirror.

* * *

I told Toby that he could wear whatever he wanted so he wore a good shirt and tie, paired with Evan's old leather jacket, jeans without holes—he went to pains to point this out to me —and combat boots. We climbed into the car and sat in uncustomary silence as Evan drove us to Stanley Park. The way was so familiar. It was a strange thing as the feelings and memories mingled. We'd spent so many rainy afternoons at the Aquarium with the kids that driving to the park felt ordinary. For all of us. But this time we weren't going to the Aquarium.

Evan pulled into a spot and paid for the day's parking. We walked a little way down a tree-lined path. The weather was clear and mild and had been for days, saving us from having to contend with the rain and mud typical of a Vancouver December. When we were far enough along the path I looked at Sulamith and asked her, "Will you help me with this?"

She nodded and took my hand and I could feel her reaching for magic as lights and colours danced around us and I pulled us through into the other world.

I looked at Sulamith and she smiled, but I could tell how nervous she was. Evan and Sheila looked around in amazement and Toby whooped and yelled, "Holy shi ...cow! That was fff ... that was amazing!" He ran ahead then ran back, "Where are we?"

"This is the world where my parents were born."

He nodded, suddenly solemn, and walked with us more calmly as I pointed the way to the castle.

Could I approach a place that had once demanded so much of me without mixed feelings? Actually, I was surprised at how distant the knocked up teen-aged girl who had once ridden to this place on the back of a unicorn had become. But somehow, it wasn't me for whom this had become "the place that lay in wait." We came around a bend in the path and the castle came into view. Sulamith walked out ahead of us. I had made her a fitted cream velvet jacket to wear over the dress and her long dark ringlets hung against her tiny waist in vivid contrast. She had bought a pair of red suede ballet flats to go with the dress and I could see the ruby flicker of her feet at the hem of her dress as she out-distanced us. Evan looked at me for a panicked moment as she disappeared through the gates of the courtyard. "She'll be okay," I told him, but took his hand as much for my own comfort as for his.

We followed Sulamith through the gates and across the lavishly decorated courtyard, in through the castle doors and up the wide sweep of stairs, to the great carved doors where Sulamith stood looking in over the threshold at the throng within. I could almost see myself on Rowan's arm, walking into that room so many years ago. "It's alright," I told her, coming up behind her. "You can go in. I'll be right here."

She looked at me, her dark eyes full to brimming with something that I couldn't quite identify at first but then I saw it, hope and wonder and love and happiness, all of the things that I'd hoped she would have. "Go," I whispered. "I'm right behind you." And she stood tall and stepped into the great hall.

She went slowly, turning this way and that, looking around her in amazement. At the fairy lights and the ladies in their beautiful dresses. At the fairies who were strange and uncomfortable to look at as well as the ones who reminded her of home. She turned her head quickly and stared up at a tall angel and I saw her smile in profile for the briefest moment. There was hush as she advanced and I could see to the end of the huge hall where my brother and sister sat laughing at the table at the base of the huge fantastical Christmas tree. I saw them look up, and saw a girl of about seventeen with long ash coloured hair turn from her seat and lock her vivid blue eyes on Sulamith. The room was quiet. Another head turned and although I hadn't seen him in nineteen years, and he had been a small child then, I knew that it was Thaylum's oldest son Quinn. He too locked his eyes on Sulamith, and I wished for a moment that I could see her face. I had the funniest most heartbreaking feeling that I might have just lost my daughter to him. The girl with the ash coloured hair rose from her place looking at Sulamith, she could have been my twin. She was Nimue and Liam's daughter, I knew just looking at her. She stepped lightly and quickly across the room going to Sulamith and taking her hands so that coloured lights danced around them and I heard the other girl laugh as she drew Sulamith, who was smiling broadly now, further along into the great hall.

We had followed Sulamith partway into the room and as her cousin drew her further in I could see my sister. I could see Nimue's eyes searching for me where I stood, clutching desperately at Evan's hand. Nimue rose and started around the table towards me. "Go on," Evan looked down at me. "I'm right here too. I'm right behind you." He smiled that charming bone melting smile at me and I turned and ran to Nimue.

We almost smacked right into each other and I worried momentarily that I was holding her too tightly but then realized that if I was holding her as tightly as she was holding me then it was fine. She was sobbing uncontrollably and I could feel the rain start to fall and I pulled back saying to her and trying to wipe her face, "Don't cry. No no, don't cry," but my own tears fell so fast that I knew it was pointless to tell her not to cry so instead I drew in magic from all around me and turned her raindrops to cherry blossoms that rained down their petals all through the hall.

"Oh I'm so happy you're here, I'm so glad you've come, oh you came, you came," Nimue babbled over my shoulder then tried to pull me down the aisle to the table at the end.

"Just a moment," I smiled at her and drew her back to where Evan, Toby, and Sheila were standing together waiting, then we made our way up to where Sulamith was surrounded by a throng of cousins and the other grown children of the friends that I'd known during that life. A delicate looking punked out adolescent girl in jean shorts over black leggings covered in skulls sauntered up to Toby, "Hey! I'm Fionnuala. I'm your 'sort of' cousin. That's my dad." She pointed to a tall blond man, and then dragged Toby away and over to a group of kids about his age at one end of the table. I looked back at the blond man not sure for a moment if I was crazy, and then realized that I wasn't. Leif stood there in jeans and a blazer. He'd shaved and cut off his dreads. He smiled at me and he looked just like our dad. Raphael was standing and grinning at me too, with Fenna next to him. Thaylum was there smiling, looking from me to Sulamith to his son, who couldn't take his eyes off of her.

I was drawn up into so many hugs and must have spent an hour saying, "This is Evan," and then watching him get whole-heartedly hugged too, and then we were introduced to *so many* children. Leif and Raphael took care of Sheila all evening long. They told the story over and over again of how she had let them into her house without batting an eye and then cooked for them. Eventually room was made around the table and we sat. Sulamith was across the table from me sitting with Lilly, my niece, and they were flanked by Quinn, and on Lilly's other side, Raphael and Fenna's oldest son Gabriel. Toby was down a ways, still with Fionnuala. I could hear him laughing. I was sitting next to Evan in between Liam and Nimue. A meal was set out and wine was poured. There was a hush and Liam stood. "So ... I'm not going to drag this out because, well, he wouldn't want us getting all sad and ... He'd be here for the party anyhow ..." Liam looked down at me for the briefest moment, and it was the only time that evening, the only moment that I felt that old sorrow, then he raised his glass and said clearly, "To Rowan."

Glasses went up and the chorus went round. Tears fell, but eyes were bright. I looked across the table at Sulamith and she looked momentarily stricken. Our eyes met and I smiled sadly at her to show that I understood. She pressed her lips together and nodded to me in unspoken agreement as a tear escaped her lashes.

I sat next to Evan and we watched Lilly and Gabriel helping Quinn teach Sulamith to dance and they laughed and laughed together. She was so happy. We sat and talked with family and old friends, hearing their stories and catching up on life, and life had been good in Nova Britannia ... after I'd left.

"So strange to watch them isn't it? So very much of *us* in them and yet ... so very much their own selves," Fenna murmured later on, watching wistfully as our oldest children, the ones who had been born and conceived in the throes and wake of the war that had affected our own lives so dramatically, danced.

I watched, seeing a strange reflection of the past. Lilly looked so much like me. And Gabriel? Well, Fenna had always looked like a female version of Rowan and Gabriel was her son, but he looked like his father too ... like Raphael. In the same way that Sulamith was so obviously both my daughter and Rowan's. I would leave it up to her to discover that she and Quinn shared a great grandparent in the sylph line of the family, the way Rowan and I had in the Dryad line. That great great grandmother who was the source of my own and Nimue's and Quinn's deep blue eyes. "It's almost hard to look at them," I admitted, and it was.

"But they're happy Krista. So happy. They have everything that they should. This world is theirs. You and Rowan did that for them," Fenna told me earnestly.

I looked back at Fenna and she smiled and took my hand.

The day wore on. Afternoon had turned to evening and evening to night. It was time to go home. "Toby? It's time to go," I called.

"I'll call you tomorrow, I promise," Fionnuala reassured him with a smile as he got up from the table where they had been playing some kind of card game. Toby came and stood by Evan and Sheila. I looked to Sulamith who was still hovering next to Lilly. "Would it be okay ..." she paused and started over, "Would you mind very much if I stayed behind?" She looked into my eyes and I could see how much she wanted to stay.

"It's up to you," I told her. "You're too old to need my permission."

"That's, not so much what I was asking," she came close to me and rested her forehead against mine. "Will you be okay ... if I stay?"

I would and I knew it. I had Evan and Sheila to help me through, and a happy home to go back to. But there was no hiding the emotions that what she was asking brought up "I'll be okay," I whispered to her. "Stay."

"Mum?" She looked at me and somehow I knew that in those moments her childhood had truly ended. She said to me, "I'll be back on the weekend. I have a commission that I need to finish. I promised Sophie that I would spend the day with her at the art gallery. I can't just leave her in the dust. I'm not abandoning my life back home. I just want ... the best of *both* worlds." She looked confident as she stood before me.

I nodded and reached into my pocket and pulled out the chain that held the two rings that her father and I had worn ... once upon a time. I placed them in her hand and folded her fingers around them. "They want to be in this world. Keep them safe for me," I told her, and then turned. I took Evan's hand and started walking out of the hall. I turned and looked back and waved once, but I'd said my goodbyes and I had

promised that we would all be back by the next winter
solstice at the very latest, so it wasn't really goodbye.

As we walked to the spot near the car Toby prattled away
about his cousins and the friends that he had made that day
and I tried to think of what I was going to cook for dinner on
Sunday as I seemed to have roped myself into cooking for
Leif, his girlfriend, and their daughter Fionuala, as well as
Yuka and her partner. I pulled us through into the world that
was home and just as that world rematerialized around us a
unicorn, *my* unicorn, stepped out of the haze of magic. "Oh!" I
gasped, and then, "My friend!" The unicorn nudged my fingers
with its muzzle and I stroked its velvety coat. I motioned to
Toby and he slowly approached, looking like a very tall little
boy as his face lit up in the unicorn's lilac glow. He tentatively
stretched out his fingers. The unicorn snuffled against his
palm and nuzzled his cheek briefly. He smiled, a very happy
childlike smile, as he smoothed the silvery mane and ran his
fingers over the unicorn's neck. I looked over the unicorn's
back and caught Evan's eyes. I'd never seen his face so full of
wonder. I smiled, and he smiled back. The unicorn gave Toby's
face one last nuzzle and then stood in front of me for a
moment, "So you want to be in this world now?" I whispered,
looking up at the impossibly beautiful creature. It gave a
whinny of triumph and then reared up and galloped away, into
the woods.

"Well, I guess I've seen just about everything now," Sheila
murmured.

"Nah Grandma. We still gotta find Dragons," Toby grinned
at his Grandmother.

We got in the car. For several minutes Evan drove in
silence. Sheila was likewise quiet and Toby seemed to have
fallen asleep. Evan turned briefly to glance at the sleeping
teenager and then said to me, "So, Toby is dead set on going
to a month long surf camp in Tofino this summer, and

Sulamith ... well, I guess she can take care of herself. So I was thinking ..." he turned to Sheila, "Hey Mum, do you mind going to Tofino with Toby?" he asked Sheila. Sheila said that she didn't mind so Evan continued, looking at me as we waited at a light. "I was thinking, lets you and I go to England? I've always wanted to walk across Exmoor and see the ocean views from there. We could rent a cottage and have uninter-rupted sex."

"I *so* did not need to hear that Dad," came Toby's muffled drowsy voice from the back. We ignored him.

"Lets do it, lets book the tickets tomorrow," I smiled, and Evan held my hand the rest of the quiet ride home.

* * *

Home is full of such simple magics. The magic of hot milky tea and falling asleep on a lover's shoulder, of smiles and warm meals. Those things that we sometimes take for granted but really shouldn't. I'd gotten a rare hug from my giant teen-aged boy and said goodnight to him, finished my tea, and all I wanted was to lie down and fall asleep next to Evan, looking forward to that brief moment just before waking when I would see Rowan's face, and then find out what the new day held. What beauty did life have in store for me next? I tried to imagine.

Epilogue

Sheila had her favourite lawn chair, a pile of good books, and a thermos full of tea. *What else could I want for?* she thought, as she looked out to sea where she could see Toby riding the waves, in his element. He would no doubt be next to her dripping wet and waxing poetic about the thrill of the water in a few minutes. So much like his father, and yet so different. Toby seemed to operate on impulse unlike Evan, who could think even the simplest decision to death. Sheila wondered where that came from. She had only known Evan's father for three weeks, but he had seemed more the impulsive type than an over-thinker. Suddenly a shadow fell across her book and Sheila looked up.

"Sorry about that. Dover ... Heel," the tall man said to the Irish wolf hound that had been nosing around the cooler where Sheila and Toby's lunch was residing. Sheila squinted up, something stirring in her chest.

"Sheila ...?" the man said, uncertainly. "Is that you?"

"Theo?" she breathed, feeling suddenly bewildered.

Just then Toby came bounding up soaked, "Holy crap Grandma, did you see that!" he yelled, and then looked speculatively at the tall auburn haired man who stood there gaping slightly. "Who's he Grandma?"

Sheila looked up at her one time lover and she could see that it was obvious to him just exactly who the tall fifteen year old boy standing there, dripping wet with his surfboard, was. Theo too looked bewildered, but he smiled.

"Toby, this is your Grandfather," Sheila said.

And here she'd been thinking that life would quiet down.

Beth Larrivée-woods is an autistic writer living on the west coast of Canada. She enjoys knitting, collecting old and beautiful things, pretty dresses, animals, and nature. When she isn't knitting or writing she is wandering the woods with her teenaged children, watching her husband diligently wrestle self-publishing platforms for her, or watching television with her mother.

You can find her @pixiedustmagpie on Instagram or at bethlarriveewoods.ca.